THE SEVENTH DAY

Published by Dark Nebula Publishing 2014 -

Copyright © 2014 Andy Malone

Andy Malone has asserted his right under the United Kingdom Copyright, Designs and Patents Act 1988 to be identified as the author of this work.

First published in Great Britain in 2014 by Dark Nebula Publishing

www.darknebulapublishing.com

A CIP Catalogue record for this book is available from the British Library

Paperback ISBN: 978-0-9930202-0-9

Also available as an eBook

ePub: ISBN: 978-0-9930202-2-3

Mobipocket: ISBN: 978-0-9930202-1-6

LIVING IN SCOTLAND, Andy Malone is a popular international speaker and technology instructor with more than 20 year's experience. Winner of the Microsoft 2006 TechEd Speaker Idol contest, Andy has delivered technical and security content to thousands of delegates worldwide. His passionate style of delivery, combined with a sense of fun, has become his trademark and has won him great acclaim with large international audiences.

In recent years, Andy's international travels have also ignited another passion, writing. Having already written articles for magazines, websites and blogs, Andy decided to take the plunge and fulfil a childhood dream to publish a novel. The Seventh Day is his first and he is already hard at work on his second.

Follow Andy on Twitter @AndyMalone
Visit Andy's website: www.AndyMalone.org

A BIG THANK you to everyone who has aided me in the production of this book. To Leone Randazzo and Hermann Jónsson for their translation services. To the real Elín Gylfadóttir, the management of The Hilton hotel Reykjavik and the wonderful folks in Iceland for their words of inspiration. Also a huge thank you to my beta readers and friends in the Microsoft communities for their endless support. Thanks also to my editors Cherry Mosteshar and her team at The Oxford Editors, Patricia Anne Rodger and Janette Calder for their tireless efforts and ideas, and of course to my girls, Patricia and Amy for believing in me.

In The Seventh Day Dougie Allan has many adventures. Although the characters are fictitious, the places and locations are real and are definitely worth a visit. You can learn more about these locations through the following websites.

The Undiscovered Alva, Scotland - www.undiscoveredscotland.co.uk/alva/alva/index.html

Schwetzingen Palace and Gardens, Schwetzingen, Germany – www.schloss-schwetzingen.de/en/

Rua Reidh Lighthouse, Gairloch, Scotland - www.flickr.com/photos/iancowe/8261096639/

The Church of Sant' Anna dei Palafrenieri – Rome, Italy - http://en.wikipedia.org/wiki/Sant'Anna_dei_Palafrenieri

The Hilton Hotel – Reykjavik, Iceland - www.hiltonreykjavik.com/

The Bridge between two continents Iceland - http://commons.wikimedia.org/wiki/File:Bridge_across_continents_iceland.jpg

In the story the Character Kate Harding reads the book, Angels & Demons by Dan Brown.

Enjoy!

For Patricia & Amy

&

In loving memory of Janette Calder 1935 – 2014

THE SEVENTH DAY

BY
ANDY MALONE

And heaven departed as a scroll when it is rolled apart; and every mountain and island were moved out of their place.

Revelations 6- 14

PROLOGUE

LOCATION: UNKNOWN. DATE: UNKNOWN.

FOR ME, THE dream was always the same. The silence and blackness were absolute. Then a shining, piercing beam of light appears; then another and another. In all, there are seven. The lights seem to emanate from above, but with no identifiable source, surrounding me with what now appears to be a large, circular marble table complete with seven high-backed chairs. Behind the chairs, seven doors suddenly swing open and seven robed figures emerge from the darkness, and proceed to take their places around the table.

The faces of the seven are similar; gaunt pale complexions with dark, almost black, hair and piercing blue eyes. As they sit, no one speaks. The seven merely stare at each other, waiting for the silence to be broken. Then one rises and speaks.

"Has a decision been made?"

The group glance at each other for a moment and turn, responding almost in unison. "We have. Their fate is sealed."

The standing figure pauses glancing around at the group and takes a deep breath. "Does it have to be this way?"

"Yes they are dangerous, of that there is no doubt." The single voice that now speaks is different to the others, cooler and less emotional. The second figure then stands and continues, "They cannot change. We have seen it with our own eyes. History has shown that they will eventually not only destroy themselves, but also the planet. That cannot be permitted."

"But, they have great potential. I have seen it with my own eyes."

"Enough! The decision is made … Besides, it has already begun."

Then the dream is over and I wake.

ONE

PRESENT DAY: ALVA GLEN, ALVA, SCOTLAND

"**W**HAT THE HELL?"

Suddenly he felt the ground tremble and crack beneath his feet. Looking down in alarm, a split appeared like an open wound and a strand of brilliant white light began to ooze through. As the shaking increased, Tom began to panic but, as he turned to leave, the shaking suddenly stopped and he froze to the spot, waiting for something else to happen.

But there was nothing, no heat, no steam, nothing, except the continuous trickle of white light from below. Tom stopped, momentarily confused and feeling somewhat disorientated. Then, as before, the ground suddenly began to shake again. This time, however, the shaking was so violent that escape no longer seemed like an option. The deafening roar of rocks and debris shattered the silence as they began to fall around him.

Then, in a moment of sheer terror, the chamber floor suddenly gave way and exploded into a plethora of brilliant white light.

Tom screamed as he lost his footing and found himself careering downwards into the nightmarish abyss. As he fell, he lunged at a protruding rock and watched in horror as the ground that he had been kneeling on only moments earlier disappeared into the nothingness below. Clinging desperately to the rock for his life, Tom gritted his teeth and with his heart thumping and fingers sweating, struggled with all of his strength to pull himself to safety. His efforts were in vain, the floor was already beginning to collapse. His fingers slipping, Tom closed his eyes in preparation for what was to come. Then losing his battle to hold on, he took a deep breath and began to fall.

Unexpectedly, from nowhere, a large hand grabbed his arm. "Let go lad, it's okay I've got ye."

For a moment Tom was confused. He thought that he should be dead.

"What?"

Opening his eyes, he looked upwards and saw a shadowy figure through the brightness. Then glancing downwards, he began to panic again as he saw nothing below – no rocks, no ground, nothing but piercing white light! Tom shrieked in alarm, "I, I can't, I'll fall."

"Nae ye won't. Trust me laddie, it's okay. You're only few meters off the ground."

"What?"

Tom suddenly yelled out in alarm as the figure released its grip and he fell downwards only to land on his feet just a metre or so below. As Tom looked up towards the shadowy figure above, his expression turned to one of disbelief as he was overcome by the intensity of the blinding light. As he tried to shield his eyes, the voice above spoke again. "Here lad, use the rope … climb up."

A coil of rope appeared and Tom grasped an end and sighed with relief as he felt himself being hauled upwards. However before he had a chance to say thank you, he found himself lying flat out on the cave floor, only centimetres from yet another gaping precipice and possible death. Coughing and spluttering Tom took a deep breath just as his rescuer came into focus. A large scruffy dark haired figure, unusually dressed in some kind of costume, cotton shirt and a pair of old fashioned breeches, possibly eighteenth century. Tom opened his mouth to speak; the big man slapped him on the shoulder and spoke, "So laddie. Who the bloody hell are ye?"

Tom Duncan just gazed at the man, not only trying to comprehend what just happened, but also who his saviour was. The figure in front of him simply grinned, "Aye, laddie that's just how I felt when I first saw it. The names Dougie Allan, what's yours?"

Still speechless, Tom merely murmured and pointed his finger towards the drop. "Er, Tom. Tom Duncan. I, I don't understand, where did you come from? What the hell is that?"

Dougie's smile faded and his expression turned serious, still aware that the sheer drop was only meters away. "If it's alright with ye laddie, I think we had better move away from this place, what do ye think?"

Tom nodded in agreement as both men pulled themselves upwards and walked out back into the safety of the passageway, then out towards the mouth of the cavern.

At the entrance, both men flopped onto the ground breathing heavily. Tom looked at his strangely dressed saviour and repeated the question. "So, Mr Allan, where did you come from? What's with the costume?"

Dougie looked at Tom with some surprise, "Why, it's nae polite tae criticise another person's clothing. Why, I could say the same about you!"

Tom didn't respond. First because he struggled to understand Dougie, the man's accent was strange, although familiar. It was unusual, old Scots perhaps, almost foreign. Second he sensed that this angel of mercy could perhaps be easily offended.

Dougie continued, "To be honest, I don't ken. One minute I was in the mine, the next ... McArthur, then I found myself here."

Tom's face turned to confusion. "Mine, but Mr Allan, there is no mine. It shut down over 200 years ago."

Offended, Dougie suddenly jumped to his feet, "Are you calling me a liar Sir? I was just there."

The cold expression on Dougie's face was deadly serious. "No Mr Allan, I'm not calling you a liar. It's just that there is, no mine, there hasn't been in over 200 years."

Dougie's mouth gaped open in bewilderment.

"Then how ..." Dougie's head dropped as he fell to his knees. "No, my Mary, my bonnie lassie, she's, gone?"

Tom stared at Dougie sympathetically, desperately trying to find the right words to offer some comfort. "Mr Allan, I'm so sorry, I don't know what to say."

"Neither do I lad, neither do I. For me it's 1710 and I've lost my whole life."

Minutes passed and the two men sat still in silence, staring at each other, each man seemingly contemplating his own future. Looking up, Tom broke the silence. "Mr Allan, may I call you Dougie?"

Dougie gave a smirk, "Aye laddie, of course ye can."

"I don't know what this place is or what's happened here. But, whatever it is, it must be for a reason and if you are in agreement let me help you. Hopefully we'll find some answers together."

"Aye, agreed." Nodding, Dougie extended his large hand and both men shook in agreement.

"So perhaps a good place to start would be at the beginning. You mentioned someone called McArthur. Did he have something to do with you being here?"

Dougie sat back and frowned. "Aye, well I suppose in a way he did. It was because of him that I took the bloody job in the first place. Ten pounds a month tae be mine manager ..."

Dougie's head dropped and he sighed. "Ten pounds. Well at the time it seemed to good tae be true."

TWO

WEDNESDAY 25TH NOVEMBER 1709 ALVA, SCOTLAND

JAMES RITCHIE WAS thoroughly miserable. The carriage ride from Falkirk had been cold, damp and uncomfortable. If that wasn't enough, it was raining and not just a light rain either. It was, as the locals would say, "bucketing down". Menacing storm clouds were casting great shadows, low across the Ochil hills. It was only half past four in the afternoon, but already the brightness of day was disappearing into night. The gloomy sky just added to Ritchie's misery, reminding him of the shorter days and long wintery nights which were fast approaching.

As a boy, Ritchie had been lucky enough to have had a little schooling and, as a result, he had found employment with John Hardie Ltd, a Falkirk-based land surveying company. In the early days, he had loved his job and found it new and exciting. When he had joined the company at the age of twelve, old Mr Hardie had remarked that he showed great promise and took it upon himself to equip Ritchie with the skills needed in the business. However, nine years later, that all changed when the old man suddenly died of a heart attack. After the funeral, William, the elder of the two surviving Hardie sons, moved quickly to take control of his father's company. From that point on, what had once been a promising career for the 28 year old became nothing more than a workaday position as a courier, responsible for the delivery of mundane documents to mundane clients.

As the carriage, bumped and jerked its way along the rough track, Ritchie drew breath, shook his head and sighed in sheer disbelief at how stupid he had been. Brushing down his once smart bottle green coat with his hand, he gazed down at the brown leather satchel sitting on his lap. In his head he could hear his wife's voice repeating over and over, "I told ye so. I told ye he would make a bloody fool oot of ye."

"Aye Jenny," Ritchie thought, "you're right, as usual."

Looking outwards towards the hills, Ritchie noticed the familiar outline of three neglected, almost derelict farm cottages, indicating their arrival in Alva. Taking a deep breath, he groped under his seat, fumbling and eventually retrieving a large wooden stick. Firmly taking hold of one end, he proceeded to bang the carriage roof three times in order to get the drivers attention. After a few momentary jerks, Ritchie felt the carriage begin to slow and eventually it rocked to a halt. The carriage shook as the driver leaned over and cleared his throat, "Are ye okay Mr Ritchie, Sir?"

Ritchie sat up and leaned out of the right side of the carriage, straining his neck as he attempted to make eye contact with the driver. "Aye I'm braw, Tam. How much further?"

The elderly driver held his breath for what seemed like an eternity while he surveyed the location. "Well, this is it, Alva! What was the name o' the chap that ye were wantin' tae see?"

Looking down at the satchel, Ritchie untied its leather laces and pulled out several pieces of parchment. After a moment of struggling with the deteriorating light, he eventually made out the name. Clearing his throat, he again strained towards the driver. "Douglas Allan," he shouted.

"Oh Dougie, aye, in that case we're just about there."

The carriage juddered again as Tam repositioned himself back into his driving seat. After a loud crack of his whip the carriage once again rocked into motion. With barely enough time to return the documents to the satchel, the horses were once again slowing. Ritchie sat up and adjusted his tunic in an attempt to make himself look a little more presentable.

As the carriage rocked for a final time, the elderly, somewhat scruffy, driver jumped down, walked around and pulled open the right hand side carriage door. Placing the satchel under his right arm, Ritchie jumped out of the coach that, even in the rain and after two hours of an uncomfortable journey, was a welcomed relief. As he looked around, Tam the driver was already climbing back up to his seat.

"What time would ye like tae return tae Falkirk Mr Ritchie, Sir?"

Pausing for thought, Ritchie replied, "Could ye please stay? I shouldn't think I'd be tae long."

Repositioning himself in the driver's seat, Tam nodded in acknowledgment and replied, "Aye, nae bother."

Ahead of him, Douglas Allan's modest but well maintained cottage; a warm inviting glow coming from inside. After hours of sitting on a cold, unpadded seat the thought of some home comfort seemed appealing. As Ritchie approached the door, the delicious aroma of home cooking, drifted by, reminding him by means of a stomach rumble that he was hungry. Placing the satchel under one arm, he paused to take a breath and then knocked three times. After a few moments muffled voices could be heard from inside along with the sounds of approaching footsteps.

The door swung open to reveal an attractive woman in her late twenties. She was tall with long, dark, platted hair. Dressed in a dark green bodice and long flowing skirt, her bright blue eyes surveyed Richie and she smiled politely.

"May I help ye Sir?"

Ritchie nodded in return, "Aye, good evening tae ye. My name's James Ritchie and I'm lookin' for a Mister Douglas Allan. Have I come tae the right place?"

"Aye Sir ye have," she replied. "Would ye like tae speak with him?"

Ritchie nodded, "Aye, ma'am that would be much appreciated."

The young woman briefly turned her head inward and Ritchie sensed that she was silently beckoning to someone inside. Then came the sound of a man's voice, "Mary, don't leave the poor man standing 'oot there in the cold, invite him into the warm."

The woman turned her head back to Ritchie and stepped back, swinging the door open.

"Aye, would ye come away in then Mister Ritchie?"

Entering the humble but inviting room, Ritchie's eyes immediately caught sight of the remains of an apparent evening meal. On top of a long wooden table stood two wooden bowls, a small loaf of bread and two mugs.

To the left, there was an open fire over which hung a large iron pot. On the right there was what appeared to be a sleeping area, divided by a large tartan blanket, tied to either side of the opening in the stone wall.

As he stepped forward, the woollen blanket parted and a tall, unshaven, powerful-looking, dark-haired man in his thirties appeared, dressed in dark tanned breeches, white shirt and a woollen waistcoat.

"Good evening, Sir. Ye'll be from Mr Hardie's office, aye?"

Feeling somewhat intimidated at the sight of this gentle giant, Ritchie placed the satchel on the table and politely extended his hand. As the two men shook hands, Ritchie couldn't help thinking that he wouldn't like to get on the wrong side of Dougie Allan.

"Aye Sir, my name is James Ritchie. Mr Hardie has sent me with a proposal for ye tae consider."

Releasing hands, Ritchie reached for the satchel. "If ye will permit me tae stay a while tae talk it through with ye, it would be good o' ye."

"Aye, of course ye can."

A moment later, the door was closed and the woman was

standing beside her husband. "Mr Ritchie, Sir, this is my wife, Mary. She makes a fine broth and you look cold Sir, would ye care for a bowl?"

Giving a courteous but enthusiastic nod, Ritchie smiled, "Aye, it smells grand, Mr Allan, that'd be braw."

Pulling out a wooden stool, Ritchie sat, as Dougie placed a tankard full of milk in front of him. Moments later, Mary returned with a wooden bowl full of steaming, thick vegetable broth. Thanking her, Ritchie picked up a spoon and eagerly ate the hot soup in barely a minute. Then, as Dougie and Mary grinned at each other, he reached for the tankard of milk and enthusiastically gulped down half the contents.

Dougie stood up and walked over to the small fireplace; he reached down towards a pile of misshaped logs, picked up two and placed them carefully on the dying embers of the fire. Seconds later, the fire seemed to burst into life again, revived like a thirsty man who had just been given a glass of water.

"It's good tae see ye enjoy your food Mr Ritchie, my wife will be pleased that ye liked her broth. Now, if ye please, tell me more aboot this proposal from Hardie that ye mentioned."

Swallowing the remainder of the milk, Ritchie wiped his lips on his sleeve and placed the tankard to the table. Turning to his left, he could see that Mary had risen and made to move towards the large blanket dividing the room.

"It's fitting if I leave ye tae your business, gentlemen," she said as she walked away.

Both men suddenly stood as if Mary had royal blood running through her veins.

Ritchie smiled and nodded with a sense of genuine gratitude. "I'm most thankful for your kindness Missus Allan."

The young woman smiled and gave a nod before disappearing behind the blanket.

As the fire crackled in the semi darkness of the cottage both men returned to their seats. Staring at each other on opposite sides of the table, Ritchie leaned across, picked up the leather satchel and untied the drawstring. Opening the bag, he reached inside and pulled out two large pieces of parchment.

"Mr Allan, ye will be familiar with the Erskine folk and their plans for the silver mine?"

Dougie smiled wryly, "Och aye I ken all aboot the plans. But I don't want tae get involved with politics."

Ritchie raised his eyebrows, "Ye will forgive me for sayin' so, but this has nothing tae do with Sir John's Jacobean interests. This is purely business Mister Allan."

"Aye, well in that case I've known aboot the plans, and that ye had a bit o' bother with safeguarding things I hear!"

Pausing for a moment as if to catch his breath, Ritchie swallowed and said, "Aye, well, if you are referring tae McArthur then ye'd be right, but there has been nae evidence tae suggest that any stealing has taken place," he paused for a second and then continued, "on the contrary, there's nae evidence at all."

Looking down at the parchment Ritchie paused and gazed back at Dougie, who looked genuinely confused.

Ritchie continued, "Mr Allan, my employer has given me power tae seek ye oot tae secure your services. Mr Hardie would like tae offer ye the position of Mine Manager for the forthcoming project and he is willing tae pay ye a most excellent salary o' ten pounds sterling each month."

Dougie sighed, stood up and walked across to where a clay pipe and a small box of tobacco sat on a table beside the fireplace. Picking up the pipe, he took out a pinch of tobacco from the box and filled the pipe. Kneeling down at the fireplace, he picked up a small piece of wood and used it to light his pipe. Moments later, small circles of bluish-grey smoke rose from the pipe as the sweet aroma of burning tobacco filled the room. He then stepped back across to the table and re-took his seat.

"Ten pounds sterling each month? That's a lot o' money Mr

Ritchie Sir. Sounds tae me like there may be more tae the matter than meets the eye?"

Well at least it was a positive comment thought Ritchie. It's obvious he was interested; after all he didn't say no, did he?

"Ten pounds for a good job done, Mr Allan – that's all. Mr Hardie just needs tae be certain that nae more mishaps take place."

"Mishaps?" said the big man, "Is that another word fer trickery?"

"Nae trickery or anything else Mr Allan, it's just that Sir John would rather see any silver taken from his land remain in his family rather than folks like McArthur getting' at it, I'm sure ye understand."

Looking at Ritchie, Dougie raised his eyebrows, "I will tell you Sir, I don't know this McArthur myself, but from what I've heard, he's a good man."

"I never said he wasn't Sir, it's just a wee bit suspicious."

Ritchie glanced down at the papers and looked back at Dougie, who was still puffing away at his pipe.

For a moment Ritchie thought he had struck a nerve and upset the big man. Deciding that he didn't want to offend any further, getting to the point seemed to be the best course of action. Ritchie said, "Until there is evidence there's nae a lot we can do. The fact is though, Mr Allan, Sir John has need of a manager." Pausing for breath Ritchie sighed then continued, "So Mr Allan Sir, ten pounds sterling per month tae manage the mine and ensure good security is maintained. Do we have a deal?"

Dougie leaned back and took one final puff of his pipe, placed it on the table and licked his lips. With a small grin appearing on his face he leaned forward, "Aye, Mr Ritchie, Sir. Aye, ye have a deal."

With the agreement made the two men shook hands. Ritchie felt satisfied, almost as if he had conquered some ancient foe and the feeling of intimidation that he experienced at the beginning of their meeting had now faded. Who knows, he thought, perhaps even Mr Hardie will be pleased at the result.

It was around 7 pm when James Ritchie finally left the Allan's. With the satisfaction of the deal done and the contract signed, Ritchie bid farewell.

"Ye should be there first thing Monday morning Mr Allan, and all the best of luck tae ye." Dougie smiled in return, "And to ye sir, and to ye. Goodnight."

Within minutes Ritchie's carriage had departed. All that could be heard was the faint muffled sound of carriage wheels disappearing into the darkness.

Dougie closed the wooden door.

"Is he away?" came a soft voice from behind.

"Aye," said Dougie softly. Mary approached and wrapped her arms around him. Her hair was soft and he stroked the back of her head as they hugged.

"Are ye sure aboot that job Dougie?"

Pulling her head gently backwards with his large hands, he stared into her blue eyes. "Aye, my love, it'll be braw and besides its nae often that its possible tae earn ten pounds for a month's work, is it?" Dougie again embraced his wife; continuing to stroke her hair, he felt her take a deep breath and then softly exhale.

"Aye, Dougie, I suppose it's nae," she whispered.

THREE

NO ONE COULD really remember how long the Village of Alva had existed. Originally called Alveth, it just seemed to be one of those villages that was always there. Like the other hillfoot villages – Muckhart, Dollar, Tillicoultry, Menstrie and Blairlogie – Alva was dominated the Ochil Hills, a range of ancient volcanoes that rose up from the land, magnificent and majestic.

Local people would say that the natural beauty of the hills changed with the seasons and that every day they would look different, and this Monday was no exception. Any colour of summer had long faded and the slopes of the Ochils were reddish brown, severe and unwelcoming. To the west, the noble peak of Dumyat rose imposing and glorious while to the northeast Craigleith looked ominous, dark and unwelcoming, it's sharp protruding ridges and crags looking foreboding and dangerous.

At first light, Dougie Allan was already at the mine entrance waiting patiently as the men assembled for work. The air was cold and he rubbed his hands together vigorously to warm them as he watched the men collect their mining tools. As the 30 or so men walked past Dougie, some of them nodded in familiar, almost respectful, recognition. Living in a place like Alva, it was impossible not to know, or be known by those who lived there – by sight at least.

However, today, there were a number of new and unfamiliar faces among the group – no doubt, thought Dougie, from Dollar or Stirling – who had travelled for work. However, as he continued surveying the group, he noticed an unusual solitary, tall figure standing slightly apart from the others, half-turned away, so that Dougie could not see his face.

Wondering who the stranger was, Dougie's initial impression was that he did not seem to be of the right build for a mining man, nor was he dressed for a hard day's labour, but was unusually slim with clean breeches and a crisp white shirt that looked almost new.

Dougie walked forward to enquire if he required assistance. Without warning, however, the figure suddenly turned, so that he was staring directly at Dougie. The man was striking – gaunt and pale skinned, with sunken eyes and untidy jet-black hair. Feeling just a little startled by his unusual appearance, Dougie became increasing uncomfortable; the man's gaze was disturbing, almost piercing.

Breaking eye contact for a moment, Dougie looked around, assessing the rest of the men, before returning his gaze to the stranger. The figure continued to stare and Dougie found himself transfixed by the man's piercing, bright-blue eyes, which shone like sunshine shimmering on water.

As the man's gaze remained fixed upon him, Dougie's discomfort turned to alarm and he began to feel the small hairs on the back of his neck rising. Who was this man? If they had not met before – and he was sure that they had not – why did he feel so uneasy, almost as if the stranger was an adversary?

Within moment, alarm turned to fear almost as if a cold hand had begun stroking the back of his neck. Hypnotised by the stranger's icy-blue stare, it was almost as if he could see directly into Dougie's soul.

Then, through the distant coldness and fear, as if from far away, he thought he heard a friendly, confident voice say, "Good morning tae ye, Mr Allan."

After a moment of silence, the voice came again, "Mr Allan is all well with ye sir?"

Dougie blinked. "Aye … aye … I'm well."

For a second, Dougie was unsure of his surroundings and then he looked around, taking a moment to register that the stranger was gone.

"Mr Allan, sir?" the voice came again. In that instant, Dougie felt that, whatever had happened, wherever he had been for those few lost moments, he was now firmly back in Alva, about to embark on a day's work.

He turned around to see two men standing just behind him. One he recognised immediately as the man he invited into his home only two days earlier, Mr James Ritchie of Hardie's of Falkirk. The other was a middle-aged man of around 40, so well dressed and of such a dignified presence that he must surely be nobility. It just took that momentary assessment for Dougie to recognise that, of course, the second man was none other than Sir John Erskine, his new employer.

Ritchie cleared his throat and smiled, "Mr Allan, may I introduce Sir John Erskine. He has been very keen tae meet ye."

Erskine extended his hand, smiling warmly. Dougie nodded in acknowledgement, took a step forward and shook the man's hand saying, "And I'm glad tae meet ye sir."

Erskine glanced first at Ritchie and then back to his new mine manager with pride, and grinned, "So, Mr Allan what do ye think of our wee operation here?"

"It seems remarkable, sir," responded Dougie politely.

"And I have heard that we can expect great things from ye, Mr Allan."

Dougie glanced down for a moment before returning to meet Erskine's gaze. "Aye, well, sir, I'm certainly prepared tae give it my best."

Erskine beamed, "That's all I ask, Mr Allan. Our initial workings seem tae show that mining this area could be very profitable … very profitable indeed … and not just for the Erskine folk but for us all."

Dougie nodded, "Aye sir, that's what I hear too."

Pausing for breath, he glanced first at Ritchie and then back to Erskine before continuing. "Well, just give me six months and if there is silver inside, then I promise tae get it oot." Erskine stiffened his shoulders and stood tall, looking joyful, "Grand, Mr Allan, just grand. That's just what I wanted tae hear."

As the two men talked, Ritchie, the man who had brought Dougie and Sir John Erskine together, pondered the success of this union. His mission, given to him just a few days earlier, had been to find a replacement for the elusive Alexander MacArthur. Although Dougie Allan had a reputation for being a hard man, he was also considered a fair man who would give one hundred per cent.

MacArthur's unexplained disappearance had caused something of a furore between Erskine and William Hardie. Accusations of time wasting and threats of contract cancellations had forced Hardie to break procedure and send Ritchie to personally negotiate with Allan. Since Ritchie's successful return however, Hardie seemed like a different man, relaxed and almost jovial.

Suddenly realising that he had been staring at the two men with a broad grin on his face; Ritchie blinked and brought himself back to the moment. "Do ye have everything ye need Mr Allan? Do ye have enough men?"

Dougie lifted his gaze, "Aye, Mr Ritchie, I believe all the men are here … but a couple of more horses would nae go amiss."

Ritchie nodded warmly, "Aye, Mr Allan, I'll see ye have them as soon as possible."

Keen to get the men to start work, Dougie glanced at both men for a final time, "Mr Erskine … Mr Ritchie, sir. If ye will give me leave, I'd best be getting on. It's been an honour talking with ye."

Smiling, Erskine extended his hand and shook Dougie's, "Likewise. Mr Allan, likewise."

Dougie acknowledged the two men with a single nod of his head, turned and walked away to where more workers were mustering.

Dougie saw a number of familiar faces – the McRae brothers from Menstrie, Robert and Stuart, fine strong lads, both of whom had worked with him the previous year in Alloa; William Donaldson from Mackie's farm, and Fraser McAndrew from Fishcross. The other thirty or so men Dougie knew by sight only. As he looked at the group, Dougie searched for the gaunt stranger who had held his attention with such intensity just a few minutes ago. Had the man left, deciding not to join the workforce, or had those moments been some kind of waking nightmare? For a moment standing with the group, Dougie questioned his own memory and wondered if the man had actually been there at all.

With Erskine and Ritchie watching, Dougie did not want to give the impression that he was hesitant or had somehow lost his mind even before the job had started. So taking a deep breath he decided to focus his thoughts on the task at hand rather than letting his imagination run wild.

Standing in front of the men, Dougie cleared his throat.

"Good morning lads it's great tae see ye all here."

The group were chatting amongst themselves, but fell silent as Dougie continued.

"Today is a historic day for Alva. It isn't every day that a good seam of silver is found. Ye lads have been chosen for I ken that ye will get the job done."

Murmurs rippled throughout the group and heads nodded in agreement. "Now, there's nae doubt that it's going tae be hard work. But I'll tell ye that, if this shaft has half the silver that's supposed tae be down there, then we'll all have a job that lasts for life."

Dougie's expression turned serious and he paused to ensure that everyone had absorbed his words and then continued, "Some of ye I ken, and some I don't, I have but a few rules for ye. In the first part, nae trickery or thieving. Any man I find stealing will be held to account, do ye hear me?"

The murmurs increased and heads nodded.

"And in the second part, ye'll get a fair day's pay for a fair day's work. And in the last part, you're nae to take any stupid risks. I don't want tae be the man tae tell your wives that you're nae coming home. So lads, are we all in agreement?"

A unanimous "Aye" rang out in a chorus of accord.

"Then let's get tae it!"

For a moment the swift rush of activity and noise overwhelmed Dougie as voices were raised, tools were picked up and the day's work began.

By late afternoon, Dougie made the decision for the men to lay down tools for the day, and having made sure that the site was cleared, he watched as the last few weary bodies dispersed on their homeward, walking through the fading light. When he had done his final check, although the daylight was almost gone, Dougie took the opportunity to walk through the Glen that he loved so much. It was in the evening twilight that he discovered a profound sense of peace that seemed to descend upon him in the cool air, and he felt that, in these moments, he could put aside any thoughts or troubles of the day.

Walking down the hill towards home, Dougie could just make out the silhouettes of two men loitering at the side of the path ahead as if they were waiting for someone. One of the men was sitting on the dry stonewall that gave a boundary to the path, while the other was standing just a short distance away. As he drew near, Dougie recognised the men as the two McRae brothers.

"Alright lads. Are ye nae going home for your supper?"

Stuart, the taller of the two, jumped down from the wall and went to stand by his brother.

"Eh, good evening Mr Allan, sir. We were wanting tae talk with ye for a moment?"

Dougie nodded, "Aye, lads, ye may talk if ye wish. Is there something troublin' ye?"

The two young men glanced at each other uneasily, almost as if to dare the other to speak first. In the end it was Stuart, the taller and elder of the two brothers, who broke the silence. "Well, ye ken, Mr Allan, the men have been talking …"

"Oh aye … and what kind o' talk would that be then?" responded Dougie, curious as to what rumours might being going round the mining crew and wondering if there had been talk of the gaunt stranger.

"Talk o' Alexander MacArthur."

As soon as Dougie heard the name, he knew what was coming. "Ach, lads, we can't be guessing on things we ken nothing aboot."

"Its nae guessing Mr Allan, sir, the men are talking …"

"And what do they say, Stuart?"

The elder lad looked uncomfortably at his brother for moral support, but none seemed to be forthcoming. "They say … well Mr Allan … they say that he just disappeared … in there … inside the mine."

Dougie sighed and nodded his head. "Ach, lads, I'm going be honest with ye? The truth is we don't ken what happened tae Mr MacArthur. For all we know the man was an idiot. Perhaps he got drunk one night and fell down the glen. Or, perhaps, he was taken away by the fairy folk, eh?"

The brothers looked at each other and smirked as the seeds of doubt began to take root.

"Aye, lads, talking aboot wild and stupid rumours isnnae going tae put food on your tables, is it? I'm sure the truth will come oot eventually, but for now, we have a job tae do, aye?"

A final glance at his brother and then Stuart turned his gaze downward and gave a sigh, "Aye, you're right Mr Allan, I'm sorry."

As the lad apologised, Dougie realised that his tone might have sounded a little harsh and critical when all these young men were looking for was a little reassurance.

He softened his tone as he continued, "Ach, look, lads, there's nothing tae be sorry for. Don't worry yourselves, for I'm sure we'll ken the truth soon enough. Now, get yourselves home before ye miss your supper."

As Dougie turned homeward once more the two young men also turned to leave. "Thank ye Mr Allan, we'll be there in the morning."

"Alright lads, and good night."

With those words, Dougie watched as the brothers turned and walked away into the darkness before he himself continued his journey homeward.

FOUR

THE DAYS AND weeks passed. Progress on the mine proceeded according to plan, albeit frustratingly slowly at times, mainly due to the onset of winter. The cold weather brought a harshness to the working conditions that many of the mining men found difficult to cope with. Bitter cold temperatures combined with snow and high winds from the north made the backbreaking work seem even harder. In the midst of their suffering, the men's tempers were often frayed and arguments broke out. The occasional black eye or bloodied nose was not an uncommon sight.

That February Thursday started just like any other day. The men arrived and got to work as normal. By 1 pm, the temperature had risen and much of the previous evening's snowfall was beginning to melt.

Dougie Allan sat on a large log near the entrance of the mine, eating bread and homemade cheese. Around him the thirty-five or so other men working at the mine also sat, finishing their food and resting. Dougie knew that once lunch was over, he had to get the men back to work, but just as he was about to stand and shout the order, his plans were interrupted by the arrival of a grim-faced lad running over to him. Seeing the lad in obvious distress and fearing bad news, Dougie jumped to his feet as the boy, face flushed, dripping with sweat, his breathing heavy and erratic, reached him. Dougie held his hand out to steady the lad.

"Whoa there, slow down laddie, you'll do yourself an injury."

"Mr Allan ... Mr Allan ... sir," the lad stood in front of Dougie wheezing and gasping for breath. Many of the men were now also standing, concern etched on their faces, made anxious by the arrival of the distraught youth.

"For the love of God laddie what's wrong?"

Bent almost double as he struggled to draw breath, the boy took a moment to recover before raising his head to make eye contact with Dougie, "Mr Allan, sir. At Woodhill ... I saw him myself ... I did, sir ... just' going into the entrance, sir."

"Who was it, laddie, who did ye see?"

But even as the question left his mouth, Dougie's heart was sinking because he already knew the answer.

"MacArthur, sir. Mr Alexander MacArthur."

For a moment time froze, the name that conjured fear and dread hung suspended in the icy air. The men stood equally stunned, waiting for the silence to be broken – something that did not seem to be forthcoming.

The lad's head dropped again. He stood, trembling as if a wave of guilt or fear had suddenly descended upon him. Dougie stood looking at the lad – and then, in an instant and with the energy of a firecracker exploding, the expression of shock on the big man's face changed to one of fury.

Spinning around to face the men, Dougie shouted, "I need six men tae volunteer." Immediately a number of hands were raised as well as a number of shouts of support.

"Stuart, Robert, William, ye come with me. Fraser, ye take two lads and go in this side o' the mine tae make sure he doesn't come oot here. The rest of ye, get yourselves back tae work, but keep your eyes open and call oot if ye see anything o' the man."

As the men began to head off to their tasks, Dougie called to Donaldson and the two McRae brothers to take up arms. In a moment Stuart appeared, brandishing three axes and a large pitchfork, "Here Mr Allan, will these do?"

"Aye, well done lad. Let's go."

First handing an axe to Dougie and another to Donaldson, Stuart leaned across and passed a large fork to his younger brother.

Armed and ready, the four men set off at speed towards Woodhill, at the other end of the gorge, where there was another access to the mine.

The men hastened through the glen at a great pace, leaving a trail of snapped twigs and branches in their wake. Under normal circumstances the distance between the two entrances was relatively short, remnants of stubborn, hard-packed winter snow remained on the path, sometimes forcing the group to take a longer, alternative route. On one of these detours, Dougie, Stuart and Robert leapt over a ridge and successfully navigated their way over a protruding rock. Donaldson, however, was not so fortunate. As he leapt, his right foot caught the edge of the rock and he stumbled forward, dropping the axe and falling heavily. The crack of breaking bone was unmistakable, and Donaldson screamed as an excruciating pain shot up his leg. A feeling of intense nausea washed over him, forcing him first onto his knees and then face down into the snow.

On hearing the scream, Dougie and both McRae brothers turned in their tracks, running back towards their fallen comrade, faces full of concern. Donaldson was on the ground, writhing in pain, his breeches torn and his knees badly cut from the fall; as he turned back Robert called out to his friend "Ach, William, are ye okay?"

Donaldson gritted his teeth in a combination of pain and anger with his friend for asking what he thought was a stupid question. "No, ye stupid galoot; its ma ankle, I think it's broke."

When Dougie reached the injured man's side he knelt down beside him and examined the damaged ankle as best he could; it was clear that the skin was bruised and badly swollen and the bone seemed to be out of place, it wasn't looking good and it meant that Donaldson was in no condition to continue the pursuit. Dougie realised that they faced a real dilemma. Were they to abandon a fallen comrade, a friend in obvious distress, or were they now to abandon the pursuit? Taking account of the bigger picture, however, Dougie realised that there really was only one choice. "I'm sorry laddie, we'll have tae go, but I'll send Robert tae get help."

Standing up, Dougie turned to Robert. "Is that alright lad? Will ye go back tae Alva and get help for William?"

Robert glanced, disappointed, first at his elder brother and then back to Dougie. "Aye, Mr Allan, of course I will."

Dougie nodded his approval before focusing his attention on Stuart, giving the elder McRae brother a reassuring slap on the shoulder. "Right, I ken he'll fetch help and we can get our done, so let's get tae it." Both men then turned and set off eastwards again, towards Woodhill.

A couple of minutes later, the two men arrived at the Woodhill entrance to the mine. Here, it looked like the mine was deserted but Dougie knew that, as a rule, almost the entire work force was working at the Silver Glen shaft and the lack of men at Woodhill was normal. There were, however, signs of recent activity at the site, with the remains of a small fire still smouldering and the gnawed leftovers of a piece of chicken lying on the ground. No doubt, thought Dougie, thrown down by the young watchman as he took fright when he saw MacArthur – or someone he thought was MacArthur. Taking a moment to catch their breath, both men stood at the entrance, with hands on knees, breathing heavily.

"Alright … Mr Allan, sir … what's the plan?"

Dougie regained his composure and stood up. "Torches, Stuart, lad. We'll need a couple o' torches." Stuart nodded and turned away towards a pile of wood to the left of the entrance.

The bright sky of that morning had faded, the light dull and diminished as darkening clouds rolled across the hillfoots. As he looked upwards, Dougie could see snow was once again falling on high ground.

"Here ye go Mr Allan." Stuart had returned grasping two bundles of wood and twigs, let from the embers of the fire, to act as torches. He handed one to Dougie and they stood motionless for a moment, facing each other secure in the warmth and safety of the flames and in the company of the other, looking for reassurance as they prepared for what was to come.

"Come on laddie, I'll go in first, ye stay behind me and keep your eyes open."

Gripping an axe in his right hand and the torch in his left, Dougie led the way forward, into the darkness. Tongues of flames from the torches licked the cold, damp air inside the cavern as the men made their way over rocky and uneven ground. As they moved inwards they could hear nothing other than their own breathing and the sound of their own feet as they trudged forward. x"Mr Allan, sir, can I ask ye a question?"

"Aye, what is it?"

"McArthur, what exactly did he do?"

Dougie had not expected this to be the question from the lad – but now that it had been asked, he started to doubt that he really knew the right answer.

"Ach, well, the man's a thief, that's all I ken."

"What did he steal?"

"It doesn't matter, laddie, the point is," said Dougie and then, he paused awkwardly, unsure of how to explain. "The man stole from Erskine and dishonoured us all. I don't know aboot ye but, well, ye ken, this is a good job and it puts food in your belly and nae one's taking that away from me."

As Dougie's raised voice echoed in the cold darkness, Stuart got the feeling that the search for McArthur was more personal for his boss than he had first imagined.

"What'll we do when we catch him?"

Aware that the torchlight was starting to fail and with his frustration rising, Dougie muttered through gritted teeth, "You'd best let me worry aboot that, laddie."

As Dougie dropped his dying torch, the two men continued to edge slowly inwards through the diminishing light by touch alone.

After shuffling along for around 20 meters, the men realised that the passage was slowly becoming smaller and smaller. As a result, they were now forced to stoop low in order to avoid hitting their heads. Eventually, they came to a point where it was impossible to continue walking upright.

"Och, where is he?" Dougie muttered under his breath.

"What's that Mr Allan?"

"Nothing lad, I'm just talking tae myself. I'm thinking that he must have crawled through tae the main shaft. We'll have tae go through here tae follow him. It's going get pretty tight for a wee while." Stuart coughed and took a deep breath, "Should we go back?"

Dougie shook his head in disagreement. "Nae that would take tae long. We'll be fine as long as we're careful."

Stuart muttered an acknowledgement and followed Dougie's lead by kneeling down on all fours and crawling forward. Sweating and cramped the men continued crawling, edging painfully forward. The claustrophobic space appeared to be wrapping around them like the coils of a serpent. Even Dougie, with his years of experience, had not been fully prepared for this.

"Are ye alright, lad?"

For a moment there was no response, then a few metres back Stuart replied, his voice quivering in the blackness. "Aye, I think so."

Without warning the crawlspace was plunged into total darkness as the remaining torch died. The blackness was now total and absolute, like a sky with no stars for guidance or moon for comfort.

Barely able to move, Dougie struggled to look back for any sign of his colleague. Although he couldn't see him, Dougie could still hear faint breathing sounds, which at least provided some reassurance.

The voice came through the darkness "Er, what do we do now?"

Dougie swallowed hard, "Just' keep goin' lad, we'll get through this … aye, we'll be through in a moment."

Although Dougie was desperately trying to sound upbeat, the situation was proving more challenging than he had anticipated and he was truly hoping that the crawlspace would eventually re-emerge into the main shaft. The lack of torchlight and the overpowering darkness were conspiring to sow the first seeds of doubt in his mind. As he inched his way forward, he could hear the sound of running water somewhere ahead and although yet unseen, with each metre covered, it could be more clearly heard. Pulling himself forward through the crawlspace, Dougie noticed that wooden timbers had replaced sharp, stonewalls of the shaft. He paused for a moment, calling back towards Stuart, who had fallen behind, "I think we'll be alright laddie, I can tell we're getting close!"

From some way behind him the young man's voice, tense and shaky, called back "That's good, sir, because I cannae take much more of this …"

For a moment Stuart's last word seemed to hang in the air, like the dying ember, then the silence was suddenly shattered with a ferocity that took Dougie's breath away. With a deafening roar the passage behind suddenly buckled and filled the crawlspace with collapsing rock and debris. The muffled screams beyond the fall could only mean one thing – and Dougie assumed the worse. Coughing and spluttering he used all of his strength to pull himself to safety in sheer desperation.

As time passed and the roar of the collapsing rocks subsided he needed to know what had happened to his companion "Stuart!"

Dougie screamed. "Stuart! Stuart, lad, can ye hear me?" There was no response.

"Stuart," Dougie shouted again, "Are ye okay?" As an apparent trickle of daylight pierced through the darkness, Dougie strained his neck to look behind. He could see that the passage way was completely blocked.

"Mr Allan." The voice was faint, weak, but unmistakable and Dougie thanked God that the young man was alive.

"Stuart lad, can ye move?" Dougie spluttered, trying to fight back the heavy dust irritating his throat.

"Aye, I can, but the way ahead is blocked. I cannot get through to ye."

"Don't concern yourself with that," Dougie shouted. "Can ye get oot from behind?"

There as a pause, Stuart took another breath and looked ahead. "Aye, I think the way back is clear, and I can make it, I'm sure I can."

Dougie swallowed, "Alright lad, tha's good tae hear. Well ye go back and meet up with the others. I'll try and find a way oot this way."

"Aye, okay sir, I'll do that. You take care."

Dougie didn't respond. In the midst of the tight dust filled crawlspace, his mind and all his willpower must now be focussed on one simple short-term goal. He must reach the source of light.

With all his might, Dougie pulled himself forward, using all his strength to work towards his goal. After about ten metres, he could see that the chink of light was now directly ahead. Looking at the light, Dougie felt good, almost as if he could feel the warmth of the sun's rays on his face. Another yard and the passageway was again beginning to open up and he realised that he could move his legs and arms more freely. He pulled himself forwards directly into the path of light, sensing that freedom was only a short way ahead. Basking in the glow, Dougie closed his eyes and smiled to himself in sheer relief.

The anticipation of knowing that this nightmare was coming to an end was overwhelming. Taking a deep breath, he opened his eyes and stared once more into the light. As he gazed, he knew that something was out of place. For a moment Dougie couldn't understand what exactly it was. And then he realised – the light source was wrong! It was not coming from above, but somehow, strangely, from below.

It was almost as if the rocks themselves were glowing. Dougie was confused. In all his years on this earth he had never been witness to anything like this. Were the rocks hot? Was it perhaps a new type of silver? Or perhaps something even stranger, or more valuable?

Confusion turned to excitement and, reaching for his axe, Dougie began to probe the illuminated rocks. After pulling away the initial surface layer of rock, it became apparent that it was not the rocks themselves that were the source of light, but something below, something unseen.

Then came a crack! The noise was deafening as the ground suddenly gave way and Dougie fell downwards, spinning, falling – then, with a thump, he landed.

Dazed and confused, he opened his eyes and looked around. The intenseness of the light was almost totally overpowering. Nothing other than white light was apparent. No shapes, no form, and even the surface on which he lay was somehow strange. Not entirely rock, perhaps some kind of polished marble. Looking upwards Dougie could see the opening where he had fallen through to this strange environment. Around him, fragments of rock and debris covered the area where he lay. With his eyes now becoming familiar with the brilliance, Dougie struggled to his feet.

"Hello, hello," Dougie's voice echoed. "What the hell is this place?" he muttered to himself. Looking around he noticed his axe a yard or two away. "Aye, well at least I can protect myself," he said in a whisper as he reached down and picked up the axe before moving cautiously forward.

The cavern was immense. Because of the brilliance, it was difficult to gauge any sense of distance or height, or anything else for that matter. All he could do was move forward. And then there it was in front of him, piercing through the light like a flame in the darkness! A black shape, like a smooth, even-sided mountain peak! Staring upwards, Dougie estimated the height to be around 100 feet and, as he walked around this amazing discovery, he counted forty strides to cover the length of one side. With his left hand, Dougie reached out and touched the object. A vibration, low and rhythmic, but definitely a vibration. As if burnt, Dougie snatched his hand back in shock and stood back. His heart was banging hard and fast in his chest, he took a deep breath. The excitement was like an energy rush. Whatever this thing was, he was sure he was the first to find it. Stepping forward once more, he touched it again. It felt cold, similar in composition to that of the floor, marble perhaps, but he couldn't be absolutely sure. The vibrations seemed to resonate through him.

"Mr Allan."

"Huh!" Quickly removing his hand, Dougie spun around in a state of surprise. Standing in front of him was a tall, gaunt figure – strange yet somehow familiar. It took Dougie a few moments of concentration before he identified him.

"Ye! Ye were at the mine before! What is this place, and what the bloody hell is going on?"

The two of them stared at each other, momentarily fixated, neither making a move. Then regaining his composure, Dougie gripped the axe handle in anticipation of, now what seemed to be an inevitable confrontation. Gritting his teeth he began to move slowly forward. "Aye, ye ... ye shouldn't be in the mine, ye're comin' with me."

The man seemed to be unarmed and showed no apparent emotion as he too stepped forward, calmly reaching into his pocket. In his hand he held a small black shape identical to the smooth sided mountain peak next to them, but in miniature.

"No Mr Allan, I am afraid I can't do that."

The dull, lifeless tone of his voice made Dougie stop dead in his tracks. Now that he had taken a couple of steps, he remembered how unnerved he had been by this person only a few weeks earlier, on that first day at the line-up. And he remembered those eyes.

Dougie felt as if he had been suddenly submerged into ice-cold water and, somehow frozen and unable to move, he just stared at the gaunt figure with its bright, piercing eyes holding him like a moth unable to escape a candle flame. In its hand, the black marble object began dissolving into a translucent liquid and within seconds, the liquid appeared to come alive as if it had a mind of its own. Terrified, Dougie wanted to run; to get away from this place, from that strange, compelling figure. He would have given anything to get away, but he couldn't move. There was an unseen force holding him, firm and absolute. He was staring at the gaunt figure in sheer disbelief at what he was seeing – and the he dropped his gaze down to his feet where he realised the oncoming liquid had now reached his boots. With thoughts of his beautiful Mary flashing through his mind, Dougie sensed that, whatever this was, it was the end for him. Unable to move, all he could do was look on in horror as this strange fluid enfolded itself around his legs and moved slowly upwards, first his knees, then his waist. All now appeared to be turning into the same translucent form. Gathering all of his strength Dougie gasped, "Dear Lord, what have ye done?"

His chest, arms and neck were all glowing. The figure did not answer, but merely continued to stare at Dougie, emotionless and silent. Finally with no pain, Dougie could feel his throat changing form.

As it did he let out one last defiant "Why?" and then Dougie Allan was gone.

FIVE

"**D**ADDY, DADDY."

"Huh?"

Through the depths of a deep sleep, Forty-four-year-old Tom Duncan became aware of the child's voice. For a moment he lay in the darkness and then, yawning and with his eyes only half-open, he glanced at his bedside clock. It read 02.40 a.m.

"Daddy, wake up, please."

"OK, sweetie ... I'm here ... just a moment."

Tom took a deep breath and reached out into the darkness attempting to locate his bedside light. After a few moments of fumbling, his fingers finally found the switch and the room filled with the soft glow of lamplight. Now fully awake, he could see his six year old daughter, Amy, standing by the bed, wearing her favourite *Dora the Explorer* pyjamas and clutching Ricky, her beloved panda teddy bear and the familiar white gauze comfort blanket. Half sitting now, Tom swung his legs out of bed and turned to smile at his daughter.

"What's the matter baby, another bad dream?"

"Uh huh."

"Do you want me to put her back?"

The soft, sleepy voice came from behind him. Looking back

over his shoulder, Tom could see the blankets moving as a tousled head of blonde hair appeared.

"No, it's OK. I'll go and lie with her for a while, you go back to sleep."

Tom stood up, scooped up his daughter into his arms and walked to the adjacent bedroom. There, by the gentle radiance of a soft night-light, it was easy to make out the shape of the small single bed, chest of drawers, nightstand and toy box. A small pinewood bed was covered with an assortment of soft toys including a large brown bear called Barney, Jenny the giraffe and cuddly Tigger from *Winnie the Pooh*.

"You know, with all these animals I'm not surprised you can't sleep. Don't they keep you awake?"

"No, Daddy, don't be silly! Of course they don't."

Tom smiled, as he pulled back the blanket and proceeded to re-position Amy back into bed.

"Now, tell me, what was your bad dream about tonight?"

"Scott."

Tom's head dropped and he gave a heavy sigh. Scott was Tom's eight-year-old son; he was everything any father could have wanted in a son – intelligent, funny and sensitive. Eight months earlier, however, he had been killed in a road accident while on a day trip to Edinburgh's Royal Mile. Just a terrible, tragic accident, nobody's fault. At least that's what everyone kept telling him.

Scott had bought a new football from a street vendor on the High Street; moments later the ball had slipped from his hands and bounced out onto the road. Despite the many warnings he had given his son on the dangers of roads, all Tom could do was watch on in horror as Scott bolted blindly into the on-coming traffic. It was all over in an instant – a large delivery van struck the boy on the head; doctors later said that he was probably dead before he hit the ground.

Although both Tom and his wife Jane were doing their best to move on, the pain was still raw in his mind; over and over again he thought: why did it have to happen … if only he hadn't bought that stupid ball, Scott would still be alive!

Shaking off his own misery, Tom tenderly stroked his daughter's soft blonde hair as he responded.

"What did you dream baby?"

Amy thought for a moment, clearly trying to remember specific details … but as with most dreams it was slipping away fast.

"I, I dreamt he was here with me. I can't remember anymore Daddy, I'm sorry."

Tom sighed and whispered softly "It's OK sweetheart, don't worry about it. Scott's in a safe place, now he just probably called on you to see how you were."

"Can he do that, come down from Heaven?"

Giving another sigh, Tom thought for a moment as he gave Amy a warm smile.

"Of course he can, in a dream. 'Cos, that's the amazing thing about dreams, Amy, God gave us the ability to dream so that those who have gone can come and visit us from time to time."

"But, will he really come back, Daddy?"

Tom swallowed hard as he attempted to push back the lump that was forming in his throat.

"Baby, I wish he could, I really do."

"Daddy, do you believe in Heaven?"

Tom looked at his daughter, her beautiful little face glowing in the soft light and wondered how to respond to such innocence. Then his heart swelled and he smiled to himself – for if Heaven did truly exist then it must be right here, right now, embodied in his darling daughter.

"I do, sweetheart, I really do."

"Well, um, so what happens when you die? Do you go to straight there, to Heaven? Mummy say's it's a magical place. Can we visit, I could take Scott some toys."

Gosh, thought Tom, how do I answer this one? He wanted to tell Amy about God and all the wondrous things that He could do … but how could he tell her about a loving, caring God when his son had been so suddenly and cruelly ripped from their lives. Looking down again at Amy he thought, no, it's not your fault. Why should I pass on my bitterness to you?

He sighed, "You know that everyone dies eventually and if you are a good person here on Earth, when you die you will go to Heaven. And yes, Mummy is right, it is a very special place, a place where you can see and be with all your family and friends again."

"But Daddy, why do we have to die? Why can't we just live forever?"

"Well," Tom paused to think for a moment. "Well … if everyone lived forever the planet would run out of room, it would get pretty cramped."

"Mrs McDonald told Rory McAllister that he was very naughty and if he wasn't good, he would go down there." Amy pointed to the ground with her index finger. "He is always being bad in class. He sat on the naughty step yesterday for a whole hour."

"Well I don't know about Rory McAllister, but I do know that Amy Duncan will definitely go to Heaven, because she is a good girl."

Amy beamed at her father, her eyes shining.

"So why, if Heaven is such a nice place, why can't we take some toys for Scott. I'm sure God won't mind, will he?"

Tom's head dropped, tears welling in his eyes and the lump he had been trying to hold back were re-emerging stronger than ever.

"I'm afraid it doesn't work like that, baby. You only get to go at the end of your life, when you are a real old lady, or, of course, if you are a boy, when you are a really old man."

A look of puzzlement appeared on his daughter's face and Tom took a deep breath, already aware of the oncoming question.

"So why did God take Scott away? He wasn't old; he was only eight. Was God angry with him?"

"Oh no, sweetie, don't think that. Scott just had an accident that's all; a really sad accident. It was nobody's fault. Sometimes these things just happen. It's just the way things work out."

"Well it doesn't seem fair."

Amy's eyes were closing, her battle to remain awake was almost finished and the curtain of sleep was descending upon her.

"No," Tom whispered, "It's not fair."

And then Amy was asleep; her breathing was steady and calm. Tom leaned over and kissed his daughter on the forehead. "Sleep well, my lamb ... God bless."

Tom gazed down at his daughter for a moment and then walked through to the bedroom he shared with his wife. Sitting on the bed he sipped a mouthful of water from a glass on his bedside table and when he had finished he placed the glass down, reached over, switched bedside lamp off and climbed into bed.

He lay there, quite still for just for a moment before he pulled the blanket upwards.

"Is she OK?" came the whisper through the darkness.

"Yes, she's asleep again now. And we should be too, g'night, honey. I love you."

The softness and warmth of his wife's hand clasped his own under the blanket. "I love you too."

Tom lay in the darkness finding comfort from the sound of his wife's breathing combined with the ticking of the bedside clock. Just before he fell asleep Tom took a final glance at that clock – even though his eyes were closing, he was able to make out the time as 03.25 a.m.

SIX

SATURDAY: 4.30AM CET SCHWETZINGEN, GERMANY

DESPITE BEING EARLY August there was a definite chill in the early morning air. Robert Jameson sat at the wheel of his black VW Passat opposite the town square. Apart for the occasional taxi passing by, the streets were empty and quiet. Robert had parked on Schloßstraße opposite the castle gardens. Normally, by day, the castle and its Baroque gardens would be buzzing with tourists, but at this time in the morning, all was quiet. If any passers-by had been paying attention they would have merely assumed that the car was a taxi waiting for hire. The only tell-tale sign that something was amiss was the collection of cigarette butts on the ground outside the driver's door. Robert, however, was becoming increasingly impatient.

The waiting was gnawing away at him. He was getting edgy. The clean shaven, stocky 48 year old Robert Jameson had worked as a staff reporter for the British *Daily Chronicle* for twelve years and always enjoyed the "romance" of these covert meetings with clients in the middle of the night or in some quiet alley, hoping for that all important scoop. But, on this occasion, he had been waiting for over an hour and he was starting to doubt whether his contact, Brauer would show.

He reached over, flipped open the glove box and retrieved another packet of cigarettes. Removing one, Robert fumbled for a moment inside his sports jacket pocket, eventually retrieving a silver cigarette lighter and continued to light the tip. As he drew breath, he felt a wave of nicotine slowly enter his lungs, followed by what he called a pleasure wave.

Robert exhaled and almost choked as he became aware of a figure moving in the shadows close to the visitor entrance. He could have easily missed him, if it had not been for the moonlight. "He came," he whispered to himself. "He actually came."

With excitement building, Robert re-opened the glove box and returned the opened pack of cigarettes. He got out of the car and walked towards the moonlit entrance gate. As he approached, the waiting man turned nervously to face him. "Herr Brauer," Robert muttered. The man walked into the light. Brauer was a large, stocky forty something with shoulder length hair. He was dressed in a dark brown, somewhat worn leather jacket, black mud stained jeans and trainers. His untidy appearance gave Robert the distinct impression that he was a man who did not stay still for very long. Obviously very nervous, his eyes darting around, Brauer responded quietly. "*Ja, ich been* Herr Brauer."

The response in a thick Bavarian accent made Robert wish he had studied harder as school. "I'm sorry Mr Brauer, I'm an American and my German is very limited."

Brauer sighed, looked around and motioned Robert to walk with him. "Then it's a good job that I took all those English lessons at school, Herr Jameson. Come this way.

The gardens will be more private." Both men walked towards a small side gate to the left of the main castle entrance and proceeded to enter the grounds.

Once inside the gardens they walked in-front the main building along the gravel drive and past the quiet flowerbeds and ornate fountains. Even in the moonlight walking through the moonlit Versailles inspired Baroque gardens was still an experience. Robert sighed, "Magnificent, aren't they?"

"Pardon me?"

"The gardens … Magnificent, wouldn't you say?"

"Er … yes, of course," said Brauer nodding.

For the next few minutes both men walked silently along the footpath enclosed by trees and shrubs, before eventually stopping outside the Temple of Apollo. The replica temple, which was built to house summer opera performances, now lay quiet behind locked gates. To the left of the temple lay an avenue of trees; they turned and walked down the path. Around 50 meters in, Robert stopped beside an ornate bench and invited Brauer to sit down. "So, Mr Brauer, I'll be honest, I was beginning to think you might not show."

Inside his pocket Robert retrieved a small voice recorder and placed it on the bench between himself and the big man. Brauer was edgy and fidgety, constantly glancing around. "Mr Brauer, there's no need to worry. It's 3.40 in the morning and no one is about. You're safe here."

As the words faded Brauer's eyes made immediate contact with Robert's, the mix of emotions he saw in them filled him with a sense of unease. Breaking the tension, Robert took a moment to switch on his recorder. As the small tape began to slowly move, Robert returned his gaze to Brauer. "OK, Mr Brauer I've been waiting a long time for this meeting so let's start at the beginning shall we?"

Brauer's head dropped and he swallowed. "Indeed that would seem like a good place to start Herr Jameson."

Jameson realised that Brauer's voice was shaking as he said, "Firstly you have to understand that by me giving you this information, you are placing yourself in possible danger."

"Are you sure?"

Robert, self-assured despite the tension in the other man, smirked as he said, "I assure you Mr Brauer, as a reporter I have heard that many times."

Brauer swung around and grabbed Roberts arm. "Do not make a joke Herr Jameson, I am serious."

As he looked at Brauer's expression in the darkness, Robert realised how earnest Brauer was and the smirk faded away, like an extinguished candle. "I'm sorry, I didn't mean to offend."

Brauer's voice dropped to a low whisper "Six weeks ago an Icelandic volcanologist wrote a paper about the volcanic activity in Iceland four years ago and of the disruption it caused in Europe. She also hypothesized about her so called Scorched Earth theory."

Robert nodded, "You're talking about Elín Gylfadóttir and of her crackpot theory of a ring of fire. I know the story, Mr Brauer, I read your email. She had some crazy notion that a series of simultaneous volcanic eruptions could bring about Armageddon. I also read that her ideas were not just disputed but ridiculed to such a degree that she was disgraced."

Brauer nodded, "All true Herr Jameson, but know this, I knew the woman and she was no crackpot. In fact she was one of the smartest women I knew."

"You keep saying, knew, Mr Brauer. Is there something you're not telling me?"

Brauer sighed, "She's dead Herr Jameson. She died, two days ago in a hotel in Frankfurt. Suicide, the police said."

Robert sighed, "Well these things sometimes happen Mr Brauer you shouldn't take it so personally."

Brauer's eye's dropped and he nodded, "I'm not, Herr Jameson, believe me. But Elin loved life; she wasn't the type of woman who would contemplate taking her own life."

"The woman was obviously under a great deal of stress."

"You are wrong, Herr Jameson, I saw her the day before she died and believe me she was not like a woman about to commit suicide."

"What are you saying? That she didn't kill herself? That she was killed? Why? Because of outlandish theories or …"

Interrupted by a muffled crack from behind, Robert turned his head to see what it was – a bird, or cat, perhaps. But in the shadows nothing moved. Robert turned back to Brauer. "Okay Mr Brauer, go on."

But Brauer said nothing. He just coughed and then, without warning, slumped forward. Alarmed Robert assumed that Brauer was sick. Perhaps he was taking some kind of seizure. "Brauer ... Brauer are you alright?" Robert reached out and attempted to pull the big man upwards. As he did so, he had the sudden sensation of warm liquid oozing over his hands. His face turned to horror, realising that the warm liquid was, in fact, blood. Robert started to panic "Brauer! Brauer! Oh Jesus!"

He placed his hand to Brauer's chest to check for a heartbeat. It was still there, but very faint. Brauer remained slumped forward, motionless. Without thinking Robert stood up, reached inside his outer pocket and pulled out his mobile phone. Then from behind, there was another crack! At first Robert thought he had been stung in the hip. "Arghh," he cried at the intense pain as he fell onto the ground. Yanking his jacket aside Robert stared at the entry wound in disbelief. "Oh my God! I've been shot."

In that moment, as he began to panic and his breathing became erratic, he knew that getting help was his only chance. As dizziness began to take hold he reached for his phone. While frantically dialling, Robert gazed at the ground. There in front of him was a set of black leather boots. Looking up, Robert finally made out the shape of a tall muscular man. Fighting for breath Robert coughed, "Sir ... Sir can you help, I think I've been sho ..."

The words faded as Robert saw the weapon. The automatic pistol complete with silencer was pointed at the ground. Robert looked at the man. Glaring back at him, the face was cold and emotionless. His skin becoming increasingly clammy and the dizziness growing worse, Robert dropped the phone and continued to stare at the figure, praying that somehow he might show a chink of reason.

Without speaking, the man simply turned to face Brauer, raised the pistol to his head and pulled the trigger. The crack rang out as the force of the shot hit him like a train, causing the slumped figure to fall onto the ground. Then he turned to face Robert, again raising his arm. Gazing down the barrel in disbelief Robert pleaded, "No … wait … wait, please don't …"

Crack! It was too late, Robert's world went dark and his body slumped forward onto the ground.

Calmly and without haste, the shadowed figure re-holstered the weapon, then crouched down and picked up Robert's phone. Observing the two dead men for a moment he then reached for the Dictaphone still lying on the bench. Putting both items in his pocket he turned towards the trees and walked away silently into the darkness.

SEVEN

SATURDAY: 10.30AM ALVA, SCOTLAND

"**A**RE YOU READY? I'm not going to wait all day."

"Sorry Mummy, I'm just coming."

Jane Duncan stood at the bottom of the tall wooden staircase looking upwards, tutting as she shook her head in annoyance at being kept waiting. Kneeling down she put on her shoes and picked up her keys. Dressed in blue Jeans, navy *GAP* T-shirt and a red outdoor waterproof jacket Jane Duncan was 38 and an accountant with a practice in Stirling – an attractive practical woman who loved her family and the outdoors. Although from Stirling, the Duncan's had lived in London for a number of years due to her husband's work with a large software company. However, that had changed eight years ago due to the economic recession. The company had decided to make "strategic cuts", as such Tom's job became "surplus to requirements."

The decision to move to Alva seemed to be the right choice at the time. Although the couple had planned to live in nearby Stirling, high property prices and a lack of affordable housing had forced a rethink. However, Alva was only a short distance from the city and did have excellent transport links, great schools and a good selection of local amenities all of which made the decision a little easier.

Personally, Jane would have liked to live a little further out of town. She and Tom had seriously considered nearby Dollar, with its splendid castle, private school and affluent coffee shop culture, but, in the here and now, Alva would have to do.

Of course, that's not to say that Alva didn't have its plus points. For both Tom and Jane probably the biggest plus, was the people. The support they had received from the local community when their son Scott had been so tragically killed, was simply amazing and had made a lasting impression on the couple.

As Jane finished tying her shoelaces, she was greeted by the sound of thumping feet coming down the stairs followed by a smiling six-year-old, wearing Jeans and a pinkish *Scooby Doo* T-Shirt. "Is this okay Mummy?"

"Yes, you look lovely. Does the T-Shirt still fit you okay?" Amy frowned, wriggled her arms for a moment and nodded. Suddenly the large wooden front door swung open and a smiling Tom Duncan stood in the doorway accompanied by an enthusiastic looking golden retriever. Amy leaped in to the air excitedly and yelled "Wallace!" The dog responded by eagerly bounding forward almost pulling Tom off his feet. "Whoa doggie ... you'll cause an injury." After a few moments of furious excitement the dog eventually calmed, allowing Tom to recompose himself. "Is everyone ready for a walk up the Glen?" Both mum and daughter grinned and shouted a unanimous chorus of "Yes!"

"Well okay then, let's get going."

Tom quickly about turned, stepped out into the waiting sunshine and took hold of his daughter's hand. Leaving the house, the warmth of the August sun felt good. The walk up to the glen was a mere ten-minute stroll, passing by Johnstone Street and Stirling Street. Once across the busy road, it was on past the popular Number 5 pub and on up into the glen.

Many locals often spoke of Alva as the best of both worlds. One minute you could be in a bustling street and the next you could be enjoying the emptiness and tranquillity of the surrounding hills. For Tom and Jane Duncan this was certainly a major factor in their decision to live in Alva. Once passed the golf club and car park. The lower entrance to the Glen is known as MacArthur Brae's. A large wooded area that is split in two by a stream or Burn as it is known locally. Now an interesting visitor attraction for tourists and walkers alike, the brae's contains a number of relics from Alva's industrial past.

In the late nineteenth and early twentieth centuries, Clackmannanshire had been part of Scotland's industrial heartland, boasting of woollen mills, coal and silver mines, all of which had employed thousands of people. Nowadays, walkers pass by these industrial relics with little thought of their heritage. But take a walk down Stirling Street and chat with a few of the old timers and visitor will soon get a flavour of what was.

The Glen itself is maintained by a local trust, mostly made up of volunteers who aim to return Alva Glen to its former glory. As a patron, Tom always reminds anyone who comments, that "we have a responsibility to maintain this historical area".

As well voluntary work the project also raises money by holding the traditional September Alva Glen Illuminations. This is an event that the entire family looks forward to. When the whole of Macarthur Brae's becomes illuminated with coloured fairly lights and candles placed in hand painted jam jars decorated by local school children.

Having now passed what seemed to be the last of a run of day-trippers, Tom released Wallace from his lead and the energetic retriever ran ahead, occasionally looking back as if to check that everything was okay. Amy skipped ahead, calling to the dog that was far too interested in the prospect of discovering a tasty morsel left by a careless child or visitor to come back. Tom took hold of his wife's hand as they continued over an old but sturdy iron bridge and continued upwards into the Glen.

Tom glanced at his wife and gave a little smirk. "What?" she said as if she had detected that Tom's sudden smirk was aimed as a joke at her. "It's nothing; I was just remembering the last time we were up here ... Remember?"

Jane grinned. It was around three months earlier and the family had been walking in the Glen when they passed a family of Orthodox Jews visiting the area on some kind of pilgrimage. Dressed in black the family seemed totally out of place and when the dog approached one of the children to play, a woman lashed out wildly, seemingly distressed that this "furious beast" was about to attack one of her young. "Have you ever seen them again?" Jane asked. "No, have you?"

Tom shook his head, "No, although I know people who have."

As the family climbed upwards the wooded gorge began to open out, revealing an array of trees and plant life. Ahead Amy had stopped for a moment, looking back for reassurance. The path ahead had begun to narrow and walking side by side was no longer an option. "Do you want to come and walk with us now, darling, it's perhaps best if you hold Mummy's hand?" As instructed Amy stopped and waited for Jane to take her hand. "Can we go to the top Daddy?"

"Do you think you can make it?" With a quick glance upwards, both mother and daughter responded with an enthusiastic, "Course we can."

"Okay you go ahead and I'll walk behind."

As the family crossed a second wooden bridge the ascent became notably harder. Jane had often remarked, that sadly most walkers did not walk this far, which is a shame because the views from the top are magnificent. On either side of the Narrow stony path the gorge appeared increasingly menacing. Sharp drops on either side would have unnerved many visitors, but Jane was convinced that the view at the top would justify their efforts. About thirty meters in front, Amy and her mother stopped and turned to look back. Jane had a puzzled look on her face. "Tom ... Is Wallace with you?"

As Tom turned to call the dog, bang! Something hit him from

behind. Initially Tom assumed it was merely a falling rock but then realised it was the dog that, in such enthusiasm, had accidentally run into him from behind. Then in what appeared to be a grotesque slow motion moment Jane and Amy's smiling faces were turning to horror. At first Tom didn't realise his situation, but then the reality hit. His foot had slipped and he was falling.

As he fell, Tom lunged with all of his strength, desperately trying to grasp at a protruding branch. Amy screamed "Daddy."

Without thinking Jane pulled Amy aside and threw herself towards her husband in sheer desperation. "Here ... take my hand ..."

"Oh my God ..." Tom yelled, "I'm going to fall."

Behind his wife, the six year old was sobbing, "Daddy."

"Tom ... Take my hand," Jane yelled. Tom realised that he had no choice but to put all of his faith into this one moment. Swallowing hard he lunged, and grappled for Jane's hand. With all her strength Jane franticly pulled, desperately trying to save her husband from what now seemed to be certain death. But something was wrong! Tom couldn't get a foothold, the ground was muddy and his grip was loosening. He looked into his wife's eyes in anguish. "Oh my God ... I can't hold on ... I'm falli ..."

"No!" Jane screamed, but it was too late, he was falling.

EIGHT

JANE ROSE TO her feet, pale and stunned, her mouth open in sheer disbelief as she struggled with her emotions to understand what just happened. Gazing down, Amy's face was white with shock and disbelief. Shaking, she knelt down and held the six year old in her arms. Sobbing uncontrollably, the child stared back at her mother with disbelieving eyes. "Where's Daddy Mummy? Will he be okay?"

Jane swallowed hard, "I don't know darling, I hope so, but let's get some help."

Reaching inside her jacket she retrieved her mobile phone and punched 112 on the keypad. After a few seconds a man's voice picked up the call.

"Emergency, which service please?"

Jane's mind seemed to momentarily blank out. "Oh … God … I don't know. My husband has fallen down a hill and I think he's hurt." While she drew breath, the reassuring voice came back, "That's okay, what's your name?

Glancing once more at her daughter Jane exhaled. "Jane … Jane Duncan."

"Well Jane, don't worry we'll get help to you. Can you tell me where you are?"

"Alva … Alva Gen, we're just past the second bridge." Jane paused to look around for a moment as if to conform the location.

"Yes … just past the bridge where the path splits into two. It was an accident, the dog banged into him and he … he fell down into the gorge. There are just too many trees and I … I can't see him."

"That's okay Jane. I have a fix on your location now. Help is on its way so please just stay where you are. We will be with your shortly."

Down below on the floor of the gorge, Tom's body twitched and his eyes slowly flickered open, "My God, I'm still alive!"

Apart from a sharp pain in his right arm and a few superficial cuts and bruises, he had thankfully not suffered any serious injuries. Staring upwards, his view of the gorge was obscured by what appeared to be and endless line of densely leafed trees and foliage. Tilting his head to the left Tom sighed in relief as he eyed a clump of dangerous looking jagged rocks that lay only a few meters from his head.

Slowly sitting up he shouted, "Hello, Jane … Amy."

With no answer, he got to his feet and made a second attempt. "Amy, Jane can you hear me?"

Tom sighed and looking around he thought that as he had fallen into the lowermost part of the Glen, the dense greenery would perhaps obscure his shouts for help. To his left, Tom could see water trickling downwards through rocks and to his right he caught sight of what appeared to be the entrance of a large cavern naturally formed into the rock. Taking another deep sigh he stood for a moment trying to focus and think of way out. Looking upwards he quickly discounted climbing out as a choice. Attempting such a steep ascent without the proper equipment or assistance would be foolhardy and dangerous. Knowing his wife as he did, Tom felt assured that being the practical woman that she was, she would probably have every conceivable emergency service on their way. No, for the moment Tom concluded that all he could do was to wait for them to arrive.

Glancing towards the normally inaccessible cavern, Tom smiled to himself and wondered that if perhaps a little exploration was called for.

Above the glen, Jane Duncan was prowling back and forth, her face pale with concern. Amy had stopped crying and was sat quietly on a nearby log. Ahead of them Wallace lay on the wooden bridge, somehow sensing that something was wrong.

"Mummy."

"Yes Amy."

"Will Daddy be okay?" Jane stopped pacing back and forth, looked down and sighed heavily, "I hope so baby, I really do."

Suddenly the glen's peaceful tranquillity was shattered as the emergency services began arriving. First the distant rumbling of engines could be heard, followed by the arrival of three Land Rovers. Entering the glen below and stopping just short of the lower bridge, twelve or so men emerged from the vehicles and started making their way upwards towards Jane and Amy.

Standing opposite the old cavern entrance, memories of childhood adventures in Wales flooded through Tom's mind. Thoughts of Saturday afternoon potholing, exploring old coal mines with his Uncle David – and of course the possibility of finding buried treasure. He never did of course, other than a few lumps of old coal, but it was still fun.

After a moment of deliberation, Tom concluded that it could take hours for the emergency services to arrive and that his rescue could take even longer. Edging closer to the cavern entrance he shook his head, "No," he thought to himself, "to miss out on such an opportunity would be crazy."

Tom had the distinct feeling that the cavern's interior would be bigger than he had anticipated. After one last look upwards for signs of a rescue party, he took a deep breath and, stepping slowly, moved into the mouth of the cavern.

Inside, Tom found his way obstructed by an aging wooden sign that read, "Danger: Keep Out! Old Mine Workings Ahead: No Access by order of Clackackmananshire Council." No doubt originally intended to warn off potential trespassers this message, however, seemed to have the opposite effect on Tom by further fuelling his curiosity.

Moving forward a few meters, he found his way was again blocked, this time by what seemed to be the remains of an old rusting iron gate. However, upon closer inspection, Tom discovered that the gate was rusting so badly that with little effort he was able to push it aside and continue further inside.

"Mummy, they're coming."

Glancing across at her daughter, Jane stopped pacing and raised her hand towards the dog that had begun to growl at the approaching men. "Wallace here boy, it's alright," she said reaching into her pocket and retrieving a piece of chopped smoked sausage. Food was something she knew the dog could not resist. As the morsel became visible the dog was instantly at her feet, tail wagging enthusiastically. While it ate, Jane used the distraction to attach a leash to its collar just as the men approached.

The rescue party had arrived! The majority appeared to be members of the Ochil Hills Mountain Rescue team and the remainder were clearly police judging by their uniforms. Most of the men were well-equipped and carried large rucksacks, tools and cords of rope slung over their shoulders. On their approach most of the group held back, with just two police officers approaching the distraught family. The first, a tall, slightly overweight sergeant in his thirties and the second, a younger constable, perhaps in his early twenties.

"Mrs Duncan?"

Jane swallowed, "Yes, that's me."

"I'm Sergeant Williams from Tullibody police station and this is my associate, Constable Bruce. I believe your husband's had a bit of an accident. Can you tell me what happened?" With Amy clinging to her mother's leg, Jane explained how the family had been crossing the gorge and how the dog had accidentally hit Tom from behind. Sergeant Williams listened intently to the explanation, occasionally nodding in acknowledgment. When Jane had finished, Williams turned to the rescue team and cleared his throat. "Gentleman, the situation is that we have an injured man down there. I need a couple of two-man teams to go down, assess the situation and formulate some options."

Immediately the majority of the group stepped forward and enthusiastically volunteered themselves. Williams nodded in appreciation, "Okay then, McAllen, Bruce, Riley and Davies, you're up. Let's move.

Within moments the four men were kitted out with ropes and tackle and were prepared to ascend down into the steep gorge. Amy stared at her mother, who despite always having projected an aura of confidence was looking distinctly shaky.

In the damp cavern below, Tom was excitedly examining pieces of old mining equipment scattered on the ground, oblivious to the commotion above. First he discovered the rusting blade of an old axe, a spade with a broken handle and a tankard. This was incredible. For Tom, it was as if the mine had somehow tapped into his childhood fantasies about finding lost treasure and delivered them to him. Tom thought that whatever had happened here had happened quickly and judging by the poor condition of the remains, it happened a long time ago. As he stood and moved forward, he carefully placed the items back where he had found them.

Continuing inwards, Tom became aware that the cavern or mine, as it had obviously once been, was starting to contract inwards. With no torch and the light beginning to fade, Tom made the decision to continue just a little further. He was forced to stoop low in order to continue. With memories of childhood adventures rushing through his mind, Tom's heart began to race with excitement, as up ahead he caught sight of a sudden chink of light.

As he took a deep breath, he placed his hand against the light bathed rock. As he moved his hand over the cold stone his expression turned to one of puzzlement. Although he could see the illuminated rock, he couldn't identify how the light was being produced.

"What the hell?"

Suddenly he felt the ground tremble and crack beneath his feet. Looking down in alarm, a split appeared like an open wound and a strand of brilliant white light began to ooze through. As the shaking increased, Tom began to panic but, as he turned to leave, the shaking suddenly stopped and he froze to the spot, waiting for something else to happen.

But there was nothing, no heat, no steam, nothing, except the continuous trickle of white light from below. Tom stopped, momentarily confused and feeling somewhat disorientated. Then, as before, the ground suddenly began to shake again. This time, however, the shaking was so violent that escape no longer seemed like an option. The deafening roar of rocks and debris shattered the silence as they began to fall around him.

Then, in a moment of sheer terror, the chamber floor suddenly gave way and exploded into a plethora of brilliant white light.

Tom screamed as he lost his footing and found himself careering downwards into the nightmarish abyss. As he fell, he lunged at a protruding rock and watched in horror as the ground that he had been kneeling on only moments earlier disappeared into the nothingness below. Clinging desperately to the rock for his life, Tom gritted his teeth and with his heart thumping and fingers sweating, struggled with all of his strength to pull himself to safety. His efforts were in vain, the floor was already beginning to collapse. His fingers slipping, Tom closed his eyes in preparation for what was to come. Then losing his battle to hold on, he took a deep breath and began to fall.

Unexpectedly, from nowhere, a large hand grabbed his arm. "Let go lad, it's okay I've got ye."

For a moment Tom was confused. He thought that he should be dead.

"What?"

Opening his eyes, he looked upwards and saw a shadowy figure through the brightness. Then glancing downwards, he began to panic again as he saw nothing below – no rocks, no ground, nothing but piercing white light. Tom shrieked in alarm, "I ... I can't, I'll fall."

"Nae ye won't. Trust me laddie, it's okay. You're only few meters off the ground."

"What?"

Tom suddenly yelled out in alarm as the figure released its grip and he fell downwards only to land on his feet just a metre or so below. As Tom looked up towards the shadowy figure above, his expression turned to one of disbelief as he was overcome by the intensity of the blinding light. As he tried to shield his eyes, the voice above spoke again, "Here lad, use the rope ... climb up."

A coil of rope appeared and Tom grasped an end and sighed with relief as he felt himself being hauled upwards. However before he had a chance to say thank you, he found himself lying flat out on the cave floor, only centimetres from yet another gaping precipice and possible death. Coughing and spluttering Tom took a deep breath just as his rescuer came into focus. A large scruffy dark haired figure, unusually dressed in some kind of costume, cotton shirt and a pair of old fashioned breeches, possibly eighteenth century. Tom opened his mouth to speak as the big man slapped him on the shoulder and said, "So laddie. Who the bloody hell are ye?"

NINE

"WHAT?"

Tom Duncan just stared at the man, not only trying to understand what just happened, but also who his saviour was. The figure in front of him simply grinned, "Aye, laddie that's just how I felt when I first saw it. The names Dougie Allan, what's yours?"

Still speechless, Tom merely murmured and pointed his finger towards the drop. "Er, Tom. Tom Duncan. I ... I don't understand, where did you come from? What the hell is that?"

Dougie's smile faded and his expression turned serious, still aware that the sheer drop was only meters away. "If it's alright with ye laddie, I think we had better move away from this place, what do ye think?"

Tom nodded in agreement as both men pulled themselves up and walked back out into the safety of the passageway and then out towards the mouth of the cavern.

At the entrance, both men flopped onto the ground breathing heavily. Tom looked at his strangely dressed saviour and repeated the question, "So, where did you come from? What's with the costume?"

Dougie looked at Tom with some surprise, "Why, it's nae polite tae criticise another person's clothing. Why, I could say the same about you!"

Tom didn't respond. First because he struggled to understand Dougie, the man's accent was strange, although familiar. It was unusual, old Scots perhaps, almost foreign. Second he sensed that this angel of mercy could perhaps be easily offended.

Dougie continued, "To be honest, I don't ken. One minute I was in the mine, the next … McArthur, then I found myself here."

Tom's face turned to confusion. "Mine, but Mr Allan, there is no mine. It shut down over 200 years ago."

Offended, Dougie suddenly jumped to his feet, "Are you calling me a liar sir? I was just there."

The cold expression on Dougie's face was deadly serious. "No Mr Allan, I'm not calling you a liar. It's just that there is, no mine, there hasn't been in over 200 years."

Dougie's mouth gaped open in bewilderment.

"Then how?" Dougie's head dropped as he fell to his knees. "No, my Mary, my bonnie lassie, she's gone?"

Tom stared at Dougie sympathetically, desperately trying to find the right words to offer some comfort, "I'm so sorry, I don't know what to say."

"Neither do I lad, neither do I. For me it's 1710 and I've lost my whole life."

Minutes passed and the two men sat still in silence, staring at each other, each man seemingly contemplating his own future. Looking up, Tom broke the silence. "May I call you Dougie?"

Dougie gave a smirk, "Aye laddie, of course ye can."

"I don't know what this place is or what's happened here. But, whatever it is, it must be for a reason and if you are in agreement let me help you. Hopefully we'll find some answers together."

"Aye, agreed." Nodding, Dougie extended his large hand and both men shook in agreement.

"So perhaps a good place to start would be at the beginning. You mentioned someone called McArthur. Did he have something to do with you being here?"

Dougie sat back and frowned, then said, "Aye, well I suppose in a way he did. It was because of him that I took the bloody job in the first place. Ten pounds a month tae be mine manager …"

Dougie's head dropped and he sighed, "Ten pounds. Well at the time it seemed to good tae be true."

"Mr Duncan?"

Suddenly turning his head in alarm, Tom became aware that there were four men directly behind them. Two of the four were police officers, the other two were dressed in rescue clothing and carrying ropes. One of the officers stepped forward and spoke again, "Are you okay Mr Duncan? Are you hurt?"

Jumping to his feet, like a cornered animal Dougie reached for a sharp rock, stood up and spun around to face the two oncoming officers. "Quick laddie, I'll take these two, ye take those."

Rushing to his feet Tom grabbed Dougie's arm. "No wait, Dougie, its okay. These men are here to help."

Above, Jane Duncan was on her cell phone and pacing back and forth, her face white with concern. "I've told you everything. Oh God I just don't know …"

"Sergeant …"

Sergeant Williams's radio suddenly burst into life followed by a series of static crackles. Jane paused and said, "Mum I'll have to call you back."

Flipping the lid of her Nokia phone closed, she returned the phone to her jacket pocket, turned heel and walked over to Sergeant Williams. "This is Williams go Ahead."

"Sir we've found them, both of them!"

The radio crackled as Williams turned to Jane whose face had a genuine look of confusion. "Both of them?" she muttered, "But there was no one else."

Sergeant Williams stood for a moment in similar bewilderment and pressed the call button again. "Bruce, please repeat your last message."

Again a pause then the radio again sparked into life, "Sir, you heard me right, there's two of em. A man wearing some kind of costume and …"

Desperate to hear news of her husband, Jane's frustration suddenly boiled over and she shrieked out, "What about my husband? Is he hurt?"

The radio went silent for a few moments and again it crackled into life "Mr Duncan … yes he's here. He's fine."

On hearing the news Jane turned, knelt down and took Amy in her arms and burst into tears. Sobbing in sheer relief she hugged her daughter, "Daddy's fine … he's fine … Oh thank God."

Williams again pressed the call button. "OK Kenny, let's get those men up here."

For a moment the radio remained quiet. Frustrated by an apparent lack of news, Williams again pushed the call button, "Constable Bruce, did you hear me? Let's get those men up here."

Again silence, then the radio burst into life once more. "Sir, we … we've found something else, you may want to see this."

TEN

KATE HARDING, THE 38-year-old, red headed editor of the British *Daily Chronicle* sat stern faced at her large 1950s light oak desk. Twiddling a pencil between her fingers, she licked her lips as she shuffled through the pages of a potential story, occasionally murmuring sounds of disapproval.

In front of her a nervous fresh-faced, nineteen-year-old reporter, Anna Blythe, was standing waiting for a response, but as the moments passed she feared the outcome may not be what she had expected. Kate sighed, "It's okay Anna but it lacks, something. I can't quiet put finger on it. I know, panache."

Anna's eyes opened wide and she had the sudden desire for the ground to open up and swallow her. Kate threw the papers on the desk and said sarcastically, "Take it away and re-write paragraphs four to nine ... and for God's sake put some feeling into it, it reads like a bloody funeral notice."

Anna's lip quivered as she quickly picked up the papers, turned and duck tailed it out of the office, muttering "what a bitch" under her breath as she slammed the door behind her.

Kate stretched back in her high-backed, red-leather chair, enjoying the feeling of power even if it was just for a moment and just occasionally, she liked it and she liked others to know it.

Harding was always destined to be in the news business. As

a child she would provide her parents with a constant stream of stories. By the time she was 13, Kate was already deputy editor of her local school newspaper, *The St Columbus School Times*. As she watched Blythe storm out, she grinned to herself as the memory of a young naïve reporter who once had a similar encounter with a former mentor.

Her moment of elation was suddenly interrupted as the phone on her desk rang. Sitting up, she picked up the receiver. "Yes, Hello."

"Kate is that you?" Speaking with a German accent, the woman's voice quivered and shook with emotion.

"Gert, what is it? What's wrong?"

"It's Robert, he's been shot. Kate … Oh my God, he's dead."

Standing up in shock, Kate's mouth fell open. "Gert … what are you saying … he was just here on Thursday."

"The meeting Kate … in Schwetzingen. You know, the supposedly big story he's been working on."

"I …"

"For Christ sake Kate, he's been murdered; along with the guy he was meeting. What the hell was he working on?"

Suddenly overcome with emotion Kate flopped down into her seat, "I'm sorry Gert. I can't talk anymore … I'll speak to you later okay?"

With tears streaming down her face she replaced the handset, stood up and walked slowly over to the glass door of her office. Pausing to take a breath she composed herself, she opened the door and walked through into the open plan office. With Sunday deadlines looming, the news floor was a hive of activity, phones ringing, staff chatting and printers churning out paper.

Kate just stood silently, staring into the room, her face red through crying, her eyes puffy with tears mixed in with traces of mascara.

"Kate, is everything alright?"

From a desk opposite her office, the young Anna Blythe had

just returned to her desk with a fresh coffee and had looked up just as Kate appeared.

Kate cleared her throat and attempted to get the attention of the room. "Excuse me everyone, can I have your attention please."

Heads turned, faces looked up from computer screens and voices went silent through the office as each person sensed that something was dreadfully wrong.

Kate's head dropped and she drew a deep breath before continuing.

"I … I'm afraid I have some bad news. Robert Jameson is dead. It appears that he was murdered in Germany last night."

Gasps of shock rippled through the room as Kate continued, "It seems Robert was to meet a contact in Schwetzingen about a story he was working on, when it happened. According to Gert Schrader from our Frankfurt office, they were both shot early this morning."

By now the room was completely silent apart from the occasional sniffle. All attention was on Kate. "Now, I know many of you knew Robert and I am sure you will agree that we were probably the closest thing to him. He was not married and had no children."

Stopping to take a breath, Kate took a moment to look around the room. She paid particular attention to making eye contact with each person before continuing. "Bill … Amanda can the two of you please put your heads together and write something nice?"

The fortyish Bill Peterson, the paper's sports editor, stood a good head and shoulders above a younger blonde woman and nodded in agreement, "Of course … No problem Kate."

Still standing opposite Anna Blythe's desk, Kate looked down at the young woman whose mouth was still agape. "Anna, I want you to find out what Robert was working on. I am sure the police will eventually contact us. I want to have something to give them."

The nineteen-year-old closed her mouth and said "Er … yes … yes of course."

Kate again looked at the sea of faces surrounding her. "I know this is dreadful thing to happen, but until we know more, there's not a great deal we can do. Right now we have a newspaper to run. Let's get back to work."

Kate nodded, turned and re-entered her office. The throng of people dispersed and noise levels rose again.

Peterson returned to his cubicle, and as he sat he reached into his pocket and retrieved a small black address book. Taking a moment to flip through the gold-edged pages, he finally stopped, placed the book on the desk and picked up the telephone handset. Glancing around for a moment, he dialled.

Moments later a man's voice said, "Hello."

"It's Peterson."

"Yes."

"As expected I'm afraid we may still have a problem. She's assigned someone else to follow up Jameson's story."

"That's ... unfortunate."

The phone clicked and the call was over. Peterson replaced the receiver and closed the pocket book. Pausing for a moment, he returned the book to the safety of his inside pocket and continued working.

ELEVEN

SATURDAY: 2.30PM ALVA, SCOTLAND

"**D**O YOU HAVE any idea what you're saying Mr Duncan?" Williams stared wide-eyed as Tom frowned.

"Yes Sergeant, I know exactly what I'm saying. For God's sake man you saw the thing."

Williams nodded, "For all we know, it could be some kind of new power station."

Tom stared in disbelief, "Power station! Have you lost your bloody mind? What about him?" pointing to his costumed rescuer. "Perhaps he's just a 300-year-old engineer Hmm?" Tom took a deep breath and paused. "Look Sergeant, you're afraid. Lord knows I'm afraid, but something is clearly going on here that cannot be explained. We need answers and you need to start making phone calls."

Glancing at the rescue team sitting nearby, Williams nodded in defeat, knowing that his attempt to place some kind of sanity label on the whole affair had failed. For the first time in his fifteen-year career he felt completely out of his depth.

"Okay Mr Duncan, we'll play it your way. However, until I can ascertain Mr Allan's part in all of this, I'll have to take him into custody."

Tom sighed and lowered his voice to a whisper, "What? Sergeant, can we speak privately?" Williams nodded and both men took a few steps away from the group.

"Look, let's think about this for a minute. That man saved my life today. He's frightened, disorientated and clearly in no condition to face a media circus."

Williams sighed looking slightly sceptical. "So what are you proposing? That I simply forget the whole thing?"

"No, of course not. All I am saying is by all means call your superiors. Let them begin their investigation, but for now let's keep Mr Allan under wraps, until we know exactly what's going on. I … I, just have a gut feeling it's the right thing to do."

Williams nodded in agreement, "Aye, alright then, but where will he stay?"

"He can stay with us."

"What? You? Are you crazy? My superiors would …"

"What's the alternative sergeant, jail?"

Williams stood up straight and nodded, "Alright Mr Duncan, you win … for now. Mr Allan can stay with you this evening until …"

"Until?"

"Until we can sort this bloody mess out." Williams turned to his bewildered-looking rescue team. "Alright lads you know the situation. It seems that Mr Duncan here doesn't require any medical attention, so you boys can go home for now. But please be aware that this … um … incident is now a police matter, so please keep your mouths shut."

The group stood, nodded in agreement and then began to gather ropes and equipment and proceeded to walk away towards the waiting vehicles.

Williams turned to face the Duncan's. "OK folks, we'll drop you at home. Do you have everything?"

Tom looked down; his wife and daughter were still sitting on the grass, Amy's head in her mother's lap. Her usual smile had faded and her eyes were red from crying. Tom smiled and knelt down. "Are you okay?"

Jane nodded, glanced at Dougie and returned a faint but tired smile. "Aye, but are you fine with all of this?"

Tom also glanced over at his saviour who stood a few paces away looking lost and somewhat bewildered. Tom sighed, turned back and nodded confidentially knowing that, in this case, it was the right thing to do. "Aye love, somehow everything's changed today and this just feels … right."

Jane smiled, "Well then, that's all I needed to know."

Tom returned the smile, stood up and faced Sergeant Williams, "Yes Sergeant, we have everything … let's go."

With the other rescue vehicles gone, the group arrived at the last remaining Land Rover.

Putting the dog in the rear compartment, everyone climbed inside except Dougie Allan who simply gazed in disbelief at this multi-coloured alien machine. "Okay … just what the hell is that contraption?"

As he was about to climb aboard, Tom stopped and stepped down. "It's okay Dougie, it's how we get around … it's a motorised carriage, we call it a car."

"A car?"

"Aye, things have changed a bit in 300 years."

"I … I can see that."

"Don't worry, it's perfectly safe."

"Well if ye say so."

In the Land Rover the sound of giggles could be heard as the big man climbed into a vacant seat. As the engine simultaneously roared into life, Dougie let out a deafening yell. Tom turned and placed a hand on the big man's shoulder in an attempt to offer comfort. "Dougie … its okay!"

Williams revved the land Rover and it sprang into life like a leopard about to hunt prey. Moments later the vehicle accelerated away from the glen and disappeared from view leaving the glen peaceful once more.

TWELVE

KATE HARDING STOOD over the shoulders of Rob Davies, the *Chronicle*'s portly, rather scruffy senior network administrator. "For God's sake man can you get me access to the bloody email or not?"

Glancing up, Davies began to scratch his greasy, dark-brown hair. "Er ... er yes, I just need to restore the files from the Server into a PST file and ... "

"Alright, I don't need a bloody post mortem just get it to me as soon as possible."

Kate turned abruptly and walked away leaving the rather flustered administrator speechless.

Minutes later she emerged from the elevator and strode on to the news floor that was buzzing as staff were frantically finalising first editions of the Sunday publication.

Kate glanced around the room, her narrow eyes darting back and forth, "Peterson ..."

"Yes Kate." Peterson raised his head above his cubicle partition and stood up.

"Have you and Amanda finished the article on Robert?"

"Er ... yes its right here, take a look."

Kate strode over and began to read from Peterson's monitor.

Staring at the on-screen headline for a moment she found her eyes beginning to water and a lump forming in her throat.

CHRONICLE JOURNALIST BRUTALLY MURDERED …

London: Staff at *The Daily Chronicle* were today shocked at news of the brutal murder of one of their own. Veteran reporter Robert Jameson was brutally shot and murdered early this morning in the grounds of Schwetzingen Castle, Germany. An unidentified man was also found dead at the scene. Police in Germany have opened a full investigation, but no motive for the crime has been forthcoming. *Chronicle* editor, Kate Harding, said, "Robert was one of the great's and he will be sadly missed."

Robert, an American who had lived in London for thirteen years had previously worked for the *New York Daily News* before taking up his post at the *Chronicle*. Kate Harding has promised a full investigation into his death and assured the authorities that any relevant information will be passed on to the police. Full story on page 4.

Kate swallowed and took a deep breath. "Good, Bill, very good. Let's run it on the front page."

Peterson looked up startled, "What about the Yellowstone follow up story? I thought …"

"Bill … this is the story, I'm not going to have a debate, not when it's one of our own."

Peterson sighed and then gave a defeated nod, "Yes, of course. I'm sorry."

Kate didn't respond. She merely nodded, turned and went back to her office. Once inside she sat down and stretched her neck and sighed. No sooner had she finished exhaling than there was a knock at the door. "Come in," she barked.

Anna flung open the door looking more anxious than ever – no doubt from their earlier encounter.

"Anna … what can I do for you?"

Anna closed the door and lowered her voice. "It's about Robert, I have some information."

Kate sat up, sighed and made a conscious effort to soften her tone. "Okay, take a seat and tell me what you have."

Sitting down the young woman cleared her throat. "Well, I looked through Robert's desk and I found this."

She opened her bag and pulled out what appeared to be a diary. "I was looking through this and I found a note. It seems that Robert had been trying to meet with a man in Germany called Brauer, Herman Brauer. So I did a little research and I found out something bizarre …"

"What?"

"Brauer was a priest …"

"A priest?"

"Well ex-priest really. He was arrested on suspicion of theft and criminal damage, but the charges were dropped and he was released."

Kate sat up and started rolling a pencil between her fingers, "Criminal damage?"

"Unfortunately, there's not much detail. But I did discover that, he seems to have associated himself with a scientist … a volcanologist by the name of Elín Gylfadóttir."

Kate sat forward and nodded, "I've heard of her, she had some wild theory about a volcanic ring of fire or something. Anyway her theories were thrown out and she lost her funding. We ran a piece last year."

Anna nodded. "That's right, but the labs in Frankfurt where she worked were torched and police suspect that Brauer was involved."

Kate stopped rolling the pencil. "So have you tried to get hold of her?"

"Yes … of course."

"And?"

"She's dead."

Kate put the pencil down. "Dead?"

"Yes, apparently she committed suicide in a hotel on Thursday night."

"Suicide!" Before Kate could continue, the phone rang. Picking up the receiver she yelled "What?"

The young man's voice on the other end sounded surprised. "Er, I'm sorry to disturb you Miss Harding ... but you said you wanted to be informed when I had access to Mr Jameson's email." Kate nodded, "I'm sorry Rob, I didn't mean to snap. What have you got?"

"Well, some of the emails were encrypted, but I managed to get in. I have attached the mailbox to your account so you should have access to everything you need."

Kate rolled her eyes and smiled, "That's great work Rob. Well done." Replacing the receiver she returned her attention to Anna. "Okay, you've done good work here, but there is something more to this. Whatever it is, there's definitely a story here. I'll look through these emails and I'll forward anything relevant to you."

Anna nodded and stood up, still feeling slightly awkward. "Kate, would you have any objections to me leaving slightly earlier this evening? I was planning to work on this from home?"

Glancing at her watch, Kate suddenly realised that their conversation had lasted slightly longer than she had planned, especially with the Sunday deadlines looming.

"Sure that's fine. We'll probably run this next weekend anyway so let's meet on Monday and discuss it."

Anna smiled, turned and left the room closing the door behind her.

By 5.40pm the office was buzzing, many of the journalists were frantically finalising copy and beginning to lay out early editions of Sunday's *Chronicle*.

Normally the editor of a busy newspaper would never leave the office early, but today was different. Feeling the heavy loss of Robert, Kate was sure that the staff could manage and that leaving

a few hours earlier would be acceptable. Besides, tonight she wanted to just go home and soak in a hot bath.

Unplugging her laptop, she placed it in her bag and zipped it closed. Then reaching up to a nearby coat stand, she unhooked her Burberry and put it on. As she did, she gave a little jump as her phone rang. She leaned over and picked up the receiver, "Hello …"

"Hello, Is this Kate Harding?" The Scottish voice on the other end was that of a softly spoken man. "Yes it is. Who wants to know?"

"Yes, hello Miss Harding. My name is McPherson, Donald McPherson. I'm a freelancer with the *Stirling Observer*. I've written a couple of pieces for you in the past and …"

"Yes I remember you Mr McPherson, you've done some nice pieces for us, but last thing on a Saturday afternoon is not a great time? Perhaps Monday morning would be more appro …"

McPherson cut Kate off abruptly. "Aye, that may be so, but I can assure you, you'll have time for this. In fact, you may want to pack yourself a bag for a wee trip."

THIRTEEN

SATURDAY: 7.35PM ALVA, SCOTLAND

THE AUGUST EVENING sky was magnificent. The Ochil's were a blaze of red as the remainder of the day's sunlight fell lower in the evening sky. In the Duncan's garden, Dougie Allan stared longingly across the tops of the hills and sighed. Although familiar, he couldn't help feeling that they, like himself, had become a strangers in a strange land.

"Are you okay Dougie?"

Dougie gave a weak smile and nodded, "Aye lad, I'm just looking at my hills. They look the same but somehow so different, if that makes any sense?"

"Of course, it makes perfect sense, especially after all you've been through. But rest assured they're the same hills, Alva's just a wee bit bigger than you remember that's all. I'm sure that if for some reason you can't get back, you'll be able to make a life here, it's not such a bad place."

Dougie's head turned and he sighed, "Oh laddie, nae without my Mary. She was my life. We'd only been married a couple of years. I can tell ye, it's going be difficult without her. Everything here is so different. I just feel so lost."

"That's perfectly understandable Dougie, but that was 300 years ago, I'm sure tha ..."

"Nae laddie, not for me it isn't. For me, it was only yesterday."

Dougie's tone sharpened and Tom realised he was starting to sound a little insensitive.

"Sorry Dougie, that's not what I meant. Look, for now you're in the 21st century, Lord knows it's going to take you time to adjust. Once you've had a little time perhaps we can do some research and maybe find some answers."

Dougie turned to face Tom, "Ye would do that? Ye would help me? Even though we've just met?"

Tom nodded, "Of course I would. For some reason, I feel that we are in this together. You saved my life today and this is the least I can do."

They were suddenly interrupted by a knock at the window, followed by the appearance of the face of a smiling 6 year old. Amy waved at the two men who couldn't help but smile back at her.

"You've got a grand family Tom, you're a lucky man."

Tom nodded and smiled at Amy, "Yes I suppose I am. Come inside Dougie, I'll put my daughter to bed and then we can talk some more."

Once back in the living room, Tom asked Dougie, "Can I get you a drink or something?"

"Nae. I'm braw cheers. That was a grand supper your wife made. I've never had food like that before."

Tom smiled, "I'm glad you enjoyed it. I'll be back in a moment."

Dougie sat down on the black leather couch as Tom turned and left the room.

"Daddy …"

"Huh." Tom looked upwards. Amy stood waiting at the top of the stairs, dressed in pink Scooby Doo pyjamas and clutching her panda. Tom climbed the stairs and led Amy by the hand into her bedroom. "Alright, my princess, have you brushed your teeth?"

Amy nodded, "Yes Daddy, see!" She opened her mouth and gave a toothy grin. "Very nice darling, they're lovely." Tom pulled back Amy's quilt and lifted her into bed.

"Daddy …"

"Yes, my darling."

"I'm glad Dougie saved you, he's a nice man."

Tom smiled as a lump formed in his throat. "Me too my darling and yes he is a very nice man." He kissed Amy on her forehead and pulled the blanket up close. "Goodnight my lamb, sleep well."

In the guest room Jane was busily making up a spare bed.

"She's all tucked up."

"That's good," Jane said and then lowered her voice to a whisper. "How is he?"

"Fine I think. Well, as fine as a person can be that's just been pulled 300 years in to the future."

Jane frowned "Are you sure about this Tom? 300 years it seems …"

"Hey, that man saved my life today. Now I don't think …"

"WHOA!!!" The stillness of the evening was suddenly shattered by the sound of a scream from the living room below. Jane dropped the blanket and she and Tom bolted downstairs. Flinging the door to the living room open the couple were met by their visitor furiously waving his fist in front of the television. "Dougie, are you alright?"

Dougie turned; his face was one of utter shock. "Alright! But, what the hell is this? There's a man inside the box."

Tom and Jane looked at each other for a moment and giggled.

"No, Dougie, it's okay. It's called television. We watch it for entertainment. I can assure you there's no one inside," Tom explained.

Dougie's face turned from alarm to confusion as he lowered his fist. "Then what the hell … how on earth does it …?"

Tom realised that Dougie must have accidentally pressed a button on the remote which had been lying on the couch. Reaching down he picked up the remote and flicked through a few channels.

"Television was invented around 80 years ago, by a Scotsman actually. It's powered by electricity. Remember I told you about that earlier."

Dougie nodded and Tom continued, "As well as electricity, television also uses a something called radio. This can transmit or send pictures and sound over great distances. We use this to communicate with each other as well as for entertainment."

Dougie nodded, "So he's not sitting in the box, he's somewhere else?"

"Exactly, like I said, there have been a lot of changes in 300 years. It's just going to take a wee bit of time that's all."

Again, Tom flicked the channel, this time to the BBC News channel. On screen the presenter was introducing the day's news headlines.

"This is the eight o'clock news from the BBC. Reports are coming in of a massive volcanic eruption in Yellowstone National Park in the USA. Early reports indicate that there may be as many as 25,000 casualties and many fatalities. The US government has declared a statewide emergency. Rescue teams have been dispatched to aid in rescue efforts. Reports suggest they should be on site within the hour."

"This is the fourth major volcanic eruption in recent weeks. Last week Tombora, in Indonesia, erupted leaving a trail of death and devastation. Scientists around the world fear that the events of recent weeks are somehow connected."

"In other news, a prominent reporter for the London *Daily Chronicle* has been found brutally murdered in Germany. Reports are sketchy, but police say that both he and another man, who remains unnamed at this time, were found shot dead at a popular German visitor attraction in Schwetzingen, Germany. A *Chronicle* spokesman said, 'Robert Jameson was one of the great's and he will be sadly missed.' The investigation continues."

"In other news ..."

Tom turned the television off. "Sorry Dougie, you must think that it's all bad news."

Dougie smiled, "Nae laddie, it's a truly amazing device."

The group sat in silence for a few moments. Then Jane stood up, saying, "So Mr Allan, may I offer you something to drink?"

Dougie smiled, "Please lassie, call me Dougie. Now in terms of that drink, another cup o' that braw tea of yours would be grand."

Jane smiled and left the room leaving Tom and Dougie sitting opposite each other. Other than an ornate clock ticking, the house was quiet.

"It's been quite a day!"

"Aye laddie, it has. I must confess though, that when I left the house this morning, I never expected anything like this."

Tom sighed and gave a smile, "No, I suppose not."

Dougie's expression turned serious. "What's going to happen with the cavern?" he asked.

"I suppose there will be an investigation. I suspect the military will be involved. We'll have to wait and see."

Dougie's head dropped and he sighed, "What do ye think they will do with me?"

"Dougie, this is a first in human history. They'll definitely want to talk to you. You never know, you might even become famous."

"Me famous?"

Before Tom could respond the living room door opened and Jane returned with a tray of tea and cakes. "Who's going to be famous?"

Tom rolled his eyes as he took the tray from his wife and placed it down on a glass coffee table. "Dougie. I was just saying that he'll be famous."

Jane nodded in agreement "Oh, aye, of that there is no doubt."

Minutes later the tea had been poured and Dougie sat quietly sipping the hot tea. "Ah braw, I'll say one thing Tom, that fine wife o'yours can make a grand cup of tea."

Jane swallowed a mouthful of tea and put her cup down.

"Dougie I've made up a bed for you in our guest room. Tom will show you the bathroom and how everything works. I'm sure you will be comfortable. I was wondering what you wanted to do about, er, your clothes."

My clothes?" Dougie looked surprised. Tom quickly broke into the conversation. "Dougie, I think what Jane means is that your clothes are perhaps a little out of time. We are just thinking that perhaps a more modern look might help you … er … blend in."

At first Dougie looked a little insulted but then his expression softened as he realised that the Duncan's were just trying to help. "Aye, I suppose that would be a plan."

Tom nodded, "Well ok then, we'll go into Stirling in the morning. I'm sure you'll find something there."

FOURTEEN

SATURDAY: PIMLICO, CENTRAL LONDON

IN CENTRAL LONDON the brightness of the day was dwindling. Low cloud had turned into ominous rain clouds. By 9.40pm, a heavy rain shower could be heard battering the windows of Anna Blythe's ninth-storey flat. Having just showered, she reached up, unhooked her white M&S bathrobe and put it on.

Although the ninth-floor property, situated as it was in an admirably affluent part of London, was worth a considerable amount of money, she never really appreciated living in the city, although she did love the views. As a child, brought up in the Dorset countryside, the young Anna would often visit London with her parents and be mesmerised by the hustle and bustle of the big city. When she was offered a job at the *Chronicle* her parents insisted she should stay in her father's city flat. Or, to be more exact, her father's company flat, until she learned the value of money and saved a deposit for a property of her own.

Sitting at her kitchen table, Anna switched on her laptop and immediately went to her Facebook account. After scanning for any interesting gossip, she entered a status update of "Another Saturday night wasted". Picking up her glass, she took a couple of sips of the Shiraz and opened her email.

Most of the incoming messages appeared to be spam, but she noticed a new mail folder labelled Robert Jameson's Email Archive.

After a moment of confusion, she realised that this was the content from Jameson's email account.

Flicking through the various messages nothing seemed to be out of the ordinary, until one headed "URGENT: Please read" prompted further attention. Opening the message, Anna took another sip of wine and began to read;

FWD: BlytheA@Chronicle.co.uk; HardingK@Chronicle.co.uk
To: JamesonR@Chronicle.co.uk
From: herman.brauer@hotmail.com
Date: July 2nd
Subject: Please meet me soon!

Mr Jameson,

I have been trying to contact you for some time, but I believe I am being watched so I have to be very careful. I know you will probably think I am a nut job trying to spread a conspiracy theory, but you have to listen to what I have to say. I believe I have uncovered an organisation that seems to be at the centre of a number of disappearances, kidnappings – call them what you will. I don't exactly know who they are and where they are based, but I do know whatever they have planned, it's big and a lot of people are going to die.

I have a friend that I want you to meet, a volcanologist from Iceland. She has some ideas about what could be causing the sudden surge in volcanic activity around the world. She will be in Germany in a few weeks. I will contact you again soon.

H

Anna sighed and leaned back, her mind whirling with questions. "What the hell's going on here?" she muttered to herself. Suddenly her cell phone burst into life. As she reached over and picked it up, her eyes rolled as the name – Boss Bitch identified the incoming caller.

"Hello, boss, what can I do for you?"

The connection was noisy, perhaps from a busy street or possibly a railway station. Yes she concluded it was definitely a railway station. "Anna, is that you?"

"Yes, is everything alright?"

Kate's breathing sounded heavy and laboured. "Nothing's wrong, I'm simply rushing to catch a train."

"A train! Where are you going?" Even before she had finished the sentence, she grimaced as she realised it wasn't really any of her business.

"I'm at King's Cross. Listen something's come up and I have to go to Scotland."

"Scotland!"

"I've got a lead on a story. Call Amanda and ask her to cover for me. Tell her she owes me a favour. It should only be for a couple of days. I'm sorry I have to go."

Anna's mind was reeling as she desperately tried to bring up the subject of Jameson's email before Kate hung up. "Wait, Kate, I've got access to Jameson's email and ..."

"Anna, that's great, but I have to run. I'm sure you can deal with it. We'll speak later, bye."

"No wait!"

As the line went dead, Anna slammed the phone onto the table and shrieked with sheer frustration, "Damn, that's so typical."

Sitting quietly for a moment in an attempt to compose herself, she leaned over and powered down her laptop. With thoughts of the past few hours whizzing through her mind she picked up her wine glass and gulped down the remainder of the Shiraz.

After her frustrating conversation with her boss, Anna was in no mood to speak to Amanda. Reaching a compromise, she leaned across the table and picked up her cell phone, located Amanda's number and sent a simple text message. "Kate Harding gone to Scotland for a couple of days re: big story. You owe her a favour." Pressing the send button Anna's train of thought was suddenly interrupted as her door intercom rang.

She walked over to the phone near her front door, "Hello."

"Hello, is this Miss Blythe?"

The voice male, although at this time of night it was no one she recognised. "Yes, who wants to know?"

"Miss Blythe I'm sorry to disturb you so late. It's Daryl from FedEx. I have a special delivery for you."

"Daryl, I'm sorry it's a little late. Could you please come back in the morning, it's not really appropriate right now I ..."

Before she could continue the voice interrupted, "I understand Miss Blythe, but tomorrow is Sunday and the office is closed. The parcel has been marked very urgent."

Anna sighed and gave a little nod, "Okay, you can come up."

Replacing the handset and pressing the entry button, she rushed into her bedroom, quickly removed her robe and pulled on a grey NIKE vest top, navy blue sweatpants and a pair of white trainers. As she finished tying her shoelaces there was a knock at the door.

Opening the door and half expecting to be greeted by a FedEx uniform, Anna was taken aback to see a tall, muscular figure, dressed entirely in black. Suddenly feeling very venerable she attempted to quickly close the door on the stranger. As she did, the intruder threw himself at the door like a wild dog.

The door flung open with such force that Anna was thrown into the air, only to come crashing down into a heavy glass coffee table. The impact was devastating. In a split second her head hit the table with such force that the back of her skull exploded, sending splinters of glass and blood in all directions.

Entering the apartment, the intruder calmly closed the door

behind him and walked over to Anna's body. Kneeling down, he placed two fingers on her neck to check her pulse.

Satisfied that his job was done. The intruder walked quickly around the apartment, stopping only in the kitchen to pick up Anna's cell phone, which he popped into his inside pocket.

Finally he picked up her laptop, walked over to the front door, switched off the lights, and slipped quietly away.

FIFTEEN

SUNDAY: 8.15AM SOUTH OF STIRLING, SCOTLAND

THE BRIGHT MORNING sun rose over the Ochil hills and apart from the occasional whispery cloud, the sky was clear and settled. Having left Larbert station the 6.40am, the British Rail Class 170 Turbostar train from Edinburgh to Stirling thundered through the countryside.

Harding sat quietly in a first class compartment, flicking through the last remaining pages of her Dan Brown novel, *Angels & Demons*. It was one of those books she always meant to read, but never quite found the time. "At least," she thought, "this journey had been useful for something." Apart from an inconvenient change of train in Edinburgh, the overnight rail journey to Scotland had been pretty uneventful.

Kate sighed contently as she flipped the last page of her book. Her hero Robert Langdon had saved the world once again.

Closing the book, she returned it to her leather laptop bag and zipped it shut. As countryside turned into cityscape, the once distant Ochil hills now loomed ever closer. The Dumblane-bound train began its slow approach into Stirling.

On her right Kate could see the Wallace Monument. Completed in 1861 and standing 220 feet tall, the monument remains a testament to Scottish hero William Wallace and his defeat of the English Army on the 12th September 1297. The popular visitor attraction remains an iconic image for both visitors and locals alike.

As the train screeched to a final halt, a number of passengers, including an early morning group of Chinese tourists, made their way towards the exit. Kate stood, reached for her coat and picked up her laptop bag and case. Then proceeded to follow the group on to the platform. After breathing re-circulated train air for the past few hours, filling her lungs with fresh air felt good.

Apart from the small group of tourists and a couple of staff, the station was relatively quiet. Kate made her way through the ticket barrier and past the ticket office towards the entrance. Once outside, the early morning sunlight felt good on her face.

Two or three white taxis were waiting for potential customers. At the front of the line a white Skoda Octavia started its engine. Sitting inside was a rather scruffy, round-faced bald headed driver who was wiping away the remains of some kind of food away from his mouth. Licking his lips, he stared at Kate like a cat about to pounce. As she raised her hand to hail the car over, a dark blue Honda Civic suddenly pulled up, the door swung open and a rather large, red-faced man climbed out. Glancing at Kate for a moment, a smile of recognition appeared on his face. "Miss Harding?"

Kate looked at the stranger, somewhat confused, she hardly expected to meet anyone who knew her. "I'm sorry, do I know you?"

She gave a nod of familiarity at the sound of his soft voice. "Yes, of course Mr McPherson. I'm sorry but it's been a long journey and I never expected …"

"Nae bother, I figured you'd be on the early train. If you'll let me take you to your hotel, we can talk en route. Where are you staying?"

Kate reached into her coat pocket and retrieved a piece of A4 paper. The Stirling Highland she replied and returned the paper to her pocket. Walking around to the back of the car, McPherson opened the trunk and motioned Kate over. "Here lass, let me take your bags." Kate handed over her two bags, walked over to the passenger side and climbed in. McPherson closed the trunk with a thud and then returned to the comfort of his own seat, closed his door and started the engine.

As the Honda departed the forecourt, Kate looked at McPherson. "So, Mr McPherson, you've got my attention. What's this all about?"

McPherson glanced at her for a moment and, gave a grunt, "I lassie, this is what they call a career maker, a real game changer."

Kate sighed and rolled her eyes in annoyance. Having heard statements like this in the past she had learnt, often the hard way, that in most cases, they lead nowhere. "Look, Donald, I've just travelled hundreds of miles in the middle of the bloody night so, no offence, but I'll be the judge of that. Now just tell me what you've got."

Glancing over at his passenger, McPherson looked a little taken aback at her bluntness. A small team ran *The Stirling Observer* in a somewhat relaxed atmosphere. He was not used to being rushed like this.

"Okay, I had a phone call, from a friend last night. He's a volunteer in the local mountain rescue team. He told me that they were called out to an incident yesterday involving a missing man. All seemed routine until they found him."

"And, then what?"

"Well, that's where things got a little weird. The team didn't just pull up one man, but two!" Kate's eye's widened, "Two?"

"Aye, but get this, the second man was dressed in eighteenth-century costume."

"What?"

"It's true and apparently he's telling everyone he's from 1710 or something."

At this point Kate's patience exploded. "Are you bloody crazy? You get me on a train in the middle of the night for this … this … cock-and-bull pile of crap. Stop the car."

Submitting to the request, McPherson pulled into the side and switched off the engine. "Wait, I know it sounds crazy …"

Kate stared in disbelief, "Sounds crazy? You must be out of your bloody mind."

McPherson took a deep breath and paused. "Look, do you honestly think I'd bring you up tae Scotland on a whim? The crazy thing is it's true. I swear it. The team also discovered something else."

Kate groaned, "What … no wait … don't tell me, little green men, right?"

The car went silent, for a moment neither spoke, then finally McPherson sighed, "They've discovered some kind of … chamber attached to an old silver mine."

McPherson's voice had changed from its usual softness and was now deadly serious. "All I know is that apparently the military have been called in to investigate … that's it. You can make of it what you will."

After a moment of consideration, Kate realised that McPherson was serious and that he may indeed be onto something. "Okay, Donald, let's say this turns out to be something, how should we proceed? Will your guy talk to me?"

McPherson turned his key and the Civic's engine spurted into life. "I think we should first get you checked into your hotel. I have a couple of family matters to take care of, but I was thinking that perhaps this afternoon we could take a drive out there, if that works for you?" Kate nodded in agreement, as the car pulled away it turned into Spital Street and then on upwards towards the Stirling Highland Hotel.

SIXTEEN

BY 11.10AM TOM and Dougie were on a mission in Stirling city centre. Tom was under strict instructions from Jane to assist Dougie in the purchase of "more appropriate attire" which would help him to blend in. As they walked through the city centre, Dougie was thrilled at constantly being asked by locals if he was part of some kind of promotional stunt. A group of Chinese tourists were absolutely delighted to have snapped a photo of a costumed Scotsman. As far as Tom was concerned walking around with his eighteenth-century companion was like shopping with a child.

In the city's Thistles Centre, Dougie simply stood memorised at the glitz and glamour of a modern day shopping mall, the lights, displays, shop windows and the people wondering about. What should have been a simple shopping trip ended up taking much longer than expected as Dougie insisted in stopping at every store window to look inside.

With time moving on, Tom finally persuaded Dougie to step into JW Menswear, a formal gentleman's outfitters. However all did not go well as Dougie accused the assistant of attempting to "Man-handle him", despite objections from the young man that he was only trying to "measure him".

By 12.45pm, Tom's patience was wearing thin. Dougie had tried on what seemed to be an endless assortment of different outfits, including jeans, trousers, shorts, sweaters and shirts. However with comments like, "I look like a bloody idiot" and "Ye cannot be serious!" constantly being shouted out, nothing seemed to suit.

As the two men made their way up Friar Street, the delicious aroma of cooking food was wafting through the air from the various restaurants and takeaways. As Tom's stomach rumbled, he turned to Dougie, "Would you like to get some lunch?"

Dougie stopped and grinned. "Och laddie, is that all ye think aboot … your stomach?"

Tom frowned, "No of course not. It's just that …"

Dougie cut Tom off in mid-sentence, "Hold on lad, this is exactly what I need."

Tom turned to look at what Dougie was staring at. There in front of him was a traditional Scottish kilt maker. McLeod's Highland Wear – Established 1858. The ageing store frontage had three large window displays that were clearly aimed at three market segments. In the first, a sign that read *Highland Dress Hire* accompanied two male mannequins dressed in traditional Scottish Highland dress. The kilts were of the Royal Stewart and Black Watch variety, while the jackets were of the Prince Charlie variety. Each display also had a selection of shoes, belts and the traditional seal skin sporran, which many traditionalists feel completes the classic look. The second window contained a more traditional selection of Men's single and double breasted suits, while the third, a selection of somewhat out dated casual wear, no doubt aimed at the younger man or teenager.

"Well, shall we go in?"

"Dougie, you can't be serious. People only wear this kind of thing for special occasions."

Dougie smiled, "Ach well, this is a special occasion isn't it? Besides we was never allowed tae wear the kilt because of, well shall we call it political reasons?"

Tom sighed, nodded and both men moved forward. Upon

opening the door, there were, as expected, rail upon rail of Kilts, jackets and men's suits. In the centre of the store stood a number of glass cabinets with wooden drawers, each containing a variety of buckles, belts and kilt pins. Overhead the walls were covered with shields from what appeared to be every clan in Scotland.

As Tom drew breath, the smell of stale air hit his nostrils reinforcing the belief that like the out-dated exterior of the shop, the inside was equally in need of refurbishment. Tom and Dougie walked around, occasionally stopping to peruse a particular jacket or kilt.

"Good morning Gentlemen, may I assist?"

The owner of the shop was a small, grey-haired, elderly man, wearing half-moon spectacles, a grey pinstripe suit and a tape measure around his shoulder. Looking at the man, Tom felt confident that if this man couldn't help Dougie then no one could.

"Er .... yes good afternoon. As you can see, my friend is in dire need of a makeover and we were wondering if you could help?"

Staring at Dougie the old man's eye's moved up and down in an attempt to gauge the big man's dimensions. "Hmm! Yes ... I'm sure I can help."

Moving away the elderly shopkeeper opened a notepad and franticly started jotting down figures. Tom suddenly had the feeling that this was going to perhaps take some time. "Excuse me but how long do you think this may take?"

The old man looked at Tom smiling, "Well, normally it can take a couple of weeks, however, looking at your friend here, it would appear that you may want something a wee bit sooner, Hmm?"

"Er ... yes that would be great."

"Well if you can be patient I think I can perhaps put something together while you wait."

Tom looked in surprise at the owner, "Wait? How long did you have in mind?"

The man tilted his head from side to side. "Hmm, perhaps a couple of hours."

"Er … okay that sounds reasonable." Tom turned to Dougie, "Are you okay with that?"

Dougie nodded, "Aye lad, I'm sure we can spare the time."

"Well, if you don't mind, I'll go across the street and get something to eat?"

The big man smiled and he gave Tom a slap on the shoulder. "Nae bother lad. On ye go. I'll be fine here."

Tom smiled and nodded courteously to the old man, as he opened the door and stepped outside. Across the street, Tom was presented with a vast array of cafes and restaurants. With hunger mounting he choose the closest, Dino's Italian Café. Forty-five minutes later Tom was back at the shop and glanced casually into the window of McLeod's Highland Wear. Inside all seemed to be quiet, and rather than disturbing them, Tom decided to continue exploring.

By 2.30pm, Tom had enough. He turned and walked down the hill back towards the shop, and opening the door Tom was met by a very surprising sight. There in front of him was Dougie, not dressed in a suit, or even a pair of trousers, but wearing a full Jacobean-style outfit of kilt, shirt and waistcoat.

"Dougie, what are you wearing?"

Dougie beamed, "What do ye think lad? Looks grand eh?"

Tom's initial reaction of shock soon turned to laughter. "Brilliant, Oh Dougie, its brilliant!" Even the old man giggled as Dougie admired himself in a mirror.

Once the purchase was complete, the owner parcelled Dougie's old clothes in to a brown paper parcel and thanked them for their custom.

The drive back to Alva didn't take too long. The A91 was unusually quiet for a Sunday afternoon. In fact, the only traffic they encountered was a road maintenance crew as they drove into Alva. The crew had erected a set of temporary traffic lights and a STOP sign opposite Cochrane Park.

Passing through the traffic lights Tom noticed two plain white Mercedes vans appearing from behind as he drove along Stirling Street. As Tom turned the corner into the back road, the two white vans also pulled in. With his house ahead, Tom caught a fleeting glimpse of his wife at the bedroom window. Her face, normally warm and smiling, was unusually pale and drawn. As Tom parked the car he smiled and gave her a wave.

Something was not quite right; she failed to respond. In fact her expression had changed to that of sheer panic as their eyes met. Tom glanced across at Dougie for a moment, "Something's not right here."

"Hmm. Sorry, lad what did ye say?"

Tom turned off the engine and was about to open the door. "I said something's not right ..."

In mid-sentence the silence was shattered as a group of heavily armed police officers in full body armour surrounded the vehicle. From all sides shouts of "Armed police" rang out. Dougie shouted, "What the bloody hell is this?"

"Don't move Dougie, do exactly as they say."

With guns aimed at the car, four officers then split into two pairs. One pair took up position at the driver's side and the other at the passenger side. Then one of the officers shouted, "Raise your hands and exit the vehicle ... slowly."

As instructed Tom and Dougie slowly, but simultaneously, opened the car doors, swung their legs sideways and slowly shuffled out of the vehicle. As his feet touched the ground Tom glanced up, only to find himself staring down the barrel of a semi-automatic machine gun. "Okay," screamed a voice from the rear, "Lie down on your stomachs."

Tom and Dougie immediately complied.

There was a sudden rush of boots overhead as officers moved in and quickly handcuffed them. As the officers above lowered their weapons, sigh of relief seemed to resonate through the air.

As two of the men assisted Dougie and Tom to their feet, another officer, who appeared to be in command, walked over and removed his helmet. "Gentlemen, I am placing you under arrest under The Prevention of Terrorism Act 2005 ..."

Tom looked at the police officer in shock and shouted. "Terrorism? Have you lost your mind? We haven't done anything wrong."

Ignoring Tom's objection, the officer continued, "I am placing you under arrest under The Prevention of Terrorism Act 2005. You do not have to say anything, but it may harm your defence if you do not mention when questioned something that you later rely on in court. Anything you do say may be given in evidence. Do you understand your rights as I've just described?"

Glancing over at Dougie, Tom nodded, "Aye, we understand."

The arresting officer then nodded a silent command and two officers, who were standing either side of Dougie and Tom, assisted them into one of the awaiting white vans.

Sitting down, Tom suddenly saw Sargent Williams, the local police officer who had assisted in their rescue only the day before.

"Williams, Sergeant Williams, for God's sake man, tell them we're innocent."

Williams shook his head, "I'm sorry Tom, it's out of my hands."

Sitting down inside the van, four police officers climbed aboard and the doors were closed. Once secure, the van's engine then roared into life and quickly pulled away escorted by two Police cars. As the remaining vehicles departed a dark blue Honda Civic sat on the corner of Park Street and Back Road. Un-noticed and semi-obscured, inside, its two occupants, a large red-faced man and a woman in her thirties, were watching the enfolding drama with great interest. Once the last of the police vehicles disappeared, the Honda's engine came to life and the car slowly pulled away.

SEVENTEEN

"THIS IS UNBELIEVABLE!"

"Like I said Miss Harding, this one's a real career changer."

McPherson grinned. As the dark blue Honda Civic made its way along Stirling Street and left towards Alva Glen, "Where are we going now?"

"I thought you might like to take a look at the Glen, you never know, you might see a little green man!"

As the car turned into Brook Street and upwards past the Number 5 pub, Donald was suddenly forced to brake. As the car screamed to a halt, three army Land Rovers blocked their path making it impossible to continue.

"What the hell …"

Two *soldiers* appeared brandishing weapons from behind one of the vehicles, and as McPherson wound his window down one of the *soldiers* approached.

Inspecting the vehicle, the young soldiers, glanced first into the car's rear and then at its occupants. "I'm sorry sir, the road ahead is closed, you'll have to go back."

Kate leaned over in order to make eye contact with the teenager, "Go back … Look Son, that's ridiculous. What on earth's going on here?"

The soldiers frowned. "Look, all I know is that dangerous

chemicals have been discovered in the Glen. The entire area's been sealed off. So please, for your own safety, turn around and go about your business."

By the tone of his voice, Kate sensed that he was in no mood to be pressed further.

Placing the gear stick into reverse, McPherson swung the car around and proceeded back down the hill. As the car was about to turn into Stirling Street Kate shouted, "Wait, stop. I have an idea."

The big man obeyed and hit the brakes. As the car stopped Kate reached into her pocket and pulled out her cell phone. Searching through her contact list she located Anna and pressed call. The phone rang for around a minute and then went on to play a recorded message, "Hi, this is Anna. I'm sorry I can't take your call. Please leave a message with your details and I will call you back."

As the beep sounded Kate cleared her throat. "Hello Anna, It's Kate Harding. Please call me back as soon as you get this message, thanks."

She then turned to McPherson and motioned backwards with her finger. "Okay Donald. Is there another way up there?"

McPherson looked surprised, his normally confident look now appearing to falter. "What, you can't be serious? That's the army up there you know. You can't ju ..."

"Donald, you and I both know there's no damned chemicals up there. Are you a reporter or what?"

McPherson sighed and dropped his head in defeat. "Well we can probably get around by going up and over Wood Hill."

Changing gear McPherson indicated left and accelerated away. As Stirling Street became the A91, McPherson turned sharply into Burnside Farm Road. At the end of the track, he finally turned into the Woodland Park car park and switched off the engine.

"Okay lassie, what's your game plan?"

Kate sighed, "Simple! Get in, see what's going on and get out."

McPherson grinned as he opened his door and climbed out. "The best laid plans ..."

"Have you got a camera Donald?"

"Of course."

"Well, you had better bring it along."

Nodding, McPherson reached inside and pulled out a small camera case and closed his door.

The warm August afternoon was calm and unusually quiet as the two reporters wandered through Woodland Park and up the steep path towards Alva Glen through dense woodland at first, then upward and out on to open grazing land. The climb was a reasonably easy one for the 38-year-old Kate. However, McPherson, being a rather portly man, appeared to be struggling. Every five or six minutes, he would make some kind of excuse, which would allow him to take a short rest. The ascent up Wood Hill took around twenty-five minutes, but once at the top, Kate thought the views were simply magnificent.

To her left, the Lothian's and the Forth Road Bridge could be easily seen in the distance. To her right, the Wallace Monument, Stirling Castle and Ben Ledi, which looked majestic in the afternoon sunlight. Kate took a deep breath, for a moment, almost forgetting why she was there, until McPherson came wheezing up behind her.

"Okay Donald. Which way now?"

McPherson signalled his hand to hint for another rest.

"For God's sake man, we'll never get there at this rate, which way?"

Holding his chest and panting heavily, McPherson was clearly stressed. "I, I can't go on ... I can't do ... this."

He sat down on the grass and looked up at Kate, breathless and exhausted. "I ... am afraid you'll have ... to go it alone lass."

Kate sighed and gave a nod in agreement, "Okay Donald, give me your camera and just point me in the right direction. You go back to the car and wait for me. I'm sure I can find my way back."

Nodding, McPherson reluctantly handed his camera over to Kate and pointed upwards. "That way, just keep following that hill around to the left and it will eventually drop down into the Glen."

"Okay, thanks. I'll see you soon." Turning, she followed McPherson's instructions and followed the hill around to the left. Momentarily glancing back, she saw the large man stand once more and begin to move downwards towards the car park. Once out of sight, she turned and continued over the hill towards the Glen. Now that she was free of her large companion, Kate found that she could move quicker and in no time had ascended over Silver Glen and down into Alva Glen. In an attempt to avoid the authorities she made a conscious effort to avoid public footpaths and walkways.

Gathering speed, she suddenly became aware of a number of male voices below. Ducking low behind a large rock, she cautiously raised her head to see a group of men around twenty metres away. The group comprised of four or five soldiers and what appeared to be two or three high-ranking police officers.

"This is great," she whispered to herself.

Reaching in her pocket for McPherson's camera, she hurriedly snapped two or three shots before placing it back in her pocket. The group below appeared to be in a heated discussion about something and in an attempt to overhear Kate crouched lower and shuffled forward so that she could hear what was being said. "Chemical leak … it's absolutely ridiculous, we'll have this place crawling with environmentalists before tomorrow morning. How on earth, do we sell that to the public?"

"Look Colonel, I know that it wasn't perfect, but we needed a story. We needed everyone out. The chemical scenario appeared to be the best option."

"Well it sounds like a bloody stupid idea to me. Has the PM been contacted?"

"Yes sir, and also the First Minister. We've been ordered to evaluate the cavern and report back. I believe the PM's called an emergency meeting of COBRA for around 9pm, I guess we'll know more then."

"Fine Chief Constable, we need the entire village cleared by 8pm and then we can start bringing in the heavier equipment … Jarvis."

"Yes sir."

"Organise a couple of men to start on a helicopter landing point, and for god's sake, ensure it's well out of sight this time."

"Will do, sir."

"Chief Constable, What's the news of Mr Duncan and our Highland friend?"

"We've picked them up sir, I believe there on their way to HQ. But I'm concerned, one of my officers is convinced that these men are simply innocent bystanders."

"Innocent, they may be. But when you combine an alien discovery with a man who claims to be from the eighteen century, right now a terrorism charge is the only thing that we can hold them on."

"False or not, it's an opportunity for us to get some answers."

"I understand."

"Good. May I also suggest that someone starts working on carbon dating the man's clothes then we'll know if he's genuine?"

"Yes sir, I'm already on it."

The sound of footsteps below indicated that some of the men were leaving.

Sitting in the crouched position, Kate was becoming increasingly uncomfortable and as she stretched, she also glanced once again over the rock. Now there were only three men left. Suddenly a walkie-talkie burst into life with a combination of a man's voice and fuzzy interference. "Bravo one to Charlie leader, over." Kate ducked and crouched back down. "This is Charlie leader, over." After a short moment of silence the voice came back. "Charlie leader, sir. Unfortunately we appear to have a security breach. There's a reporter down here and I don't think he's alone. Just a minute …"

As the walkie-talkie fell silent, Kate rolled her eyes, knowing full well what was coming next. "Sir, its confirmed there's another, a woman, by the name of Kate Harding. She's a reporter for the Chronicle. Realising she had no option but to run, Kate began crawling on all four's away from the scene. Then she heard, "Pull it together man … find her."

A moment later Kate had reached the top of the hill, as she stood in preparation to run, her phone suddenly began to ring. Fumbling in her pocket, desperately trying to shut the phone off she muttered, "Oh God, not now!" Then suddenly she heard a shout from below. "Sir, she's up there!" Kate didn't stay to hear the sentence completed, but bolted over the hill back towards Woodland Park. Leaping across rocks and broken branches, she thundered downwards at breakneck speed.

Almost down and her breathing was becoming heavier and erratic so she slowed down in a desperate attempt to ease a growing cramp building inside her stomach. Then below, she caught a fleeting glimpse of two soldiers and ducked quickly down behind a hedge. Wincing in sheer agony and desperately trying to remain quiet, she again forced herself to lie low and wait for an opportunity to escape. After a minute or two, it became apparent that the men weren't going to leave quickly and that she would have to seek an alternative escape route.

Waiting for the right moment, she prepared herself to move once more. Then reversing backwards, slowly on all fours she turned to run. In a moment of sheer shock, she shrieked as she found herself looking at an army officer pointing a rifle directly at her forehead. "So, you'll be Miss Harding I presume?"

EIGHTEEN

DOUGIE WAS RUNNING, his chest heaved in and out as he gasped franticly in an attempt to fill his lungs with air. Leaping over a fallen branch he ran towards a clump of trees in sheer desperation to hide from the figure chasing him. But it kept coming, relentlessly onward. Glancing back momentarily, Dougie could just make out the shape emerging from the early morning mist, its face still obscured in the semi darkness. Its pale, drawn features just visible along with its eyes gleaming like diamonds.

Once through the tree's Dougie emerged into an unfamiliar landscape, which had suddenly changed. He no longer found himself on a Scottish hillside but in a land dominated with lava rock. On his left, although just out of sight, Dougie heard the rumbling of a powerful waterfall. Ahead, distant hills and mountains sprawled upwards with jagged and dangerous ridges. Stopping for a moment in sheer puzzlement, Dougie muttered, "What the heel." Looking at the rocks below his feet, he knelt down and picked one up. Standing up he rolled the blackened rock in his palm. It felt solid enough; it's surface, cold and uneven.

Dropping the rock, it hit the ground with a dull thud. Dougie muttered to himself, "I must be dreaming, but it's so real."

As his words faded, Dougie was aware that he was no longer alone. Turning sharply, he again found himself confronted by a tall, sinister, dark-hooded figure standing directly behind him.

This time Dougie wasted no time. In sheer desperation he turned left and sped away towards the sound of the waterfall. Reaching it, he now realised that this was no ordinary waterfall. It was immense! The force of the water was thundering down on three sides, generating a permanent misty rainbow. The sound of the thundering water itself was deafening. Downhill, Dougie followed the rocky uneven path sensing that perhaps this could be a possible means of escape.

Arriving at the end of the path, Dougie's mouth fell open in a mixture of horror and frustration. Ahead, a sheer drop led the way into watery abyss below and what seemed to be certain death. "Dougie …"

"Huh!" Turning around, Dougie froze as the hooded figure appeared once again in front of him. Suddenly and without warning the figure lunged forward. Stumbling backwards in astonishment Dougie shouted, "You. Nae, it's impossible …"

"Dougie … Dougie"

"Huh!"

Opening his eyes, Tom's face came into focus. "Dougie, are you awake?"

Dougie sat up and rubbed his eyes. "Aye, lad, I am, sorry I must have nodded aff. What time is it?"

"Ten past five, hang on they're coming back."

Dougie and Tom were in a police interview room. The room itself was sparsely furnished with off-white painted walls, a basic desk, four wooden chairs and a wall mounted closed circuit TV camera. As Dougie repositioned himself in his seat the sound of voices could be heard approaching outside the interview room.

The heavy, blue door suddenly swung open and two men entered the room. The first, an older tall man in his fifties, the other a younger, leaner, almost sporty looking man in his thirties, both dressed in business attire. Standing for a moment, the two men then sat opposite Dougie and Tom. "Good afternoon gentlemen.

I'm Inspector Andrew McLeish from Central Scotland Police and this is Robert Wilkes, Senior Anti-Terrorism officer with MI5."

Tom looked at McLeish wide-eyed, "Terrorists, what the hell are you talking about? What gives you the right to frighten me, and my family, half to death? It's a bloody disgrace."

Wilkes slid forward in his chair and sneered, "I am sorry for the inconvenience, I'm sure, but this little … incident is now a matter of national security. Let's be frank here shall we. You didn't think that you and your time travelling friend here would simply go un-noticed did you?"

Tom glared at the man opposite, "No, but … "

"Alright gentlemen" McLeish interrupted, "I apologise for the dramatics, but events are moving quickly and my superiors want answers."

McLeish sighed and then sat back in his seat, "We just want to know what the bloody hell is going on. Just tell me what you know."

Dougie cleared his throat. "Well, for me this wee adventure started a couple of months ago, in 1710," Dougie smirked. "You ken I still can't believe it. Anyway, I was hired by Sir John Erskine tae manage the silver glen mine …"

For the next 30 minutes the two officers sat mesmerised as Dougie meticulously explained every detail of his recent adventure. From his initial meeting with James Ritchie to the stranger in the line-up at the first day of work and the dramatic pursuit of Alexander McArthur through the mine. Finally Dougie explained the discovery of the cavern, the black mountain peak and of how McArthur had transported him to the future. He also explained how he had met Tom and how he should not be held responsible for any involvement.

When he had finished talking the two men sat in complete silence, occasionally glancing at each other.

It was the taller man who spoke first, "Gentlemen, do you mind if we step out for a moment?"

Dougie nodded, "Of course, nae bother."

McLeish and Wilkes stood, walked over to the blue door, opened it and stepped outside closing the door behind them. The two men stood in the corridor looking at each other for a moment in silence. "So what do you think?"

The younger man sighed, "Too be honest I didn't understand half of it, his accent is unusual. But, they certainly seem sincere. I think they're telling the truth. The question is what we do with them. The terrorism charge will never stick and you know it."

McLeish nodded, "I agree and the results from the carbon dating confirm that his clothes we picked up from the kilt shop are of that time."

"This is crazy. How the hell do we explain this?"

McLeish's head dropped, "We can't, and at the moment we have too many questions with no answers."

Wilkes nodded in agreement, "What about this so called McArthur and what if this black pyramid actually exists? These could be significant leads. Has the team discovered anything like this?"

The elder man shook his head, "No, I don't think so, but the search area is immense. It could take some time to ..."

"Well, perhaps under the circumstances they could be persuaded to assist us."

Wilkes nodded, "Perhaps, but I'll need authorisation. I'll make some calls. In the meantime, sound them out and see if they'll agree. Oh, and Inspector, we have another small problem. I was informed that a reporter was caught snooping around near the site and may have overheard more than she should have, I believe she's on her way here. I think, in order to avoid any further lapses in security, perhaps they should be kept together, at least for now."

McLeish nodded in agreement, opened the blue door and stepped back inside the interview room. Wilkes turned heel and walked away down the corridor.

Inside the interview room Dougie was still sitting at the table and Tom was pacing around the room. As McLeish re-entered the room Tom returned to his seat.

"Inspector, I want to call my wife. I believe I'm allowed at least one phone call," he said.

McLeish nodded, and said calmly, "I am sure that can be arranged Mr Duncan, although I think you should know that all the formal charges are in the process of being dropped."

"Dropped?"

Tom looked at McLeish in utter surprise.

"Yes."

McLeish paused awkwardly, "Okay, look, I'm probably breaking protocol by telling you this, but at this stage I've gone past caring. Mr Allan I've no doubt you are aware of stories in the media of the increased occurrences of natural disasters currently taking place around the world?"

Dougie nodded, "Aye, I've seen the man in the box."

"Well, since the cavern was discovered our people think that perhaps these two events are linked. Now you mentioned a black mountain top or pyramid?"

Dougie nodded, "Yes"

"This is something we have yet to discover. I wonder if you would agree to assist us in finding it."

Dougie looked at Tom and then back at McLeish. "Of course, but tae be honest I stumbled on it by accident. Also, what about Tom's folk? Before I make any kind of deal you'll first have tae reunite this braw man here with his family."

As McLeish opened his mouth to respond his mobile began to ring. Reaching inside his pocket, he pushed the answer button.

"McLeish speaking."

The room went silent for a few moments. Dougie and Tom looked at each other while the officer listened intently to the voice on the other end of the phone. "I see, okay thanks for letting me know. I'll make the arrangements."

McLeish ended the call and returned the phone to his pocket.

"Well Gentlemen, you are being released. Mr Duncan, your wife has been informed and one of my officers is on the way up to take you home. You should know that the military are evacuating Alva."

Tom looked at McLeish with concern, "Evacuating, why?"

"I'm afraid the decision came from above. Mr Wilkes was correct when he called it a threat to national security. The cover is that there has been a chemical leak. A bit thin, I know but we can't have the public wandering around up there."

Tom nodded, "What about my family?"

"They are being returned home as we speak. However, I must ask you not to repeat anything I have told you. It's a matter of national security. Do you understand?"

Tom nodded. "Yes of course but ..."

McLeish cut Tom off in mid-sentence, "There is another small complication. A reporter was caught snooping around the site and we think she knows what's going on. My superiors have asked me to somehow contain the situation. To be honest the only way to ensure this is to keep you all together, I ..."

Tom stood up, "Now look here Inspector, you can't honestly expect me to ... "

"I understand your reluctance, but this is an extreme situation. I assure you it will only be for a couple of days."

Tom glanced at Dougie and then back at McLeish. Giving a small sigh he nodded in agreement, "Very well, just for a couple of days."

The moment was broken by a knock at the door. McLeish shouted,

"Come in," McLeish shouted.

The familiar shape of Sargent Williams entered the room. He first nodded at Tom and Dougie and then fixed his gaze on his superior, "You sent for me, sir?"

"Yes Sergeant, can you organise the release of Miss Harding and these two gentlemen then see that they are driven back to Alva."

Williams nodded, "Yes sir, I'll take care of it myself."

McLeish stood up, "Well gentlemen, if you'll excuse me I have other matters to attend to. Mr Allan, we'll see you tomorrow morning, around 11am. I'll get someone to pick you up. I am sorry, once again, for the dramatics."

McLeish acknowledged his officer with a nod, turned and left the room.

Williams looked at the two men awkwardly. "Tom, I'm sorry about this afternoon. You must see I was just doing my job."

"Of course, we just want to get out of here."

"Well then, if you will just follow me please."

The two men stood and followed Williams through the blue door and down a long, dimly lit corridor. As they approached another blue door, this time marked Reception, the voice of an angry woman could be heard approaching from behind. "This is bloody ridiculous, you have no right to keep me here. I demand to ..."

Turning the corner the woman suddenly stopped dead as she found herself confronting the three men. "You!"

Sergeant William's straightened his back and gave a courteous smile, "Miss Harding, may I introduce Tom Duncan and Dougie Allan. Mr Duncan has kindly offered you accommodation for the duration of your stay."

Upstairs, Inspector Andrew McLeish stood by the window in his office and watched silently as the group got into a Range Rover and sped away. McLeish returned to his desk and sat down in a somewhat worn looking black leather chair. Positioning himself comfortably, he reached for the phone and punched numbers into the keypad. After a few moments a voice at the other end said, "This is Colonel McNeil."

"They've just left. I've done as you asked."

"I trust there were no complications?"

"No."

"Excellent, until tomorrow then."

McLeish replaced the receiver, sat back and sighed in quiet satisfaction.

NINETEEN

TOM, DOUGIE AND Kate sat in silence, staring into space as Jane Duncan appeared with a tea tray. Glancing at her husband she cleared her throat in an attempt to subtly gain his attention.

"Ahem ..."

Shaking himself out of his momentary trance, Tom said, "I'm sorry, let me help you."

He took the tray and placed it on the table, he then picked up the china teapot and proceeded to fill the cups with the hot tea.

"Miss Harding, do you take milk?"

"Huh."

"Tea, milk?"

"Oh, yes please, sorry ... and please call me Kate."

Taking the cup from Tom, she proceeded to sip the hot liquid. After a few sips she placed the tea on the table and glared at the two men. "This is incredible, just incredible. I could sell a million copies tomorrow."

Tom glared at Kate, "Miss Harding, I mean Kate, please!"

Kate smirked, "I'm only joking. Besides the readers would think I'm crazy. Which, to be honest, doesn't feel a million miles away from the truth right now. Can I ask a small favour?"

"Of course, anything."

"With all that's happened today I haven't checked in for a while. Don't worry I won't say a word about this."

Looking at Dougie first, then Jane, he nodded, "Aye of course."

Kate took her mobile phone from her bag and walked into the semi darkness of the dining room and sat in a large brown leather armchair. Staring at the phone for a moment, she flipped the lid open and began to browse the contact list, eventually stopping at Anna. Taking a deep breath she pressed the call button then waited for an answer. As before, the phone rang out for about a minute and then played the familiar recorded message.

As the answering machine beeped, Kate shook her head in frustration and said, "Anna ... Anna, are you there? Where the hell are you? Call me back, please!"

Ending the call she continued browsing the contact list and stopped at Amanda Harris, the *Chronicle*'s assistant editor and pressed the call button. This time, the line only rang for a moment before being picked up.

"Hello."

"Amanda, is that you? It's Kate."

"Kate, where the hell have you been? Everybody's been trying to contact you."

Kate shook her head, trying desperately not to say too much about her current circumstances. "Amanda, it's complicated. I need to speak with Anna, I've been trying to call her and ..."

"Oh my God, you don't know!"

For a moment the line went deadly silent and Kate felt a shiver run up her spine.

"Know what? What are you talking about?"

"It's Anna."

"Amanda, for God's sake what is it?"

"Kate she, she's dead!"

For a moment Kate struggled to comprehend what Amanda was saying. The thought that perhaps this was all part of some grotesque joke popped into her mind for a moment but then faded as if a dark cloak of reality had been thrown over her. Then it happened, the grief, the shock was incredible. Hitting her hard. She dropped her head into her left hand, desperately trying to hold back tears.

"How? What happened?"

"I don't know exactly, she was attacked in her apartment last night. The police think that perhaps it was a bungled robbery."

Kate sniffed. "Robbery?"

"Well it's weird, the only things taken were her mobile and her laptop."

"Her laptop …"

"I know it's weird."

Kate's mouth fell open as if everything suddenly fell into place. "Oh my God, the emails."

On the other end of the phone Amanda was sniffling, "Kate what emails? What are you talking about?"

Kate's head dropped as she attempted to recover. "Nothing, it's not important. Listen it's late, try and get some sleep and I'll call you in the morning. Hopefully by then the police will have some more information."

"Okay, are you sure, you'll be alright?"

Kate sighed and exhaled slowly in an attempt to regain her composure. "Yes I'll be okay. I just need a little time to think."

"Of course, I understand, bye for now."

Kate remained in the seat motionless for a few minutes, feeling numb.

Suddenly a knock came from behind. She turned her head to see Tom over her shoulder looking concerned.

"Kate, are you okay? We heard you crying."

"No, I'm not. It's one of my staff, she's … been murdered."

Tom's mouth fell open as if unsure what to say. "I'm so sorry, is there anything that I can do?"

"No, I'll be okay. I guess I just need some time."

Tom nodded and turned to leave. Suddenly Kate had a thought and stood up.

"Tom wait! Did the police return my things, my laptop?"

"Yes of course, it's upstairs in the guest room. Do you want me to get it for you?"

"Please," Kate went back into the living room as Tom went to get her laptop.

"Are ye alright lass?" Dougie asked.

Kate swallowed, wiped a tear from her eye, and said, "Not really, I'm afraid I've just received bad news."

"I'm sorry tae hear that."

As the three stood in awkward silence, Tom reappeared with a leather bag and handed it over to Kate. "Thanks."

Kate took out her laptop, plugged in a Wi-Fi dongle and powered it up. Tom looked at Jane and Dougie for guidance.

"What is it Kate? Is everything okay?"

"What? Huh, I just need to check something that's all."

After a short wait she logged on and proceeded to open her email, to find a large number of emails begin to pour into her in-box. Then a folder appeared titled Robert Jameson's Email Archive. Opening the folder she began browsing through the contents. At first nothing seemed unusual, until she spotted an email headed "URGENT: Please read." Opening the message, Kate began to read.

FWD: HardingK@Chronicle.co.uk ;BlytheA@Chronicle.co.uk

To: JamesonR@Chronicle.co.uk

From: herman.brauer@hotmail.com

Date: July 2nd

Subject: Please meet me soon!

Mr Jameson,

I have been trying to contact you for some time, but I believe I am being watched so I have to be very careful. I know you will probably think I am a nut job trying to spread a conspiracy theory, but you have to listen to what I have to say. I believe I have uncovered an organisation that seems to be at the centre of a number of disappearances, kidnappings – call them what you will. I don't exactly know who they are and where they are based, but I do know whatever they have planned, it's big and a lot of people are going to die.

I have a friend that I want you to meet, a volcanologist from Iceland. She has some ideas about what could be causing the sudden surge in volcanic activity around the world. She will be in Germany in a few weeks. I will contact you again soon.

H

For a moment Kate forgot where she was, until she glanced up. Staring at her with an obvious concern Tom, Dougie and Jane simply stood silently waiting. As a reporter Kate always credited herself with the ability for smelling a rat and uncovering the truth. It's what her mentor called her "Sherlock Skills". Feelings of sadness were now changing into something more – anger perhaps.

Something was not right here. Somehow Anna's death was linked not only to Robert Jamieson but also Herman Brauer and the volcanologist Elín Gylfadóttir. More than that, it had something to do with this email, but what was it?

It was Jane who spoke first. "Kate is everything okay? Not more bad news I hope."

Kate shook her head, "No, not bad news, just another mystery!"

TWENTY

LAYING DOWN A cream A4 folder bulging with documents onto an ornate oak side table, James Walton leaned over, picked up a blue ceramic mug of steaming coffee, took a sip and returned the mug to the table. Swallowing the warm liquid he slowly leaned back into the comfortable soft leather couch, rubbed his eyes and sighed. The lack of sleep was beginning to take its toll.

As he gazed around at the drawing room's pale yellow walls, Walton pondered how his predecessors would have dealt with this unfolding ecological nightmare. Over the past three years, it seemed that he had received a constant stream of bulletins from worried scientists and advisors informing the government of unusual tectonic activity. Earthquakes and volcanic eruptions were occurring at an alarming rate in South America, Asia and now the United States.

Taking a deep breath, he wondered how Churchill, Thatcher or even Blair would react under similar circumstances. The simple truth was that these incidents appeared to be planet wide and random. In war, there are sides, boundaries, but in this brave new world disaster can strike anywhere and at any time. However, he was not Churchill, this was his time and he alone would make the call to evacuate the population if it became necessary. From somewhere within he prayed and hoped that it would not come to that.

Rubbing his eyes for a second time he sighed heavily as a knock came to the study door. Clearing his throat he sat up, "Yes, come in." The large glossed white painted door swung open and a smartly dressed woman in her twenties entered. "Excuse me Prime Minister, you said you wanted to be informed when they arrived."

Giving her a tired but friendly nod in acknowledgment, Walton picked up the cream folder and stood. "Very Good Lisa, lead on."

The young woman turned and Walton followed her down a winding staircase and along a wide carpeted corridor. At 46, James Walton was a relatively young man and many in the party would have preferred someone older in the driving seat. However, when the crucial vote came, his nomination for party leader had been successful and the rest was history.

Walton had been in office for two years and had presided over more than his fair share of dramas, but somehow current events appeared, on the face of things, more desperate and unpredictable.

He paused for a moment outside the Cabinet room, pondering the situation. Closing his eyes, a sense of calmness descended upon him and, for a moment, he almost forgot the reason for the meeting. Opening his eyes once more, reality returned like a heavy burden, he knew that behind the door was a gathering storm, a storm that was not simply going to go away.

"Sir, are you okay?"

"Yes thank you, I'm just gathering my thoughts."

As the door swung open, the reality that now presented itself was not entirely as he had expected. Around the room's large, oak conference table sat a mixture of ministers and military advisers, all in complete silence.

As Walton entered the room the group stood and spoke in unison. "Prime Minister."

Walton nodded in acknowledgement and sat in a hard, green leather chair towards the centre of the table.

"Good evening ladies and gentlemen."

He then leaned over and picked up a small, glass bottle of water, opened it and proceeded to pour the contents into a tall glass. Taking a sip, he leaned back into his seat and sighed.

"Firstly, thank you all for coming in so late. I'm sorry for this interruption to your weekend, but something has come up. If you'll forgive me I'll pass this briefing over to the Home Secretary and General Carey who will explain."

At that moment Anne Petrie, a woman in her forties, stood. Dressed in a smart, navy skirt and jacket she walked to the head of the table and addressed the group.

"Good evening ladies and gentlemen. Firstly the contents of this briefing are classified and are not to be discussed in public. What appeared to be a simple missing persons report in central Scotland yesterday afternoon has developed into what can only be described as an unexplainable event. While rescuing a local resident of Alva, which is around 7 miles from Stirling, the local police discovered a second individual, a man who claims to have time travelled from the 1700s.

"At first it was assumed that this man was, of course, lying or perhaps crazy. However, the individual, a Mr Douglas Allan, provided officers with not only an incredibly detailed account of his adventure but also the location of what can only be described as an underground labyrinth containing some kind alien structure. I can also reveal that despite purchasing new clothes, the local police forensic team managed to recover his original attire and that carbon dating tests confirmed that his clothes do in fact originate from, or around, 1700.

After an initial survey the ranking officer has made the decision to seal off the area for further investigation. At the moment we have around 100 police officers and 70 Army personnel onsite. In order to avoid a difficult situation with the public and the media a cover story was devised and the village has been subsequently evacuated."

"Where is he now?"

"Prime Minister?"

"Where is Mr Allan now?"

Petrie attempted to recompose herself, "He, along with another man, a Tom Duncan, were initially arrested. However an MI5 agent and the local Chief Constable concluded that neither were a threat. Indeed both men were quite keen to assist in the investigation. I believe that Mr Allan is this evening with the Duncan family at their home in Alva."

"Anything else?"

"Yes, one other small issue. A reporter was caught snooping around at the site and has been detained. A Kate Harding, Editor of *The Daily Chronicle* here in London."

"Harding?" The voice, with a soft Welsh accent, came from the far end of the table. It was Roy Clark, the Foreign Affairs Minister. Tall and smartly dressed in a grey pinstripe suit, light blue shirt and red tie.

"You know her?"

"Yes Prime Minister, and so do you. She interviewed us both just before the general election. It was at the Dorchester, remember?"

Walton sat up and the confusion on his face suddenly cleared. "Of course, a formidable woman. She gave us quite a hard time, especially you Roy."

Walton smiled and Clark nodded in acknowledgement. "Yes, she certainly did. The question is …"

Walton interrupted, "The question is, Roy, how and why she just happened to be in Alva at this precise moment. Surely, not a coincidence?"

The room remained silent as Walton turned back to his Home Secretary, prompting her to continue.

"Indeed! Another point of concern, are the reports of the

murders of two prominent *Chronicle* reporters, including correspondent Robert Jameson who was killed in Germany only a few days ago and a young woman, Anna Blyth, in what appears to be, on the face of it, a bungled robbery, at her home only yesterday."

Walton leaned forward and interrupted. "Do you think she's involved?"

"She's clearly involved in something. At this point I'm just not sure what. I must admit though that I'm a little concerned for her safety."

Clark again interrupted, "Well Prime Minister, it sounds like she's in the best place, for the moment."

"Roy?"

"I mean, the village has been cleared and secured, yes? Well then it sounds like they have a small army protecting them."

"True, although, I think Anne is right. A further investigation would perhaps be prudent."

"Of course Prime Minister."

"Thank you Ann. Ladies and gentlemen, I will pass over the remainder of this briefing to General Richard Carey."

Anne Petrie returned to her seat and an ageing, but handsome, tall grey-haired man stood. Dressed in uniform, brandishing an array of colourful braid, he stepped forward to where the Home Secretary stood only a few moments earlier.

"Prime Minister, ladies and gentlemen, the situation is that late yesterday evening at the behest of the Scottish First Minister, police officers discovered what appeared to be an un-natural cave structure in the Ochil hill range next to the village of Alva."

"Un-natural? General what do you mean?"

"I'm not sure Sir. It's like nothing we've encountered before. Firstly, it appears to be an enormous labyrinth. Secondly, it appears to be bathed in what's been described to me as 'brilliant white light' with no definable source."

Walton again interrupted, "Enormous? Just how big are we talking here, General?"

"Well. According to this Mr Allan, it's miles long, sir."

Walton's eyes widened, "Miles?"

"To be honest we just don't know. We have a team of scientists in transit and they are scheduled to be on-site tomorrow morning. Allan and Duncan have agreed to assist in locating what Allan referred to as a black, pyramid shaped object.

"A black pyramid?"

"Yes Mr Clark, a pyramid. But what it is and where it came from is unknown at this time." Carey glanced around the room and paused for a second before saying, "Hopefully we'll know more tomorrow. We have additional military personnel arriving tomorrow who will bring in heavier equipment which should make exploration a little easier to …"

Suddenly there was a knock at the door and the General stopped talking in mid-sentence. The door swung open and a pale-faced Lisa Harkins, the Prime Ministers twenty-something aide, entered the room looking visibly shaken. Walton stood, "Miss Harkins is there something wrong? What is it?"

"H … Hawaii … Sir, it's Hawaii."

Moving towards the young woman in an attempt to provide some comfort, he felt his stomach drop and an awful sense of nausea run through his body.

"What is it? What's happened?"

The young woman crumpled onto the floor. By sheer luck, Walton just managed to reach her, narrowly avoiding what would have been a nasty head injury. As he caught her, the entire group rose and were moving to assist their leader.

"Switch on the television, please."

Even before the words have left the PM's mouth the 51-year-old Deputy Prime Minister, Derek Johnson, had reached for a remote control and was in the process of flicking through television channels. Within moments he had located the BBC News channel.

"Oh my God …"

Everyone looked at the television, their faces turning white with shock. A shaky helicopter mounted camera was transmitting pictures of sheer devastation.

Rivers of lava combined with a massive wave of seawater ripping through buildings, streets and entire neighbourhoods as if they were children's playthings.

The reporter's voice shook with emotion as he attempted to describe the scene.

"It's unbelievable, just unbelievable. The Hawaiian islands of Maui and Oahu have been utterly destroyed in what appears to be a disaster on an unprecedented scale. At 7.12 am local time, there was a massive underwater earthquake off the coast of Hawaii. Monitoring stations have measured the quake as 10.6 on the Richter scale. What made matters worse is that the quake has not only triggered a massive volcanic eruption but also a huge tsunami wave which as I speak is heading towards the US mainland cities of Los Angeles, San Francisco and Seattle. The US government has declared a national state of emergency and a massive exodus is already underway in these cities. However, the tsunami is moving so fast it's not clear whether the authorities will be successful.

"In terms of lives lost here, it's still too early to say … but figures could run into the hundreds of thousands …"

Taking the control from his deputy, Walton pressed the standby button and the room went deathly quiet. For a few moments the group stood motionless in complete silence before Walton turned to face the group.

"First please send a message to the UN and say that we stand ready to assist if required. Anne can you please get some help for Miss Harkins and Roy … get me the President of the United States on the phone."

TWENTY ONE

MONDAY: 6.40AM ALVA, SCOTLAND

L YING IN A strange bed, Dougie was restless. His thoughts
were for his wife, Mary. Although only three days had passed
for him, the realisation that he was somehow stuck 300 years
in the future was becoming a harsh reality. There was now no
doubt in his mind that life without her would be difficult.

As an outdoor man, early mornings were usual for him,
whereas lying in bed waiting for others to rise was not. After a few
minutes, he decided that enough was enough, an early morning
walk would perhaps be a good idea, and so, after taking a deep
breath, he pulled himself out of bed and got dressed. Opening the
bedroom door he quietly went downstairs and attempted to open
the Duncan's front door. After a couple of failed attempts fumbling
with various keys, he eventually succeeded.

"Dougie, where are you going?"

"Huh."

Dougie turned as Tom came downstairs looking concerned.
"Are you okay?"

"Dougie smiled, "Aye lad, I'm braw. I just thought that some
early morning air would be a good idea."

"Do you want some company?"

Normally Dougie would have said yes, however in light of
recent events, perhaps a little alone time would be a better option.

"Nae lad, I'll be braw, I just need a wee bit of time tae collect my thoughts if that's okay?"

Tom smiled and gave an understanding nod, "Aye, of course."

Closing the door behind him, Dougie turned and began to walk. The air was cool and an early morning summer mist had descended upon the village. Dougie looked for reference points, a rock, and tree, something … anything that would trigger a memory and guide him to a familiar spot; but there was nothing. It all seemed so different. Open spaces had been replaced with streets containing row upon row of unfamiliar buildings.

As the village had been evacuated the streets were eerie and quiet. The only noticeable sounds were that of early morning birdlife and Dougie's feet as he paced up the street. His mind was reeling. He needed a place to start, a reference point. A church, yes churches, they have graveyards and graveyards have stones. Perhaps, just perhaps, there would be one for Mary.

He strode along Stirling Street with a sense of purpose, occasionally glancing upwards at the Ochil's in an attempt to spot a familiar landmark. He remembered that in 1710 the cemetery was relatively new and only had a small number of graves, but hopefully it would be a good place to begin.

As he passed by St Mary's, the small Roman Catholic Church on Stirling Street, he noticed a small brown sign on the left that read Cemetery. From the sign, he could see Lovers Loan, a residential street leading up to the cemetery.

As he walked up the gradual incline, he found himself standing opposite large black gates and wrought iron green painted railings. Once through the gates and inside the cemetery, he began to slowly walk among the graves and neatly kept flowerbeds. As he walked he carefully examined each headstone for a familiar name.

The cemetery itself was much larger than he had expected and as he walked a lump began to form at the back of his throat. The realisation that she was truly gone was becoming a harsh reality.

Stopping at a small wooden bench, Dougie took a deep breath and again swallowed in an attempt to stop the tears welling up.

As he was about sit down he noticed a small gold plaque fixed to the bench, which read, "In loving memory of Margaret Robertson – 1944 – 2006. With love from Robert, Emma and the Girls."

Dougie smiled, "Aye lass, it looks like ye will be missed to."

Quietly staring out over the neatly kept gardens and sea of gravestones, Dougie became aware that he was no longer alone. Glancing around, the morning mist remained tenacious, yet as he focused, he could just make out the feint outline of an approaching figure on the far side of the graveyard.

He assumed that it was perhaps a local out for an early morning walk or someone paying their respects to a loved one. But no, in what could only be described as a moment of pure fear, the whispery figure came into focus like a ghostly apparition.

Gazing in horror, the hairs on Dougie's neck stood on end, as a tall-cloaked figure approached. "Was this yet another dream?" he whispered to himself as he squeezed his eyes shut, like a frightened child in the night hiding under its blanket. With his heart pounding and forehead beginning to sweat, he took a deep breath and opened his eyes. Standing in front of him was the nightmare he had come to fear.

Gazing downward, almost afraid to look the sinister, hooded figure in the face, he could see the bottom of the black cloak. Swallowing hard, his eyes gradually moved upwards.

The hooded spectre remained motionless, its face hidden. Dougie took a deep breath and tried frantically to speak. "Who, who are ye? What do ye want with me?"

The figure raised its hands, and slowly pulled back its hood, revealing, to Dougie's surprise, not the terrifying creature he had expected, but a familiar looking woman with flowing, long dark hair and piercing bright blue eyes.

Dougie's mouth fell open as he dropped on to his knees. "Mary? My god, is it really ye? How is this possible?"

The woman merely gazed in silence at the man kneeling before her. Her large eyes glistened in the early morning sunlight.

"Dougie, it's difficult to explain. But what you see here is a shadow of someone you once knew, someone, who is long since gone."

Pulling himself up, Dougie stood looking confused, "What are ye talking about lass, you're my wife I can see ye as clear as day."

The woman sighed and her expression turned serious, "No Dougie. The woman you knew died a long time ago. I'm here because it was felt you would interact better with a familiar face."

"But …"

"There are things you need to know. Some of these you may find difficult to believe or even understand, but it's vital that you listen to what I have to say."

The initial excitement of discovery was slowly evaporating into a look of puzzlement and concern.

"What are ye talking about lass? Just tell me how you got here?"

"That's not important right now. Your arrival here Dougie, it was no accident. The mine, McArthur, the Pyramid … I know of all of these things."

Dougie stood, in surprise and said angrily, "But how do ye ken?"

"Like I said, I know everything. You were sent here because we need your help."

"We, who do ye mean we?"

"There are events happening to your world … events that are about to change everything."

Dougie stood.

"Who, what are ye?"

"Think of us as, keepers"

"Keepers?"

"Dougie, it doesn't matter who I am, what does matter is that you listen to what I have to say. Within days, everything will change, all of this will be gone"

Dougie's mouth opened as if to speak but he could not find any words. The woman sighed, "We came to your world before it had form. There were ten of us then. Now there are only seven.

"Seven?"

Some of our numbers became lost and one took a wrong path.
"

"What?"

"One in particular. His ideas were different. Where we sought to create and develop life, he sought conflict and destruction. In the end he became reckless, dangerous. It was decided that he should be banished."

Dougie interrupted, "MacArthur, you're talking about Alexander McArthur aren't ye? That's why you're here?"

The woman nodded and took a few steps away from the bench and turned back to face Dougie, "Partly. But there are those among my people that believe that humans have become a virus that has infested and damaged this planet to the point of destruction. If left unchecked they feel that this damage could have serious consequences for other species. It has been decided that this cannot be permitted to continue."

"What exactly are ye saying, Mary?"

"It has been decided that another, less violent species should be given an opportunity to, develop."

Dougie stood, with a look of grave concern appearing on his face. "Develop! What do ye mean? What does it mean for these people? For me?"

"The process of removing humanity was to take place over several hundreds of your years, through a series of natural disasters, conflicts and so on. However, due to unforeseen circumstances this process has been, accelerated …"

"Ye mean McArthur?"

The woman nodded, "He disagreed with the others. He felt

that removal should take place immediately. When his plan was discovered, I tried to stop him, unfortunately, he escaped and I failed. You were my last chance, and that's why you're here now."

With nausea building inside him, Dougie swallowed to avoid throwing up. He stood, paced back and forth for a few moments, in an attempt to control his breathing.

"How long Mary, how long?"

Mary sighed. "It's already begun. In just over a week, all of this will be gone."

As the words left her mouth, Dougie lost his footing and collapsed on to a nearby grass verge. Sweating and breathing heavily, his head dropped and the feeling of nausea became so overpowering that he was physically sick.

After a few moments of coughing and spluttering, he turned his head up towards Mary. Too his surprise her face remained unusually calm and unemotional, as if either unaware or unmoved by his reaction. Pausing to catch his breath he merely stared at the woman who looked so much like his wife.

"Surely, there must be something that we can do?"

At that moment the look in Mary's eyes changed, as if she had suddenly found something, a lost treasure or a prize perhaps. Although it stayed only for a moment, it sent a shiver up Dougie's spine.

"Perhaps ... perhaps there is a way," she whispered.

Struggling to fight back the dizziness, he again stood and stumbled back to the bench and sat down. "For God's sake lass, what is it, tell me?"

Dropping her gaze for a moment, the woman reached inside her cloak and pulled out a piece of worn parchment and handed it to Dougie. He carefully opened the document then looked up in confusion. The page was written in a language he was unfamiliar with. There were no words, just symbols. Even though he knew in his heart that this woman was not his Mary, his heart still skipped a beat when she gazed upon him.

"Go to the light and find the key to join the world, only then can I guide you home."

"Wh ... what do ye mean? I don't understand."

"My time is up. Now I must go."

Dougie stood, somewhat distressed on hearing this.

"Nae wait, please don't leave. Mary I don't want tae lose ye again."

Raising her hood as she turned to leave she smiled, "I must. Go to the light and find the key to join the world."

Before he could respond, she was moving swiftly away, back past the rows of gravestones and neatly kept flowerbeds, eventually disappearing once more into the early morning mist. She was gone! He had lost everything.

Raising a hand to his mouth he fought hard to contain the stinging tears now welling up behind his eyes. Returning to the bench his head fell into his hands and he sobbed uncontrollably.

The slow walk back to Tom's was a sombre one. With the realisation that Mary was gone and the magnitude of the task ahead, he felt as if the weight of the whole world was on his shoulders.

Opening the small iron front gate to Tom's house he gazed at the front door and wondered how on earth he could tell his new found friends that they were probably all going to die within a week and that his glorious Scottish homeland may be lost forever.

Closing the gate, Dougie gazed at the magnificent Ochil's with a new sense of awe. As the early morning sunshine hit the high peak of Craig Leith something moved inside him. For the first time he no longer felt confident, but venerable and afraid – almost as if he was a stranger in a strange land.

"Dougie did you enjoy your walk, is everything alright?"

Dougie turned to face Tom.

Tom's smile fell away as Dougie stood in front of him, his expression blank and empty. Dougie sighed and swallowed "Nae, I'm afraid it's not."

TWENTY TWO

"**D**ADDY! MUMMY SAY'S that breakfast is ready. Daddy do you hear me?"

For a moment Tom simply stood and silently continued to stare at Dougie with an increasing look of concern on his face.

"Daddy ..."

Tom shook himself out the momentary trance and turned to face his daughter, "Hmm, what's that? Oh I'm sorry my darling, tell mummy we'll be right there."

Tom turned back to Dougie and spoke softly "Do you want to talk about it?"

The big man shook his head, "Nae lad. This isn't the time ... perhaps after breakfast."

Tom nodded sympathetically and turned back towards the open door, politely inviting Dougie inside.

After breakfast, Jane cleared away the remaining dishes and decided to take Amy and an enthusiastic Wallace for a walk, leaving Tom, Dougie and Kate sitting in silence around an empty breakfast table.

Tom sighed and twiddled his thumbs back and forth waiting for either Kate or Dougie to initiate a conversation. However, as the minutes passed, both just sat quietly staring into space. Finally, for Tom, enough was enough and he broke the awkward silence. "Okay let's have it, before this drives me insane."

Kate was the first to look up "Huh … what's that? Oh I'm sorry Tom."

Then with a sudden change of mind she sat up and said, "You know, what the hell … perhaps you can help."

Tom looked at Dougie who pursed his lips and nodded, then Tom answered, "Okay, go ahead."

"Well, in the past week, two members of my news team have been murdered. The first was gunned down in Germany and the other in London. At first I thought I was going crazy and that they weren't related. Then I started digging into a story that Robert Jameson had been working on."

Tom's eyes widened. "Hey, I've heard of him. He was shot or something! It was on the news yesterday."

Kate nodded, "Exactly! It's like a bloody onion. For every layer I find an answer to another layer appears. It's only been few days and already I'm looking at four unexplained deaths."

Kate sighed and paused for a moment.

"You know, I'm sorry Tom, you don't need to hear this today. You have other things on your plate."

Tom shook his head, "If it was any other day I would agree. However today is no ordinary day and as I said to Dougie yesterday, we've been thrown together for a reason and I have a gut feeling it's a good one."

"Aye lad. You ken that's exactly what it is."

Both Kate and Tom turned to Dougie who was leaning forward looking re-energised. Tom and Kate looked at each other in semi confusion and then turned back at Dougie who was now on his feet.

"Dougie is everything okay?"

Pacing up and down, Dougie shook his head "Nae lad, it's not. However she wouldn't have told me, unless, unless I … I mean, if we had a chance at stoppin' it."

Tom glanced at Kate who was now raising her eyebrows as if to ask what on earth he was talking about.

"She? Dougie what do you mean?"

At this point, Dougie stopped pacing and merely gazed down at Tom and Kate, desperately trying to decide on what his next sentence should be. He wanted so much to tell them everything, but how, how would they react? Would they understand or would they just think he was some kind of madman.

"Wait, the paper … the paper she gave me," he suddenly burst out as he sat back down, reached inside his shirt and took out the piece of parchment and placed it on the table.

Tom picked it up and turned to Kate shrugging his shoulders, "What is it?"

Kate merely stared blankly. Taking back the parchment Dougie unfolded it and placed it face up on to the table. Clearing his throat he glared wide-eyed at Tom and Kate.

"Don't ye see? It's the end of the world laddie … it's a message about the end of the world."

As his words faded it was now Kate now took and inspected the parchment with interest..

"What happened to you this morning Dougie … you … you go out for a walk and then come back, with this … this story?"

"If I told ye laddie, you'd never believe me. Hell at this stage I'm nae even sure I believe myself"

"Wait …"

Dougie and Tom turned towards Kate.

"Dougie who gave you this?"

"It was given to me this morning by … my wife."

Both stared at him and said in unison, "Your wife?"

"Aye one minute I was sitting alone in the graveyard and the next there she was … Telling me that I was sent here for a reason and that she needed my help."

There was an awkward silence before Tom spoke.

"What kind of help?"

Dougie sighed, "All I ken is that whatever she or … it is,

she isn't human. She told me that another like her, a 'keeper' or something has come tae destroy us …"

"This parchment … I saw something like it once when I was younger." As she spoke, it was now Kate who stood and started pacing back and forth. "It was when I was a student at Oxford. We visited the National Museum of History in London, I remember it so well because my professor at the time made a big deal of telling us about of a number of pre – Egyptian civilizations and how they had mastered one of the earliest forms of symbol based communication. If these symbols do indeed contain a message that can save us then we have to find out what it means."

"Go to the light and find the key tae join the world only then can I guide ye home."

Both Tom and Kate turned to face Dougie. "What's that Dougie?"

"That's what she said. She told me that within days all of this would be gone. When I asked if there was anything I could do she simply give me that and said "go to the light and find the key tae join the world. Only then can I guide ye home."

Suddenly Tom banged his fists on the table and yelled, "Of course!"

"What is it laddie?"

"The light, It's the cavern Dougie. We've both seen it. Don't you get it? The cavern is the light?"

"That's braw reasoning laddie, but what does it mean? What is this key that she wants me tae find and what the hell do I do with it when I find it?"

Kate stopped pacing, sat down and placed the parchment on the table. "I'll bet the answer is in here somewhere. The question is how on earth we translate it?"

The room slipped again into silence. After a few moments it's was Tom who spoke first. "Well, what about your old professor Kate, could he help?"

"Professor Bird? Oh God I don't know. I don't even know if he's still alive."

"Well you could try giving him a call. It's something."

Kate glanced over at Dougie who nodded in agreement.

"I suppose I could try."

Tom stood and picked up the parchment. "Perhaps we should make a copy or two, you know just in case it gets lost or damaged. I have a photocopier in my office."

Kate nodded in agreement. "That's a great idea."

Dougie, who was now the only person still sitting at the table raised his hand in apparent confusion. As he moved towards the kitchen door Tom glanced back and noticed Dougie's puzzled expression. "Is everything alright Dougie?"

Dougie lowered his hand. "Aye, but if ye don't mind me asking lad … what's a photocopier?"

His mind was made up. For Donald McPherson, today was the day he was going to discover the truth. After his encounter with Kate Harding and being needlessly detained for several hours by the authorities on Saturday, enough was enough!

Now he wanted answers and today he was damn well going to get them. What the hell was going on in Alva anyway? A whole village cleared for what? The official line, of course, was that dangerous chemicals had been discovered in the glen. Harding wasn't convinced and neither was he.

As McPherson straightened his tie and put on his grey suit jacket, a sense of determination was flowing through him. Filled with new purpose MacPherson strode over to his couch, picked up his leather laptop bag, and opened the white painted oak front door and stepped out into the bright sunlight. Closing the door behind him and taking a deep breath, the large man strode down the gravel path towards his familiar blue Honda Civic.

Arriving at the car, he fumbled for a moment looking for his keys, eventually pulling them out of an inside pocket. Unlocking the rear door, he placed his laptop bag on the back seat and slammed the door shut.

"Mr McPherson …"

"Uh!"

Turning around McPherson was momentarily startled by the sudden appearance of a tall, muscular man dressed in a black leather jacket, grey top and black jeans.

"Are you Donald McPherson?"

"Aye … er, yes I am. Can I help you?"

Smiling the man approached and nodded. "Yes my name is Brooks … David Brooks. I work with Kate Harding at the *Chronicle*, I believe you know her?"

McPherson sighed in relief, "Yes … yes. Bloody hell man you scared me half to death, I thought you were."

The man gave a sneer, "Who … who did you think I was Donald?"

For an uncomfortable moment Donald McPherson was lost for words. "I … I thought you were the police."

The man gave a hollow laugh, "No Donald I'm definitely not the police. I'm simply trying to find her."

Something was wrong here, McPherson couldn't put his finger on it, but this felt all wrong. Brooks was just out of place. His clothes, his appearance, even the way he spoke just didn't seem right for a reporter. With the hairs on his neck slowly rising, Donald glanced around hoping that a neighbour or passer-by might perhaps suddenly appear and offer him a reason to get away. But as he glanced up and down the unusually quiet street, McPherson realised that he was unfortunately on his own.

"I … I don't know where she is. I've not seen her."

A lie, a blatant lie and as he gazed back at the sneering stranger, McPherson knew that his words were transparent. Brooks' sneer fell away, and as he stepped closer to McPherson he sighed. "Pity … I thought you could help me. Especially because a taxi driver saw you pick her up at the station, not to mention the nice lady at the hotel who saw you drop her off. So you see Donald I know you know where she is."

McPherson's head dropped as alarm bells began ringing inside his head and a wave of nausea gripped his stomach. "Okay, okay, all I know is that she was arrested in Alva and that she was later released." As he spoke the man stepped closer and he got a whiff of the stranger's foul breath.

"Where is she now?"

The large reporter continued to stare at the stranger's black leather, military style boots. Closing his eyes for a moment he sighed and then reopened them. "Tom Duncan ... I believe she's staying with Tom Duncan and his family. I don't have an address, I swear."

Brooks' sneering smile reappeared. "There you see Donald, that wasn't too hard was it?"

"Can I go now?"

"Of course you can go Donald I don't want to detain you any longer than necessary." Breathing a sigh of relief he turned swiftly towards the safety of his blue Honda Civic, opened the vehicles front door and climbed into the driver's seat. Shutting the door he sat for a moment before placing the key into the ignition.

As he turned the key to start the engine, a knock came at the window and Brooks' grinning face reappeared. Turning off the engine McPherson rolled down his window, "Yes what is it?"

"Now Donald, you didn't honestly think I was just going to let you go did you?" McPherson just sat looking blankly "But ... I don't understand I've told you everything you wanted to know."

He could feel the fear growing inside, he should have driven away when he had the chance. Why did he switch the engine off?

"I believe you."

"Then why can't I go?" he muttered.

McPherson noticed that the man had something in his hand, but couldn't quite make out what it was.

"If I let you go you could warn her that I was coming, and I can't allow that."

A syringe! In his hand was a syringe! Feeling sick with panic McPherson gazed up at Brooks, "W … what's that for?"

"Why, it's for you Donald."

"You don't have to do this, I won't say a word to anyone I promise."

Brooks sneered, "It's okay Donald, I know you won't."

Suddenly the man thrust a leather-gloved hand over McPherson's mouth like a vice. Thrashing wildly, McPherson tried desperately to scream, but it was in vain. Brooks' grip was just too overpowering.

With his other hand he calmly raised the syringe and plunged the needle into McPherson's large neck emptying the entire vial into him. McPherson's body first went limp and then suddenly erupted into a series of grotesque, violent spasms.

After a few seconds his body relaxed and his throat gurgled as he gave one final breath. Glancing up and down the quiet street, Brooks calmly placed the syringe back into a small leather case and returned it to an inside pocket.

He then straightened McPherson's clothes and closed his eyelids. When finished, it would appear to any passers-by that McPherson had simply fallen asleep at the wheel. Closing the Civics door, Brooks calmly walked back towards his own vehicle. Once inside the silver Mercedes he reached for his mobile phone, dialled a number and waited for the call to be picked up.

"Yes."

"It's Brooks. I know where Harding is."

"Good. Were there any complications?" Brooks glanced towards McPherson's blue Honda and sneered. "No, no complications. She's staying with a family in Alva."

"You know what must be done. It ends with her."

"And the family?"

"I want things clean; understand? If they get in the way then that's ... unfortunate."

"I understand."

Brooks placed the phone down onto the passenger seat and started the engine. Pulling away the sleek silver Mercedes headed eastwards towards the Wallace monument, the A91 and the Hillfoot village of Alva.

TWENTY THREE

MONDAY: 11.20AM ALVA, SCOTLAND

DESPITE THE PROMISE of a brighter day, the warm start had prematurely given way to the arrival of menacing dark clouds and blustery winds over the Ochil's. Two police Range Rovers had arrived outside Tom's house and as Jane returned home with Amy and Wallace, her husband and their two visitors were climbing aboard the waiting vehicles. As the engines roared into life, Tom waved to his wife and daughter who responded with corresponding smiles and waves.

The drive to Alva Glen only took a few minutes. On arrival, the cars parked adjacent to a large temporary mobile police unit that had been positioned in the Alva Golf club car park adjacent the Glen entrance.

The car park was a flurry of activity as a variety of police and military personnel were busy erecting various temporary structures and assembling equipment. Dougie, Tom and Kate were met by Inspector Andrew McLeish and the young MI5 officer, Robert Wilkes.

"Good Morning Gentlemen. Miss Harding I hadn't realised you were joining us this morning. I don't think that ..." McLeish began.

Kate shook her head and abruptly cut McLeish off in

mid-sentence. "Oh please Inspector, don't be so naïve. I wouldn't miss this for the world."

McLeish shook his head in frustration and glanced disapprovingly across to his young colleague for support, but with none forthcoming he merely nodded in defeat. "Very well, but may I remind you that this is still a classified situation and that any violation …"

"Yes, yes, man, I understand. You don't need to keep repeating yourself."

McLeish rolled his eyes in annoyance and nodded in agreement, "Very well then, if you'll please follow me we'll get started."

Leading the group across to a waiting Army Land Rover, McLeish proceeded to introduce them to three people waiting at the vehicle. "Mr Allan, Mr Duncan, Miss Harding may I introduce Colonel James McNeil, Professor Helen Moore and Dr Richard Quest, scientific advisors from the Home Office."

McNeil appeared the typical career military man. In his late forties, tall, smartly dressed and well spoken. As Kate eyed the senior officer her first thought was Sandhurst, the British army's royal military academy, located in Surrey, a short distance from London.

For generations it was responsible for training elite officer cadets. Alongside McNeil stood Professor Moore. An attractive, dark-haired, thirty something who, by her slightly stuffy appearance, looked as if she preferred a good book rather than a night out with the girls. By her side Richard Quest, a semi-attractive man perhaps in his mid-forties. Dressed informally in fading black jeans and a short sleeved, buttoned down powder blue shirt. He looked relaxed and gave the impression of being in control.

McNeil stepped forward and formally extended his hand, "Gentlemen, Miss Harding, delighted to meet you."

Tom, Dougie and Kate nodded politely and shook hands with the officer. When finished the Colonel stood aside and Moore stepped forward and approached the tartan clad Dougie and grinned. "This is just incredible. Mr Allan, may I call you Dougie?"

Dougie nodded, "Aye lass of course ye can."

Placing her hand on his cheek, she stroked him as if he were made of gold.

"This is just incredible. Is it true, where you're from? I mean, I guess I should say when?"

Dougie glanced first at Tom and then at Kate and nodded, "Aye it's true."

As Dougie blushed, she moved away and her colleague stepped forward.

"Easy Helen, you may get whisked back in time. I'm sorry but it's not every day we get to meet a real life time-traveller. Please, call me Richard ... we're not ones for titles."

Quest shook hands with the group and stepped back. A moment later Inspector McLeish returned carrying what appeared to be a selection of large maps. Stepping in front of the Land Rover he unfolded one, placed it onto the car's hood and motioned Dougie and Tom over to take a look. "Here you are gentlemen, a complete map of the Alva and Silver Glen mine project. I though you may find it useful."

Walking to the front of the car Dougie gazed in amazement at how the small mine had developed through the years. "Och laddie, look at this ... I had nae idea ..."

McLeish grinned. "Alva was famous for silver Dougie. In its day it was one of Europe's finest, all partly thanks to you."

Pointing at the map he said, "Here ... Tom this is where you were picked up after your fall. The problem is how do we find your pyramid Dougie?"

Glancing down, Dougie nodded, pointing at the map. "Hmm there's nae point going in there, for me that was the way oot. No ye need tae find the way in, and as far as I remember it was here."

Dougie placed his index finger on a spot slightly to the left of

Wood Hill. McLeish stroked his chin and shook his head, "But there's nothing there, we've already checked."

Dougie smiled as he recollected his recent adventure, struggling through tight crawlspaces. Eyeing McLeish he nodded, "Believe me laddie, it's there … but we had a cave-in so you'll need some lads tae help clear it."

McLeish looked eagerly at Colonel McNeil, "Don't worry Dougie that won't be a problem. Colonel, could you spare some men?"

"Absolutely."

"Well then, let's get started."

Additional vehicles including a large khaki-coloured Army personnel carrier and two additional Land Rovers now joined the Land Rover. As the group climbed aboard and the engine started, the convoy pulled away eastwards and up towards Wood Hill.

As the vehicles juddered and jerked there along the single mud track road towards the mine Dougie's mind wandered. Thoughts of a life, now long gone merged with images of his beautiful Mary and the faces of his workmates and friends preparing for work.

He recalled the McRae brothers, James Ritchie and the breathless teenager, desperate to warn him about the Rogue Alexander McArthur. A man, who now as it turns out, is not even a man but some kind of freak intent on the destruction of everything he held dear.

As the cars shuddered to a halt, he recalled the cemetery encounter and the instruction given to him – "Go to the light and find the key to join the world. Only then can I guide you home."

"Dougie, are you okay?"

The cars had stopped and everyone but Dougie had left the vehicle. Tom stood holding the rear door open, waiting for his new friend to climb out. Quickly shaking himself out of his momentary trance, Dougie answered, "Aye, sorry. I was miles away."

As he climbed out and Tom shut the door, the group stood

for a moment watching the flurry of activity as military personnel assembled in front of the somewhat dilapidated mine entrance.

Dougie looked at the soldiers, who by the looks on their faces and the weapons they were carrying were expecting trouble. Turning to McLeish and the Colonel Dougie raised his hand in protest. "Colonel what is this? Are ye expecting a war? I don't think that this is …"

Colonel McNeil stepped forward raising both hands in way to allay Dougie's fears, "Don't worry Mr Allan, this is merely standard procedure in this type of situation."

"What type of situation is that then?"

As he waited for an answer, it was Kate who finally broke the silence. "Don't you see Dougie? "It's what all men fear. The unknown."

Both the Colonel and McLeish glanced at each, "Exactly Miss Harding,"

The mine entrance itself was exactly as he remembered. Apart from a rusting green gate which had been placed across the entrance and a sign which read *"DANGER! OLD MINE WORKINGS. KEEP OUT!"*, today could have been like any other day.

As the Colonel turned towards the men, the squad stomped their feet to attention and an older, smartly dressed officer stepped forward and gave a salute.

"Company assembled sir."

"Thank you Major. Good morning gentlemen, I believe you have already been briefed so I won't labour. Needless to say we face an unknown situation here. Our orders are simple, get in, determine the threat and report back to the powers that be. I would also like to introduce Dougie Allan, Tom Duncan and Kate Harding, who have agreed to assist us in the investigation. I believe some of you already know Professor Moore and Dr Quest, our scientific advisors from the Home Office. "

The group of assembled men nodded in recognition.

"Major do you have all the equipment you need?"

The smartly dressed Major nodded and stepped forward. "Aye sir, we've everything we need."

"Excellent ... well then, let's get started shall we."

With that, the Major turned on his heels and commanded "Davies, Thomson, remove that gate. Robertson, Muir, fire up the mole. I want that tunnel checked and cleared as fast as possible. Well, what are you waiting for? Move!"

The scene erupted into a flurry of activity as one group of men dragged a large robotic drilling machine from inside one of the Land Rovers over to the mine entrance. At the same time, a tall muscular red headed corporal took a large axe from the back of the personnel carrier and calmly walked over to the ageing metal gate. Swinging the axe with such force, the large padlock on the gate shattered as if it were made of glass.

As the gate swung open, the officer held up two fingers and began a series of hand gestures. Two armed soldiers ran forward and took up flanking positions outside the cave entrance. One of the young soldiers then unclipped and ignited what appeared to be a flare and tossed it inside the entrance and he and his partner advanced forward beyond the sight of the rest of the group. Again following the Corporals hand instructions, two further members of the squad took up position outside the entrance assumedly to provide support if required.

Standing adjacent to the Land Rover, Dougie stood with the rest of the group surveying the scene with interest. As he leaned over to speak to Tom, his words were overlain with static as a nearby radio burst into life. After a pause the static was replaced by a young man's voice "Charlie one to Charlie leader over."

The Major unclipped a radio from his belt, held it up to his mouth and pushed the transmit button. "Aye lad, what do you see?"

Again a moment of static crackles came back followed by the young man's voice, "Sir ... it's clear here, but the passageway ahead is blocked. We'll need the mole to proceed further."

"Understood, Stand by."

Releasing the transmit button, the Major glanced at McLeish and the Colonel who seemed to be in conversation. Having finished his conversation, McLeish turned to Dougie, "Well Dougie, what do you think?"

Clearing his throat Dougie nodded, "My lad's must have sealed the entrance for a reason, perhaps to stop MacArthur getting oot, I'm nae sure. Assuming your lads can get in there ye shouldn't have any problems. I may warn ye though, that it'll get a bit cramped in there."

McLeish nodded in response and said, "Send in the mole Major."

"Aye sir."

The Major pushed transmit and the radio burst into life with a series of crackles.

"Charlie one, out you come lads, we're sending in the mole."

With that the Major clipped the radio back onto his belt and gave a hand signal to the remaining troops to move the drill inside the opening. Once in place, the Major ordered, "Right lads, step back."

As instructed the group stepped away and the large, red-headed corporal, once again strode towards the entrance carrying what appeared to be a small portable computer. As the device powered up, Dougie turned to Tom and whispered, "What's happening lad?"

Tilting his head Tom murmured, "It's a machine Dougie, a drill designed to burrow through rock. The corporal there is operating it through that control device. I'll bet you could've used one of those in your day eh?"

Dougie gave a wry smile, "Aye, it took me and the lads a six months tae tunnel though a shaft once … amazing."

The drill roared into life and began rumbling slowly forwards. The ground reverberated as the drill hit the rock and the roar changed to a shrill screeching. From inside the entrance, billows of thick, choking dust poured outwards causing members of the group to cover their eye's and mouths. The drilling continued for several minutes, until a sudden change in sound gave the Corporal an indication that the machine had cleared the obstruction. As the he pressed a key on the keyboard, the drill began to slowly reverse out of the mine and came to a halt a few meters away from the group. As the roar of the engine fell silent, the officer placed the computer into a small bag and walked across to one of the Land Rovers, opened the door and placed it onto the front seat. After closing the door he strode over to the Major, "All clear sir."

"Excellent Corporal. Send in the recon team."

The Corporal turned and again motioned the four, armed troops to again take up flanking positions. Dougie gave a sigh and shook his head stepping forward away from Tom and Kate, "For goodness sake colonel, you're nae afraid of the dark are ye?"

Turning, McLeish and the Colonel glanced at each other, before McNeil answered, "I'm sorry Mr Allan its simply military procedure that we …"

Shaking his head with frustration, Dougie cut the Colonel off in mid-sentence. "Look Colonel, I ken these caverns like the back of my hand. By all means send in your laddies if ye like, but time's wasting here."

Glancing at McLeish for guidance he attempted to object but was immediately interrupted by the MI5 officer, Robert Wilkes. He had been standing quietly nearby, but now stepped forward. "He's right Colonel."

Glancing around the group, the Colonel yielded, turned to the Major and gave a reluctant nod. Once again the Corporal sprang into life.

"Right lads, let's get these civvies kitted out. McRae, Jones you two will take point. Jarvis get the lights and ropes."

Within minutes, Dougie, Kate, Tom, Moore and Quest had all been provided with khaki coveralls, radios and torches. Despite complaints, the Colonel had decided that, for safety reasons they would be accompanied by four military personnel – Major Johnstone, Corporal Jarvis and two squaddies armed with rifles.

By 12.15 pm, the clouds had thickened and a light drizzle had turned into a persistent shower. After what seemed to be, in Dougie's opinion, "an eternity", the group finally appeared ready. Dougie felt an eerie sense of the familiar as he stepped through the entrance. In front, the two soldiers edged carefully onwards, guiding the five civilians past the enormous pile of debris by the mine entrance.

The mine was as Dougie remembered. Cold, damp and unnervingly quiet. The shadows of the group's torches danced off the grey walls and as they moved forwards the only noticeable sounds were those of heavy boots up ahead, echoing as they trudged onwards.

As Dougie had foretold, the walls of the mine had begun to close in and the group were forced to stoop low in order to continue. A few more steps and it became almost impossible to stand and they were finally forced down on their hands and knees. For Kate, who was clearly unaccustomed at crawling through dark passages, this was almost too much.

As she moved, Dougie noticed her heavy breathing. "Are ye all right lassie? Do ye need tae take a rest?"

She stopped for a moment and took a deep breath, then tilted her head back and wheezed, "No, I'm okay, and I'm just not used to crawling around like this, that's all."

The conversation was interrupted by a shout ahead, "Sir, wait there's something here."

The group fell into silence as the Major shouted, "What is it lad, what have you got?"

After a pause the echoed voice came back from the shadows, "It appears to be the remains of a body."

Before the Major could respond, Dougie cried out, "Where, where is it? Let me see."

Pushing forward he edged past Tom and almost pinned the

Major against the cavern wall as he came elbowing through. As he moved towards the soldiers, the chamber began to open out and he found that he could just about stand.

"What is it lads, what can ye see?"

"It's here Mr Allan, here look!"

As Dougie approached, the young soldier directed his torchlight towards the grim remains. Gazing down Dougie's mouth fell open in dismay, "No!"

At the same moment, the rest of the group arrived. Standing behind him, shining torches downwards, each gave a gasp of surprise. On the ground in front of them lay the semi-clothed, near perfect skeletal remains of a man.

As Tom gazed down at his friend, he saw Dougie lean over and pick up a piece of worn, but distinctive red and blue tartan cloth. Placing a hand on his friend's shoulder, Tom crouched down to take a closer look. "Are you okay? Did you know him?"

For a moment the big man said nothing, as he swallowed hard in an attempt to fight back the tears now welling up in his eyes. Slowly he turned to Tom. "Aye, it's Stuart – Stuart McRae. He was a good lad. He must've got stuck when the beams gave way. I should never have left him."

Kate stepped forward and stooped lower for a closer look. "Dougie, you shouldn't blame yourself. It's not your fault."

"Kate's right Dougie, if you had gone back, you'd probably be dead as well. You were right. You were brought here for a reason and it's important."

Dougie sighed, wiped his eyes and stood. Glancing first at Kate, he then pulled himself up, "Aye … you're right lad … of course, you're booth right, thank ye."

Turning to the Major he pointed at the remains and lowered his voice. "Major, if ye don't mind, I'd appreciate a proper burial for my friend here. He was a good lad."

The major pursed his lips and smiled reassuringly, "Of course Mr Allan, I'll take care of it."

"Sir, you have to see this!"

About fifty metres ahead of the group, one of the men stood motionless looking shocked and pointing at a chink of daylight. Stepping forward the group shuffled along the passageway with interest. Shaking his head in apparent disbelief the Major turned away. "It's just daylight you idiot, come on let's get moving."

Staring at the light, Dr Quest raised his hand in an attempt to gain the group's attention. "Wait a minute … it's not, look!"

Turning around, the Major noticed everyone staring at the light source in the same weird way. Then he suddenly realised what was wrong. The light not was coming from above, but was emanating from below. Then as everything became clear, he knew exactly what needed to be done. "Jarvis you and the lads set me up a perimeter."

The large, red-headed Corporal swung around, "Aye sir. All right lads, you heard the man. This is what we're here for. Get me those ropes and a pick axe."

TWENTY FOUR

10 DOWNING STREET, LONDON

"THIS IS THE One o'clock news from the BBC. The world was in shock today, as the United States became the latest victim in the series of worldwide disasters. The paradise islands of Hawaii have been completely devastated. Yesterday at 7.12 am local time a massive volcanic eruption and underwater earthquake hit off the coast of Hawaii measuring at least 10.6 on the Richter scale. Despite their best efforts, the United States Government is now estimating there are at least seven million dead.

"The quake triggered a huge tsunami that hit the US mainland cities of Los Angeles, San Francisco and Seattle a short time afterwards. Having had only hours to evacuate, it's feared the damage and death toll will be high. A short time ago President Richard Bryant made a statement to the world's media. This is what he had to say."

As he watched, the shot moved from the newsreader to a scene inside the White House. Standing at the press podium was the President, a tall well-built man in his early 50s with jet-black hair and striking blue eyes. Dressed in a neat grey suit, white shirt and red silk tie, he looked tired and abnormally pale. As he spoke his voice shook with emotion.

"My fellow Americans, today our homeland has once again fallen victim to another cruel and devastating event. The islands of Hawaii have been completely destroyed. At this point we are looking at an unimaginable loss of life. I have ordered FEMA and our armed forces in the Pacific to aid in the rescue effort. We have received pledges of assistance from countries including Japan, China, Russia and the United Kingdom, for which we are very grateful.

I am also saddened to inform you that as a consequence of the disaster, our western seaboard was also hit with a large tsunami. Although the force of the wave had weakened by the time it hit land, the cities of Los Angeles, San Francisco and Seattle have suffered extensive damage and loss of life. In this, one of our darkest hours, I have called for a countrywide national emergency and I would ask that all Americans co-operate with the authorities to aid the recovery effort. We are a strong people and we will prevail. God bless you all and God bless the United States of America."

As the screen switched back to the studio the newsreader shuffled in his seat and continued reading. "With the world still reeling from a series of catastrophic disasters, the scientific community are to meet world leaders including President Bryant in Reykjavik on Saturday to discuss the causes and solutions for these catastrophic events."

Switching off the television, James Walton sighed as the screen went blank and his office fell silent. He leaned back in his chair, closed his eyes and rubbed his forehead, trying desperately to understand the events of the past few hours. The silence was interrupted by a knock at the door. Opening his eyes, he sat up in his chair and shouted, "Come in."

The door swung open and his assistant, Lisa Harkins, entered carrying a silver tea tray with a white china teapot, two matching cups, saucers and a plate of chocolate digestive biscuits. "I thought you might be in need a cup of tea, Prime Minister."

Walton smiled, "You read my mind. There are two cups. Are you joining me?"

The young woman shook her head and smirked, "No such luck sir, I'm afraid. It's for the Home Secretary, she's waiting outside."

Walton rolled his eyes, "Rats, I forgot about that."

"Shall I show her in sir?"

Sitting up, he straightened his tie and nodded in acknowledgement, "Yes please Lisa."

"Sir."

Harkins placed the tray down on a coffee table, turned and opened the door, "The Prime Minister will see you now, Mam."

The Home Secretary, Anne Petrie, stepped through the door. "Good afternoon Prime Minister."

Walton stood, smiled and stepped forward shaking the woman's hand. "Anne, nice to see you. You're just in time for tea."

"Yes please, it's been quite a day."

As she sat down, Walton filled the two china cups with steaming hot tea. Placing the cups and saucers on his desk he then proceeded to offer a biscuit to his visitor, "No thank you. If I get started on those, I'll never stop."

"So, what's the news from the US?"

Picking up the cup, Petrie took a couple of sips and sat back looking sombre. "Not good Sir. So far early reports indicate that they are looking at a 95 per cent loss of life in Hawaii and around 4.2 million dead in Los Angeles, San Francisco and Seattle with another 300 thousand or so missing."

"My God. Do we have any idea how this happened?"

"Not yet, but the scientific community are speculating that the increased volcanic activity in the southern hemisphere in the past few years has somehow triggered a shift in the Earth's tectonic plates."

Walton Leaned forward looking concerned, "Do we have a hypothesis as too how this may end?"

Petrie sighed, "No sir, I'm afraid not. Perhaps the meeting in Iceland on Saturday will be more fruitful."

"What about our response?"

"Well, we're doing as much as we can. The HMS Illustrious and the Daring are on their way to the US west coast; they should arrive sometime on Wednesday. The plan is to join with the combined US, Japanese and Chinese task force and hopefully rescue as many people as possible."

Picking up his cup, Walton took a couple of sips and placed it back down. "The Chinese, I never thought that I would see the day when …"

"To be fair sir, they have suffered as well. I'll be the first to admit that they have been extremely helpful."

"Yes, I agree, they have."

The room fell silent as Petrie picked up her cup and sipped the warm liquid.

"What about the incident in Scotland? What's the latest?"

"The latest I heard was that the team were on site about 40 minutes ago. Other than that, nothing more yet, sir."

Walton stood, stretched his arms and sighed, "What about Kate Harding, anything there?"

At the mention of Kate's name, Petrie appeared to perk up. "Indeed, as you know I love a mystery. Well, I've done a little digging and after contacting *The Chronicle* I think I've found out what she's been working on. She was investigating Robert Jameson's death. He was shot in Germany last week, along with a man named Herman Brauer, an ex-priest as it turns out."

"A Priest?"

"Yes. He appears to have been involved with an Icelandic scientist, Elín Gylfadóttir, a volcanologist."

"Well, shouldn't we contact this Elín Gylfadóttir? Perhaps she could shed some light on all of this."

Petrie shook her head, "I wish we could, but I'm afraid she's dead!"

"Dead!"

"Yes sir, apparently she took her own life. I contacted the authorities regarding all three cases and I've been promised a report. Hopefully that will provide a little more insight."

Walton began pacing up and down. "This doesn't feel right Anne. Five deaths within a couple of weeks, what does it mean?"

Petrie sighed, "I'm not sure, but as I said yesterday I'm concerned that Kate Harding has uncovered something that's put her in danger."

"Is there anything we can do?"

"Well we do have an MI5 asset on-site, Robert Wilkes. I could ask him to have a word with her. It would also perhaps be prudent to inform the commanding officer of the possible threat. He could then take appropriate measure to ensure her safety."

Walton nodded in agreement and returned to his desk. As he sat, he gave a sigh, "Yes, okay let's proceed. You'll keep me informed of any developments?"

Petrie stood and nodded, "Of course Prime Minister."

As his Home Secretary left the room, James Walton sighed and inclined back in his leather chair. Sitting quietly going over the meeting, he picked up the TV remote control and pressed the on button.

As the A91 Stirling to St Andrew's road had been closed since Saturday, the only vehicles to approach the checkpoint outside Alva had been either of a military or police variety. It was therefore with some surprise to the two young soldiers on duty at the checkpoint that, they spotted the silver car approaching. As his companion drained the last few drops of cola from a can, Private Graham McLeod raised his hand. "Scott, look lively. We have a visitor."

The other soldier, a blond-haired youngster, perhaps no older than 19, tossed the empty can into the front seat of the Khaki Land Rover and picked up his SA80 rifle. Graham McLeod was 23, both he and his younger companion, Scott Calder, were members of the Royal Regiment of Scotland and should have, in his opinion, been somewhere more interesting in the world than Stirlingshire.

As the silver car rose over the top of the hill like a wolf in search of prey, McLeod could see that it was a silver Mercedes, perhaps an SL class coupe with a single occupant.

"Nice car."

"What's that McLeod?"

"I said, nice car, come on!"

In their current position, the Land Rovers were parked adjacent to each other in the middle of the road. As the car approached, the soldiers stepped forward in front of the vehicle. McLeod raised his hand, in order to indicate the car should stop. Pulling in as instructed, the car came to smooth halt and the driver, a tall man, perhaps in his 30s, switched the engine off and wound down his window.

Dressed in a black leather jacket and dark grey T-Shirt, he took off his sunglasses as McLeod stepped forward and cleared his throat.

"I'm sorry sir, the road ahead is closed. I'm afraid you'll have to turn back."

Brooks sneered, "Closed … for what reason?"

"Contamination sir! So if you'll just …"

As his door swung open, Brooks placed a foot on the ground and started to stand. Confused and somewhat alarmed, as to why the man was exiting his vehicle, the younger Private raised his weapon and shouted, "Sir, stay in your vehicle."

But, even before the words had left his mouth, Brooks was out and standing in front of the two youngsters.

"Easy, I just want to know what's going on; I'm just trying to find a friend of mine."

Glancing over at his younger companion, McLeod nodded, "Easy Private. That's fine sir, but please return to your vehicle."

Brooks sneered and nodded, "Of course son, no problem."

As he turned to his car, McLeod raised his hand to motion his companion to lower his weapon. As the youngster complied the scene suddenly exploded like a firecracker. Brooks moved like an animal. His speed and prowess were like nothing the young soldiers had ever seen before, let alone been prepared for. From nowhere he came at them like a Cobra striking its prey.

First he struck the teenager with a blow to the head with such force that the youngster's nose exploded in a shower of blood and broken bone. As he fell, the youngster's weapon flew out of his hand and he hit the ground with a thump. Alarmed, McLeod raised his weapon to fire. As he aimed he panicked, realising that the safety was still on. That was all the time Brooks needed. Like a streak of lightning he'd drawn a revolver, complete with attached silencer, and was aiming it directly at McLeod's head.

Sneering like a cat that is about to play a deadly game with a mouse, the man hissed, "Now then, didn't your father tell you not to play with guns?"

Leaning forward McLeod carefully placed the rifle on the ground below his feet and kicked it away. Standing up he looked down, staring at the man's black boots, wondering desperately what to say. "Okay sir, let's keep things nice and calm shall we. What is it that you want?"

Staring at the young soldier, Brooks' sneer fell away, "Like I said, I'm looking for a woman by the name of Kate Harding."

Looking directly at Brooks in defiance, he swallowed and then shook his head. "I don't know her, I only know what they tell us."

"And what do they tell you?"

"I'm only a grunt okay; all I know is that there is an operation in the glen. I know that there are civilians helping, but I don't know any details."

"Where are they staying?"

McLeod shrugged his shoulders, "Hey man, if you're looking for an address, I don't know okay, okay … try Back Road. That's all I know, I swear! Come on put the gun down."

Brooks nodded and smiled, "Yes thanks, you've been very helpful."

The muffled shot hit McLeod in the forehead. Reeling backwards like a charging bull had hit him, he struck the front of the Land Rover with a dull thud and slowly slumped forwards on to the ground. Turning, Brooks then focused his attention on the youngster who was covered in blood lying on the ground out cold. Like a true predator and without any emotion he calmly walked over to the boy, raised the weapon and fired two shots straight into his head.

The sound of the bullets was like the plopping sounds of rocks being thrown into a pond. For a few moments Brooks stood calmly and silently. Holstering his weapon, he opened the trunk of his car and with little effort lifted each of the soldiers' bodies, one at a time, and placed them inside. Finally he collected the two SA80 rifles and placed them alongside the bodies. Closing the trunk he made a final sweep of the scene that included washing away a few patches of blood on the road with a bottle of water from one of the Land Rovers.

If anyone turned up, he would ensure it looked like the men had simply deserted their post. Scanning around one final time, he climbed into his car and slammed the door. Starting the engine, he drove into the village, first past a Welcome to Alva sign and onwards into the unnaturally quiet Stirling Street. Once turned left onto Park Street, he discreetly parked the silver Mercedes in an off street-parking bay and got out and slipped quietly into the shadows.

TWENTY FIVE

AS THE CORPORAL'S pick axe struck the rock, there was an almighty crack and the ground shuddered so violently that the group yelled out in surprise. As the impact reverberated through the cavern, a large section of rock fell away causing debris to crash downwards into the emerging nothingness. Simultaneously with the sound, the darkness within the cavern exploded into a blinding white light. Jarvis dropped the pickaxe in shock; the intensity seemed overpowering, causing Dougie, Tom and the rest of the group to reel backwards in an attempt to shield their eyes.

One of the younger soldiers screamed out, "Help, I can't see."

Dougie shouted, "It's okay lad, hold on it'll get easier in a moment."

Shielding his eyes while simultaneously leaning across to a pile of debris, Jarvis picked up a large rock and hurled it towards the source of the light. A moment later, the unmistakable sound of a dull thud signified that it had hit something solid. "Major, I estimate about 20 meters down, sir."

Edging slowly past the civilians, the major stood beside the corporal.

"Okay corporal, what do you say we get those ropes secured and let's take a look?"

"Aye sir."

Removing the large coil of rope from his shoulder, Jarvis proceeded to tie one end to a large protruding rock. Once attached, he tossed the remainder over the edge.

"McRae, Davies, recon, let's move."

As instructed the two, armed soldiers stepped up and nervously lowered themselves over the edge and disappeared down into the light. Ten metres away, Dougie, Tom, Kate and the two advisors simply stood and looked on in wonder.

As her eyes become accustomed to the brilliance, Kate said, "Dougie, this is incredible. Is this the same as you remember?"

"Aye, it is."

First 10 minutes passed, then 20. Staring at each other nervously, the group waited in anxious silence for the recon team to report in. The longer the wait, the tenser the situation became. Cramped spaces were now becoming intolerable. Moore stood up to stretch and accidentally struck her forehead on a protruding rock. The pain was sharp and intense, "Damn it!" she shrieked, in a mixture of frustration and intense pain. "For God's sake, how long are we going to stand around Major?"

Looking very uneasy, the Major turned to Jarvis and was about to ask, when the Corporal's radio spewed out a burst of static. "Char … ader … Ch … ne."

Jarvis unclipped his radio, held it to his mouth and pushed the talk button. "Charlie One, this is Charlie Leader, say again, are you alright lads?"

To everyone's relief the response was clearer. "Charlie Leader … Yes sir, the area is secured."

Jarvis grinned and again pushed the talk button. "Great lads, get back here. We're coming down."

As he gave Jarvis a thumbs up, the Major, unclipped his radio and pushed the talk button "Charlie Control, this is Charlie Leader over."

For a moment the radio was silent but then a series of crackles came back mixed with the voice of Colonel McNeil. "This is McNeil, what do you have Major?"

"Sir, we've made it through to the cavern. Colonel it's… it's incredible. We're going down to investigate."

As he released the transmit button the radio crackled and then the voice of McNeil came back. "Understood Major, I'll inform the powers that be. Take care, McNeil out."

Turning back to face the group, the Major cleared his throat, "Alright ladies and gentlemen this is it. Please step forward and Corporal Jarvis here will lower you down."

Pausing, he then turned to Dougie and motioned him forward, "Mr Allan perhaps you would like to lead the way?"

Glancing first at Tom, who smiled with a look of encouragement, Dougie turned back to the Major and nodded. "Aye, of course."

Stepping forward to the opening, Jarvis placed a harness and a length or rope around Dougie's waist and secured it with several clips. As he took the strain, Dougie took a deep breath, stepped over the edge and was lowered downwards into the light.

Above, the car park was a flurry of activity, as a group of police officers began placing large halogen lamps around the perimeter and military personnel were busy dragging large boxes with bright yellow stickers with the words Danger Radiation – X-Ray Equipment to the mouth of the mine.

Robert Wilkes stepped out from inside the mobile police unit and walked across to the Colonel who was nervously pacing back and forth.

"Any news?"

McNeil stopped pacing and turned, "I believe they are descending now. We should have a preliminary report soon."

Wilkes nodded and gave an uncomfortable sigh. "Good.

Colonel I'm sorry to bring this up, but I need your help with a small problem?"

McNeil stepped closer looking intrigued, "Problem, what sort of problem Mr Wilkes?"

"Sir, I've just received some intelligence regarding Miss Harding."

"What kind of intelligence?"

"It appears that her life could be in danger and I've been ordered to ask you for assistance."

"We're in the middle of, well I don't know what, and you're telling me that I've got to protect a bloody reporter as well?"

"Look Colonel, all I'm saying is that this comes from the top. They feel that this is a credible threat."

McNeil sighed, "Very well Mr Wilkes. I'll inform the men. In the meantime, I'll leave it up to you and the Chief Inspector to make the necessary arrangements for her safety."

As Wilkes opened his mouth to respond, but he was swiftly interrupted by a young soldier. "Excuse me sir, I'm sorry, but could I have a quick word?"

Glancing back at Wilkes, McNeil nodded, "Excuse me for a moment."

Stepping out of earshot, Wilkes observed as the two men talked. When over, the soldier signalled to a colleague and the two men climbed into a Land Rover and drove away. Re-joining Wilkes, McNeil shook his head apologetically. "I'm sorry about that Mr Wilkes, but it appears that we seem to have a couple of missing men."

"What?"

"From checkpoint one. Probably off chasing some bloody girls." Wilkes stroked his chin as he paused for thought. "Perhaps. Sir if I may, given the circumstances, I'd like to organise a couple of extra patrols."

"Of course, if you feel the need."

Wilkes nodded, turned and headed back to the mobile police

unit. Opening the door, he stepped inside and walked up to where the Chief Inspector was in the process of concluding a team briefing. As the officers stood to leave, McLeish cleared his throat and stood up. "Well Mr Wilkes, did you tell him?"

"I did ..."

"And what was his reaction?" Wilkes rolled his eyes and gave a sigh, "He said that he would inform his men. But to be honest, I think it'll be up to us."

"I see. Well, as soon as Harding returns, we'll have a chat, okay?"

Wilkes nodded and turned to leave. As he reached the doorway, he abruptly turned towards McLeish, "Sir, just one other point"

"Of course, what is it?"

"Well, it's probably nothing, but the military are reporting that two men are missing from their post at the Stirling Street checkpoint."

"Missing really?"

"It's probably nothing. I'm sure they'll turn up. But in the meantime I'd like to organise a couple of extra security sweeps, just in case we encounter any ... unwanted guests."

McLeish nodded and walked over to the desk where a young officer had just finished a phone call. As she placed the handset down, McLeish tapped the constable on the shoulder. "Jenna, do me a favour and send a couple of units out to do a sweep of the village. Also arrange for a car to take a drive by the Duncan's place."

Looking back at Wilkes he shrugged, "It wouldn't do any harm."

McLeish then turned back to the constable. "Ask them to report anything out of the ordinary will you, anything at all?"

"Yes sir."

"Oh and one other thing Jenna call, headquarters and ask them to pull the CCTV tapes for Stirling street. The past 12 hours should do it. It may reveal something."

"Aye sir."

Nodding, she shuffled back in her chair to get comfortable, picked up the phone and began to dial.

As Dougie descended into the light, the intensity and brightness were momentarily overpowering. Echoing voices emanating from above fused with the disorientating radiance. As his feet touched solid ground everything changed. Reverberating caverns gave way to an unnervingly silent abyss. Standing still, Dougie opened his eyes.

Where he now expected blinding light, he gasped in surprise as he found himself consumed in utter blackness. Then, a single beam of light appeared from above shining down on him. As his eyes focused, he found himself standing before three hooded figures seated around a large, marblesque table.

Their pale faces were hollow and gaunt with eyes that glistened like sun-tinged watery pools. For a moment Dougie simply stood frozen in terror. "What the bloody hell is this? What do ye want with me?"

The unnerving silence continued as the group merely stared at him as a child observes an insect on the ground.

"I said what the bloody hell do ye want with me?"

Despite his pleas, the three continued to stare, seemingly unaware or uncaring that he was even there. With a combination of fear and frustration Dougie felt as if he had endured enough and said, "Tae hell with this, I demand you …"

Without warning the big man flung himself at one of the hooded figures. To his surprise, the impact was not as he expected. It felt more like reaching into a pool of water but with no wetness. Reeling backwards, Dougie shuddered as if his body had just received an electric shock. Before him the scene rippled, as if a great stone had been thrown into a still pond. As he stood puzzled, the ripple effect subsided and once again, became still.

"Dougie."

Dougie felt a hand touch his shoulder, "Huh?"

As he spun around in surprise, he lashed out. Then, to his horror, he felt someone grab hold of his arm. Looking upwards, the beam of shimmering light began to pulsate. Slowly at first, then faster and faster, eventually the scene exploded and the blackness was once again replaced by brilliant white light. Shielding his eyes he yelled in surprise and crumpled on to the ground.

"Dougie its Tom. You're alright?"

"Huh, Tom?"

As his initial shock eased and his eyes re-focused, Dougie found himself on the ground looking upwards into the concerned faces of Tom and one of the young soldiers.

"What happened?" he asked.

Tom released Dougie's arm and knelt to assist his friend. "You were being lowered down and you blacked out for a moment. Here let us help you up."

Tom stood and both men reached out and helped Dougie to his feet.

"Are you okay? Do you need a Doctor?"

Dougie shook his head, "What do ye mean blacked out? I never blacked out. Didn't ye see them?"

Tom turned, to the soldier who simply shrugged and then back to Dougie shaking his head. "Them?"

"Och laddie, ye must have seen them, they were right here."

"Who?"

"The aliens, or whatever ye want tae call them. They were sittin' right there watchin' me."

As Dougie spoke the rest of the group had completed their descent and were in the process of assembling just behind Tom.

"What was that?"

Stepping forward, Moore raised her hand. Dougie glanced at Tom, as a moment of doubt flashed through his mind. But no, he was absolutely sure. They had been there.

Raising his hand he pointed to a spot approximately ten meters away. "Aye, there were three of them right there."

Looking at Tom for support, Dougie's head dropped in disappointment as he realised from the expression on Tom's face that neither he nor the soldier had seen anything.

"But ye didn't, did ye?"

Tom shook his head, "No, I'm sorry."

"Maybe I'm going mad; I was sure that …"

As Dougie spoke, Dr Quest stepped forward and cut him off in mid-sentence. "For God sake, look at where we are. Why are we even debating this? It's quite possible that because of what he's been through he can perhaps perceive or see things that we can't."

The Major stepped forward and asked, "So Doctor, are you actually suggesting that they could be watching us right now?"

Quest swallowed and nodded, "Yes major I am."

The group began to shuffle nervously, glancing around in all directions. Turning to Dougie, Professor Moore cleared her throat and said, "Dougie, perhaps you could tell us what these individuals looked like? What did you see?"

Glancing at Tom and Kate, Dougie nodded. "Well, they all look the same. Tall with dark hair, white gaunt faces and have the most intense blue eyes."

"In your report to the police, you mentioned a man, an Alexander McArthur?"

"That's right."

"Did he look the same as …?"

Dougie nodded as he answered her unfinished question. "Aye, he did." Pausing for a moment, she sighed and turned to the Major and nodded. "Major, I recommend caution."

The Major laughed sarcastically, "You think so? Okay … Corporal, setup the beacon and let's move out."

As instructed, Jarvis took off his rucksack, pulled out a small metallic box and placed it on the ground just below where the group had descended from the cavern. Sliding the box open, he pushed a small black button, which began to flash intermittently. As he closed the box, Jarvis stood and raised his arm in order to gain the group's attention. "Alright everyone, this is a radio beacon that will allow us to find our way back here. If you become separated, use channel 101 on your radio handsets. We will use channel 18 for comms. Does everyone understand?"

The group murmured a simultaneous acknowledgment and Jarvis turned to his two soldiers, "Alright lads, you take point and keep those eyes peeled."

"Sir"

As the soldiers moved out, the others stepped forward into the brilliance. Striding forward to join his friend, Tom tapped Dougie on the shoulder and lowered his voice. "Dougie."

"Aye lad, what is it?"

"I'm confused."

"Oh, what about?"

"Mary."

Dougie turned to Tom with a look of confusion. "What about her?"

"Well, you never mentioned her. You didn't even mention your encounter in the cemetery." Dougie shrugged, "Look lad, I want tae get my facts straight before I go off spreading wild stories about the end of the world."

Tom gave a sceptical look, "But you have to tell them. You can't keep this to yourself. People have a right to know."

Dougie looked at Tom, opened his mouth to speak but then paused as if he had a change of heart.

"Alright lad, but nae here, nae now. When we get it I'll explain it to the doctor, he seems like a reasonable man."

Tom nodded in agreement, "Aye, he does."

The group carried on walking, generally in silence, for around forty minutes. For Dougie, it was as he remembered, sheer brilliance with no rocks or walls, in fact no discernable landmarks whatsoever.

"Sir, sir, up ahead, look."

Around thirty metres ahead, one of the soldiers was pointing to something as yet unseen. Then, rising up like a great bird, the black pyramid emerged from the brilliance. For Tom and Kate the sight was simply breathtaking.

For the first time since meeting their time-travelling friend, any doubts about his legitimacy were completely eroded. Gasps of shock and awe resonated throughout the group as military personnel and civilians alike simply stood with open mouths. Doctor Quest stepped forward and whispered to the Major, "My God Major, this is going to change everything."

Ahead the young soldiers, just like the others, had stopped and simply stood staring in silence at the thirty plus meter high structure.

As the group began to circle the pyramid, it was Professor Moore who broke the silence. "Wait do you feel that?"

For a moment, nobody said a word. Then, the deep rhythmic vibration could be felt resonating through them like an electric current. Grabbing Dougie's arm in fright Kate yelled, "What is it?"

"It's coming from the pyramid," Quest shouted.

The major stepped forward, "Maybe it's a weapon, a bomb. Corporal."

"No, wait. I don't think so. To me it's like some kind of generator room."

The Major raised his hand for the Corporal to stand down. Who looked as if he was about to leap forward, with all guns blazing. "I'm forced to agree with Richard."

Placing her hand onto the surface of the pyramid, Professor Moore jumped back excitedly. "It's cold! My God, feel it. The power that's going through here must be incredible."

As she spoke the Major, Corporal Jarvis, Tom and Kate stepped forward and in turn, placed their palms onto the cold black surface. As the minutes passed and the group investigated the pyramid, Dougie's mind was churning. Somehow this discovery had to mean something. Was the pyramid a tool that could be used for man's destruction, as foretold by his encounter in the graveyard, or was it in fact, as the good Professor suggested, some kind of powerful generator? And if it was, then to what end.

As he walked around the structure, he stared at his almost perfect reflection in its black marble surface. For him this is where his adventure began. Why had McArthur attacked him and why had he been thrown forward in time? So many questions! Mary had warned him of man's failings and how they now faced imminent destruction within a matter of days. Why tell him? What could he possibly do that could save humanity?

"Go to the light and find the key to join the world. Only then can I guide you home."

"What key, I don't understand?"

Looking at his reflection, he closed his eyes for a moment in an attempt to silence his thoughts. As he took a breath Dougie raised his hand, exhaled and placed it onto the cold surface of the pyramid.

Suddenly, the sense of disorientation was overwhelming. Instead of touching a cold solid surface, his hand appeared to dissolve into a translucent state as if it had been plunged it into iced water. The sense of power and energy was incredible. All around his hand, the surface of the pyramid became translucent and as suddenly as it had begun, it was over.

Dougie wrenched his hand away as if he had snatched it back from the very jaws of death itself. As he did so, the jet-black surface rippled and became solid once more. Breathless and sweating, he looked at his closed fist as it once more became solid.

Then in a moment of utter shock he opened it, only to discover that it was no longer empty! For there lying in his palm was a small, but perfect, miniature representation of the black marble pyramid.

"My God, the key. It's got tae be. I've found the key!"

Stepping back, he glanced around and gazed back upon the object in his hand.

"Mr Allan, is everything okay?"

Dougie reeled with surprise, "Huh …"

To his right, Corporal Jarvis stood looking concerned. Quickly closing his fist around the object, he nodded, "Aye, I'm braw thank ye."

"You would be better off sticking with the group. We don't want to lose you …"

Dougie gave a nervous smile, "Of course lad, I'm sorry."

As the Corporal turned away, Dougie quickly placed the small object in a fold of tartan and followed the officer to the other side of the pyramid where the Major was addressing the group.

"Alright Ladies and Gentlemen, I think we've seen enough for the time being. It's time for us to head back to the surface. There will be plenty of further opportunities to see more however, for the moment, Moore and Quest will return for a more thorough investigation. That is after we've made a full report to the powers that be. Corporal, let's go."

Jarvis nodded and cleared his throat, "Aye sir. Alright folks, let's get back to normality."

TWENTY SIX

MONDAY: 3.55PM ALVA, SCOTLAND

BY LATE AFTERNOON, the drizzle and dark cloud, which had smothered the Ochil's for most of the day, had lifted and the village was once again enjoying the warm August sun. Sitting on a traditional, oak garden bench in her back garden, Jane Duncan was struggling to brush Wallace, their overzealous Golden Retriever, who seemed determined to make a game of the whole affair.

"Wallace, for goodness sake, stay still boy."

Inside, Amy sat on a large mat on the living room floor, surrounded by an array of colourful crayons and a seemingly endless supply of drawing paper. As she finished one drawing she paused and looked up for a moment. Surprise turned to shock, as there at the window staring in at her was the sneering, cat-like smile of a stranger. Without hesitation she screamed "Mummy" and sprang for the door.

Jane pushed the dog aside, dropped the brush and bolted for the back door. Once inside, she was met by her visibly shaken six-year-old.

"What is it darling, what's the matter?"

"There's a man, at the window."

Standing up she gestured Amy to remain still and slowly edged ahead of her into the living room, glancing first to the back window and then to the front. There was nothing, other than the outline of the Ochil's. Stepping back into the hallway she made her way to the front door. Unlocking it, she swung the door open to reveal, no face, no man, nothing.

Closing it again, she moved back to where Amy was sitting, alongside a tail wagging Wallace. "There's no one there baby, are you sure?"

"Yes Mummy, I told you he was there. I'm not telling lies honestly."

Jane sighed and gave a comforting smile, "I believe you baby. I tell you what, come and see there's no one there."

Scooping up her daughter, Jane went into the living room and pointed to the window, "Look sweetie, nobody there. Okay?"

Next she moved to the front door, unclipped the latch and swung open the door.

"Jesus!!"

Standing on the doorstep, looking utterly surprised, were two young police officers. "Mrs Duncan, are you alright?"

"Yes, yes thank you, you just startled us, that's all."

The two officers glimpsed at each other and continued, "Sorry, but we wanted to check that everything's alright."

Jane put Amy down. "Aye, we are fine. Actually while you're here I wondered if you've any news about my husband and the others."

The younger constable shook her head, "No, I'm sorry. But I'm sure it won't be long now." Jane nodded and gave a smile. "Thank you."

The officers smiled and walked away and closing the door Jane picked Amy up again and headed towards the back garden.

"There you see darling, the nice police officers were just checking to see if we were alright. Now, I could really use your help with Wallace. What do you say?"

Amy smiled, nodded and ran towards the back door. "Okay Mummy."

As the police 4x4 pulled away, a tall sinister figure emerged from behind the Duncan's double garage. Taking a moment to ensure he couldn't be seen, he sneered to himself as a plan to return later began to formulate in his mind. Making one final check of the area, he stepped forward and slipped quietly away.

As the group emerged from the mine, it was smiles all around, apart from Dougie and Doctor Quest, who both emerged somewhat agitated. Arriving at the mobile police unit, the group slipped off their khaki coveralls and returned them to a waiting officer. The hut door opened and Colonel McNeil, Chief Inspector McLeish and Robert Wilkes stepped out to greet the group.

"Major, what's the news?"

Clearing his throat the Major approached his senior officer. "Sir, it was as Mr Allan described. A labyrinth that must go on for miles, sir."

"And the pyramid?"

"It's, just incredible Colonel."

McNeil gave a nod and then turned to Moore and Quest. "Professor, Doctor, the equipment you requested has arrived. What do you want done with it?"

Stepping forward Quest cleared his throat, "Thank you Colonel, we would like to perform an additional assessment of the pyramid as soon as possible. If you could kindly have your men set up the X-ray and the drilling equipment, it would be much appreciated. We need to determine the composition and purpose of the structure as soon as possible."

Stepping forward, Corporal Jarvis gave a brief salute, "Sir, I can arrange that for you. Just give me six good lads and we'll get it done."

"Excellent Corporal, take whoever you need."

"Sir." Jarvis gave a final salute, turned heel and strode away towards a group of soldiers mustering near the mine entrance.

As Jarvis departed, the Doctor again cleared his throat, "Mr Wilkes, if you have a few moments I would like a quick chat with you and Dougie."

Turning to Kate, the young MI5 officer nodded, "That suits me Doctor. Besides, I believe the Chief Inspector wanted a quick chat with Miss Harding."

"Me?" Kate gave a baffled look, "What have I done now?"

McLeish stepped forward, signalling for Kate to follow him, "Relax Miss Harding … this time we're trying to help you solve a puzzle."

Glancing at Tom and Dougie her eyes rolled. "Very well, but if I'm not back in twenty minutes, send out a search party."

Kate picked up her bag and followed the Chief Inspector inside the police unit.

As Kate disappeared, the Colonel said, "Well Mr Allan, if you will excuse me I must report in. For the moment I'll leave you in the capable hands of Mr Wilkes and the good Doctor here. I'm sure they can provide everything you may need."

Shaking the officer's hand, Dougie smiled, "Aye, thank ye colonel."

Wilkes motioned the Doctor and Dougie to follow him towards a parked Range Rover nearby and said, "I thought this would be a little more private."

As the three men climbed inside and slammed the doors, the Doctor spoke first, "Okay Dougie, tell him what you told me."

Dougie's head dropped, "There's nae easy way tae say this and you'll probably think I've lost my mind. I don't ken how or why but I've been told that within five days, all of this … everything ye ken will be gone. I also believe that somehow, someway, I've been sent tae stop it."

Wilkes sniggered and rolled his eyes, "That's ridiculous."

Before he could continue, Quest broke in, "For God's sake listen to him, he's serious! Think about what's happening to the world, disaster after disaster …"

"Coincidence Doctor, that's just coincidence. You have no proof."

Dougie interrupted, "But I do. Since my arrival, I thought I've been goin crazy with visions, dreams, call them what ye will, but I'm now convinced that there is a greater power at work. I believe these beings may have been here for millions of years and they somehow blame humanity for damaging the planet."

"Listen to what you are saying? That's preposterous."

"Is it? She came tae me and told me that within days all of this, everything will be gone. She also told me that what's happening should have happened over centuries, but one of their kind has gone ... rogue and has caused the whole process tae be somehow accelerated."

Wilkes shook his head, "An interesting fairy tale, but you still haven't provided any proof."

Dougie nodded and reached inside a fold of tartan from around his waist and pulled out the small piece of parchment given to him by Mary and handed it across to Wilkes.

"Well, what about this?"

Taking the material from Dougie, Wilkes examined it for a moment, shrugged and passed it to the Doctor.

"What do you make of it Doctor?"

Staring at the symbols, the scientist's jaw dropped, "This is incredible. I've never seen anything like this. It's very old, I'll tell you that."

Dougie glanced at Wilkes and rolled his eyes, "Aye laddie, it is that. But I need tae ken what it says. Can ye translate it?"

Quest shrugged, "I ... I don't know. Perhaps if I had time."

Dougie shook his head, "Time, unfortunately, is something we don't have."

Wilkes nodded, "Alright Dougie let's say that this is all true. What can we do? Is there perhaps a way to reason with these beings?"

Dougie thought for a moment and shook his head, "How do you reason with a God Mr Wilkes?"

"In this case, we have to."

"Gentlemen, I've lost everything, including my wife. I can't and won't believe it's all been for nothing. I'm an ordinary man, nae different from ye and the doctor here, so why send me 300 years into the future? Ye have technology here that I could never understand. If anyone's in a position tae make a difference then surely it's ye?"

Suddenly the door of the police unit re-opened and the Chief Inspector, Tom and Kate stepped out into the afternoon sunlight. Walking towards the Range Rover, Wilkes rolled down his window and McLeish leaned in.

"Gentlemen, I've arranged for Miss Harding and Mr Duncan to be taken home for the evening. Would Mr Allan like to join them?"

Glancing first at Dougie and then at the Doctor, Wilkes shook his head, "Actually Andrew, we'd like to keep Mr Allan here a little while longer. I can drop him off when we're finished, assuming of course that's okay with Mr Allan?"

Dougie shrugged his shoulders and gave a nod, "Aye lad, that's braw by me."

"Perfect, thank you gentlemen."

Giving a smile, McLeish turned towards Tom and Kate and motioned them towards an awaiting police vehicle. As they climbed inside, Dougie caught a brief glimpse of Kate through his side window. Her expression was one of anxiety. Suspecting that something was amiss, he leaned forward and cleared his throat. "What's wrong with the lassie Mr Wilkes, she seems a wee bit upset?"

Wilkes shuffled uncomfortably and turned to Dougie. "Well, we received some intelligence regarding a possible threat to her."

"You're talking about the man in Germany?"

A surprised Wilkes interrupted, "Just how do you know about that?"

"She told us, just this morning actually. Is that why she's here? Are ye worried about her?"

As the police car departed, Wilkes paused and gave a nod, "Yes, I must confess to being a little concerned."

Sitting forward, looking anxious, Dougie cleared his throat, "Now laddie, if you're telling me that she's in some kind of danger, then what about Tom and his family? Surely ye should."

"Whoa, hold on Dougie, let's not panic. It won't help anyone. Remember the village is locked down and we have around 210 personnel on-site. I can assure you, they'll be perfectly safe."

As the car fell silent, Quest turned to Dougie, "I'll do a little investigating regarding the symbols and I'll come back to you. Also, if you are in agreement, we should have you meet with a police artist. It would be useful for us to have an idea of what these beings look like."

Dougie nodded, "Aye that seems reasonable."

Quest turned to face the young MI5 officer, "Perhaps, you could make the necessary arrangements Mr Wilkes?"

Wilkes nodded, opened the car door and climbed out.

"That's a good idea Doctor. Let me check inside, I'll be back in a moment."

Closing the door, Wilkes walked up to the mobile unit, opened the door and disappeared inside. In the car the two men sat in silence for about five minutes. Then from behind, the police car that had taken Kate and Tom home returned and parked a few meters away.

As Dougie watched with interest, Chief Inspector McLeish emerged with a younger officer and walked briskly towards the police unit. As they arrived, the door swung open and the two officers were met by Wilkes and for a few moments the men talked. Once finished Wilkes returned to the Range Rover, opened the door and leaned in. "Gentlemen, unfortunately we have no official police artist on-site. We do, however, have a talented constable who's a bit of an art enthusiast. She's willing to have a go … If that's alright with Dougie?"

Dougie nodded enthusiastically, "Aye lad, of course."

As he climbed out of the car, Doctor Quest joined him.

"Well gentlemen if it's alright I'd like to re-join the professor, I'm sure she'll be waiting for me."

.As the Doctor left, Wilkes beckoned Dougie towards the police unit. "Right Dougie, if you'll follow me, I'll introduce you to our budding artist."

Brooks crouched silently behind a neighbour's stonewall and coolly contemplated his move. To him this was not personal, but merely a job, a means to an end. With his target identified, he could make his move. He would have preferred not to have involved the family, but in this case he couldn't take the chance of them talking, there was too much at stake. Orders were orders and he always followed them, no questions asked. "What of the child though? Should he let her go?"

He recalled a job in Mexico two years earlier, where he faced a similar dilemma. In that case it was a boy of 7. Having initially let the boy go he had to return a month later to clean up. Apparently the child gave the authorities an almost perfect description, which resulted in him almost being captured. As his mind cleared, his expression changed to one of pure indifference.

Recalling the phone call, the instructions that were given were clear, "I want it clean."

He knew what he had to do. Opening his jacket, he un-holstered his Colt Double Eagle pistol and attached its silencer and prepared to make his move.

TWENTY SEVEN

DOUGIE ALLAN SAT patiently on a slightly worn, but reasonably comfortable swivel chair inside the police unit. He was waiting for Wilkes to finish a seemingly endless conversation with the Chief Inspector and two of his aides. Just when he had almost lost all hope, the conversation was over and Wilkes strode across to where he was sitting.

"I'm sorry to have kept you waiting. If you'll follow me I'll introduce you to our budding artist."

Dougie followed the officer over to where a young police constable sat armed with an assortment of pencils, crayons and a large sketchpad.

"Jenna. I'd like to introduce Dougie Allan."

"Dougie, delighted to meet you."

Dougie nodded, "Aye lass, a pleasure."

"Well, if you take a seat we can get started."

"Alright, what do ye need tae ken?"

"Just describe what they look like and I'll do my best."

For the next ten minutes, Dougie methodically described the cloaked figures in detail. Their pale gaunt faces, sunken expressions and bright blue eyes. While he talked, the constable listened intently and attempted to interpret Dougie's description into a coherent and meaningful image. When finished the constable turned the pad around to show the result. On seeing the drawing he gasped in surprise. The likeness was chilling. The figure was almost exactly as he had seen.

"Och lassie, that's perfect. You've got it just right."

Nodding, the constable passed her sketch to Wilkes who looked at the image and smiled. "That's really excellent work Jenna. Let's get this scanned and placed into the file. I want London to have a copy of this as soon as possible."

"Thank you sir, I'll get this circulated right away."

Wilkes motioned Dougie towards the exit. "Right Dougie, let's get you back."

Before he finished the sentence, a worried Chief Inspector appeared. "I'm sorry to disturb you Robert, but I need a moment. There's something you need to see."

Turning back to Dougie, Wilkes shook his head, "I'm sorry Dougie, I'll be back in a minute."

He turned away and followed the Chief Inspector over to a monitoring station manned by two constables. The desk contained an array of monitors and communications equipment. Standing behind one of the officers, McLeish cleared his throat.

"Okay Charlie, show him."

"Sir, we just received this recording from headquarters," the older constable said as he pulled up on screen a rather grainy black and white image from what appeared to be a traffic camera. "What are we looking at constable?"

"It's the A91 sir. It's from the Stirling Street number one camera, taken at about 11.45 am. The check point."

"It's a very bad picture. I can't see a bloody thing."

"Just a moment sir. Keep your eye on this area here."

As he spoke, the constable placed his forefinger onto the screen. Wilkes now established that he was looking at two Army Land Rovers and, yes, there were two men – presumably the aforementioned missing soldiers. As he watched the recording, a vehicle approached the checkpoint and stopped in front of one of the Land Rovers. It appeared to be a light coloured car – a

Mercedes perhaps. Then a third figure appeared from the vehicle. As he watched, Wilkes began to sway on his feet, sensing that something awful was about to happen.

In the pit of his stomach, the awful sensation of nausea began to grow.

As he watched, the two, stick-like figures seemed to bolt towards the car. His face then turned to horror as the scene exploded into a flurry of violence. The intruder raised his arm and appeared to fire a weapon at one of the soldiers. As the figure slumped forward, the stranger then fired at the second soldier. As the grotesque scene unravelled, the screen finally flickered into darkness as the recording ended.

For a moment neither man spoke, then the Chief Inspector whispered, "Oh my God, he's here."

Coolly, Wilkes turned to the Chief Inspector and whispered, "Sir, you'd better issue me with a weapon."

For a moment McLeish seemed visibly unable to respond. Sensing that time was slipping away, sheer frustration gave way to courtesy as Wilkes shouted, "Sir, issue me with a weapon … NOW!"

"Er … yes of course. Constable, issue this man with a firearm right away."

As ordered, the taller of the two constables stood, and moved across the room to where a large black metal box lay on the floor. Once opened, he picked out a Smith & Wesson M&P Compact, along with a box of 9mm shells and handed them to the MI5 officer.

"Sir, will this do?"

Nodding with gratitude, Wilkes opened the box, took out a handful of shells and stuffed them into his jacket pocket. Pulling out the gun clip, he then loaded thirteen shells, twelve for the clip and one for the chamber.

Once complete he pushed the clip back into the gun firmly

and stuffed it under his belt. On hearing the uproar, Dougie strode across to where Wilkes and the Chief Inspector were standing.

"What the bloody hell's going on?"

Wilkes shook his head and motioned for Dougie to stay put.

"We have an incident. I must ask that you stay here for your own safety."

"Incident my arse, it's him isn't it? He's coming for her."

Wilkes shook his head, "Dougie, this is police business, please stay here."

Ignoring politeness, Dougie stepped in front of the officer and raised his voice, "Don't give me that laddie, these are my friends, I'm nae to going simply sit back while you."

Wilkes briskly shook his head and barked, "Alright, if you must. But for your own sake, stay in the bloody car. Do you understand?"

"Aye, alright."

Moving quickly towards the door, Wilkes turned and faced McLeish, "Andrew, can you spare a couple of lads for back up?"

McLeish nodded, "Of course."

"Good. Ensure they are armed. Have them meet us at the Duncan's."

Flinging the door open, Wilkes and Dougie ran towards a police Range Rover. "Get in. Remember what I said."

Slamming the car door shut, Wilkes started the engine and pressed his foot on the accelerator. Then, like some ancient beast the car roared into life and sped away.

In the Duncan's dining room, Kate Harding sat opposite Tom in silence. The only audible sounds were those of a ticking baby grandfather clock, given to Jane as a wedding present by her grandparents, and the clink of cups from the kitchen.

As she swallowed a mouthful of hot tea, her mind whirled with the events of the day. Gazing at Tom she sighed, "So what do you think?"

Tom rubbed his head. "Too be honest, it's a lot to take in."

As he finished talking there was a knock at the front door. Standing up, he smiled and threw his hands up into the air, "At last, he's back."

Tom dashed down the hallway and as he unlocked the door he shook his head, "Dougie, I thought you would never …"

The figure standing on the doorstep was not Dougie, but a tall, muscular stranger dressed in black jeans and a black, leather jacket.

"Good afternoon, I'd like to speak with Kate."

Tom's expression turned to one of puzzlement as he attempted to fathom how on earth anyone local would even know who Kate was, let alone come knocking at his door for her. "I'm sorry, but who are you?"

The question was met with a cold silence and a cruel sneer that made Tom feel very uncomfortable. Something was wrong here and Tom felt that he had to act. Quickly and simultaneously he attempted to shut the door while screaming out, "Kate!"

Moving like a crazed animal, Brooks threw himself against the door with incredible force. The impact threw Tom backwards and after hitting a wall he crumpled to the floor in pain, looking up, Brooks stood above him snarling, and said, "Fool, this could have all ended so quietly."

Suddenly, the kitchen door opened and Jane appeared, screaming, "Tom, Oh my God!"

As instinct kicked in, she rushed to defend her husband, but as she moved, Brooks' response was brutal and unforgiving. Like a snake he lashed out at her, his fist smashed into her cheek: the impact was devastating, her nose and cheekbone exploded in a shower of blood and as she stumbled backwards, crashing through a plate glass door.

With tears streaming down his face, Tom screamed for his wife, but as all he could see was her blood-stained body slumped on the kitchen floor covered in glass. Then, Tom's face turned to horror as Brooks suddenly aimed a gun at his wife's body.

"No, you bastard."

With all of his strength, Tom pulled himself up and lunged at the intruder.

As the Range Rover thundered along Back Road, Dougie's face was white with concern for his new friends.

"Come 'on lad ... can't this thing go any faster."

Wilkes didn't answer, he simply pushed his foot down on the accelerator even harder, forcing the vehicle to leap forward.

As Wilkes swerved to avoid a pothole, the Duncan's house came into view. With the front door seemingly ripped off its hinges, Wilkes whispered, "Damn he's here."

As the car drew up in front of the house, he pushed his foot down on the brake and the car screeched to a halt. Flinging the door open, he reached for his gun and leapt out.

"Stay here."

With his adrenaline spiking, Wilkes sprinted from the car and jumped over Tom's gate and raced towards the house. From the door, he could hear the sickeningly familiar sounds of violence. Sounds that, over the years, he grew to hate and would do anything to forget. In his early military career, violence and killing were an expected part of everyday life. But working as an agent for the security services, those days were now fortunately gone. His current post was, for the most part, desk based. The need to be issued a weapon, let alone actually use one, was almost unheard of. However, there's a saying "A soldier never forgets". Taking a deep breath, he raised his weapon and slowly edged forward, carefully positioning himself so he could see within the Duncan's hallway. Inside, the cowering figure of Tom lay crumpled on the floor, bleeding and bruised.

Standing over him like a conquering gladiator, was a powerful and cruel looking figure. As Wilkes looked on in horror, the intruder suddenly wielded a weapon and was in the process of pointing it directly at Tom's head.

"Don't move. Armed police."

As Wilkes voice bellowed out, the intruder spun around in surprise and fired two shots directly at him. Wilkes darted out of the way just in time to see the bullets harmlessly ricochet off a garden wall. Then, wasting no time, he sprang around, raised his own weapon and returned fire.

The Smith and Wesson sounded like firecracker as the bullets left the chamber, but, to Wilkes's frustration, the target was already gone and the bullets had simply embedded themselves in a cavity wall. "Damn!" he muttered to himself as he slowly edged down the hallway towards the dining room.

As he approached Tom's body, he knelt down and carefully placed two fingers on his neck to check his pulse. He was alive, thankfully. Then as he stood his mouth fell open as he caught sight of Jane's seemingly lifeless body in the kitchen. Although blood spattered and covered in broken glass, he couldn't get to her. He just prayed that she would be okay. Then summoning all of his courage he raised his weapon and kicked-open the dining room door. However, to his disappointment, any hopes of an easy resolution faded as there, standing in front of him was the intruder smiling chillingly, holding a distraught Kate by her hair, his gun held to her head.

"Put the gun down, or she's dead …"

Wilkes didn't move. He'd seen this type before and, in his experience, if he lowered his weapon the intruder would not only kill the woman but probably him as well. No, he had to buy time. After all, back up was on its way.

"No, I don't think so."

"I tell you what," Brooks snarled, "it's this one I've come for. Let me have her and I'll leave the rest, including the child."

Disgusted by his sickening threat, Wilkes almost forgot himself and was about to pull the trigger, when he looked at Kate. Her expression was one of sheer terror, her eyes bloodshot and filled with tears.

Wilkes sighed, "You know I can't do that. Besides haven't you killed enough? The pair in Germany, the girl in London. How many more have to die?"

Brooks' sneer fell away and his expression turned serious, "I'm a soldier, nothing more. Just following orders, like you eh?"

Wilkes shook his head, "No, I'm nothing like you. You enjoy it too much."

"This is all very touching, but I've a schedule to keep, I'll say this one last time, back up."

Biting his lip in frustration, Wilkes knew he was beaten. He couldn't risk a shot hitting the woman so, as instructed, he backed slowly out of the dining room, into the hallway, stepping carefully aside to avoid Tom. As Wilkes moved back, Brooks held on to Kate's hair with a vice-like grip and dragged her outwards, towards the front door.

Sobbing uncontrollably, she gazed at Wilkes, "Oh Jesus. Please don't let him kill me."

As he reached the step, Wilkes backed up and moved outside into the afternoon sunshine. "Now, drop the gun and back away."

Wilkes took a deep breath and lowered the weapon, hoping and praying that he was doing the right thing. Tossing it onto the ground, he stepped back. "Okay. Now let the woman go. Surely we can work somethi…?"

His hand moved like lightning. Before Wilkes could complete his sentence, the bullet had already left the chamber and had slammed clean through his shoulder. The force of the impact took his breath away and threw him backwards.

As he hit the ground, Brooks pulled Kate forward and viciously threw her to the ground next to Wilkes.

Sobbing and pleading, Kate screamed, "No, Please don't."

As he stepped out into the sunshine, he aimed the gun and with a cruel sneer hissed, "Goodbye Miss Harding."

The blow to the head appeared to come from nowhere. Dropping his gun, Brooks reeled backwards and collapsed to the ground in agony.

"I don't think so laddie; enough is enough."

Standing above Brooks, was the unmistakable tartan-clad shape of Dougie Allan.

Snorting like an enraged bull Brooks rolled quickly away and lunged towards his gun. Dougie, however, was one step ahead and instinctively threw himself into his path. As Dougie landed, he lashed out with his fist, catching Brooks on his cheek, while simultaneously managing to kick the weapon away. In retaliation, Brooks howled in fury and sprang at Dougie like a bear, kicking and punching him in the groin.

As Dougie struggled, Brooks grabbed his throat and attempted to choke him. However the sound of approaching vehicles forced him to end his attack and flee. He released Dougie just as a police Range Rover came screeching to a halt outside Tom's house.

In one final act of defiance, he punched Dougie on the cheek and grabbed his hair, hissing, "This isn't over. I'll see you again. Soon!"

Turning, he sprang over a wall and bolted across a field towards a clump of trees, finally vanishing out of sight.

Moments later three police officers tore into the driveway, weapons drawn screaming, "Armed Police, nobody move."

Breathing heavily, Dougie sat up, pointing towards the trees, "That way, he went that way …"

Nodding the young officer stood and gave a hand signal towards his companions, "You two, over there. Get after him."

Finally finding his breath, Dougie scrambled to his feet and moved towards Wilkes.

"Are ye okay lad?"

Visibly shaken but sitting up, Wilkes nodded, "You saved my life."

"Nae lad, I think we were just lucky today that's all."

"Thank you anyway."

"For what?"

"For not staying in the car."

Dougie's smile turned to horror as he realised no one had checked on the family.

"Tom! What about Tom and his family?"

Wilkes spluttered and sat up breathing heavily, "Constable, get the medics, the family inside, hurry."

The officer motioned to a colleague and they both ran inside the house. Dougie then moved across to where Kate was recovering. Although not badly bruised, she was visibly shaken. As Dougie knelt down, she leaped forward hugging him warmly.

"Thank you. Oh God, thank you Dougie. I thought I was going to die."

Placing his arms around her, he stroked her hair and whispered, "Hey, it's okay. You're safe now."

As the constable emerged from the house, Dougie let go of Kate, stood up and rushed forward. "How are they?"

"They're all okay. Mr Wilkes here was very lucky. It appears the bullet went straight through his shoulder – it should heal nicely. Mr Duncan is badly bruised that's all. But, Mrs Duncan's in bad shape, she'll need a doctor."

"What of the bairn?"

The officer smiled and gave a nod, "She's fine, fortunately she was upstairs the whole time with the dog and had the sense to hide. Now, if you'll excuse me, I must go and organise an ambulance."

TWENTY EIGHT

MONDAY: 4.40PM 10 DOWNING STREET, LONDON

STANDING BY THE window, James Walton gazed out at the large oak trees and ornate garden shrubs of the number 10 garden. At this time in the afternoon he would normally have taken a pre-dinner drink on the terrace, however, due to a recent downpour, he had been forced to remain indoors. Returning to his seat he picked up a cup of hot tea, took a sip and placed the cup down. Leaning across, he opened a folder marked "Classified" and took out a sketch, portraying a cloaked, rather frightening looking gaunt figure. Although only a drawing, it unnerved him. As he pondered over the picture, the phone on his desk began to ring. Leaning across he picked up the receiver, "Yes?"

"Excuse me Prime Minister, but it's a Doctor Richard Quest for you."

Siting up with interest, he placed the sketch aside and cleared his throat and said, "Yes please Lisa, put him through"

After a short silence a man's voice came on to the line. "Hello."

"Yes, hello Doctor, what's the latest news?"

"Well, sir, we've completed out preliminary investigation and the device and the threat do appear to be, genuine."

Walton swallowed, "I see."

"Sir, due to the urgency of this situation, it would be perhaps prudent for both myself and Professor Moore to present our findings directly to COBRA."

Walton didn't like the sound of that. During his term as Prime Minister he had chaired many sessions of the British Government's emergency committee COBRA, but never in living memory had one been called at such short notice.

"You think it's that serious?"

"I do, sir."

Walton paused for a moment and gave a long sigh, "Very well, its 4.40 pm now, shall we convene here at 9.00 pm?"

"Yes Prime Minister, that sounds fine. If you'll excuse me I'll go and organise a flight. Good bye."

Before Walton could reply the line clicked and the call was over. Walton sat for a moment speechless, firstly, as premier, he was not used to having the phone put down on him and secondly Quest sounded worried, which in itself was unusual, as in all the years he had been advising the government Quest had been the cool one with all the answers.

Placing the drawing back in its folder Walton leaned back in his chair and was about to call on his assistant, but was interrupted as a large ornate chandelier hanging above his desk began to rattle. At first he thought was that it was nothing more than a passing vehicle, but as the shuddering increased and the chandelier began to shake he became more concerned.

On his desk his cup and saucer toppled on to the floor, smashing and spilling its contents onto an undoubtedly expensive Indian rug. Then, without warning, books and papers began spilling out of a tall oak bookcase onto the floor of his office.

As he stood to investigate, the door to his office burst open and two uniformed police officers rushed in. "Sir ... It's an earthquake. If you will follow us, we'll get you to safety."

"An earthquake?"

"Sir, this way please!"

Grabbing the cream folder, Walton hurriedly ran towards

the waiting officers. Without warning the shuddering suddenly increased. As he glanced back, he looked on in horror as cracks began to appear in the walls and the glass chandelier above his desk suddenly gave way, crashing onto the floor sending glass fragments flying across the room.

"Sir, please!"

The tone of the officer's request jolted Walton back to reality and the three of them bolted out of the office and ran along an upstairs corridor. At the Grand Staircase, Walton looked dismayed as huge cracks appeared along the usually pristine plasterwork. The yellow painted walls, normally occupied with treasured portraits of Prime Ministers past, were now eerily empty, as many of the framed pictures and paintings lay strewn below on the black and white tiled floor. Running ahead of the Prime Minister the two constables attempted to clear the way of any debris.

At the bottom of the staircase, the officers escorted the Prime Minister down into the safety of the basement. Once in the passageway, they walked along and eventually assembled with the rest of the personnel in the old fortified war room.

"Is everyone alright?"

One of the constables nodded and cleared his throat, "Sir, apart from the Deputy Prime Minister and a couple of kitchen staff, this is everyone."

Gazing on at the frightened faces of the assembled staff, Walton raised his hand.

"Can I have your attention? It appears that we've just experienced some kind of earthquake. We don't know the extent of the damage, so for now let's keep calm and not panic. Constable, you mentioned some missing personnel. Have you checked?"

The officer nodded, "Yes sir, The Deputy PM is in Westminster and the two missing kitchen staff are on sick leave."

"Okay, good. The shaking seems to have eased for now. Mr Jefferies will you kindly muster the house staff into the auxiliary dining room and get them organised with a cup of tea. I'm sure that it will help calm nerves. If I could have all members of the senior staff remain in here please."

Stepping forward as instructed, the smartly dressed, senior butler, Mark Jeffries, cleared his throat and says, "Okay ladies and gentlemen, can the house staff please follow me. This way please."

Within moments the house staff had left the room leaving the Prime Minister, members of the Cabinet, and a small team of aides. Turning to the Foreign Secretary, Roy Clark, Walton placed a hand on his shoulder, "Roy, see if you can find out what damage has been done?"

As Clark moved away, Walton opened his mouth to continue but was interrupted by Lisa Harkins, his assistant, who stepped forward, looking at her cell phone with a grim look on her face.

"Sir, I just received a text message from my sister. I think you had better switch on the television."

Walton nodded as the young aide stepped forward, picked up a remote control and switched on the television. As the picture flickered into life, a young BBC reporter shuffled in his seat as he began to speak.

"Reports are coming in of a massive earthquake which has hit at the centre of Paris. The quake's tremors were felt as far away as London and the south east coast of England. At the moment we have no news of casualty numbers, but speculation suggests that these could be very high.

"The French government has called for a country-wide state of emergency and a short time ago I spoke with our correspondent Marie Delaney, who described the centre of Paris as 'Hell on Earth'. Many of London's famous landmarks, including Trafalgar Square and Buckingham Palace, were damaged but, luckily, there are no reports of any fatalities. We will of course keep you up to date of any developments as they happen."

Walton raised his hand and Harkins switched off the television. As the screen blanked out, the group remained standing in silence, unsure of what to say, let alone what to do. The normally confident

Walton looked around the room, desperately grasping for answers. Glancing across at Clark, a man who Walton had known for many years, a man that could always be depended on for ideas, simply stood in stunned silence. Walton took a deep breath and slowly exhaled.

"Lisa, I'd like to convene an emergency COBRA meeting this evening at 9 pm. Can you please arrange a suitable room? I want everyone to attend, no excuses. Can you please also check on the state of the house?"

"Of course Prime Minister."

"Roy, contact the French and find out how we can help."

Nodding, the Minister took out his phone and began dialling.

"You're worried?", Anne Petrie asked, concerned all over her face.

Walton nodded and lowered his voice to a whisper, "Yes, I've never seen anything like this before. Indonesia, the US and now Europe, what the hell's going on?"

Petrie sighed, "I don't know."

"I spoke with Richard Quest a short while ago. He and Helen Moore seem very keen to speak to us."

"What about?"

Walton sighed and shook his head, "I don't know, although he sounded pretty rattled. The more time continues, the more I fear these events are related."

Petrie's eye's narrowed, "Prime Minister?"

"Well, increased disasters, evidence of possible alien life and to top it all an assassin. Come on Anne you have to admit it, there has to be a link."

Shaking her head, she sighed, "I don't know sir, but perhaps Quest and Moore can shed more light on the whole affair."

Walton nodded, "I hope so Anne. I hope so."

"Prime Minister!" The couple were interrupted by a grim-faced Clark, "Sorry to interrupt, but I've just spoken with Jacques Martin in Paris. Sir it's a bloody mess over there."

"What's happened?"

"Sir the earthquake. It appears to have taken out more than half of Paris."

Walton's mouth fell open, "What?"

"Apparently they are looking at a huge amount of damage and loss of life …"

"What of the government? What about President Broussard? Has he been contacted?"

"Sir …"

Clark's head dropped and he took a long sigh, "James he's dead, along with three of his ministers."

Walton face turned to shock, "Dead! How?"

"He was in a meeting at his residence when the earthquake struck. The roof collapsed. Apparently they were hit by falling masonry."

As he finished, the Prime Minister's assistant approached the group and cleared her throat. "I'm sorry to interrupt sir, but I have the police Commissioner on the telephone for the Prime Minister."

Walton nodded, excused himself and stepped across to a telephone. Picking up the handset, Walton cleared his throat, "Yes, Sir Michael."

"Prime Minister I'm afraid I've just received some disturbing news."

Walton rolled his eyes and sighed inwardly, unsure of how much more bad news he could actually take.

"What is it?"

The voice on the other end of the phone paused as if trying to sum up the courage to answer the question.

"Sir, I've just been told that due to earthquake damage, the Thames Barrier has been damaged and may not operate."

"Well that's alright I guess we just arrange for the contractor to go out and fix it."

"No sir, it's not quite that simple. If there are aftershocks, or indeed another quake, the barrier would not hold."

Walton looked up for a moment as if trying to comprehend the full meaning of the Commissioner's words.

"So what are you saying?"

"I'm saying that if another event occurs, London will be under water. In my opinion it's a disaster waiting to happen, with ramifications far worse than the floods of 53. Sir, we may need to consider evacuation as one possible option."

"Evacuate! Sir Michael you're talking about millions of people, do you realise what you're saying, what that means?"

The other end of the line remained silent for a moment as Walton dropped his head and sighed, inwardly already fully aware of what the Commissioner's response would be. "Yes sir, I'm afraid I do."

TWENTY NINE

MONDAY: 6.00PM FORTH VALLEY ROYAL HOSPITAL LARBERT

THE ATMOSPHERE IN the A&E waiting room was sombre and as depressive as the storm clouds gathering in the skies above the hospital. The £300 million facility not only boasted first class healthcare, but also a first in the use of robots for the more mundane tasks in the hospital.

Normally bustling with patients, staff and visitors, the department had been closed for security reasons. Taking into account recent events as well as his own injury, Robert Wilkes had decided not to risk any further security mishaps and had insisted on a heavier security presence, both outside and inside the hospital. Unfortunately this meant that regular patients were being temporarily shuttled between other departments.

Inside the modern, brightly-lit waiting room, Kate Harding was sitting on a white plastic moulded seat watching Wilkes as he paced up and down the polished floor, occasionally stopping to glance at a large flat-panel television fixed onto the corner wall of the room. Although the volume was muted, the news broadcast displayed disturbing scenes of shattered Paris streets, injured Parisians and grotesque images of twisted metal that will long be remembered as the once-great Eifel Tower.

As she sat waiting for news of the Duncan's, a faulty fluorescent light tube flickered continually on and off above her head.

Glancing up she tutted in annoyance, "A multi million pound hospital and they can't change a bloody light bulb."

Wilkes stopped pacing and turned his head, "Huh, what's that?"

Kate shook her head, "Nothing, and for God's sake man will you stop that, you're depressing me."

Wilkes expression turned to a one of surprise, "Stop what?"

"Pacing up and down like that, you're starting to make me feel dizzy."

Wilkes shrugged and sat down beside her. "Sorry. Actually, I was thinking."

Kate raised her eyebrows, "About what?"

"I just want to know why this man wants you dead so desperately. I mean, with the military and police presence, why take the risk?"

Kate shook her head and sighed, "I don't know. It seems to have all started a couple of days ago with Robert Jameson. He met a man called Herman Brauer in Schwetzingen. Apparently, Brauer had contacted Robert with details of some sort of dark plot involving a terrorist group. Brauer had been in some kind of relationship with a scientist, a volcanologist named Elín Gylfadóttir. I believe that…"

Wilkes sat up straight and interrupted, "What was that?"

Kate looked at Wilkes and repeated, "A Volcanologist."

As he glanced back to the disturbing television images of a devastated Paris, his mouth fell open, "That's it Kate, if I may call you Kate. Don't you see? It must be something to do with her."

Kate shook her head, "Possibly, but why kill so many people, I just don't understand. What's the big secret? My assistant did some research and the whole affair seems to circle around the woman. The police's theory is that she committed suicide, but why? It doesn't make any sense."

Wilkes nodded, "From the look on your face, am I to think that you don't believe it was suicide, do you?"

"No, not really, call me a sceptic, but it just doesn't add up."

Wilkes began to pace up and down again. "Tell me more about this scientist. What else did you find out?"

Kate thought for a moment and shrugged, "Nothing really, we were just getting started when all this began."

"I see."

"Although, I've heard that her theories were somewhat ridiculed by the scientific community."

Wilkes stopped pacing and turned, "Theories?"

"Something about a volcanic ring of fire."

Wilkes reached inside his jacket pocket and pulled out a mobile phone and began to dial.

"Do you think it's significant?"

Wilkes coughed, "I'm not sure but it's a possibility." Suddenly he turned away as his call was picked up, "Yes, Doctor, it's Robert Wilkes. No I see ... I ... yes, I understand Doctor but just before you go. I'm in need of some information regarding an Icelandic volcanologist, Elín Gylfadóttir. I don't know if you're familiar with the woman or her work? Good. I see ... well apparently she had some rather outlandish theories."

Wilkes paused and turned back towards Kate, who was rubbing a bruise on her forehead.

"It appears somebody is going to great lengths to hide any correlation between her theories and current events and I want to know why. Now it may be nothing, but then again it could be important. If you wouldn't mind seeing what you could dig up, it would be very much appreciated ... Of course ... Thank you very much."

Wilkes placed the handset back inside his jacket pocket. "He's at the airport, just about to board a plane to London."

Kate nodded, "I see."

As he was about to continue, Wilkes spotted Dougie, Tom and a young doctor walking towards them. As they approached Wilkes and Kate stood up.

"Miss Harding, Mr Wilkes."

The doctor smiled and momentarily glanced at Tom. "The good news is that there is no permanent damage. Other than a few broken bones, Mrs Duncan should make a full recovery. But if it's alright I'd like her to remain in hospital for a few days for observation. Fortunately Duncan here was very lucky, escaping only with a couple of cracked ribs. Now, if you'll excuse me, I'll get back to work. If you need anything more the ward Sister will be able to help."

Smiling, the doctor turned and disappeared back along the corridor leaving the group standing in silence.

Kate's head dropped as she said, "I'm so sorry Tom, I had no idea that this would put your family in danger."

Tom glanced at Dougie and shook his head, "Kate, don't be. There was no way to know."

"Yes, but …"

Before she could continue, Wilkes stepped closer and interrupted, "Tom. I'm very sorry about your wife. Is your daughter okay?"

Tom nodded, "Yes thank you, she's staying with my wife's parents in Dumblane. I think that perhaps, under the circumstances, we'll stay there for a few days."

Wilkes nodded in agreement, "I understand. I also think that perhaps it's best that Dougie and Kate be moved away for their own protection, as well as yours."

Tom shook his head and raised his voice, "What, no, that's the most ridiculous thing I've heard."

"Tom, you've seen what's going on. Paris, the US. If there's even a chance that Dougie's predictions are correct then God help us all. I believe, like you, that he's here for a reason and we need to work out what that reason is. I've just received information that the body of a missing reporter, Donald McPherson, was discovered in his car earlier today. It looks like the work of our friend."

Kate raised her hand to her mouth in shock, "Donald, No!"

Wilkes continued, "The point is the police and security services will do everything in their power to protect you and your family. But you have to understand this individual is a professional. It may not be enough. He will try again and I don't want to be responsible for the possible consequences."

Stepping forward, Dougie placed a hand on Tom's shoulder and spoke gently, "Tom, he's right lad. We have tae get away to try and work things oot. You're family's safety is important. We haven't much time now and ye need tae be with them now."

Tom turned reluctantly towards Dougie and sighed. "Aye okay."

Then turning to face Wilkes, he cleared his throat. "Where will they go?"

Glancing, first at Dougie and Kate, Wilkes returned his gaze to Tom "Somewhere safe, I'm sure there will be a number of options, I ..."

Before he could continue, Tom leaned forward and interrupted, "Rua Reidh ..."

Wilkes turned to Tom with a confused look, "Pardon me?"

"Rua Reidh, Mr Wilkes, if you're looking for a place to hide them, I may have just the place ... Rua Reidh lighthouse, in Melvaig."

"Pardon?"

"Jane's grandfather was a keeper in the lighthouse service for 30 years and when he retired the government sold many of them off. Well, he couldn't let go and persuaded his wife to buy one as a holiday home. We've been renovating the place. It's not the palace hotel at the moment, but it's pretty remote. I wouldn't imagine anyone would go looking for them there."

Wilkes glanced at Kate who was looking a little lost and then at Dougie who simply shrugged his shoulders, "What's a lighthouse?"

Turning back to Tom he nodded, "You know that might just work. Well done, Tom. However, if we are going to move them, it'll have to be done quickly, tonight perhaps."

Tom raised his hand, "Tonight?"

Wilkes nodded, "Yes, I'll see if our army friends can arrange a flight!"

Dougie's eyebrow's raised in apprehension, "Fl ... flight?"

Tom slapped his friend on the shoulder and smiled, "Don't worry Dougie, you'll love it."

Wilkes nodded, "Okay folks, if you'll excuse me I'll make a couple of phone calls."

Turning away, the young MI5 officer walked through a large automatic revolving door marked Exit and strode outside. Inside the waiting room, Kate sighed and walked back across to where she had been sitting and re-took her seat below the flickering light tube. "I feel terrible, I've caused so much trouble."

Dougie glanced first at Tom and then Kate and sighed, "Look lassie, its nae your fault that beastie attacked ye. Don't blame yourself. I'm just thankful you're okay."

Tom sat down next to her, "Look Kate, If Dougie's right, none of this will matter anyway. It's up to you and him now, you have to help."

Raising her head, she wiped a tear away, "I will, I promise, thank you."

Taking a deep breath she stood up and exhaled, "I need some air. Do you mind if we step outside for a moment?"

Dougie and Tom nodded simultaneously. As she stood, she stepped forward, stopping for a moment to gaze once more at the annoying flickering light. Then with Dougie and Tom at her side, they made their way through the exit.

After sitting inside the sterile waiting area for so long, the cool evening air was a welcome relief.

Filling his lungs, Dougie turned to Tom and gave a weak smile, "Well lad, I must admit I'm going miss ye and your family. I feel like I made some real friends here and I want tae thank ye for that."

Tom nodded in agreement, "Aye, me too. I'm just sorry it was under these circumstances." Shaking his head, Dougie said, "Don't worry, if there's a chance of stopping this, I'll do my best."

Turning to Kate momentarily, Tom nodded and smiled, "I know you will Dougie, besides, I have a strange feeling our paths will cross again."

As the two men shook hands they were re-joined by Wilkes.

"Okay Kate, Dougie. I've made a couple of calls, and the RAF will shuttle you to Melvaig this evening, assuming of course, that the weather remains clear. Tom, Inspector McLeish has also agreed to maintain the level of security around the hospital, so your wife and family will be protected."

Tom shuffled forward, "Thank you Mr Wilkes I appreciate that. The keys for the lighthouse are at home, if you can drop me off I'll get them for you. As it turns out there's not much I can do here right now, Jane is sleeping so I may as well go home and tidy up a bit."

Wilkes nodded, "Of course. The move should only be for a couple of days, until we can find a more permanent solution. OK folks, if you'll follow me I'll get you back to Alva."

As the group climbed inside a nearby police car Dougie looked up in awe as an enormous flock of birds of varying varieties flying overhead. Hundreds, maybe, even thousands momentarily turning day into night. "Whoa, look at that?"

Raising their heads, they looked up at the sheer numbers. Turning to Dougie Tom pointed, "What does it mean? It almost looks like a storm."

Dougie breathed in and slowly exhaled, "Aye lad, you're right it does."

THIRTY

B Y 7.05 PM, the British Airways Airbus A320-200 had reached its assigned altitude of 32,000ft and was cruising smoothly through a cloudless sky. This evening the Edinburgh to London Heathrow bound flight was unusually quiet, with only a quarter of the seats sold. Doctor Richard Quest looked uneasy. Flying was never his favourite mode of transport and today was no exception.

"What's the matter Richard? You seem very uneasy."

Quest shrugged, "Oh I'm sorry Helen. I was just thinking about something that Wilkes said just before we boarded."

"What was it?"

"He was rambling on about an Icelandic scientist, Elín Gylfadóttir. Have you heard of her?"

After thinking for a moment her eyes widened, "Actually I have! I once attended a conference in Iceland on global warming and she delivered a rather spirited session on her theory of a volcanic ring of fire."

"And?"

"Too be honest she was pretty much ridiculed. She took a lot of criticism, especially from a couple of Germans in the audience. I remember she got rather upset and ran off stage." Pausing for a moment Quest glanced through the window and sighed. "What was her theory, do you remember?"

Moore shook her head, "Richard, the woman was a crackpot she …"

Quest raised his hand to interrupt, "That may be so, but please tell me what her theory was?"

Moore sighed, "Well, as you know the planet is made up of seven continents, which in turn are made up from a series of tectonic plates. As a volcanologist she theorised that the ring of fire that surrounds the Pacific Rim could potentially be expanded to encompass the entire planet. She thought that if the tectonic plates were pressured or manipulated to such an extent, it could start a chain reaction that would send a series of earthquakes and volcanic eruptions reverberating through the Earth's crust."

Quest nodded and thought for a moment.

"Okay, let's say for argument's sake that she was right."

"Oh for Christ's sake Richard, please!"

"Helen, I said for argument's sake, just suppose she was right, what would these warning signs be?"

The professor took a deep breath and continued, "Well, she theorised that at first there would be a swarm or several smaller earthquakes. As the plates become more unstable the composition of gasses in volcanic regions would increase causing tectonic movement and stronger earthquakes."

"Resulting in?"

"The Earth's core is essentially solid iron encompassed in liquid iron. She theorised that if this core was manipulated, it could initiate a chain reaction which would place enormous pressure at the core, eventually causing a simultaneous worldwide pyroclastic flow."

Quest looked puzzled for a moment, "Pyroclastic?"

Moore sighed and lowered her voice, "It would be ten million times worse than Pompeii. Ash, debris, gasses. It would happen so fast that it would kill everything, not even bacteria or viruses would survive. A ring of fire literally would mean, Hell on Earth!"

Quest shook his head, "Jesus!"

Placing her hand on his arm she sighed, "But Richard, Gylfadóttir's theories were only that, theories. They are ridiculous, and besides she said that initiation points would need to be simultaneously activated across the planet and they would have to be more powerful than …" Suddenly, her face turned pale and she went quiet.

"Helen, what is it?"

Moore didn't respond, she just continued staring ahead, silently.

"Helen?"

"The Pyramid, Richard, oh my God! Why didn't I see it?"

"Now Helen, let's not jump to conclusions. Surely this ignition point would have to be near a major fault line or a volcano."

"But it does, look!" reaching down, she lifted up a brown leather briefcase onto her lap. Unclasping a brass clip, she took out a blue A4 folder. She shuffled through various documents and finally handed one to Quest.

"Look, I pulled this off the internet. It clearly talks about the Ochil Fault line and ancient lava flows."

Quest scanned through the document and shook his head, "Helen, you're talking about events that occurred millions of years ago. You don't honestly believe that …"

"But I do, that's the point. Look, Dougie said that these beings had been on Earth for millions of years, right? Well, what if the pyramid had been placed there at the same time?"

Quest sighed and shook his head, "Even so, as powerful as one pyramid probably is, it's hardly enough to rip the world apart …"

Quest's words faded as a stewardess came past with a drinks cart. Turning her head upwards the professor smiled and said "No thank you."

As the stewardess moved on, Moore continued. "Well, what if it's not?"

"What?"

"What if it's not the only one? What if there was at least one pyramid on each continent. What if these, when combined, somehow affect the Earth's magnetic field?"

"Helen, please, that's a lot of what ifs!"

"I'm serious Richard. Maybe Gylfadóttir was onto something. What if these devices are designed to not only manage the core, but also manipulate it? Think about it. A gigantic magnet could literally rip the tectonic plates to pieces."

For a moment Quest said nothing, then dropping his head, he took a sharp intake of breath and slowly exhaled, "Jesus Helen, what are we going to do?"

Moore sighed and shook her head, "I'm not sure. I don't think there's anything we can do. Just prepare for the worst and hope for the best."

Suddenly Quest reached inside his jacket pocket and pulled out the piece of parchment given to him by Allan. "What about this? It's got to mean something?"

Taking the sheet, she opened it and carefully examined the symbols.

"I just don't know, I'm not a symbolist, it looks pre-Egyptian to me."

"Perhaps we're going about this the wrong way. Maybe it's something they want us to find. I mean, why give it to Dougie? He's clearly no scientist."

Moore shrugged and gave a nod, "What if it's some kind of test, a chance to stop the disaster?"

Quest nodded and snapped his fingers, "Exactly!"

Sitting back, Moore scrutinised the symbols further before carefully folding the delicate paper, and handing it back to the doctor.

"Well, I just hope we can find the answer Richard, I really do."

By 7.45 pm, Dougie, Kate, Tom and Wilkes had arrived back at the Duncan's house. The local police had already cleared up the majority of the damage caused by the intruder and, to Tom's delight, someone had replaced his damaged front door. Once inside, Tom retrieved an envelope containing a set of keys and location details for Melvaig from a desk drawer in his office. Handing them to Wilkes, he continued to gather food and other essentials for Dougie and Kate's journey north.

Upstairs, Kate was busy packing, and as she placed her clothes inside her navy blue travel bag, her mobile phone slipped onto the floor. Leaning over she picked it up and was about to place it with the rest of her things, when she paused, realising that she had not contacted her colleagues at the *Chronicle* for some time. Deciding that the moment was right, she flipped open the cover, dialled her office number and placed the phone to her ear. After a few moments, the line clicked and the call was answered by a familiar voice, "News desk, Bill Peterson speaking."

"Bill, its Kate Harding."

"Kate, is everything alright? Everyone's been so worried."

Kate grimaced at Peterson's sincerity. Unlikely she thought to herself. She ran a pretty tight ship and, if anything, the staff would be pleased at her absence.

"Thanks Bill, I don't suppose Amanda is still in the office, is she?"

"No, I'm afraid not. She went to see her mother. Apparently her house was damaged in the quake and she's gone to spend a few days with her. Can I give her a message?"

Kate swallowed and gave a nod, "Yes okay, please tell her that I'm still working on that story and I will need a few days longer. I hope she can manage."

"Can I say where you can be contacted?"

Pausing for a moment, unsure of what to say, she took a deep breath, deciding that it probably wouldn't do any harm. "I'll be staying at a lighthouse in Melvaig. It's about 2 hours northwest of Inverness."

For a moment there was silence before Peterson continued, "I see!"

"Bill, you will tell her where I am and not to worry?"

"Oh yes, Miss Harding, I'll make sure she gets the message. Goodbye."

"Goodbye Bill and thank you."

Satisfied things were on course, she wandered downstairs into Tom's kitchen, where Tom was busy placing various items of food into a cardboard box. "It's not much, but it will keep you going for a few days."

Dougie glanced at Kate and gave a smile, "Thank ye lad, it's much appreciated."

Kate stood beside Dougie, "Yes, thanks for everything Tom. I do hope Jane makes a good recovery."

Tom looked at them both and acknowledged with a weak smile, "Thank you. Well, what can I say it's been quite an adventure?"

Dougie smiled as he shook hands, "Aye, it has."

Tom then turned to face Kate and gave her a hug.

"It was a pleasure Kate. Good luck."

"Thank you Tom."

"I just hope you can find an answer. Good luck!"

"We'll do our best, I promise,"

Just then Wilkes re-joined the group and said, "Okay folks, they're ready for you so if you'll gather your things and kindly follow me."

As instructed, the pair collected their bags, including Dougie's bag of "essentials" as Tom called it and followed Wilkes into the hallway and out through the front door. As they stepped out into the cool evening air, Dougie took one final look at the Ochil's and sighed, wondering if he would ever see them again.

Tom closed the door behind and walked with the group through his garden gate and to the left towards a clearing. There waiting for them was a RAF Sea King helicopter along with three army personnel, including the red-headed Corporal Jarvis.

As the group walked towards the aircraft Dougie grabbed Tom's arm and spluttered, "What the hell is that?"

Tom placed a hand on Dougie's shoulder and smiled, "It's called a helicopter. It's a machine that flies. Don't worry Dougie you'll be perfectly safe."

Dougie rolled his eyes and continued walking as a seed of doubt began to grow in the pit of his stomach.

At the helicopter, Jarvis strolled across to the group, took the box of food from Tom and placed it, along with their belongings into the aircraft's hold. Then turning to face Wilkes he cleared his throat. "OK Mr Wilkes, everything's arranged. The flight shouldn't take more than a couple of hours. As you'll be the only officer on-site, the Chief Inspector wanted me to hand you this." Bending down, Jarvis picked up a black leather briefcase and opened it.

"It's a satellite phone sir. We figured that it'll be pretty remote out there. Also the inspector insisted you take a weapon so we've included a 9mm M&P Compact."

As a couple of junior officers assisted Kate aboard the helicopter, Jarvis closed the briefcase and handed Wilkes a piece of paper with the case's code combination. "I think that's all sir, have a good flight."

"Thank you Corporal."

Wilkes climbed aboard the helicopter, took a seat and fastened his seat belt. As the engines started up and the blades began to rotate, a reluctant Dougie turned to Tom looking worried, "Are ye sure about this lad?"

Tom nodded and gave a reassuring smile, "Dougie, you will be fine."

As he looked at his friend, Dougie could feel a lump forming in his throat. Although he was in Alva, he felt so far from home and although Tom was not family, the thought of leaving his new friend was painful. Dougie swallowed and glanced towards the helicopter and then back at Tom, "Thank ye lad, for everything."

With the speed of the blades increasing and volume of the engine roaring, Corporal Jarvis raised his hand and yelled out, "Dougie, it's time to go."

Shaking hands and giving one final wave, Tom stepped away from the aircraft and as instructed, Dougie turned and climbed aboard. Once seated, Jarvis assisted him with his seatbelt. Having secured it, Dougie could hardly move, but in his present situation he thought that perhaps it wasn't such a bad thing.

As Jarvis turned to Kate, he gave her a smile, "Are you okay Miss Harding?"

"Yes, thank you Corporal I'm fine."

Giving a nod in acknowledgment, Jarvis leaned forward and gave a thumbs up signal at the pilot, "Okay Captain, you're good to go!"

Leaning across, he slid the large exit door closed and stepped away from the aircraft. As the helicopter slowly began to rise, the sensation in Dougie's stomach turned nauseas, forcing him to close his eyes tight. Then as the helicopter increased speed and pulled sharply away, Dougie yelled out in shock and his face turned almost grey.

"Don't worry Dougie, it's always like this the first time. You'll get used to it."

Breathing heavily, Dougie held on tightly to the arms of his chair, almost as if his life depended on it. Then opening his eyes and swallowing, he nodded and gave a weak, rather unconvincing smile, "Aye well, I'm sure it bloody does."

Bill Peterson was furious. How this man, this so called professional, could make such a mess out of a simple job was quiet beyond him. Why was she still alive? The instructions had been, in his opinion, clear and unambiguous, eliminate Elín Gylfadóttir and everyone involved with her project. This unfortunately now included Kate Harding and other members of the *Daily Chronicle*'s news team. His employer was going to be outraged! Taking a deep breath, Peterson opened his desk draw and took out a small, black notebook, flipped through a few pages and finally stopped. Reaching over to his phone, he lifted the receiver and proceeded to dial a number. A moment later the line clicked and the call was picked up.

"Yes?"

"Brooks, its Peterson. When were you going to tell me what happened today?"

"Sorry?"

"Sorry! You had simple instructions, what happened?"

"It was complicated. The place was crawling with police and military. I was discovered and had to break off, now unfortunately they've been moved to an undisclosed location. Don't worry, it's only a matter of time before I find her."

Peterson rolled his eyes and banged his desk with his fist, "Time, unfortunately is the one thing we don't have. But fortunately for you, she just called in. So I suppose it's lucky that she suspects nothing."

There was a sigh on the other end of the line, "So where is she?"

"She's in the process of being moved to a safe house."

"Safe house?"

"Yes, and to a fairly remote place. Rua Reidh Lighthouse, it's perfect. It's about two hours northwest of Inverness, ideal for a man of your skills. However, I'm sure she will be protected, but I assume this won't be a problem?"

For a moment the voice on the other end of line remained silent. Then as Peterson opened his mouth to speak, the cold voice on the other end of the line responded, "No. It's not a problem. I'll take care of it."

THIRTY ONE

ETHEL OBRIEN, THE 48-year-old White House Chief of Staff, looked pale and anxious as she strode along the glass enclosed, East Colonnade of the White House's east wing. Today had been a nightmare, not just for her country, but also for her personally. Her elderly parents had lived in Los Angeles and, despite being in a position more fortunate than most, her efforts in tracing their whereabouts had been, so far, fruitless.

It had been two whole days since she'd spoke with her father, which for her, seemed almost like an eternity. Since the earlier tsunami, communications from the west coast had been sporadic to say the least. But, she was hopeful that there was a chance, however slim, that they were still alive.

Today, her normally pristine attire had been abandoned. Her navy blue jacket, left in one of the west wing's meeting rooms and at the moment, any thoughts of retrieving it were the least of her concerns.

"Mrs Obrien."

She turned to see a tall smartly dressed Secret service agent approach.

"Yes?"

"I'm sorry to bother you Mam, but your presence is needed

in the situation room right away." She nodded and smiled at the agent, "Very well, thank you."

Created under the orders of President John F Kennedy during the Cuban missile crisis and renovated in 1995, the situation room was now one of the most advanced communication centres in the world. As she quickened her pace, her heart leapt. Perhaps it was news of her parents? Perhaps they'd been discovered and were safe. But alas, as she opened the heavy door and stepped inside her heart sank as Melissa Bailey, the president's aide approached and cleared her throat, "Mrs Obrien, they're waiting for you in conference room four."

Nodding in acknowledgement, she sighed and gave a weak smile, turned and walked past the busy communications centre and headed down a dimly lit corridor. As she approached the conference room, she knew instantly that inside the President was waiting to chair a meeting. This was not down to an ability to see into the future, but through simple deduction. Outside the room, two smartly dressed secret service agents stood guard. This would only be the case if the President were inside. As she approached, the eagle-eyed agents surveyed her and gave a nod of acknowledgement. Then standing aside, one of the men leaned forward and opened the door.

As the door swung open, she half expected to see a room full of generals and other military advisors scuttling around the conference table. But no, on this occasion the room was occupied by three others only. A concerned looking President, Richard Bryant, dressed in jeans and a casual shirt, was nervously pacing around the room. Michael Thomas, the elderly Secretary of Defence and John Baker, the President's head of scientific affairs. As she stepped inside, the two men at the table looked up and the President stopped pacing and turned to face his Chief of staff.

"Mr President, you sent for me."

Pulling out a chair from under the table, he sat down and gave a sigh. "Yes thank you Ethel, I did. Okay John, tell her what you just told me."

Baker opened up a blue folder in front of him, pulled out a document and passed it across the table. Leaning forward Obrien picked up the A4 sheet and gazed at a photograph of what appeared to be a black marble pyramid.

"I don't understand Mr President, I've seen this already, it was found in Yellowstone last year."

"No Ethel. We've just received this from the Brits. This is another one, discovered in Scotland just a few days ago."

"What! Two of them?"

"Yes."

"Do the Brits know about our one?"

Baker shook his head, "No."

"Well, surely you have to tell them. They have a right to know and besides it may be important."

Baker glanced at the President who nodded in agreement, "I agree, send them our findings. Hopefully they can shed some light on all of this."

As the President spoke, his science advisors head dropped and he shook his head. "You disagree Mr Baker?"

Baker looked up, "No, not at all sir. It's not that, I was just thinking that it would be perhaps prudent to bring the Icelandic summit forward a day or so in order to give us more time."

The President sat back in his chair and glanced across at the Secretary of Defence who had been uncharacteristically quiet throughout the conversation. "What do you think Mike?"

The elderly man glanced at the others and shook his head, "Hawaii, the west coast and now France. With all that's happened Mr President, we need answers and we need them soon. If this gathering can provide them, then I say let's give them as much time as they need."

"I agree. Ethel, could you make the arrangements?"

"Of course Mr President. I'll start making some phone calls right away."

As the group stood to leave, Baker raised his hand, "Er, Mr President, there's just one other small matter that I have not mentioned."

The group returned to their seats and turned to face the middle-aged science advisor.

"What is it John?"

"Well, as impossible as it sounds, the Brits who found the pyramid, also say that they have discovered an individual who claims to have time travelled, from the 1700s!"

Obrien leaned forward, her mouth wide open, "What?"

Baker shuffled uncomfortably and nodded, "You heard it correctly Ethel. I don't know if this is genuine, I'm waiting for confirmation. I heard that the British Government are taking the matter very seriously and have dispatched not only the military but also a couple of science advisors to the site near Stirling, a Doctor Richard Quest and Professor Helen Moore. I actually had the pleasure of meeting both of them at a dinner in Prague recently. Just before our meeting, I tried to contact the doctor, but was told both he and the Professor are en-route to London."

Throughout Baker's briefing the President looked uncomfortable and distant, as if the conversation had somehow stirred up bad memories. Noticing his leaders apparent discomfort Baker paused, "Mr President, is everything alright?"

Rubbing his eyes, the President nodded, "Yes, I'm sorry John, my mind just wondered for a moment. Please continue."

"It's totally understandable sir. Well, as I said, I believe they are en-route to a briefing. I will pass on a request for a conference call and hopefully we can collaborate on our findings." Sitting up straight, the President picked up a glass of water, took a sip, swallowed and placed the glass back on to the table.

"Very well, let's start making plans to depart for Iceland tomorrow morning and John let's see if we can find out a little more about this so called time traveller shall we. Ethel can you please update the Vice President on our movements and brief his team on the changes."

"Of course Mr President, I'll take care of it."

As the President stood, the others stood in a unison as a sign of respect.

"Very well, Ethel if you could please stay back for a moment. For the rest, let's schedule a follow up with the Brits later this evening?."

Nodding both men uttered, "Yes, Mr President," before turning heel and leaving the President alone with his Chief of Staff. As the door closed, the President motioned Obrien to sit down. "How are you holding up Ethel?"

"Mr President?"

"You're parents, have you received any news?"

Obrien's eye's dropped and she sighed. "No not yet. I was hoping that this was all just a horrible nightmare and that I would just wake up and everything would be back to normal. But I'm afraid it's not is it?"

As a politician Richard Bryant had always prided himself on being able to hide his true feelings. Even on his various campaign trails or party conventions he was able to maintain, what he called a "professional distance". But this time it was different. The world had changed and today it seemed raw, more personal.

"No, I'm afraid things may never be normal again."

Taking his Chief of Staff's hand, Bryant sighed, "Hey I know your parents remember? Your folks are fighters. If anyone survived, I'm sure they did."

"You don't have to say that Mr President, it's alright. I know the reality of the situation. "

"Hey, I'm not just saying that, I mean it. Don't lose your faith Ethel, not now."

She swallowed in an attempt to fight back the tears. Then

sniffing, she gave a weak smile, "You're right, of course you're right. Thank you."

Standing, the President smiled and placed his hand on her shoulder and patted her on the back. "Anytime, come on, let's get back to work. It'll take your mind off it."

7.50PM CHECKPOINT: ON THE A96 JUST OUTSIDE ALVA, SCOTLAND

"CLOSED? YOU'RE JOKING man, I have tae get home. Your bloody diversion will take me hours."

Standing in front of him a young soldier looked on with little sympathy. After already explaining three times why the road was closed, he was tired and in no mood for an argument or any verbal abuse, especially from a farmer. Gritting his teeth the youngster raised his weapon and hissed menacingly, "I told you sir, the road ahead is closed. Now, I suggest that for your own safety, you return to your vehicle and leave now!"

Sensing that he had lost this battle, the middle-aged farmer turned and muttered, "asshole" under his breath as he reluctantly climbed back into his car. Slamming the door with a thud, he turned the key, pushed his foot down on the accelerator and his dark grey Toyota RAV 4 sprang away towards Stirling.

Graham Wallace was a farmer through and through and one of his pet hates was letting his staff down, especially at this busy time of year. As he sped along the A91 towards Stirling his mind churned with thoughts of which route home would be the quickest. Should he go via Alloa or out on to the M9 and then upwards towards Perth?

Suddenly, his mind returned to the present as an image of a man lying beside the road flashed before his eyes. Within a moment, any doubt to whether or not the man had been real was gone. Yes, he was sure. He had definitely been there. Slamming on the brakes, the RAV came to a screaming halt and the man leaped out of the car and ran back towards the spot where he thought the injured man was.

In the deteriorating light it took a moment for him to focus but, yes, there, about 20 meters ahead to the right, a man appeared to be lying face down at the side of the grass verge. Wearing black jeans, boots and a black leather jacket the figure remained motionless as Wallace approached and knelt down. His face turned to one of puzzlement as he surveyed the scene. With no apparent cause of injury or trauma, the farmer shook his head and muttered, "He must be drunk!"

Then placing a hand on the man's shoulder Wallace attempted to shake him, in order to wake him up. "Sir, sir, are you alright?"

To his alarm, the figure on the ground twitched, swung around and sprang to his feet. Staring at the sneering figure, Wallace staggered back in shock "What the hell, is this, some kind of sick joke?"

Smirking cruelly at the farmer Brooks sneered, "No joke, I just need a car."

"A car, what?"

The attack was sudden and brutal. Brooks leapt at Wallace like an animal and the resulting pain was sharp and sudden. Spluttering and gasping, Wallace staggered backwards and glanced with horror at his attacker. Then looking down, he saw it in his hand. The knife covered red, with blood, his blood. With his eyes unable to focus and an increasing sense of panic overcoming him, he moved his hand to his stomach. But in the fading light it was difficult to see; however, he sensed the warm liquid over his hands was blood. With dizziness and nausea gripping him, he found himself unable to stand any longer and he dropped to his knees. Looking up, at his attacker, his eyes stared at the stranger's unemotional face, pleading for answers, "Wh … Why?"

Then Graham Wallace's battle for life was over, he took one final gasp and slumped forward onto his stomach. Staring at his victim in silence Brooks stepped across and calmly grasped the farmer's body under his shoulders and dragged it with apparent ease further into the undergrowth, where his body would be hidden from view. Then coolly and without haste, he walked along the road to where the grey RAV was sitting, its engine still purring.

Once inside, he slammed the door shut and surveyed the scene one final time. A cruel sense of personal satisfaction came over him as he pulled on a seat belt. Then leaning across to the car's dashboard he smirked as he enabled the car's satellite navigation system and punched in his destination. Melvaig. After a moment, the screen flickered and the result of the six-hour journey appeared on screen. Nodding confidentially to himself, he whispered, "Perfect!" Then he pushed his foot down on the accelerator and the car sped away with a new sense of purpose.

THIRTY TWO

THE LANDSCAPE WAS eerie and quiet; like nothing Dougie had ever experienced before. Scorched earth and blackened volcanic rock sprawled out as far as the eye could see. In the distance tall, dangerous volcanic rock formations looked ominous and foreboding in the early morning light. Breathing in, the air was thick with the unpleasant aroma of rotten eggs. Around him small pools of hot sulphurous water gurgled angrily. As he stepped forward the only other sounds were those of his boots as they crunched along the ground. Turning full circle, he scrutinized the landscape, but saw no animals, no vegetation and no companions. He was completely alone. Was this a dream? If so, it seemed so real. The landscape, the smells, the very essence of the place seemed to be so authentic and alive.

"Hello Dougie."

"Huh?"

Spinning around, Dougie jumped in alarm as there, in front of him, stood an ominous looking cloaked figure. As Dougie turned to run, the figure called out again, "No Dougie, wait!" Recognising the voice, Dougie stopped and spun around. As in the cemetery, the figure lowered its hood to reveal a familiar and beautiful face. Dougie's heart leapt and he rushed forward.

"Mary, what is this place and why ye are here?"

The woman smiled, "Congratulations Dougie, you have found the key!"

Nodding, the big man reached inside the fold of his kilt and took out the miniature black pyramid and held it in the palm of his hand. He didn't know why, but he could almost sense the immense power of the original pulsating through him, almost as if they were both connected.

"I don't know. I just placed my hand on the pyramid and this came tae me."

"Of course. It was waiting for you."

"Waiting? I, don't und …"

Raising her hand, she interrupted, "You don't have to. You were destined to find it, as it was destined to find you. You are both connected."

"Connected? But what is it. What does it do?"

The figure turned and took a few steps back, seemingly unsure how to respond. Then, as Dougie opened his mouth to repeat the question, she turned and continued.

"It's a key to a new beginning Dougie. Remember what I said. Once found it will join the world in a way that you cannot possibly imagine and together we will forge a new beginning."

Glancing downwards at the bubbling water below his feet, Dougie remained motionless. "What of MacArthur? I assume if he's here, he's at least going to try and stop me?"

As Dougie glanced back at the familiar face of his wife, he became aware of her expression. An almost cruel smile, similar to the one he'd seen in the cemetery, back in Alva.

"He already knows you are here."

"He does?"

"Of course and he will do anything and say anything to stop you. But Dougie, and this is very important, trust no one. No matter what happens you mustn't fail in your task. For if you do then humanity will fall and he will have won."

Dougie again turned away from the cloaked figure, glanced at the bubbling water below his feet and sighed, "Join the world. I don't know. How do I do that exactly?"

As he turned to face her, she stepped a little closer and answered. "When the time comes, you will know."

His attention was suddenly diverted as a large Geyser erupted to his left, sending a huge plume of boiling hot water and steam high up into the air. As the upsurge subsided, he returned his gaze to where the cloaked figure had been standing. But to his dismay, she was gone and he was again, alone. Sighing in disappointment, he gazed through an increasingly dense plume of rising white steam, desperately attempting to relocate her.

However, within moments the plume became so dense that seeing anything in front of him became almost impossible. As he stepped forward, the ground suddenly shook and he was thrown forwards. His body juddered, as if an electric current had been passed through it.

Opening his eyes, he took a sharp intake of breath, as he once again, found himself back aboard the helicopter.

Wilkes sat forward and gazed at him with a look of concern. "Are you alright Dougie?"

Dougie breathed heavily and rubbed his eyes, "Aye, sorry, it was just a bad dream, I guess."

"You don't think you can actually stop me do you?"

"What? Huh!"

Momentarily confused by the cold voice, Dougie wondered what on earth would motivate Wilkes to make such an outrageous comment. His face grimaced in horror as Wilkes was suddenly gone and in his place sat a terrifying black-robed figure with blazing bright blue eyes.

As panic set in, Dougie desperately fumbled with his seatbelt in an attempt to free himself. Once unclipped, he leaped up in a bid to escape. But it was too late. The figure sprang at him with such force, that it sent him flying backwards against a bulkhead. Then, with what seemed like a feat of superhuman strength, it grasped his throat and lifted him clean off his feet.

Kicking wildly in the air, Dougie squirmed and choked as he watched in terror, as his captor calmly used its other hand to slide open the helicopter's side door. Then, with apparent ease, it lifted him out onto the ledge as if he were nothing more than a child's plaything. Feeling his life slowly draining away, Dougie coughed and spluttered as the sneering figure came closer and hissed, "You pathetic fool, you're too late."

Desperate to save himself, he thrashed his body wildly from side to side in a futile attempt to break free. But his attacker was too strong. As the cold wind whipped the back of his head Dougie gave one last defiant scream as the creature released him. Clumsily stumbling backwards, he fell out of the aircraft, tumbling into nothingness.

With a shudder, his head forwards and his body jerking, Dougie opened his eyes and, to his relief, found himself still safely aboard the helicopter! Across from him was Wilkes who, as before, sat facing him, but with his eyes closed. Taking a deep sigh of relief, he muttered "What a nightmare."

He glanced briefly over at Kate who, like Wilkes was sleeping. As he again closed his eyes to rest, his stomach suddenly churned as if it had been separated from his body. The helicopter unexpectedly jerked sharply to the left, forcing him to grab on to the armrest of his seat. As his knuckles turned white, the voice of the pilot came over the loudspeaker.

"Sorry about that folks, just a little turbulence. As I feared the weather's beginning to close in. We have about 25 miles left to run and will be landing in around 10 minutes so please fasten your seat belts in preparation."

Dougie watched, as Wilkes rubbed his eyes, sat up straight

and tightened his seat belt as instructed. Then glancing across at Dougie he asked, "Everything alright Dougie?"

He gave a weak smile at the thought of still being alive, especially after the whole falling out of the helicopter nightmare, "Aye lad, I'm braw. I'm just nae used tae being in one of these contraptions, that's all."

Wilkes grinned, "I know what you mean. You'll get used to it."

"Especially Robert, in first class which, I'm afraid to say, this is most certainly not!"

Wilkes rolled his eyes, as an image of a troublesome Kate Harding, barking orders at an air-hostess flashed through his mind. Glancing at Dougie he grinned and responded to the comment with, "Kate, I'm sorry it's not up to your usual standard, but I'm afraid we're in a recession you know."

Kate responded with a tut and folded her arms like a spoilt child on a day trip.

As the Aircraft descended through the stormy skies, the pilot struggled with the cyclic stick, desperately trying to keep the Sea King steady in the driving wind and rain. Ahead, he could just make out the light of the Melvaig lighthouse reaching out like a tear of sheer brilliance through the darkness.

The elements battered the aircraft and it shuddered and shook like a puppet. Inside, the pilot increased the speed of the helicopters windscreen wipers in a frantic attempt to fend of the rain so he could see. As he flew lower, he hit a switch and two powerful floodlights revealed angry, thrashing waves below. Reducing speed, he could now just make out a group of sprawling, dangerous rocks ahead.

Then like a shark rising from the depths, he took a sigh of relief as the search lights struck the white painted walls of the lighthouse ahead. He had been told he would be able to put down on a landing pad, but what his superiors had failed to mention was, that at present, the lighthouse was unmanned and thus the pad would not be easily visible.

"Damn," he muttered to himself as he pulled up the collective control and the Sea King lurched higher into the air. Then, as he was about to turn away and attempt a different approach, the pad suddenly became visible. With great skill, he carefully manoeuvred the large aircraft over the pad and reduced power. A few moments later it had gently touched down and there was a collective sigh of relief throughout the cabin as the pilot leaned backwards towards the group, raised his thumbs and yelled, "Okay Mr Wilkes, we're down. Please ensure you and your companions walk away towards the front of the aircraft and keep away from the tail area."

After braving the weather, Wilkes had discovered a good supply of fuel in a nearby out house and proceeded to light a fire in the old keeper's cottage. The group now sat huddled in silence around the warmth of the fire, listening intently to the storm as it battered against the tiny windows. Sipping hot tea, they looked at the fire, mesmerised as tiny sparks leaped and danced from the hot coals.

"So, Robert, just how long do we have to endure this godforsaken place?"

"Kate, with all due respect, you're damn lucky to be alive. I would have thought that you would have been a little more grateful."

Kate's eyes dropped in realisation at how arrogant her last statement must have sounded. "I'm sorry, I didn't mean that quite the way it came out."

"Very well. To answer your question, you 'll have to stay here until we can find a more, permanent solution."

Kate's eyes widened in alarm, "Permanent?"

"There is a professional hit man out there trying to kill you. Right now, in London, an entire team of my colleagues are painstakingly trying to work out why. I believe that this is probably the safest place on earth for you to be."

Feeling that perhaps silence was a better option, Kate simply sat back, nodded and took another sip of tea.

"And what about me laddie, how long will I have tae stay here as your guest?"

"You Dougie are of national interest. Once Professor Moore and Doctor Quest report to the government, the investigation can continue."

Like Kate, Dougie went silent. Then standing up, he walked slowly over to the fireplace, stood quietly for a moment and sighed. Staring at the crackling embers he turned once again to face Wilkes and Kate.

"Ye know, I was just remembering a time when I stood in front of a fire nae unlike this one. It was that night when young James Ritchie came knocking at my door tae offer me the job as mine manager. I have tae tell ye right now, that there are times when I wish I'd never taken the bloody thing, its brooght me nothing but pain."

"Like Tom said, Dougie, perhaps it was just destiny."

"Ye ken Kate, that's all I keep hearing. That it's my bloody destiny. Well if it is, then I can assure ye, I don't want it."

Glancing across at Wilkes, Kate stood and walked across to where Dougie was standing and took hold of his hand. Looking into the flames memorized she whispered, "Don't be afraid of your destiny Dougie. On the contrary you should embrace it, perhaps one day it may change the world."

THIRTY THREE

"**P**RIME MINISTER, YOU simply can't ignore the facts."

Walton sat back and threw his hands up into the air, "Doctor, I appreciate your insight, I really do. But really, time travellers, marble pyramids, it's all just a bit too much to take in that's all."

Quest glanced across the large oak table and at Helen Moore who cleared her throat and rose to her feet.

"Prime Minister, sir, I understand your misgivings, but Dr Quest's conclusions are correct. Having witnessed the chamber for ourselves, along with detailed discussions with Mr Allan, I honestly believe that our planet may be on the verge of a catastrophic disaster."

Walton gazed around at the look of shock on the faces of his inner cabinet colleagues.

"Can you say to what end Professor?"

Moore looked around, at the concerned expressions, before clearing her throat, "Extinction, sir."

The silence in the room was shattered, as ministers on both sides of the table, stood and began to panic. Waving hands, along with shouts of "What are we going to do?" and "How long do we have?" reverberated throughout the room.

Standing up, Walton raised his hand, "Ladies and Gentlemen, please calm yourselves, this will not help the situation."

As the room again fell silent, the Prime Minister retook his seat and said, "Okay Professor, let's just suppose that for arguments sake these assumptions are correct. How would this disaster, unfold?"

"Earth is made up of seven continents, these are essentially tectonic plates floating on a sea of liquid iron with a solid iron core. We believe that if the core were somehow manipulated, the trigger effect would generate what volcanologists call a swarm, or several smaller earthquakes to occur across the planet. Indeed, this is what we believe maybe happening right now throughout the US and Europe. If these events continue, then pressure inside the Earth's core could create a cascade reaction, resulting in the generation of a planetary pyroclastic flow or Wilson cycle, which would happen so fast, that it would literally cause global extinction within days. Not even bacteria would survive."

The professor paused, took a deep breath and continued, "The Doctor and I believe that the chamber discovery may not be an isolated incident. If this is indeed the case, then the cumulative power of these devices would be enough to start the chain reaction."

As she finished, she drew breath and retook her seat. For a few moments the room remained deadly silent.

Leaning forward in his seat the Deputy Prime Minister cleared his throat and asked, "Doctor Quest, you mentioned in your conversation with Mr Allan that he has had contact with one of these beings. Do you think that it's possible for us to somehow communicate or even negotiate with it?"

Quest glanced across at his colleague and sighed. "No Minister, from what Mr Allan has said, the decision seems to already been made. I, we both believe that we are already seeing the early stages of the process. However, with that said, I got the distinct impression that one of these beings did not entirely agree with this decision and had perhaps offered humanity an olive branch of some kind."

"An olive branch Dr Quest?"

The group now turned to face a bank of large wall monitors at the end of the room.

"Mr President?"

"I asked, what form does this olive branch take?"

Quest cleared his throat, "Well, er, in the form of a symbolic message Sir. Mr Allan gave me a piece of parchment that had been given to him, containing a series of ancient symbols. We are still trying to decipher them."

Walton sat forward and interrupted. "In the spirit of transparency, I can arrange for a copy to be sent to you Mr President. I think that at this stage we need all the help that we can get."

The face on the large monitor nodded in agreement, "That would be appreciated Prime Minister, and in the same spirit of transparency my people will also forward to you details of a similar chamber discovered in the Yellowstone region last year."

At this revelation an almighty gasp reverberated throughout the room and Quest's mouth fell open.

"Oh my God! In that case, this would confirm our fears Sir."

The President nodded, "Indeed."

The room again fell silent as the Prime Minister stood. "Do we have any idea of how long we have?"

The faces of the entire room turned to face the Doctor.

"Sir … I'm not sure … perhaps weeks, possibly days it's hard to say."

Walton shook his head, "But, what about the people, surely we have a responsibility to warn them."

At that moment Anne Petrie cleared her throat and rose to her feet, "Forgive me Prime Minister, Mr President, but given the time scales, informing the general population would surely make matters worse. It would create mass religious hysteria, generate panic, crime ..."

"Mr Prime Minister, I am afraid that I'm forced to agree with the good lady's comments, it would clearly just make matters worse."

Glancing across to the monitor, Walton nodded in agreement, strode across to his seat and sat down.

"I agree. For the time being let's keep this on a need to know basis."

The President sighed and gave a nod, "Ladies and Gentlemen my government has made the collective decision to bring the Icelandic summit forward. As you know it's designed to bring together a collection of the greatest scientific and political minds on the planet. Hopefully with one aim survival! I think that under the circumstances we should give the scientific community more time to come up with ideas. Mr Prime Minister, I would appreciate it if we could meet in Reykjavik on Thursday, if you are in agreement of course."

Looking around the table the ministers all nodded in agreement.

"Yes, Mr President, I agree."

"Thank you Prime Minister. One small after-thought before we finish, perhaps it would be prudent to bring this gentleman, Dougie Allan along. I personally would like to hear what the man has to say."

For a moment Walton eyed Professor Moore across the table for any possible objections. After none appeared forthcoming, he turned back to face the President and gave a nod, "I don't see that being a problem Mr President. I'll make the necessary arrangements."

"Very good, Mr Prime Minister. I'll see you in Reykjavik. Ladies and Gentlemen, good evening and good luck to us all."

The screen went blank and the two-way video link was over. Facing his colleagues around the table, Walton cleared his throat.

"Okay, ladies and gentlemen, it's late and we're all tired. Let's reconvene at 9.00 am, and in the meantime let's make the travel arrangements for Reykjavik. I'll see you all in the morning. Thank you."

The group stood and spoke in unison, "Prime Minister" and began to disperse.

"Professor, Doctor, Anne do you have a moment?"

Fastening the clasp on her briefcase the professor glanced at her associate and nodded, "Of course, Prime Minister."

As the others left, Petrie and the two advisers retook their seats. Walton slowly walked across to the far side of the room where a large portrait of Winston Churchill dressed in a smart grey suit, hung on the wall. Walton stared into the eyes of the once great leader. Then, taking a slow deep breath he continued to ponder the picture.

"You know, I've looked at this painting more times than I can remember and every time I look at it, his expression seems to change. I know that sounds ridiculous. But I look into his eyes for inspiration, advice and sometimes I even feel as if he's talking to me."

"Well, it's a very powerful picture Prime Minister, inspiring."

"Yes I suppose it is, isn't it."

Turning, Walton walked back across to the large oak table, retook his seat and gave a sigh. "He had Europe to worry about. I feel as if I have the entire weight of the world upon my shoulders."

Quest cleared his throat, "That's completely understandable, Sir. But humanity is an amazing species. There still may be a way."

Looking Quest in the eye Walton nodded, "Do you think Allan will co-operate?"

Quest nodded, "Yes I do."

"Doctor, those symbols you spoke of, have you been able to identify them yet?"

"No Sir, but we sent them out to a number of experts around

the world. We've even reached out to the Vatican, hopefully we will have an answer soon."

Leaning forward Walton unscrewed a bottle of spring water and filled a glass. Then, replacing the top, he placed it back on to the table

"Anne, where is Allan now?"

Clearing her throat the Home Secretary's head dropped for a moment before she continued. "Sir as you know, there was an incident involving an attempt on Kate Harding's life. Fortunately there were no fatalities. However, in the aftermath the intruder unfortunately escaped."

"Escaped? How could that happen? I was told that there is a small army there."

"Indeed, but it appears that the man was a professional."

Walton took a sip of water and held the glass in his hand for a moment. "So where are Mr Allan and Miss Harding?"

As she was about to answer she glanced uncomfortably at the two science advisers. "Sir; the information is currently classified for your eyes only."

Walton gave an awkward glance across at Quest and Moore, "I, of course, sorry. Doctor, Professor, thank you so much for your help. I know you've both had a very long day. If you'll please excuse us, I'll see you both tomorrow."

Quest stood and nodded, "Of course Prime Minister, Thank you."

Then standing, Walton shook hands with Quest and Moore before they both turned heel and left the room, leaving the Prime Minister and his Home Secretary alone.

As the door closed, Walton walked across to a Silver drinks tray, picked up a bottle of Taylor's forty-year-old port and proceeded to pour himself a glass.

"Anne, would you like one?"

Shaking her head, she grimaced, "Oh God no! I can't stand the stuff. Besides, it will keep me up all night. No, just a glass of water will be fine for me."

As Walton replaced the bottle, Petrie poured herself a glass of sparkling mineral water and watched as Walton returned to his seat, took a sip of the rich dark liquid, swallowed and gave a sigh. "Mmm that's good. Okay, tell me, where Allan and our troublesome reporter friend are held up."

Placing her glass down on to the table, she leaned across and flipped open a blue A4 folder. Taking out a couple of documents she handed one to the Prime Minister.

"It's called Rua Reidh and please excuse the pronunciation. It's a lighthouse, in Melvaig, North West Scotland."

Walton sat up looking surprised, "Lighthouse?"

"Believe me I was a little surprised as well. But, according to MI5, it's owned by the Duncan family and in in the process of being renovated. Now, in terms of a safe house, it's perfect, very remote."

Walton took another sip of the port and swallowed, "When did this happen?"

"This evening Sir. The Army CO in Alva arranged for them to be flown to Melvaig by Sea King, along with an armed officer."

Walton nodded, "I see. One thing comes to mind though. How on earth are we going to get them to Iceland?"

Petrie thought for a moment.

"Well, the closest airport is probably Inverness. I guess we could arrange for Mr Allan to be airlifted there tomorrow and transferred to a Reykjavik flight."

Walton nodded in agreement, "That sounds like it would work. What of the woman?"

"Kate Harding? Sir, to be honest, something's been bothering me about this whole affair.

I just couldn't put my finger on it."

Walton placed his glass onto the table and sat back. "But Anne, the last time we spoke you seemed so sure that she couldn't possibly be involved. From what I've heard she was almost killed earlier today. What's changed your mind?"

Sitting up straight, the Home Secretary shook her head and said, "I'm not for one minute suggesting that she's involved. It's just that something doesn't fit here, that's all. I've gone ahead and ordered the security services to proceed with an internal investigation at the Chronicle. You know, standard wiretaps, mail intercepts and so on. If anything is amiss then I'm sure it will come to light."

"Fair enough. What about Reykjavik? Do we bring her along?"

"I suppose it wouldn't do any harm. She doesn't need to attend any of the briefings and it would certainly provide us with the opportunity to protect her and monitor her movements."

"Okay Anne, make the arrangements and let's meet in the morning after the briefing."

Standing up Anne Petrie nodded, "Very good, I'll make the arrangements. Goodnight Sir."

"Goodnight Anne."

The pair shook hands and Petrie left the room, leaving Walton alone to ponder the future as he again stared at the painting on the wall.

7.15pm (Eastern Time) – The White House – Washington DC

President Richard Bryant was uneasy. Sitting at the "Resolute Desk" in the Oval Office, he fumbled with a $1 dollar bill in his right hand. On one side he scrutinised an image of what historians called the Great Seal, the image was of an all Seeing Eye floating above an ancient pyramid. Through the years, symbolists and theologians speculated that the great seal was somehow associated with mysterious groups such as the Freemasons or the *Illuminati*, or that it was possibly the symbol of some new world order. However, Bryant was a sceptic. He didn't believe any of those things. For him it was just a further example of humanity's need to belong.

Placing the note back on to the desk, the silence was interrupted as a knock came to the door.

"Come in."

Ethel Obrien stepped inside. "I'm sorry to disturb you Mr President, but it's just to inform you that Air Force One is scheduled for a one o'clock departure to Reykjavik tomorrow. Marine One will be on standby at 12.15pm to shuttle you across. I've also arranged for a press briefing at 10.30am."

Bryant nodded and smiled at his Chief of Staff, "Ethel, you are a model of modern efficiency."

"Why, thank you Mr President. Will there be anything else?"

Bryant shook his head, "No thank you Ethel. Oh, one other thing, please inform the Vice President that I need to reschedule our meeting to 8am and not 9am."

"Of course Mr President."

As the large white door closed, Bryant stood for a moment in silence, staring again at the $1 dollar note on his desk. After picking it up, he folded it and placed it inside his trouser pocket. Then, turning to the right, he opened the door to a small private bathroom and walked through.

Once inside, he twisted the cold-water tap and proceeded to sprinkle a few drops onto his face, then picking up a white cotton towel, he dried himself. Looking at his reflection in the mirror he sighed as his normally handsome demeanour suddenly began to change. First, his eyes turned to an almost penetrating shade of bright blue and his face began to mutate into an almost unrecognisable translucent state. Finally, his skin turned increasingly gaunt and pale. Even his normally well-kept grey hair was now an uncharacteristic shade of black. Then as he gave a confident nod to his reflection, his clothes began to change. Within moments his smart business suit had gone, to be replaced by a long, black hood and cloak. Observing his reflection in the mirror the figure stepped closer; its eyes blazing like two halogen beams piercing the darkness. Then it spoke or, to be more accurate, it hissed to itself, "Dougie Allan, right on schedule."

THIRTY FOUR

TUESDAY: 12.10AM RUA REIDH LIGHTHOUSE, MELVAIG, SCOTLAND

STANDING ON THE upper platform of the lighthouse's top deck, Dougie and Wilkes looked out at the storm. Below, powerful white foamed waves crashed against dangerous protruding black rocks.

"It's a wild place this, nae for the faint hearted that's for sure."

"Absolutely. I won't argue with that Dougie, I'm only glad we're inside and not out there."

Dougie turned towards the door and both men slowly made their way back down the rusting iron spiral staircase.

"It's amazing don't you think that these used to be manned. Keepers would come and stay in places like this for weeks or months at a time."

As Dougie emerged off the staircase he turned his head back, "Months?"

Wilkes sighed and nodded, "Oh yes, and as you can imagine it must have been a hard life … but from what I've heard, it was a pretty satisfying one."

Listening to the howling gale outside, Kate rubbed her eyes and sat up as the two men walked through the door into the room. Closing the book, she sighed and sat back. "Did you find anything interesting?"

Dougie smiled, "Well, Robert here was just tellin' me about the life of a lighthoose keeper, it sounds like a tough life."

As Kate nodded in agreement, "I was just reading about this place. Rua Reidh was designed and built by David Stevenson in 1908, but it wasn't until four years later that its light was lit.

Apparently, you can still see the original lens in the Heritage Museum down the road in Gairloch. There's also a quay and a ramp which was used to take on supplies."

Dougie couldn't help himself and yawned.

"Dougie, am I boring you?"

"Ach lass, no it's just been a long day."

Kate smiled as she interrupted, "I'm sorry, I should have realised how late it was. I think we could all use a little sleep."

The two men nodded in unison. Then standing, Wilkes moved towards the door. "Well, the weather is supposed to ease tomorrow, so hopefully after a good night's sleep we can explore."

As he stepped through the doorway, Wilkes stopped and turned back to face Dougie and Kate with a serious look. "I'm not anticipating any problems out here, but I think that given the circumstances, we should all remain vigilant. So with that, I'll say goodnight and I'll see you in the morning."

"Aye lad, we will. Goodnight."

Dougie stared at the fire and sighed," I wonder how Tom is. He was a good friend, I'll miss him."

"Now, you mustn't talk that way Dougie, you'll see him again. My father always told me that things have a funny way of working out in the end."

Dougie shook his head, "That's what my Mary used tae say."

"Well, she sounds like a smart woman."

Kate stood directly in front of Dougie and smiled. For an instant, Dougie did a double take as he thought he saw a familiar look, almost as if it was someone he had known in a previous life.

"What is it?"

He shrugged and shook his head, "It's nothing, and I'm sorry lass. For a moment ye reminded me of someone that's all."

Kate gave an awkward smile and took Dougie's hand, "You're a good man Dougie. Thank you for today, good night."

Kissing him on the cheek, she turned and walked away, leaving Dougie alone by the fire to collect his thoughts. As he gazed once more at the crackling flames, he watched memorized as its snake like tongues shot out and licked the darkness.

He then walked across to a small adjacent room, and once inside he closed the door and without undressing, lay down on a small but comfortable looking single bed and closed his eyes. As he lay in the darkness he could hear the relentless storm outside. The wind whistled wildly as it battered against the windows of the lamp room above and outside he could hear the sound of the waves as they crashed against the rocks. Then, as he began to drift off to sleep, he smiled to himself as images of Tom, Jane and little Amy ran through his mind. Then, as his eyes became increasingly heavier, his mind cleared and Dougie Allan drifted off to sleep.

12.40am: The Hilton London Euston Hotel, London

In room 301 of the London Euston Hilton, Richard Quest poured himself a glass of sparkling water and retook his seat opposite the replica of an 18th century oak desk. Other than flying, Quest's other pet hate was staying in tourist hotels, especially those that insisted on using what he called tacky period furniture aimed purely at the American tourist. Too be fair though, after all that had happened, the hotel had survived the worst of the recent quake and seemed to be in pretty good shape.

On the desk in front of him, he laid out various items including the piece of parchment provided by Dougie Allan along with various books and articles on ancient writings and civilizations. After taking a sip of water, he returned the glass to the desk, sat back and rubbed his eyes. Then, sitting up straight again he scrutinized the symbols on the paper and murmured to himself, "What's your secret? Just what are you trying to tell me?"

Quest sighed and picked up a copy of *The Ancient Languages of Syria-Palestine and Arabia* by Roger D. Woodard and proceeded to flip through the pages until he reached page 83, and continued reading a section on Plautus. As he was about to flip the page, his concentration was interrupted by a sudden knock at the door. Placing his book down, he rose and walked over to the door opening it to reveal a tired looking Professor Helen Moore.

"What's the matter, can't you sleep?"

She gave a weak smile and shook her head, "You're kidding, right? My mind is reeling."

As she stepped inside Quest nodded, "I know what you mean."

She walked over to the desk, glanced down at the sprawl of paperwork and picked up Quest's copy of *The Ancient Languages of Syria-Palestine and Arabia*.

"A little light reading Richard? No wonder you can't sleep."

Quest sat down on the corner of the bed opposite and smiled, "On the contrary, it's helped me nod off on many an occasion."

Returning the book to the desk, she sat down, yawned and turned to face her colleague. "Have you heard anything about the symbols?"

"No, I'm afraid not yet and to be honest Helen I wasn't really expecting anything just yet."

"I know, I just thought."

Reaching out, he took hold of her hand, "Hey, it'll be okay you know. There has to be an answer. It's just a matter of time."

She swallowed and gave a hollow smile, "That's what I'm afraid of, time. I mean. It's the one thing we don't have a lot of."

"Now steady on Helen, I've not given up yet and I don't think you should either."

"I haven't given up Richard, well not yet anyway. It's just the tiredness talking, or maybe I'm just a little scared that's all."

Quest sighed and gently squeezed her hand.

"Helen, we're all scared. It's perfectly normal. Perhaps after a good night's sleep we'll both feel better, you'll see."

Letting go of his hand, she stood and began to walk slowly towards the door. "Oh, I meant to say that we've been asked to present our findings direct to the science council on Friday Morning in Reykjavik."

"Of course, we can discuss it on the flight tomorrow."

As she opened the door she turned back towards him and smiled, "See you in the morning. Let's meet for breakfast at 7am. They are sending a car for us around 8am. Goodnight Richard."

Slipping out into the corridor, she closed the door and was gone even before Quest finished saying, "Goodnight."

Standing for a moment in the empty room, he returned to his desk and flipped to page 84 of, *The Ancient Languages of Syria-Palestine and Arabia* and continued reading.

02.10AM: SLATTADALE, JUST WEST OF LOCH MAREE, SCOTLAND

THERE WAS NO doubt that even in semi darkness, the scenery was dramatic. Tall mountains and rolling hills appeared to sprawl out from every angle. Perhaps in a different life, or under different circumstances Brooks could have stopped to enjoy the views, but not today.

The tall, muscular figure behind the wheel of the grey Toyota RAV was no tourist. He was a man on a mission, a man with a purpose and as the car sped along the A832 towards the Gairloch Brooks only had one thought on his mind – completing his task. Unfortunately there were obstacles – the big man in costume and the armed police officer.

Glimpsing the Sat Nav, he licked his lips in anticipation as it read 21 Miles and an estimated arrival time 41 minutes. Of course he had no intention of driving up to the lighthouse directly, only a fool would do that. No, he would park out of sight, perhaps a mile or so away, then he would approach discreetly on foot. Even the weather, was perfect. "With the storm, they'll never hear or see me coming."

Then, looking across at the passenger seat, he gave a confident sigh as he admired his favourite Colt Double Eagle pistol complete with attached silencer. "Yes" he thought to himself. "This is just perfect."

THIRTY FIVE

HAVING FINISHED AN early breakfast of boiled eggs, toast, orange juice and what appeared to be insanely strong black coffee, Father Antonio Demarco sauntered back to his simple, but comfortable, single room. Morning mass would not take place for another 45 minutes, just enough time for him to check his email and daily schedule. Once inside his room, he hung his jacket on a brass wall peg, closed the door and walked across to his desk and powered on his laptop computer.

The 32-year old Demarco had joined the priesthood ten years earlier. His choice had been controversial to say the least and had caused much friction in the Demarco household. His father, Pietro, an accomplished professor of mathematics at Rome's Sapienza University, was furious at the thought of Antonio wasting what he considered to have been a promising career in mathematics. However, Antonio disagreed and had tried repeatedly to explain to his father that his calling to the priesthood would, if anything, help combine his love of God with his passion for mathematics and Symbology. His father refused to listen and, after leaving the family home, the rift between them only grew wider as time progressed.

Over the years, Antonio had of course attempted to patch things up, but after a number of failed attempts he became "comfortable" with the situation and eventually stopped trying. Even at his mother's funeral, two years earlier, his father had refused to talk. For Antonio, that was the final straw. Of course, he tried to seek advice – his mentor and long-time friend Bishop Jean-Louis Bouchard even suggested that a little time off would provide an ideal opportunity to try again. But, after numerous attempts and subsequent failures, even Bouchard finally accepted to the reality that Antonio's best efforts would never be enough and that he would find a better resolution through prayer, meditation and his work.

Although he was young, Antonio's knowledge and skill in mathematics had gained him much respect within the inner sanctum of the Vatican's hierarchy and as the years progressed, his reputation finally paid off as he was rewarded with access to the Holy See's most treasured artefacts, the Vatican secret archives. As his computer finally flickered into life, he logged into the Vatican network and opened up his email account. After a few moments, scores of emails began to populate his inbox. Most were fairly routine – Mass schedules, network maintenance, or requests from junior clergy requesting unedited copies of his most recent article, *Understanding Christ through Symbols*, which appeared in last months *Inside the Vatican* magazine.

There was even a request for lunch from an old school friend, Dario Cotronei. As he was about to log out, an unexpected email grasped his attention.

To: DemarcoA@asv.va
From: Richard.Quest@homeoffice.gsi.gov.uk
Subject: Symbol Identification Request
Status: Confidential

Father Antonio

My name is Doctor Richard Quest. I am a science advisor
with Her Majesty's government based in London. I am aware
of your expertise in historical and ancient Symbology and
wondered if I could ask you for help in identifying the enclosed
graphic. It is a piece of parchment that came into our possession a few days ago. Thus far the symbols and writing remain
incomprehensible to my team. If you could kindly take a look at
the enclosed and respond with your feedback as soon as possible it would be greatly appreciated.

Kind regards

R Quest PHD, MSc
United Kingdom Home Office

Even as a child, Antonio loved a challenge and this would definitely
fall into that category. Leaning back into his seat, he pondered over
the email, before double clicking the attachment. As the symbols
appeared, Antonio's mouth dropped, "Mio Dio!"

Suddenly his adrenaline levels spiked and he sprang forward to
switch on an adjacent printer and proceeded to print two copies
of the symbols. He always printed two copies of anything that
he considered to be of importance. This was a habit he picked
up while in college. His friend Dario Cotronei used to call him
"*spendaccione* Antonio" or "Wasteful Antonio" as often he would
just end up throwing the second copy away.

Shutting his laptop down, he hurriedly placed it inside his
rather worn leather satchel, took his jacket off the peg and put it
on. Then grabbing the papers from the mouth of the printer, he
stuffed them into his pocket and rushed for the door.

Pulling the handle, he stopped in mid motion, closed the door
and retrieved his mobile phone from his desks top draw. Scrolling

through his list of contacts, he eventually stopped at Vescovo Jean-Louis Bouchard and pressed the call button. After a few moments, the call was answered. The voice of an elderly woman said, "*Sì?*"

"*Vescovo Bouchard per cortesia.*"

"*Temo, che il Vescovo sia andato a servire messa.*"

Glancing at his watch the time now read 6.31am. "*Diamine!*" Antonio thought. He was meant to be serving Mass with the Bishop in 30 minutes. But, somehow, he had to get out of it. Surely if he explained the situation, his friend would understand. "*Grazie signora.*"

After thanking the Bishop's housekeeper, Antonio placed the phone inside his jacket pocket and bolted out the door. Once out into the corridor he ran off, gathering speed.

At the end of his floor he continued at top speed down two flights of stairs, almost knocking over two elderly priests on their way to mass. After stopping briefly to apologise, he sped off once more into the early morning sunshine.

Five minutes of dodging members of the public and early morning clergy and Antonio arrived at the Church of Sant' Anna dei Palafrenieri. He moved quickly through the magnificent building in an attempt to locate Bouchard. Serving Mass in Vignola's masterpiece was, in his opinion, not only a great honour but also a deeply spiritual and humbling experience.

Today, however, his mind was focused firmly on other matters. Opening the heavy door to the vestry, he sighed in relief as he was greeted by his mentor, Bishop Jean-Louis Bouchard. "*Buongiorno* Antonio, I was beginning to think that perhaps you'd forgotten my friend."

As he opened his mouth to respond, the door opened behind him and three middle-aged altar servers appeared and Antonio was forced to remain silent.

"*Signori buongiorno.*"

Nodding in respect the three spoke almost in unison, first to

Antonio and then to the Bishop, "*Buona giornata Padre buono, Buona giornata sua grazia.*"

Moving quickly to the corner of the room, the three servers began to assemble the various items that would be required for the morning's service. As Bouchard appeared to have finished preparing himself for the service, Antonio stepped across and attempted to discretely grasp his mentor's attention.

"*Avrei bisogno di parlare con sua grazia.*"

Turning his head, Bouchard smiled, "Of course Antonio, is everything alright my friend?"

"*Sì*, I mean, yes your Grace, I was wondering if I could ask a small favour of you?"

Briefly glancing at the three men, who had finished their preparations and were now in the process of leaving the room. As the large heavy door closed behind them, Antonio sighed and pulled out the folded printouts from inside his jacket pocket and handed them to the bishop. "Of course my friend, what is it?"

"Jean-Louis, would you be deeply offended if I asked to be excused from Mass this morning?"

For a moment the Bishop looked puzzled, "No, of course not, but, has something happened?"

"If you take a look at those, you may begin to understand."

Unfolding the documents, Bouchard first read the email from Doctor Quest and then gazed in amazement at the symbols on the second sheet.

"I ... I see what you mean. Do you think you can decipher these?"

"I don't know. However, I'm sure I've seen something like it before, but the trouble is I can't remember where. I figured that perhaps the library would be a good place to start. That's where I wanted to go now. But, if you need me for Mass ..."

Bouchard shook his head, "No, my friend, of course it's fine. I'll manage here. Let's meet up later and perhaps we can discuss your findings."

Nodding enthusiastically, Antonio shook the Bishop's hand, *"Grazie amico mio, apprezzo molto e sono in debito per questo."*

At that moment, the large door at the corner of the vestry opened once more and the three altar servers re-entered the room and gave a nod in the Bishop's direction, *"E' arrivata l'ora Vostra Grazia."*

"Grazie, fate strada."

Antonio discretely slipped out of the church via a side entrance and proceeded to walk across the courtyard towards the Vatican Library.

On arrival at the *Archivio Segreto Vaticano*, Antonio headed directly to the Leone XIII Index room and handed an unusually long list of requirements to the elderly counter clerk, who gave the young priest an annoyed glance as he disappeared to search for the requested materials.

After what seemed to Antonio to be hours, but in reality was probably only minutes, the clerk returned carrying a huge pile of books and documents. Feeling slightly embarrassed at asking the elderly man to locate such a long list so early in the morning, Antonio grasped half the pile and apologised for the inconvenience. He was then escorted up the adjoining marble staircase to the *Sisto V* reading rooms, where he was finally led into one of the small adjacent private rooms normally reserved for staff or for papal use. Antonio reached inside his jacket pocket, retrieved the email from Quest and spread the sheet containing the unknown symbols on the desk.

He took a seat and started to flick through the various volumes in an attempt to identify not only from which point in history these symbols perhaps originated, but more importantly, just what was the message they were trying to convey.

THIRTY SIX

THERE WAS SOMETHING wrong. After taking a sharp intake of breath, Wilkes opened his eyes and slowly exhaled. His mother always said that her "Robbie had a sixth sense".

What she meant exactly he was not entirely sure, but he definitely sensed that something here was not right. Reaching across to a small side table, he picked up his watch to check the time, 05.55am. Placing the watch on his wrist, he unzipped his sleeping bag and swung his legs out on to the cool wooden floor. Sitting up straight he rubbed his eyes and for a moment and sat quite still before reaching across to a pile of clothes and got dressed.

After slipping his shoes on he reached under the bed, fumbling for a moment in an attempt to locate the black leather briefcase given to him by Corporal Jarvis. Once retrieved, he opened it and took out the 9mm M&P Compact pistol, briefly checked the weapon and placed it discretely under his black Nike sweatshirt. With his sense of unease growing, he stood and quietly opened the door and stepped out into the hallway. His first thoughts were that he should make a sweep of the area and, as such, he headed for the lighthouse's tower. Climbing up the rusting spiral staircase, he stepped off on to the top platform where the view that greeted him was quite different to the previous night.

The storm was over and the last remnants of any dark cloud

were giving way to a more promising looking day. From this high position, Wilkes could not only see for miles but it was also a good vantage point to systematically scan each of Rua Reidh's out buildings for signs of life. Looking below, an earlier ferocious sea had given way to more placid looking waters and the dangerous craggy cliffs looked a little less intimidating in the daylight.

From his current position, everything seemed to be in order. Even so, he decided that perhaps it wouldn't do any harm to take a closer look. So cautiously and quietly he made his way back down the staircase. Before venturing outside, he glanced into the adjacent bedroom where Kate was still sleeping. Everything seemed quiet and normal, but Wilkes continued to feel uneasy. He even thought about making a call to his office with the satellite phone, but shrugging the idea off, he realised that it would take at least an hour for any help to arrive. "No", he told himself. There was no point being alarmist, just because he had a "gut feeling".

Unlocking the front door, Wilkes stepped out into the morning sunshine and closed the door behind. Now that he was outside, he was impressed, not just at the overall size and number of buildings that the site enjoyed, but also, to Tom Duncan's credit, at how well the lighthouse had been maintained. Bright whitewashed walls and recently painted doors gave the impression that the Duncan family had visited recently and that for Tom, this was perhaps a labour of love.

To his right, he could see the raised single-track road that led back towards Melvaig and to his left, the path that continued downwards out of sight – no doubt to the small jetty.. Taking a deep breath, Wilkes stealthily continued his slow and methodical walk around each of the outhouses, occasionally stopping briefly to peer through a window. His inspection had thus far revealed nothing, however his sense of unease remained. The third door he approached had a small brass plate attached to the wall adjacent to the door that read Generator Room. Trying the door, Wilkes was surprised to find that it was unlocked.

As the door swung open, he reached under his sweatshirt and pulled out the M&P pistol. Glancing inside the room, nothing looked out of place and he was about to close the door when out of the corner of his eye he spotted a small navy blue rucksack lying on the ground, next to one of the large diesel generators. Holding the pistol at arm's length, Wilkes held his breath and edged slowly into the room. The room appeared to be otherwise empty. He slowly walked across to where the bag was lying, then, kneeling on one knee, he cautiously began to pull open its drawstring laces.

The blow seemed to come from nowhere! For Wilkes it felt like he had been hit with a hammer. Reeling forward in pain, he crumpled to the ground. The gun flew out of his hand and rebounded off the floor, eventually coming to rest underneath one of the large generators. Struggling to focus, Wilkes raised his head and gazed in horror at the familiar sneering figure now standing above him in the doorway.

"So the policeman, we meet again."

Spluttering blood, Wilkes coughed, "You? But how?"

The intruder looked down at Wilkes with an empty, cruel gaze as if he was nothing more than a wounded animal squirming for survival. Then, with a twisted smirk he raised his weapon and hissed, "How many?"

His mouth filling with blood, Wilkes spluttered, "Just the three of us."

"And the woman?"

Wilkes wheezed and gave a reluctant nod, "Inside … she's inside."

With a sense of cruel satisfaction the intruder lowered his weapon and sneered, "Perfect. Thank you, you've been very helpful."

The man raised his leg and brought his heavy booted foot smashing down into the side of Wilkes' head, causing the MI5 officer to pass out. Then, calmly and carefully, the intruder dragged his limp body into a position where it would not be easily discovered. With one final check of the generator room, he cautiously stepped outside, checked that the door was closed and then slipped silently away, feeling somewhat smug with the knowledge that his final goal was now within easy grasp.

6.30AM MI5 HEADQUARTERS: THAMES HOUSE, LONDON

CLAIRE HAMMOND WAS tired, overworked and underpaid. At least that's how she felt after working for 13 hours straight without a break. Claire, a 24-year-old junior analyst, had joined MI5 as a graduate from the University of York. At the university's milk round she had been both excited and intrigued at the thought of working as a "spy".

Well, as she found out the hard way, being a junior analyst is a far cry from the pages of an Ian Fleming novel. Unfortunately for her, there were no exotic locations, no gadgets and definitely no encounters with tall mysterious strangers. For the past 13 hours, Claire had been instructed to do nothing more than to analyse the phone records for *The Daily Chronicle*. Initially, and rather foolishly, she assumed that the apparent simple task would only be a two or three day job at most. She was horrified to discover that the actual number of calls involved was enormous, meaning that she would be staring at her computer screen and listening to dull recordings for many more days to come. Giving her tired eyes a rest from the screen, she stretched her arms out and yawned. Then leaning across her desk, she retrieved a half-finished cup of coffee and placed it to her lips. After talking a sip she grimaced, it was cold. Placing the cup aside, she rubbed her eyes, got to her feet and walked to a nearby vending machine.

After briefly pausing to survey the drinks menu, she ignored the alternatives and decided to go with a cup of "old faithful". Slipping a paper cup out from the dispenser, she placed it into position and punched in 26A, her "survival code", as she called it. Extra white coffee with no sugar – guaranteed to keep you going. Well at least that's what she told herself.

Returning to her desk, she placed the cup down and retook her seat. Like many large media companies, *The Chronicle* had a policy of recording both incoming and outgoing calls.

This was in most cases documented as for "security and training purposes". As well as trudging through seemingly endless logs of phone numbers and cross-referencing them against databases of known criminal organisations, she was also on the lookout for anything irregular that might provide clues as to why Harding and her team had been targeted in such a brutal way.

So far she had drawn a blank and as she brought up record number 507 she feared that this record would be no different. "*Daily Chronicle* Call Log – Record Number 507: Date / Time Index: Saturday – 13.20pm." As she scrolled through the call log, she noticed a sound file. Reaching across she picked up her headphones, placed them over her ears and clicked play. Most of the calls she had listened to were dull and fairly routine. However, from the outset, she knew this one was going to be different.

"Yes, Hello."

"Kate is that you?"

"Gert, what is it? What's wrong?"

"It's Robert ... he's been shot ... Kate ... oh my God, he's dead."

"Gert ... what are you saying ... he was just here yesterday."

"That meeting Kate ... in Schwetzingen. You know, the supposedly big story he's been working on."

"I ..."

"For God's sake Kate, he's been murdered; along with the guy he was meeting. What the hell was he working on?"

"I'm sorry Gert ... I ... can't talk anymore ... I'll speak to you later okay?"

The highly emotional call ended and Claire sat motionless, somewhat shocked at what she had just heard. Replaying the recording twice, she indexed the call as coming from the office of the newspaper's editor, Kate Harding. Sitting back for a moment, she pondered over the recording and remembered that this had been in the news only days earlier. Perhaps if she searched for related calls and cross-referenced the results it would provide additional clues as to possible motives. Claire always prided herself on her eye for detail. Indeed, before joining the service, she seriously considered an investigative or forensics career with the police, but the "romance" of working for the security service won her over. Now, unfortunately her current analytical post keeps any aspirations that she may have had firmly in check.

Clicking into the search box, she typed in Kate Harding, Editor, and refined the search criteria to include senior staff and known associates. Then as she clicked the search option, she picked up her coffee, took a sip and sat back waiting for the results to appear.

"Good morning ... Miss Hammond, isn't it?"

"Huh?"

Turning her head somewhat taken aback, that anyone apart from her team would be in the office so early, let alone a member of senior management actually knowing her name. Gazing upwards, she was surprised to see it was her boss, Deputy Director Robert Marshall.

That is, he was actually her boss's boss. She, of course, knew of Marshall, but had never actually met the man in person. In her position, it was far more likely that he would consort with senior staff rather than her directly. "Er yes, good morning, Sir."

To her further surprise, meeting the middle-aged Deputy Director was not entirely as she imagined. Firstly, he had spoken to her! A lowly, junior member of staff and secondly he actually smiled at her.

"Now Miss Hammond, please tell me that you haven't been here all night, have you?"

"Yes Sir, I'm afraid so … I was working on something and I … I guess I must have got carried away."

Marshall looked intrigued, "What on earth could possibly keep a young woman like you at her desk for so long?"

"Well Sir, I was instructed to work my way through *The Chronicle*'s call logs in the hope of shedding some light on the recent deaths."

"Yes, I'm afraid you have me to thank for that one. I'd been contacted by the Home Secretary and instructed to start an investigation."

"I see."

"So tell me, have you discovered anything relevant?"

Looking at the smartly dressed Director she shook her head in defeat, "No Sir, Not yet." Reaching inside his jacket pocket, Marshall pulled out a silver business card holder, opened it and handed a card to the young analyst.

"I understand, but if you discover anything of relevance, please let me know immediately. There's a lot people interested in this one."

Claire nodded, "Of course, Sir."

As Marshall walked away towards an elevator, she turned back to her computer, which had now completed the search and was displaying the results, including two entries for the previous day. Picking up her headphones, she proceeded to record number 612. "*Daily Chronicle* Call Log – Record Number 612: Date / Time Index: Monday – 19.50pm." Glancing through the record, she again spotted a sound file. So after placing the headphones over her ears and taking a farther sip of coffee, she placed the cup down and clicked the on play button. After a moment of silence the playback began.

"Bill, its Kate Harding."

"Miss Harding … Is everything all right? Everyone's been so worried."

"Thanks Bill, I don't suppose Amanda Harris is still in the office is she?"

"No, I'm afraid not, she went to see her mother. Apparently her house was damaged in the quake and she's gone to spend a few days with her. Can I give her a message?"

"Yes okay, please tell her that I'm still working on that story and I will need a few days longer, I hope she can manage."

"Can I say where you can be contacted?"

"I'll be staying at a lighthouse in Melvaig. It's about 2 hours northwest of Inverness."

"I see!"

"Now Bill, you will tell her where I am and not to worry?"

"Oh yes Miss Harding, I'll make sure she gets the message. Goodbye."

"Goodbye Bill, and thank you."

The phone clicked and the recording ended. Taking off her headphones, she entered a note to say that in her opinion the call was within standard operational parameters and contained no evidence of any criminal intent. After saving and closing the record, she continued on to entry number 613. After double clicking the entry, there was a short pause before the record appeared. "*Daily Chronicle* Call Log – Record Number 613: Date / Time Index: Monday – 19.56pm." After reviewing the log it became apparent that the call was made to a mobile.

"Yes?"

"Brooks, its Peterson. When were you going to tell me what happened today?"

"Sorry?"

"Sorry! You had simple instructions, what happened?"

"It was complicated. The place was crawling with police and military. I was discovered and had to break off, now unfortunately they've been moved to an undisclosed location. Don't worry, it's only a matter of time before I find her."

"Time, unfortunately is the one thing we don't have. But fortunately for you, she just called in. So I suppose it's lucky that she suspects nothing."

"So where is she?"

"She's in the process of being moved to a safe house."

"Safe house?"

"Yes, and to a fairly remote place. Rua Reidh Lighthouse, it's perfect. It's about two hours north west of Inverness, ideal for a man of your skills. However I'm sure she will be protected, but I assume this won't be a problem?"

For a moment the recording remained silent. Then a cold voice responded, "No … It's not a problem. I'll take care of it."

The recording ended on a chilling note, and Claire sat white faced and somewhat stunned at what she had just heard.

"Jesus!" she whispered.

As her heart began to race she glanced at the date / time index of the recording and realised that the call was placed only hours earlier. Her colleagues would not arrive for at least another hour. She had to do something, but what?

For a moment she struggled with the idea of contacting Marshall. What if she was wrong? She could lose her job for not adhering to correct protocols or wasting the Deputy Director's time. On the other hand, not informing him could be just as serious.

"No, don't be bloody ridiculous," she told herself confidently. This was critical information and under the circumstances she was sure that he would agree. Lifting up a pile of papers, she retrieved the deputy's business card from underneath, picked up her telephone handset and carefully dialled his number.

After short pause the call was answered, "This is Marshall."

"Sir, its Claire Hammond."

"Claire, I had no idea we would be speaking so soon. What

can I do for you?" Thinking carefully on how to phrase her next statement, she cleared her throat and continued. "Sir, you said that if I discovered something pertinent that I should contact you. Well I think I have."

"What have you found?"

Claire sighed, "Sir, I think it would be easier to explain if you just came to me."

There was a short pause and Marshall continued, "Of course, just give me a couple of minutes and I'll be right down."

"Yes Sir."

Placing the handset down, Claire stood and feeling slightly flustered, began to quickly tidy her desk, feeling almost as it was her flat and her parents were coming to visit for the first time. Just as she had finished stuffing the last few sheets of paper into the top draw of her desk, the elevator "pinged" behind her, indicating Marshall's arrival. As she sat down, the elevator doors slid smoothly open and the smartly dressed Deputy Director strode confidently out.

"Okay young lady, let's see what you've got."

Standing, Claire sighed and offered her seat to the deputy.

"Sir, if you'll take a seat, there's something I need you to listen to."

As Marshall sat down, Clair leaned over, lifted her headphones and handed them to the deputy who duly placed them over his ears, then, locating entry the first call she clicked the playback button. Marshall listened intently to the call. When complete, he nodded and Claire proceeded to open the next file. As the recording played, Marshall's relaxed expression fell away and his face turned to a distinct shade of grey. For a horrible moment Claire thought that he was about to throw up. Thankfully to her relief he didn't. As the recording finished he slipped off the headphones, placed them onto the desk and stood up.

"Christ! Wilkes is up there all alone."

"Sir?"

"Robert Wilkes, Claire, he's one of ours."

To Claire, the scene appeared to explode. Marshall sprang towards Claire's phone, picking up the receiver he punched in a number and waited to be connected.

"Colonel, its Robert Marshall. I'm afraid the cat's out of the bag and they've been discovered. Please scramble an extraction team immediately."

Watching Marshall carefully, Claire sighed, feeling somewhat relieved to have made the correct decision. As the conversation continued, Claire watched and listened intently as Marshall's face began to flush red and his voice became sharp with anger and apparent frustration.

"Two hours? Sir, with all due respect, it could be too late by then. We need that team up there and we need them now."

Slamming the handset down, Marshall turned to Claire and gave a nod, "Well done Claire, you've just earned yourself a promotion. I just hope we're not too late."

"Sir?"

Marshall shook his head, "Get your team in Claire. This is priority number one, understand."

"Yes Sir, but my ... team Sir?"

Marshall rolled his eyes and strode quickly across to the elevator and pressed the call button. As the door slid open he gave her a sly smirk and yelled out, "That's right Miss Hammond, Your team! Get them in now!"

THIRTY SEVEN

TUESDAY: 7.10AM RUA REIDH LIGHTHOUSE, MELVAIG, SCOTLAND

"**K**ATE. LASSIE, WAKE up."

Kate's eye's slowly flickered open to see the tall, silhouetted figure of Dougie Allan standing above her. As she opened her mouth to speak, Dougie shook his head and placed a forefinger to his lips, indicating to her to remain quiet. Then he whispered, "Lassie, Wilkes is missing, you'd better get dressed."

She nodded and Dougie turned his head away. Swinging her legs out of bed, Kate grabbed her clothes and quickly got dressed as instructed. Once fully clothed she whispered, "Okay Dougie, I'm ready. What now?"

Quietly opening the bedroom door, Dougie peered carefully into the hallway and then motioned her to follow him. "First things first lassie, let's find Mr Wilkes, he may need our help."

Nodding in agreement Kate stood and followed Dougie into the deserted hallway.

After taking a few moments to check inside the various rooms for any sign of Wilkes, the pair then made their way towards the front door. However, as the door swung open Dougie froze and Kate gave a stifled scream. Standing in front of them was the cold, sneering face of Brooks.

"The costumed Scotsman, I told you I'd see you again."

Dougie glared at the intruder and his gun and snarled, "Aye, ye did laddie, but if ye had any kind of honour, you'd put that weapon away and fight me like a real man. That's if ye have the guts."

Brooks' smirk fell away as he glared at Dougie and hissed, "Don't test me Scotsman, my argument isn't with you, it's with her. Now, step aside!"

As he spoke he stepped backwards, motioning Dougie with his gun to move away. With Kate continuing to cling to his arm, Dougie realised that there was no point negotiating with a man like this, a man, in his opinion, without soul or honour. He had but one chance to escape, separate the man from the gun.

"I beg tae differ Sir, but if ye think I'm going simply step aside and watch ye kill an innocent lassie then you're out of your bloody mind. Nae laddie, if ye want her, you'll have tae come through me first."

A cruel smirk appeared on his face, like a sly fox luring in its prey, Brooks slowly lowered his weapon and grinned. "A challenge? Well, I was going to kill you quickly, but I agree, this way would be far more enjoyable."

In a somewhat surprising move, he holstered his weapon. For Dougie and Kate, any initial relief was short lived, as from behind his back he now brandished a large and very sharp looking blade.

Kate screamed out, "Who are you? Why are you doing this?"

Dougie released Kate's arm and shoved her back towards the doorway.

"Kate, get inside and lock the door."

Before he could finish, Kate screamed as Brooks suddenly sprang at Dougie lashing out at him with such force, that Dougie lost his balance and was sent reeling backwards crumpling to the ground in agony. As the sneering Brooks moved in for the kill, Dougie yelled out, "Get inside!" and quickly rolled away, just as Brooks' foot came smashing down on the ground where his head had been only a moment earlier.

Kate wasted no time and bolted for the doorway, but as she

scrambled to close the door, Brooks leapt at her. With his full body weight, he came crashing through the doorway sending her hurtling forwards into a wall. As she slumped to the floor, she screamed out in terror as he grabbed her ankle from behind and hissed, "Time's up!"

As he raised the knife, to deliver his final blow, Kate somehow managed to kick her way free and landed a devastating blow to his face with her foot causing his nose to explode.

Bloody and in agony, Brooks howled in pain and released her. Taking advantage of her split second of freedom, she quickly scrambled to her feet and ran forward towards the lighthouse's tower. As she franticly began to climb the rusting spiral staircase, she could hear his footsteps getting ever closer, his blade clanging and scraping threateningly against the metal staircase as he roared at her chillingly, "I'm going to kill you, you bitch."

On reaching the upper platform, she scrambled onto the floor, desperately looking for something … anything that she could use as a potential weapon. But, as Brooks' blooded face appeared at the stairwell opening, Kate realised there was no escape and absolutely nothing that she could do. As he rose up towards her, she cowered on the opposite side of the huge lamp and closed her eyes waiting for her, now seemingly inevitable fate.

As he moved in for the kill, his smug expression suddenly fell away as he yelled out in shock. A hand suddenly appeared from below and grabbed his foot causing him to lose balance and come crashing down, face first onto the deck. Astonished at still being alive, Kate opened her eyes and watched stunned as Brooks' knife spun uncontrollably out of his hand and fell harmlessly away down the iron staircase. Without thinking, Kate saw an opportunity to escape and scrambled to her feet.

Darting towards the staircase, she clambered past the bewildered intruder, narrowly escaping his grappling hand. Seeing Dougie's head suddenly appear at the top of the staircase made her cry out in relief, "Dougie, help me!"

He quickly moved aside and yelled out, "Quick lassie, this way."

Wasting no time, she carefully manoeuvred past him and franticly made her way downwards. As she disappeared along the hallway, Dougie yelled after her, "Kate! Find somewhere tae hide."

As Dougie began to climb down, the enraged Brooks screamed in fury and suddenly spun around, kicking Dougie squarely on the right shoulder sending him tumbling down the spiral staircase. Landing in a stunned heap on the floor he opened his eyes to discover the intruder's knife on the floor frighteningly close to the side of his head. Hastily reaching across, he grasped hold of the handle, picked himself up and ran off down the hallway. Snorting like an enraged bull, the injured Brooks wasted no time in getting to his feet and scrambling down the staircase. Rushing out of the doorway with a callous expression on his face he bellowed, "There's nowhere to hide, I'll find you."

His mistake, he now realised was to "play with them", rather than doing what he should have done in the first place, which was to simply kill them quickly and get it over with. Tilting his head back for a moment to quash the flow of blood from his nose, he reached inside his jacket, unclipped his leather holster and pulled out his Double Eagle pistol, checked the weapon and stomped off, determined to put an end to this once and for all.

The military helicopter roared above the early morning, Highland countryside. Inside the cabin the red-headed Corporal Jarvis sat alongside three other heavily armed members of his handpicked extraction team. Biting his nails, he leaned across to the co-pilot and shouted "C'mon man, can't this bloody thing go any faster?"

Turning to face Jarvis the young pilot shook his head, "We're doing our best Corporal. There are currently air traffic restrictions in progress and …"

Jarvis shook his head and barked, "Restrictions? Look man I

don't care if you've been ordered to slow down by God himself, I'm telling you right here and now that if you don't push this bird to the max, I'll shoot you myself. Do I make myself clear?"

Nodding nervously the youngster stammered, "I, I understand. I'll do my best."

"Can you give me an ETA?"

The officer glanced at the instrument panel, and then back to the Corporal, "About 40 minutes."

Jarvis rolled his eyes, "Forty minutes? In 40 minutes, they could all be dead. You have to give me more."

Nodding the pilot sighed, "Like I said, I'll do my best Sir."

Sweating heavily and feeling sick, Kate huddled nervously behind one of the smaller out buildings. Then scrambling behind what appeared to be an external storeroom, she edged slowly along to the corner of the building and gradually positioned herself to where she had a clear view of out front. Suddenly, she froze in terror as about twenty meters away, the blooded angry face of the intruder reappeared.

Swiftly, she edged backwards and remained absolutely still. Panting heavily, she closed her eyes in a desperate attempt to calm her nerves and slow down her breathing. Then to her relief, she heard his footsteps move away. Once sure that he was gone, she decided that it was time to find an alternative hiding place. Opening her eyes she moved quickly out from behind the wall, occasionally stopping to glimpse inside the small windows of the adjacent whitewashed buildings. She checked each door to see if it was unlocked. Unfortunately, to her disappointment, most were not, except the last one. Glancing at a small brass plate that read Generator Room, Kate took a deep breath, turned the handle and swung the door open.

Stepping inside, the room appeared to be empty apart from three large oil drums and a couple of rather ancient looking diesel generators. Stepping forward, her expression suddenly turned to one of horror – lying just behind the door was the badly bruised body of Robert Wilkes. "Oh my God!"

Quickly closing the door, she knelt in front of the young MI5 officer and began to search for signs of life. "Mr Wilkes … Robert, are you okay?"

With Wilkes unresponsive, she tried desperately to recall her basic first aid training from the girl guides.

"Er, ABC, er, Airway … Breathing … Chest."

Repeating to herself over and over, she then placed two fingers on Wilkes's seemingly lifeless wrist to check for a pulse. Her heart leapt as she felt the first definite signs of life. Breathing a sigh of relief she muttered, "He's alive!"

She realised that there was nothing she could do now except find Dougie and help him. After all he had saved her life twice now and she owed him at least the effort of trying.

Rising with a new sense of purpose and renewed determination, she made her way back to the door, opened it and stepped carefully outside. Unfortunately, even before she took another step, Kate sensed that it was somehow too late. "So, Miss Harding, I see you found the policeman."

The voice was cold and unemotional. Turning to face him, she was already coming to terms with her now seemingly unavoidable fate. Behind the doorway, deliberately waiting for her was the hideous blood stained, sneering face of the intruder. "Now, you didn't actually think I was simply going to let you go did you?"

Slowly shaking her head, she swallowed hard and whispered, "No."

Smirking like a crazed Cheshire cat, Brooks appeared elated with himself. Now he could finally put an end to this whole troublesome affair. Raising the gun barrel to her temple, he hissed, "Where's the other one?"

Kate swallowed, desperately trying to remain composed and at the same time hold back her tears. "I don't know."

Gritting his teeth, Brooks pushed the tip of the silencer harder against her head, "Don't lie to me bitch. Where is he?"

With a tear rolling down her cheek, she sniffed, "I don't know, I swear it."

Brooks seemed satisfied that she was telling the truth and relaxed the pressure of the barrel against her head. Licking his lips, he pondered if he should just kill her here and get it over with, or should he use her as bait to lure in the Scotsman. After a moment, he concluded on the latter. "Turn around."

As Kate turned, he placed the gun to the back of her head and barked, "Move!"

He marched her whimpering and white faced down towards the small concrete jetty. Her eyes frantically darted across the terrain for signs of her tartan-clad hero. But, as they approached the end of the walkway she felt that now more than ever that she was truly alone and that no one was going to save her this time.

"Stop there."

With the tide out, the dark rocks below looked more ominous and dangerous than ever, Kate took a deep breath and closed her eyes in preparation for the inevitable. Aiming the gun directly at her head, Brooks sneered, "Call for him. Call for him now."

Taking another breath, Kate yelled out, "D ... Dougie, help me!"

Brooks lost patience and pushed the gun harder against the back of Kate's skull. "Well Harding, it appears your hero won't be coming to save you today. Goodbye!"

The knife flew through the air like a flash and struck Brooks in the upper right shoulder. Falling to his knees, Brooks screamed out in agony.

The force of the knife entering his flesh felt like an electric shock forcing the gun to fly out of his hand and fall onto the rocks below. Turning his head, Brooks looked on in disbelief as Dougie leapt out from behind a rock like a giant bird about to snatch up its prey. Landing on top of Brooks, Dougie smashed his fist into the he intruders face.

"That's for Tom and his family and this one's for Kate."

The second blow struck Brooks clean on the cheek and he howled in furious pain. As Dougie raised his hand for a third blow, Kate screamed as Brooks suddenly leaned forward and head butted Dougie with such force that it sent him reeling backwards onto the ground. Then with all of his strength, Brooks reached behind and grasped the handle of the knife. Then taking a deep breath he quickly pulled out the blade causing him to let out another furious howl.

As Dougie struggled to his feet, Brooks lunged with the blade but, luckily for Dougie, he stepped backwards just in time, narrowly missing what could have been a fatal blow. Then Brooks came at him again, but as he swung the blade this time, Dougie was ready. As the blade swished past his chest, Dougie stepped forward and swung his fist hard. For Brooks, the blow was dreadful.

The knife flew out of his hands and he reeled backwards onto the edge of the jetty. Before he could scramble to his feet, Dougie was already towering above him. Grasping hold of the intruder by the scruff of the neck, Dougie growled, "And this one's from me."

Dougie swung his fist and struck the intruder in the cheek. Brooks, stunned and disorientated suddenly lost his footing and slipped on a loose rock. His twisted, cruel smirk fell away and was replaced by a grotesque expression of shock as he tumbled like a rag doll over the edge onto the rocks below.

As Kate burst into tears, Dougie ran across and took her into his arms.

"Kate. Kate its okay, it's over now. He's dead."

She didn't speak, but merely embraced him tightly, sobbing into his chest.

"I thought I was going to die."

Stroking her hair, Dougie raised her head with his large hand, smiled and said, "Shhh, it's okay now. He can't hurt ye anymore."

Softly kissing her cheek, he released her and turned his head towards the jetty for one final glimpse of the intruder. However, his relief abruptly turned to shock as there was no sign of the body on the rocks below.

"Fools, did you honestly believe you could win?"

Whirling around, Dougie and Kate's mouths fell open in dismay as there, standing in front of them, was the blooded, snarling face of the intruder, complete with his pistol pointed directly at them. Turning to face Kate, Dougie's head dropped and he whispered, "I'm sorry lass, at least we tried."

Taking Dougie's hand she shook her head, "Don't be, it's my fault, I'm the one who should be sorry."

"You know this is all very touching, but I've a schedule to keep and thanks to you I'm right on-time. Goodbye and good riddance."

Closing their eyes in expectation, Kate squeezed Dougie's hand.

Suddenly, three loud shots rang out and Dougie opened his eyes in surprise. They were both still alive! Then as he glanced at the spot where the intruder had stood, his heart leapt as there, lying on the ground, was the bullet-riddled body of the intruder. Behind him, standing with a raised pistol was a bruised, but thankfully alive Robert Wilkes.

Sighing in relief, Wilkes lowered his weapon, walked across to the intruder's body and kicked his gun away. Stooping low, he placed two fingers on his neck and gazed up at the couple, nodding with a sense of quiet satisfaction with the knowledge that it was finally over. "He's dead."

Exhaling with relief, Kate smiled, "Thank you."

Wilkes acknowledged Kate with a nod and then glanced across at Dougie and cleared his throat.

"Dougie, perhaps it would be best to take her inside."

"Aye lad, but will ye be alright?"

Wilkes sighed and gave a weak smile, "Yes thanks, don't worry about me I've had much worse."

Dougie escorted Kate back to the safety of the Keeper's cottage.

Once out of sight, Wilkes picked up the intruders weapon and began to thoroughly search through his clothes, looking for something, anything that might give him a clue as to who this man was and why he had so brutally targeted Harding and her team at *The Daily Chronicle.*

Reaching inside Brooks' left pocket, Wilkes retrieved the man's brown leather wallet. Flicking through its contents, there was nothing immediately obvious, a few pounds, driver's licence and a couple of credit cards. Just as he was about to close the wallet, he found what appeared to be a hidden compartment. Lifting out the credit card section, he noticed a small zip and opened it. Inside, were two additional plastic cards –a United States issued American Express credit card and a United States identity card.

Wilkes almost choked, as he realised the card clearly identified the dead man as David James Brooks, an employee of the United States Central Intelligence Agency,

Along with the wallet, Wilkes also recovered the Colt pistol, address book and a mobile phone. Picking up the items, Wilkes made his way back up towards the lighthouse. As he approached the doorway of the Keeper's cottage, the tranquil August silence was shattered with a deafening roar from the sudden appearance of a military helicopter overhead. As it landed, four heavily armed soldiers leapt out and ran towards him.

Behind, the cottage door swung open and a somewhat bewildered Dougie and Kate stepped out to stand alongside Wilkes. Wilkes gave a sigh as he recognised the squad's leader, Corporal Jarvis,

"Are you folks okay?"

Glancing across at Dougie and Kate, the bruised and somewhat battered Wilkes nodded, "Yes, but there's a body on the jetty. Perhaps you can take care of it."

Jarvis nodded in acknowledgment and spun around to face his companions, "Stephens, Davies, see to it will you."

"Aye Sir,"

Nodding, the two youngsters turned heel and ran off in the direction of the jetty. Turning back to Wilkes Jarvis continued, "Sir, apart from the rescue, I've also been ordered to take Mr Allan and Miss Harding to Inverness airport. You are, of course, welcome to join them."

"Airport?"

Glancing first at Wilkes and then across at Dougie he grinned, "The Prime Minister has asked for these two to join him at the upcoming Icelandic summit."

Dougie's mouth fell open, "Iceland, but why?"

Jarvis shook his head, "I don't know Sir, all I've been told is that No. 10 has arranged for a flight to Reykjavik for the three of you and we have to transport you to Inverness as soon as possible. So if you want to get cleaned up and gather your belongings, we can get going as soon as you're ready."

As instructed, Dougie and Kate turned and walked away to collect their things. As Wilkes was about to walk away, he stopped, turned and returned to where the Corporal was standing. "Corporal, I have to contact my office urgently regarding this incident. This case is a little more complicated than I had anticipated."

THIRTY EIGHT

"**Y**ES MR WILKES … I understand, I'll run a report and get back to you as soon as possible. Thank you, goodbye."

Replacing the handset, Claire Hammond sat back, stretched out her arms and rubbed her eyes. Working for 14-hours straight had begun to take its toll and she was exhausted. But, in her opinion, to leave now would not only be inappropriate but also potentially career ending, especially in the light of her recent promotion. Having found an apparent mole within *The Daily Chronicle*, she was intrigued to discover exactly what this deadly relationship was between the brutal David James Brooks, the *Chronicle*'s Bill Peterson and the CIA.

Turning to her computer, she entered Bill Peterson – *Daily Chronicle* into her database search engine. After a moment, the results appeared on screen giving details of Peterson's employment record, recent credit card transactions and more importantly his home address in Carlisle Place, SW1. Reading through his details nothing seemed noticeably out of the ordinary. On the contrary, his record appeared impeccable and rather mundane which, given the circumstances, was unusual in itself – almost as if someone had put a great deal of effort into creating the record.

Peterson, she read, had joined the Chronicle 18 months

earlier. Before that he had been a staff writer for a number of international broadsheets including *The Times*, the *Herald Tribune* and *Die Welt*. He never stayed more than two years in any one position, which to be fair was not overtly unusual for a journalist.

"I wonder," she murmured as she clicked on Edit Search Parameters and typed in William (Bill) Peterson – Central Intelligence Agency. As the screen flickered, Claire almost choked at the result "CIA: Unauthorised Access – Level One Top Secret clearance required."

Scratching her head, she leaned back and muttered, "Top secret clearance, for a reporter? Gazing at the screen she concluded that under the circumstances and after putting in so much effort, she could not simply just walk away. No, the man had questions to answer.

Finally deciding that the best course of action was to bring him in for questioning. Scrolling to the end of his record she clicked on Issue National Arrest Warrant.

This option would not only generate an authorised warrant, but also send it to every airport, port and police station in the land.

There was a good chance, all being well, that within 24-hours Peterson would be in custody. Glancing at her screen, she mused at how only a couple of hours earlier, it would have been almost inconceivable for her to have access to warrant information, let alone have the clearance to issue one. Yet here she was, not only issuing it but also coordinating the investigation. With a sense of mild achievement she finally clicked save and closed the record.

Back at the main menu page she clicked on new search and entered the name that Wilkes had provided, David James Brooks – Central Intelligence Agency.

As before the screen momentarily flickered and finally displayed a result, albeit not quite the result she had hoped for.

"CIA: Unauthorised Access – Level One Top Secret clearance required."

Staring at the screen she muttered, "Not again!"

Deciding that whatever this was, it was above her pay grade and although she didn't have the clearance herself, she wondered if perhaps the Deputy Director could help. Collecting her notebook, she logged off her computer and walked across the white polished tiled floor towards a large elevator behind her desk and pushed the call button.

After a moment a loud "ping" rang out and the doors swished smoothly open. Stepping inside she pushed the button for level four and the doors closed, immediately causing the elevator to rise and begin its smooth journey upwards.

Stepping out of the elevator she strode down a brightly lit corridor and paused outside the Deputy Director's office. Taking a deep breath she knocked, somewhat sheepishly, on the large oak wood door and waited for a response. After a moment, the door swung open to reveal a tall, slim, middle-aged woman, perhaps in her early fifties. Claire concluded that this must be Marshal's personal assistant.

"Good morning, can I help you?"

"Yes, good morning. Is it possible to have a quick word with the Deputy Director?"

The woman frowned, thought for a moment and responded with a smile, "Well, he's on a conference call at the moment, but I think it's almost finished. You're welcome to come in and wait if you like?"

Claire nodded, "Yes please."

The woman swung the door aside and Claire stepped through. Once inside, the assistant gestured for Claire to sit down in a small waiting area that comprised of two black-leather couches and an elegant smoked-glass coffee table.

"If you'll just take a seat Miss, er?"

"Hammond, Claire Hammond."

"Very good Miss Hammond, I'm Gillian McDonald, the Director's personal assistant. If you'll just make yourself comfortable I'll inform Mr Marshall that you're waiting. He shouldn't be too long."

"Thank you!"

Claire walked across to one of the couches and sat down, while McDonald returned to her desk.

Having to wait 10 minutes wouldn't normally have been a problem for Claire. However, today's unusually long fourteen-hour shift had made her drowsy and as she leaned back on the comfortable couch her eyes began to gain weight and before long her battle to keep awake was lost and she drifted off to sleep.

INVERNESS AIRPORT: SCOTLAND

The arrival at Inverness airport felt somewhat surreal as there were no queues, no passports checks and surprisingly, no questions asked as Dougie, Kate and Robert Wilkes were whisked through the airport by military personnel and escorted to a small private VIP waiting area adjacent to gate six which had been "pre prepared" for their exclusive use.

As Kate poured herself a coffee, Dougie sat opposite and watched Wilkes being treated by a young medic. As the youngster cleaned a large cut on the officer's forehead, Dougie looked on somewhat concerned "How do ye feel laddie? Do ye nae think you'd be better off in your bed?"

Wilkes looked across at Dougie and shook his head and said, "As I said I've had worse. I'm just thankful that I got to you both in time."

"Believe me laddie, so am I."

"Like I said Dougie, I'll be fine, it's all part of the job."

Kate returned with a large cappuccino and sat down next to Dougie.

"Oh I'm sorry, would any of you gents like a drink?"

Dougie glanced first at the coffee, then at Wilkes and shook his head. "Coffee, is that all they've got?"

Kate smirked and shook her head, "No. Actually they've a pretty good selection, they even have alcohol, if you feel the need."

"Aye, I do. Nae offence, but after all we've been through today a wee dram soonds grand and by the way Mr Wilkes is looking, he could use one to. What do ye say lad?"

Wilkes looked up at the young medic, smiled and nodded, "I'd love one."

Standing up, Dougie grinned and strode across to a large glass table laden with a dizzying selection of whiskies, beers and soft drinks. Picking up a bottle of *Kenmore Blended Scotch Whisky* he removed the cap, took a sniff and continued to pour two large glassfuls of the dark amber liquid.

Returning the bottle, he picked up the glasses, marched back across to where Kate, Wilkes and the Medic were sitting and handed one of the enormous glasses to a stunned looking Wilkes. "Dougie, you don't expect me to drink all that do you? There's almost half a pint here!"

Retaking his seat, Dougie took a large gulp of the amber liquid, swallowed slowly and leaned in closer to Wilkes, grinning.

"Och laddie! Ye have tae mind I've nae had a drink in over 300 hundred years. I'm just makin' up for lost time. Besides, I'm nae looking forward tae getting into another one of those flying contraptions."

Glancing at Kate, Wilkes grinned and nodded in agreement, "Fair enough!"

As Wilkes took another mouthful, the medic sighed disapprovingly, "Well Mr Wilkes, that's the best I can do for now. Luckily for you, the damage was only superficial. But, when you return home, I recommend you book a check-up with your doctor."

Giving a nod, Wilkes stood. "I will and thank you, it's appreciated."

As the medic walked away, the door to the lounge swung open and a smiling stewardess stepped in.

"Good morning folks your flight to Reykjavik is ready for boarding. If you will follow me, I'll escort you to the aircraft."

Placing her cup down Kate collected her things and followed Wilkes to the entrance of the lounge. Then, watching Dougie with a rather disapproving look, she rolled her eyes and grinned as he walked back across to the drinks table, calmly lifted the bottle of "Kenmore" and re-joined the group, mumbling "Well … I have medical needs as well, ye ken."

"Miss Hammond, Miss Hammond are you alright?"

"Huh!"

Opening her eyes, Claire stared into the concerned face of Marshall's assistant and promptly sat up.

"Oh, I'm terribly sorry, I must have nodded off."

"No need to apologise Miss Hammond. It wouldn't be the first time that's happened. The Deputy Director is ready for you now. You can go in."

Feeling somewhat embarrassed at falling asleep, Claire stood and followed Marshal's assistant through to a large, spacious office surrounded with large glass windows overlooking the London skyline.

"Claire Hammond, Mr Marshal."

Rising, the Deputy Director stepped forward and motioned to Claire to come in and take a seat.

"Miss Hammond. I feel as if I've seen more of you this morning than my wife."

With her face turning a plum shade of red, Claire sat down as instructed, "Yes Sir. Sorry Sir."

Pouring a glass of water, Marshal picked up the glass, took a sip and returned to his seat. Taking a deep breath, he exhaled and sat forward.

"Okay. What do you have?"

"A puzzle Sir."

"A puzzle?"

"Yes Sir. I've just spoken with Robert Wilkes in Inverness and he's informed me that the intruder who attacked Harding has been apprehended and killed."

"That's good news."

"Not exactly Sir."

"What do you mean?"

"Well, Wilkes asked me to run a report on the dead man, based on an identity card he discovered on the body."

"So, what's the problem?"

"Well Sir, the problem is that the ID card recovered suggests that the man, this David James Brooks is, or I suppose I should say was, in the employ of the CIA"

Marshal spluttered, "CIA? What?"

"I'm afraid that's not all Sir."

"There's more?"

"Well, when I tried to run the report for Mr Wilkes, the system reported that the file has been classified as CIA Top Secret. I would need CIA level-one clearance to access it."

Marshal sat up, "I see."

"I also ran a similar report on Bill Peterson from *The Daily Chronicle*."

"And?"

"It's sealed as well. But I thought that as Peterson is based in the UK and is probably still in the country, we could bring him in for questioning. I've issued an arrest warrant hoping, that if he was picked up we could find out more about what his role was in all of this."

Sighing, Marshal stood and starting pacing around his desk.

"I have a gut feeling Claire, that we'll never see Mr Peterson again."

"Sir?"

"CIA, Claire, he's probably got diplomatic immunity. They're a law unto themselves you know. I tell you what. Leave this one with me and I'll make some phone calls. I know a couple of people who owe me favours."

Claire placed her hand over her mouth and yawned, "Oh. I'm sorry Sir, it's been a long night that's all."

Marshal shook his head, "Claire you've already impressed me, you don't need to work 24-hours."

"Sir?"

"I don't want my staff fighting fatigue Claire. You're no use to me sick, you've done great work here today, now go home and get some rest. I'll do some digging around and see what I can find out and I'll give you a call when I know more."

Claire stood and gave another yawn, "Yes Sir, thank you Sir."

As she turned and left the room, Marshal leaned forward and picked up his phone. After pondering for a moment, he punched in a phone number and sat back, waiting for the call to be answered.

"Gerry, Gerry it's Robert Marshal … Yes … it's good to hear your voice as well. Gerry I have a small puzzle that I was hoping you could help me solve!"

THIRTY NINE

TUESDAY: 10.30AM TERMINAL 5 HEATHROW AIRPORT, LONDON

THE BBC NEWS was on the big overhead TV and the newsreader was reporting on the latest developments.

"Government leaders and representatives from the world's scientific community are converging on Reykjavik In preparation for an emergency summit aimed at discussing the recent spate of disasters which have struck many parts of the world. It is hoped that the conference will not only help identify the cause, but also offer possible solutions. Among the UK delegation is the Prime Minister, members of the Cabinet and a number of Britain's most influential scientists. The summit is due to start tomorrow and I can now pass across to our reporter on the ground in Reykjavik, James Hall, for the latest. James can you give us the latest?"

"Yes thank you David. As you said we are expecting the Prime Minister and the UK delegation to arrive within the next hour at what is now understood to be the most important summit since the end of the Second World War. Delegations from China, Russia, France and Italy arrived earlier and are preparing for tomorrow's historic meeting. Later this afternoon we are expecting the arrival of US President Bryant. We will of course bring you that arrival live on the BBC."

In the British Airways business lounge on the first floor of Heathrow's Terminal Five, Bill Peterson turned away from the television screen and after ensuring that no one was within earshot, dialled a number and waited for the call to be answered. After a moment, the connection clicked and a man's voice said, "Code in please."

"Code is One, Alpha, Five, Charlie, Zulu, Seven."

After a short pause the voice on the other end continued, "Confirmed. What is it Peterson?"

"I need to talk with him now!"

"I'm afraid that's not possible, he's travelling."

"Look, I'm just about to board a flight, I need to speak to him now, it's urgent!"

The line went quiet and Peterson heard the man sigh.

"Just a moment."

The line clicked as the call was routed to another number. Then, as before, the line rang for a moment and was again picked up.

"Yes?"

"Mr President, it's Peterson, Sir, I'm sorry to call your private cell Sir, but you said to call if it was urgent."

"That's alright, Peterson, what is it?

"I'm sorry Sir, but she may have got away ..."

"Do you know where?"

"I believe to Scotland Sir. Brooks followed her northwards, but I've not heard from him for some time. I can only assume he's been compromised."

"That's unfortunate ..."

"Yes Sir."

"What's your situation?"

"I'm using an alternate passport and I am about to board a flight to Newark. I should arrive around 4pm."

"What about the *Chronicle*? Have you cleaned up?"

"Yes Sir."

"Good. I'm just about to board the flight for Reykjavik. Once you arrive in the States, make your way back to DC. I should be back in a few days and we'll talk then. In the meantime, keep a low profile, understand?"

"Of course Sir. But what if ...?"

There was a momentary silence and the President responded coldly, "We'll cross that bridge when we come to it."

"I understand. Thank you Sir. Goodbye."

Placing the phone back in his inside pocket, Peterson walked towards the exit. As he approached the doorway, his mouth fell open in shock as a set of automatic smoked glass doors opened to reveal four heavily armed police officers accompanied by two plain-clothed officials.

As Peterson stopped dead in his tracks, one of the plain-clothed men calmly walked up and pulled out an identity card. "Mr Jenkins? Or should I say Mr Peterson? MI5 Sir. Would you come this way we would like a word."

TUESDAY: 9.40AM (EST) ANDREWS AIR FORCE BASE

"I HOPE IT wasn't bad news Mr President?"

Placing his personal phone back inside his pocket President Richard Bryant sighed and shook his head. "No Ethel, it wasn't."

As the President's black limousine came to a stop, the car door suddenly swung open and a young Marine stood to attention and saluted as the President stepped out of the vehicle and made his way across the tarmac towards the front steps of the Presidential Boeing 747.

Within minutes of take-off, Air force one was airborne, soaring eastwards across an early morning Virginia skyline. After being served coffee and warm croissants, a small team of advisors joined the President around the conference table.

Taking a sip of coffee, the President swallowed and cleared his throat., "Okay, where are we up to?"

Opening her briefcase, Obrien stood and addressed the group.

"Mr President, ladies and gentlemen, we should be landing in Reykjavik around 4pm local time. Although the conference doesn't officially start until tomorrow, the Icelandic Government has arranged an initial press conference and informal dinner for this evening. "

"This evening?"

"Yes Mr President. It's to be a fairly informal affair. I believe it was primarily intended to allow the scientific delegations to have an opportunity to get acquainted."

Bryant nodded, "Very well, in that case I'm sure it'll be fine."

Turning back to the group Obrien continued, "Mr President, overnight we received an update on the search for survivors in Hawaii."

"And?"

"It's not good news I'm afraid. We're now looking at a loss of around 98 per cent of the population, Sir."

As the words left her mouth, the room reverberated with gasps of shock.

"I'm afraid that's not the end of it. As feared, and as you already know, the west coast was also hit hard. Although there's been a steady trickle of survivors into our rescue centres, it's not what we'd hoped for."

Bryant's head dropped and he sighed deeply, "Do we know how many?"

Obrien shook her head, "No Sir, it's still too early to say, but it looks bad."

"What about your folks, any news?"

With painful memories of her missing parents flashing

through her mind, she gazed into the eyes of President for a moment, as if they were both somehow spiritually connected. Then slowly exhaling, she swallowed and solemnly shook her head, "No Sir, no news."

"I'm sorry Ethel."

As Obrien opened her mouth to respond, the group was suddenly interrupted by rather worried and somewhat pale-faced member of the flights aircrew.

"I'm sorry to interrupt you Mr President, but I thought you should know that CNN are reporting another huge quake."

The conference area fell silent.

"What ... Where?"

"In Germany Sir."

"Germany!"

"Yes Sir. Just south of Frankfurt. Early reports indicate that we are looking at damage in the area of around 8.2 on the Richter scale."

Bryant's face turned white and his mouth fell open, "My God ... What about casualties? Do we know?"

"No Sir, but the media is reporting that the German Chancellor has abandoned his trip to Reykjavik and is returning to Berlin to deal with the crisis."

Taking a deep breath, Bryant picked up his coffee and took a farther sip.

"Mr President, Sir, with all that's going on, don't you think that it would be more prudent to perhaps reschedule?"

Turning, somewhat surprised at the comments of his elderly Secretary of Defence, the President took another sip of coffee, placed the cup down and exhaled.

"On the contrary Mike, the world's depending upon us. We can't just turn with our tail between our legs and fall at the first hurdle."

"Mr President. I didn't mean to ..."

Raising his hand, Bryant cut the old man off before he could finish.

"It's okay. There's no need to apologise, but understand that turning back is simply not an option"

As the elderly man nodded, the President retook his seat and turned once again to face his Chief of Staff.

"Ethel, please send a message to the Chancellor. Tell him that the people of the United States stand by, ready to assist if needed. Also contact our military on the ground. Instruct them to offer what assistance they can."

"Of course Mr President."

As Obrien stood and walked away towards the plane's communication centre, John Baker, the President's head of scientific affairs, said, "Have we had any news from the Brits regarding their discovery in Scotland?"

Bryant thought for a moment and shook his head, "No, I'm afraid not John. However, I do know that they have a team en-route to Reykjavik. I'm sure their science team will be more than happy to share their findings with you."

Baker nodded and gave a sigh, "Yes Sir."

For a moment the group fell silent. Then sitting forward Baker raised his hand.

"John, you're not at school, you don't have to raise your hand."

Baker smiled feeling somewhat embarrassed. "I'm sorry Mr President ... I was wondering if Quest and Moore had any luck deciphering the symbols on the parchment." Bryant glanced around the table and shook his head, "No, I haven't. Have you had a chance to look at them?"

The middle-aged science advisor sighed and shook his head in apparent disappointment, "Yes Sir, I have, but Symbology was never my strong point. I only hope that when we meet, they have found an answer."

Standing, Baker picked up his coffee mug and turned away.

"Well, for once I hope we find a solution and soon. I've heard that the Brits are bringing their time traveller along for the ride. I just hope that he can shed some light on this whole affair."

As Baker and the rest of the advisory team stepped away from the conference table, the President picked up his coffee and took a final sip. Placing the cup down he slowly exhaled. "Oh I'm sure he can John, I'm sure he can."

FORTY

N A SMALL private study room inside the *Archivio Segreto Vaticano*, Father Antonio Demarco sat back and rubbed his tired eyes. He had been wading through a seemingly endless pile of books and journals, looking for something, anything that might provide an insight as to what the mysterious symbols were and what was the hidden message contained within. After examining various books containing Egyptian hieroglyphics, Mayan writings, Greek symbols and even Stone Age carvings. Antonio was tired and frustrated.

He had once considered himself fairly knowledgeable, but now frustration and doubt were beginning to creep in. Just what was the origin of these symbols? At this point he was unsure. They were like nothing he had ever seen before. As he stared once more at the email from Richard Quest, he even contemplated that perhaps he may have been the victim of some elaborate prank. He sighed heavily as memories of Pietro, his father flooded into his mind, playing similar tricks on him as a child.

Actually, "tricks", Antonio thought, was a rather harsh word to describe his father's teaching practices, Perhaps puzzles would have been more appropriate. For years, Antonio would be forced to solve mathematical puzzles before being allowed to play with friends or participate in sport. Although, at the time he hated the practice, he eventually grew to appreciate the strange ritual and as a teenager began looking forward to it. But that was long ago and, unfortunately, it would not help him solve this puzzle in the here and now.

As Antonio yawned and shuffled his chair back into position, he was suddenly interrupted as a knock came to the study room door. "*Sì, sono disponibile.*"

As the small rooms door swung open his friend and mentor Bishop Jean Louis Bouchard stepped inside. Pushing his chair back, Antonio rose to his feet and greeted his friend and long-time mentor.

Raising his hand as if to tell Antonio not to fuss, the Bishop stepped forward.

"Va bene amico mio, Ti prego rimani seduto."

Returning to his seat Antonio smiled, "*Grazie, tua grazia.*"

"So what have you discovered, Antonio?"

Antonio sighed and shook his head in disappointment, "Unfortunately, nothing of significance your Grace."

"Nothing?"

Lifting up the printed sheet of symbols, Antonio, again repeated, "*Sì.* Nothing. I've looked through dozens of books for clues as to what they mean, but I just can't find the key."

Placing a reassuring hand on Antonio's shoulder, the Bishop smiled and spoke quietly, "My friend, if anyone can unravel their secrets, it's you. Just pray and have faith. Then when the Lord is ready to speak, you will be ready to listen."

Nodding, Antonio smiled, "You know I was just thinking of my father. When I was a child he would have me solve puzzles. At the time I hated it. But now, I feel that if anyone could help, it could perhaps be him."

"Then why don't you try calling him again?"

Antonio gazed up at his mentor with a look of surprise, "*Vostra Grazia?*"

Smiling down at the young priest, Bouchard nodded, "God moves in mysterious ways my friend. Even you must know that."

TUESDAY: 1.15PM KEFLAVIK AIRPORT, ICELAND

Stepping onto the tarmac, Dougie, Kate and Wilkes were escorted quickly through security and past the awaiting media scrum to the terminal building's main entrance. There, to meet them was an Icelandic chaperone. A jolly, slightly overweight middle-aged, blond man named Herman Michelson. After greeting the visitors he escorted them to a waiting silver 4x4. As the group climbed inside, Michelson placed their bags into the rear and climbed into the driver's seat.

Strapping himself in, Michelson started the engine, turned to face his passengers and cleared his throat, "So, has anyone been to Iceland before?"

Dougie was quick to answer, "Nae lad, I've never been out of Scotland before so this is a first for me."

Smiling cheekily, the Icelander nodded as he stared at Dougie's somewhat unusual attire.

"I can see that Dougie, isn't it?"

"Aye lad it is. But you're staring' at me as if you've never seen a Scotsman in a kilt before?"

"No … er, not really. Well not around here anyway."

In an attempt to diffuse a potentially embarrassing situation, Michelson turned frontwards, placed the car into first gear and pushed his foot down on the accelerator.

"Well then I hope your first visit to our country will be an interesting one," he said.

"Oh, I'm sure it will be lad."

The car made its way along Reykjanesbraut towards Reykjavik city centre. As he drove, Michelson insisted on providing an enthusiastic running commentary on the surroundings – perhaps, due to nerves or even Icelandic pride, the group were unsure.

On any normal day the gesture would have been appreciated, but not today. Not after almost being killed by a manic in a lighthouse and certainly not after two nights of getting little sleep. Although tired after their journey, the group were conscious of not wanting to cause any offence to their new host and so politely sat back and nodded, pretending to be interested as he droned on.

"On the right here you can see the remains of the American base. They moved away a few years back and it's now used for student accommodation for the university."

"University?"

"Yes Miss Harding, I work for the university, well at the Institute of Sciences actually. They're co-sponsoring this summit. The department is one of the foremost authorities on Volcanic research in the world and ..."

As Michelson spoke, his cell phone suddenly began to ring. "Oh, sorry ... Excuse me a moment."

Reaching inside his jacket pocket he took out his phone and pushed the answer button. "*Halló ... þetta er Hermann ... já ég er á leiðinni til Hilton, Hilton núna. ég ætti að vera þar eftir um 20 mínútur. .Ekkert vandamál, Bless.*"

As the call ended Michelson placed the phone back into his inside pocket and continued, "That was my boss. He just wanted to make sure I had collected you. We've arranged rooms for you at the Hilton. I'm sure you will be quite comfortable."

Wilkes nodded, "Thank you Mr Michelson, that's much appreciated."

With a grin appearing on his face, Michelson shook his head, "Oh please, there's no need to be so formal. Call me Herman. Actually that reminds me Mr Wilkes, I was instructed to pass on a message to you. Your office in London called. When you get a moment they want you to call in."

"Thank you Herman, I appreciate that."

As the car continued its journey along the highway, the conversation faded and the group fell silent. Kate was beginning to enjoy the silence when Michelson once again continued his commentary.

Becoming increasingly agitated at having to listen to the man's continual drawl, Kate finally snapped and sat forward in a journalistic attempt to get Michelson to talk about something more useful than just the scenery.

"Herman, you mentioned that you work at the university. Are you by any chance familiar with Elín Gylfadóttir?"

As she spoke, Wilkes suddenly interrupted, "Kate, I don't think this …"

"For God's sake man I'm only asking a question. I'm a bloody journalist remember."

Wilkes shook his head angrily, "Yes but, what I mean is that this is perhaps not the time or the place to."

"Elin," said Michelson. "Yes, of course I know her … You forget Miss Harding that Iceland only has a population of three hundred thousand. Living here you get to know a lot of people. Of course I knew her. I worked with her!"

"You worked with her."

"Yes, for about a year. Actually when she left, we were all very disappointed. She did some great work here. But I suppose if I'd received an amazing job offer with a crazy salary I probably would have jumped at the chance too. Have you seen her?"

For an awful moment Kate sat still, realising that he hadn't heard of her death. Taking a deep breath she glanced across at Dougie and slowly exhaled.

"You haven't heard then?"

"Heard what?"

"I'm afraid Elin is dead Herman. She was found in a Frankfurt hotel room last week. I believe the police are investigating. I've been out of touch for a few days and I'm really not up to date with the facts."

Michelson's face turned pale and his voice drifted away, "I see …"

"I'm very sorry Herman."

From that point, the conversation in the car died and the remainder of the journey into the city continued in silence. Staring sympathetically at Kate, Dougie gave her hand a supporting squeeze and turned to gaze outside at the passing countryside as it sped by.

As he gazed out at the bleak moon like landscape, he could see distant and dangerous looking mountains surrounded by what appeared to be an endless sea of grey lava.

"Oh my God."

Kate turned in surprise and gazed at Dougie's grim expression. With questioning eyes, she whispered, "Dougie what is it. What's wrong?"

With his face contorted and the horrible realisation that he had seen this landscape before, he took another deep breath, "This is it lassie, the nightmare. It was here!"

In the front seats Herman and Wilkes gave each other a puzzled look and Wilkes turned his head to the rear, "What did you say Dougie?"

Dougie swallowed and slowly exhaled, "It's here lad. Whatever's going happen, I ken it's going happen here?"

The arrival at the Hilton Nordica Hotel was not quite the experience that Michelson had expected for his passengers. Normally bustling with tourists hoping to visit one of Iceland's famous landmarks, the hotel appeared to be surrounded by TV crews, all frantically scurrying forward, all desperate to be the first to interview one of the many arriving dignitaries.

As the silver 4x4 pulled up to a makeshift security checkpoint, Michelson rolled down his window and presented his security pass to a waiting police officer. After carefully scrutinising the ID, the officer gave a satisfied nod, tuned to his colleague and signalled him to raise a metal barrier. Once through, the vehicle swung around and came to a halt outside the main entrance of the hotel.

As the engine fell silent, the group left the vehicle and followed Michelson into the hotel's spacious foyer.

After checking the group in he handed each of them a room key and explained the layout of the hotel and also instructions about not wandering above the fifth floor as the those rooms were reserved for the world's leaders and were classed as high security areas. Finally, happy that he had explained everything, he shook each of their hands and turned to leave.

"Well, I'm sure you will be quite comfortable here. If you need anything, don't hesitate to ask. Everything's been taken care of. The conference begins tomorrow. I understand that Doctor Quest is on his way with the UK delegation and he has asked for Mr Allan to be available tomorrow to meet some of his colleague's, if that's all right of course?"

Glancing somewhat overwhelmed at Kate, Dougie gave a nod and a weak smile, "Aye of course lad, thank ye."

"Oh Miss Harding if you were to visit the university tomorrow I could arrange it. If you like?"

"Yes please Herman that would be appreciated."

"Well then, until tomorrow."

As Michelson left, the group were escorted to their respective rooms on the third floor. Having never stayed in a hotel before, Dougie was somewhat dumbfounded at the size and apparent luxury of his assigned room. As the porter left and the door closed, he placed his small bag of belongings onto what appeared to be an enormous king size bed and walked over to a large picture window. Carefully, he nervously placed his fingers gently against the enormous wall of glass and as he gazed downwards at the concrete forecourt below, his stomach churned with the sudden realisation, that if it wasn't for the glass he could so easily fall out. But after gently pushing his fingers a little harder against the surface, he sighed in quiet relief that the glass was indeed strong enough and he was safe.

Gazing down at the gathering below, he sighed and refocused

his eyes outwards across the city and over the dark water in the bay towards the sharp and foreboding mountains in the distance. As he looked out across the bleak landscape, memories of his wife, McArthur and of a stolen past life combined with a sense of destiny. Then, taking a deep breath, he slowly exhaled and gritted his teeth, "I don't know who you are and I don't know why you're doing this. But it ends here understand! I'm going to fight you … I swear it!"

FORTY ONE

BY THE TIME Father Antonio had arrived at the Ristorante Maria, the small family restaurant was almost full. To his surprise, his father had not only arrived earlier than expected, but had rudely proceeded to order without waiting for him. As he walked across to where his father was sitting, Antonio slipped off his jacket and glared angrily at his father who was taking a mouthful of spinach cannelloni. Gazing at the old man in annoyance, Antonio shook his head. For him, this arrogance seemed so typical of his father and was yet another perfect example of why their relationship had fallen into disarray all those years ago.

Fighting the urge to just turn and walk away, Antonio gave a heavy sigh as he heard the voice of his mentor inside. Although, Antonio would never admit it, he knew Bouchard was right of course – he always was. But this time it was different. He knew deep inside that somehow he had to get through his father's stubborn shell. If there were at least a chance that he could help decipher what appeared to be an impossible puzzle, then just perhaps this meeting would be worth it.

"*Ciao Padre* …"

With a somewhat fleeting glance at Antonio, the old man took another mouthful of food, swallowed and returned his cold gaze to the table.

"So, you've arrived then! I'm sorry, but I was hungry and couldn't wait."

Without responding, Antonio pulled out a wooden chair and sat opposite his father. As he shuffled in closer, a waiter approached and gave a friendly nod.

"*Buona sera Buon Padre, gradisce qualcosa da bere?*"

Taking a moment to decide, Antonio nodded, "*Sì, grazie, un quartino di vino rosso dei Castelli Romani.*"

Within moments the waiter had returned and proceeded to pour two generous glasses.

"*Grazie*" The waiter nodded and smartly turned and left the two men alone. Antonio then picked up a glass, took a sip and returned it to the table.

"So how have you been father?"

With the same steely glare that Antonio was all too familiar with, Pietro Demarco swallowed the remainder of his spinach cannelloni and wiped the corner of his mouth with a napkin. Then gazing at his son with a look of cold suspicion sat back in his chair.

"You don't need to be concerned with pleasantries Antonio. You and I both know that the only reason I'm here is because you need my help."

"It's true father I do need your help, but it's not the only reason I'm here. I thought that …"

Sitting forward, the old man interrupted, his voice raised, "Thought what, Antonio? That after all these years we would just sit down and have a cosy chat and that your mother would be back and everything would be perfect?"

Without responding, Antonio picked up the wine glass and gulped down a large mouthful. Returning the glass to the table he reached inside his pocket, took out the folded email and slapped it down it on the table in front of his father.

"No, it's obvious that despite my best efforts, things between us will never change. You're right father, perhaps this is just a waste of time."

Pushing his chair aside, Antonio stood almost disbelieving his father's seemingly unyielding attitude. As he gazed at the cold-faced old man, Antonio picked up his jacket and handed a 20 euro note to a passing waiter for the bottle of wine. Turning to face his father one final time he pointed to the paper, "Here father. See what you can make of it ... *Addio.*"

As Antonio stormed away furious, the old man reached across to the piece of folded paper and picked it up. Unfolding it his eye's widened and his mouth fell open as he gazed upon the strange symbols with an unusual sense of familiarity.

"A*spett*a, Antonio ..."

Stepping outside the Ristorante Maria into the early evening sunlight, Father Antonio stopped for a moment to gather his thoughts. After stomping his foot on the ground in what appeared to be an accumulation of fury and frustration, he took a deep calming breath and walked briskly away towards St Peter's Square. As he walked, he suddenly began to feel somewhat light headed. Fearing that he had perhaps taken too much wine, he stopped for moment to steady himself. As he stood motionless, he realised that it was not just him swaying – it was everything. Then as quickly as it had started, it stopped and everything became still again. So still in fact the whole world seemed to take a breath and fall into an eerie silence. After a few moments and just as before, the swaying began again. Only this time it was much stronger. Swaying buildings now began to shake. Behind him faces of worried bystanders turned to horror as the chilling sounds of women screaming and children wailing began to blend with the sounds of falling debris and breaking glass.

Then in sheer panic people began to run. Cars smashed into each other in desperation to escape the carnage. Ahead, Antonio could see a plume of thick black smoke rising into the air like an awakened serpent.

"*Dio mio … Padre.*"

With an awful sense of dread growing inside him, Antonio quickly turned and ran back towards the restaurant. Running back along the crumbling street, the air became dense with thick white dust, and he narrowly escaped being hit by blocks of falling concrete and twisted steel from above. With his eyes stinging and gulping desperately for air, Antonio moved quickly through a sea of blooded and bewildered faces. In the thick of the chaos, all Antonio could think about was his father. Whatever the issues that had been between them were now gone. Antonio didn't care anymore – he just wanted to reach him, to be with him. He had to be alive; he just had to be.

Antonio felt like he had been running for hours, but in reality it was only for a couple of minutes. As he approached the Ristorante Maria the shaking had now subsided and the scene had become still once more. In front of him, the normally well-maintained family restaurant had been replaced with a grotesque pile of rubble, broken glass and twisted steel. In the silence he screamed out, "*Padre!*"

Moving slowly through the nightmare, Antonio breathed heavily as he laboured to lift tables, concrete blocks and heavy beams away, but with each step taken and each dead body passed, his hopes of finding his father alive were now beginning to fade. Standing still with a sense of helplessness and with his eyes filled with tears and stinging dust, Antonio stood amid the rubble.

He lowered his head and began to pray, "Father in heaven if you can …"

"Antonio?"

The voice was weak, but definitely there.

"Antonio …"

Yes, there it was again, "*Padre.*"

Turning quickly, Antonio listened intently, desperately trying to home in on the sound. Then suddenly there he was, his father, just ahead lying on the ground covered in rubble. But as Antonio approached, his elation turned to sadness. Kneeling down by his father's side, Antonio could see that his father's crushed chest lay beneath a hefty steel beam. With a heavy heart he realised that even if he could conjure up a miracle to move the beam, his father would probably not survive. Taking out a handkerchief, Antonio began to wipe blood and dust off his father's face.

"*Padre* … I'm sorry, I'm so sorry."

Gazing up at his son, the old man wheezed and winced in pain. "D … Don't be … Antonio. We all m … made our choices. As it happens, I … I made some bad ones and I'm sorry for that now. But, now you have to l … listen Antonio. The sym … symbols …"

As he wiped tears from his eyes Antonio shook his head and interrupted, "No … Father … Don't worry about that now, just lie still. Help will be here shortly."

Gasping heavily the old man gave a weak smile and shook his head. "N … No … You listen … Antonio, th … the symbols. Antonio, they're not … symbols. They're numbers!"

Antonio held on to his father's hand for the last time as Pietro Demarco wheezed and took one final breath.

FORTY TWO

FOR JAMES WALTON staying in the Hilton Nordica Hotel felt a little unusual. Not that there was anything wrong with the hotel, in fact quite the opposite, it was fairly prestigious for the most part. It was just that after sleeping at Chequers or the White House, staying in a regular hotel room felt a little curious. If his mother had still been alive, she would have scolded him for acting like a snob and reminded him that he should be thankful, especially in these difficult times. Maybe it was true. He hadn't stayed in a regular hotel room for years and even if he had, he was normally accommodated in the Presidential Suite or a private annex tucked away from the prying eyes of the general public.

But today there were just too many dignitaries visiting the city, and as a result he was in Room 924 of the Hilton Nordica. To be fair it was a nice room. An executive room, apparently. Walton sighed and gulped down a mouthful of freshly squeezed orange juice, before walking across to what appeared to be, in his opinion an insanely small desk and sat down to put the final touches to his speech.

Placing the glass down, he leaned across to pick up his pen. Just as he did, a knock sounded at the door.

"Come in."

Lisa Harkins entered accompanied by a somewhat stern faced Anne Petrie.

"Good morning ladies, is everything ready?"

Petrie nodded, "Yes Prime Minister, they're ready for you now Sir."

After meeting Quest, the two men stepped through the doorway into the packed hotel ballroom. Standing for a moment, engulfed within an intensely bright spotlight. The two men felt somewhat overwhelmed by the overzealous applause of the audience. As they walked the length of the ballroom they stepped up onto a raised platform and Walton stopped in front of a brightly lit podium while Quest took a seat behind the Prime Minister.

As he approached the microphone, Walton waited for a moment until the applause subsided and began.

"Ladies, Gentlemen, Dignitaries, thank you for that warm welcome. It appears we have reached an unprecedented moment in human history. Over the past few months and even weeks, a series of catastrophic events has touched every corner of our world. Even today, we have received yet more distressing news of a devastating earthquake in Italy. In a single week, we have seen death and destruction never before seen in the history of the human race. For those in the affected areas our hearts and prayers go out to them.

"The human race is an amazing species and it's in that spirit that this conference has been made possible. We have brought together some of the brightest minds on the planet and together we will work tirelessly to formulate not only a cause but hopefully a solution. Standing here I am truly humbled that so many world leaders and members of the scientific community have travelled to be here and I'm hopeful that together, we can work through this, our darkest hour."

As his words faded, the room again erupted into rapturous

applause. As the clapping receded and the room again fell silent, Walton continued, "As you now know late yesterday evening the United Kingdom, the United States, China and Russia took the first steps in releasing details of a number of apparent alien chambers which are buried underneath each of the Earths tectonic plates. Each of which make up our seven continents. As you can imagine this information has not been made public and I urge each and every one of you to ensure that these findings remain absolutely secret."

"In the public domain this knowledge could cause untold panic and have dire consequences for each of our home nations. For our part we have hypothesised that these chambers are somehow linked into our planets core and that something or someone has initiated a process that has triggered this chain of catastrophic events that we are all now experiencing. Who these beings are and why they have made this aggressive decision is for the moment unclear. I know that many of you are afraid ... But we can no longer be consumed by our petty differences, greed, politics, race or religion. If we are to survive we must come together as equal members of the human race and begin a new era of true openness, understanding and cooperation."

As Walton paused to take breath, his words were met with a farther round of applause.

"Now I would like to introduce a man who needs no introduction to the scientific community. I'm proud to call him one of Britain's brightest minds. Over the past week he and his colleagues have made startling discoveries in Scotland and I think it's important that he shares them with you. So please welcome to the podium, Doctor Richard Quest ..."

In his room on the third floor, Dougie lay on his bed and was really in no mood for company. So when a knock came to his door, he rolled his eyes and reluctantly stood up, walked across the pinewood floor and opened the door. As expected it was Kate Harding, but having hardly slept for at least two nights, he was not in any condition for another adventure. With everything that was going on, he would have just preferred to be left alone.

"Good morning Dougie, I wondered if you'd like to go for some breakfast."

Not wishing to appear rude, Dougie gave a weak smile and shook his head, "Actually, do ye mind if I say nae lass. I'm tired and I fear I would nae be good company."

Kate's expression turned to one of concern. "Dougie, of course I perfectly understand. With everything that's happened, it's perfectly natural for you to want to be alone."

Sighing, Kate glanced up and down the empty corridor before continuing. "I wondered if I could talk with you, just for a moment."

Giving a reluctant nod Dougie smiled, "Of course lass, come away in."

Kate entered the room and walked across to the picture window and gazed down at the horde of reporters and security personnel below. Dougie walked across and sat down on one of the two easy chairs. Taking a deep sigh Kate continued to stare down below.

"I can't believe this is happening … it … it's like some horrible nightmare that I can't wake up from. A week ago I would have been out there among them. But now I don't even know if there's going to be a tomorrow."

"Hey … now lassie, dinnae worry. It's nae over yet. As Tom said, if it was the end then why go tae all the trouble tae bring me here and have these beings reveal themselves? I'm convinced that whatever are whoever's behind this has brought us together for a reason. Now that I have the Key, we'll find a way you'll see."

Suddenly Kate turned to face Dougie with a puzzled look.

"Key … You never mentioned anything about a key."

Suddenly Dougie's head dropped and with eyes full of guilt, he sighed, "I didn't want tae say until I knew what it was"

"What was are you talking about?"

Reaching inside the fold of his kilt Dougie took out the small black pyramid that had revealed itself to him only a few days earlier in Alva.

"My God! Why didn't you tell anyone, Doctor Quest or ... or the police. Surely someone has to be told."

"Perhaps, but don't ye see. It was foretold, that it would find me. In the cemetery in Alva, Mary told me that once I found it, I would ken exactly what tae do with it when the time comes."

Kate stood silent for a moment before returning her gaze to the reporters gathered outside the hotel.

"It's here isn't it? Whatever's supposed to happen, it's going to happen here?"

Dougie frowned and began to pace back and forth.

"I don't ken Kate, I just don't ken. At times I feel like I'm riding on the back of a great horse and nae matter what I do I can't make it stop."

Giving a wry smile, Kate turned and sighed, "Like I said Dougie, perhaps you're not meant to. Perhaps it's just your destiny."

Flopping back down on the easy chair Dougie sighed and shook his head in disagreement. "Nae lass, its nae destiny, of that I'm sure now ... it's a bloody curse!"

Standing on the 13th floor balcony of the Presidential Suite at the Grand Hotel Reykjavik, Richard Bryant took a deep breath and exhaled.

"My God, just smell that air Ethel, isn't it marvellous?"

Obrien cleared her throat and stepped up behind the President, "Mr President?"

"The air ... Ethel, can't you smell it, so clean. You'll never get air like this in DC, I'll tell you that."

Obrien grinned, "No Sir ... I suppose not."

Turning to face his Chief of staff, the President motioned his finger in the direction of the Hilton and cleared his throat.

"So tell me again why we're not over there?"

"Simple logistics Mr President I'm afraid. The Chinese beat us to the Presidential Suite at the Hilton."

Bryant grinned and rolled his eyes, "That explains everything."

"Yes Sir. But you should know that many leaders ended up in ordinary rooms. It was sheer luck, and a little persuasion on my part that I managed to get you in here."

Stepping back inside the large suite, Bryant smiled. "Well I appreciate it thank you."

Then walking across to a drinks trolley, he picked up a half-finished cup of black coffee and sat down on a large cream coloured leather couch.

"What's on the agenda today?"

Walking briskly across to join the President, Obrien picked up a red leather bound diary and sat opposite. "Well Sir, as you know the conference has already begun. In fact I believe the British are delivering an opening speech as we speak. This will be followed by an address by the Russian President at eleven followed by your address at eleven thirty."

Swallowing a mouthful of coffee, Bryant nodded, "Sounds busy. Anything else?"

"This evening you have a formal dinner engagement at seven as well as a request from the British Prime Minister for you to meet this Dougie Allan, the gentleman from Scotland."

At the mere mention of Dougie's name the President's face turned almost white. At first Obrien thought she had said something to upset him, but then she thought that perhaps he was feeling ill.

"Is everything alright, Sir?"

Taking another gulp of coffee, he said nothing for a moment almost as if in deep thought. But then as he swallowed, he exhaled and continued, "Actually Ethel I would like to meet Mr Allan, but not here and not today. Perhaps in a day or so, when these meetings are over."

Obrien gave an agreeable but slightly confused nod, "Of course Mr President, whatever you say."

Sensing that the meeting was now over, Obrien stood and made her way towards the door. "Ethel!"

Suddenly realising that perhaps he hadn't finished and that her decision to rise was a little premature, she released her hand from the door handle and turned back to face the President. "Yes Sir."

"I think I would like to meet Allan alone. Perhaps, somewhere away from all this."

"Sir?"

Obrien was shocked. In all her years of service, he had never made a request like this. Conduct a meeting alone and unescorted in a foreign country? It was preposterous.

"Mr President, I don't think ..."

As The President raised his hand and she suddenly fell silent like a scolded child.

"Ethel, he is like no one we've ever encountered before. This man may have the answers to our questions. I simply want to meet him as an ordinary man and not the President of the United States. In doing so I can ascertain who he is and what exactly his intentions are. Understand?"

Nodding reluctantly, Obrien gave a dry smile and opened the door, "Of course Mr President I'll make the arrangements."

As Obrien left the room and closed the door behind her, Bryant sat back on the couch with a sly, almost smug look of confidence appearing on his face.

"Perfect!" he whispered.

FORTY THREE

LYING COVERED IN dust, Father Antonio Demarco's eyes slowly flickered open. Disorientated and unable to remember how he came to be lying there, he took a moment to focus before he sat up and surveyed the grim scene.

As his senses slowly returned, he concluded that a piece of falling debris must have struck him from above and knocked him out. Raising his arm to read the time on his watch, he rubbed a layout of grey dust off the glass and gasped as the dial read 12.10pm. Rolling his eyes in despair at the thought of laying in one spot all night he mustered all of his strength, he sat up and gazed solemnly at the grim scene.

All around, streets were covered with sporadic groups of wailing Romans desperately searching through mounds of rubble and blocks of fallen concrete for possible survivors. Close by he watched in despair as a distraught young woman screamed out in anguish as she discovered the blood-soaked remains of a small child.

Antonio coughed and spluttered as he slowly climbed to his feet and glanced down at his own ripped and dust covered clothes. He gazed out at the awful scene he wondered what he could do. What difference could he possibly make? Today he was lucky, he was still alive and he thanked God for that. As he began to walk and move slowly through the chaos, his father's final words kept repeating over in his mind.

"The symbols. Antonio they're not symbols, they're numbers!"

Around thirty minutes later, he arrived at the remains of the St Peter's Basilica. Gazing in horror at the scene, he struggled to comprehend how a single earthquake could lay waste to centuries of magnificent architecture. Stumbling past rows upon rows of bloodied and bewildered survivors, images of his dying father kept replaying in his mind.

Despite the terrible loss and their long-term differences, something at the end brought the two men back together. For Antonio, grief would have to wait. For now he had to translate the symbols into something meaningful. Something that he was sure would make a difference. Thanks to his father he felt that had now been given a second chance and this time he was determined not to waste it.

As Antonio approached the remains of his small apartment, his head dropped in despair. Despite hoping for the best, the building, like the others, now lay in ruins.

"Antonio!" Suddenly a voice echoed from behind and when he spun around to investigate, his mouth fell open in relief to see the bloodied and bruised, but still alive, face of Bouchard. "*Antonio, amico mio, sei ancora vivo!*"

Sprinting across to Bouchard, Antonio embraced his friend warmly, "*Sì, amico mio.*"

"I'm okay Antonio. But your father, did you see him? Is he alright?"

"*Sì*, I saw him ... But ... I'm afraid he did not survive."

Bouchard placed a comforting hand on his shoulder and nodded. "I'm so sorry my friend." Taking out the piece of paper out of his pocket, Antonio unfolded it and gave a weak smile. "But ... I think I may now know what these might be."

"Antonio, that's marvellous news, but now is hardly the time. Look around you. We need to help these people."

Antonio shook his head in disagreement and explained, "I understand the urgency your Grace. However, I think my efforts would be better served in trying to decipher this. I think this has to do with what's happening to the planet. You have to trust me, this is important."

Glancing at his friend, Bouchard sighed. Inside he knew Antonio was probably right and that if he had indeed discovered something of great importance his efforts should be allowed to continue.

"*Sì*, very well. But if you are indeed going to make a difference, you can't do it here."

"But your Grace, I can at least help for a while."

Bouchard raised his hand to silence his friend, "No, you are right my friend. Take the symbols and go."

As he spoke two police cars and an ambulance came screeching to a sudden halt about twenty meters away and a group of emergency personnel leapt out and ran across to assist a group of injured tourists. Then, spotting the two injured clergy, an officer at the wheel of the second police car jumped out and ran across to offer aid.

"*Padre, Vostra Grazia … State bene?*"

Wiping blood from his forehead, the Bishop raised a hand in order to allay the officer's fear.

"*Sì*, I am fine, however, it's very important you get my friend to safety. He has critical information for the international authorities."

For a moment the young officer looked bewildered before continuing. "*Sì*, er *Sì* of course. Please get in the car. I'll take you to safety right away."

Turning to his friend, Antonio embraced the Bishop and cleared his throat.

"Will you be alright?"

"Antonio, I'll be fine my friend. Now please go!"

Turning to the officer Antonio nodded and the two men dashed across the courtyard towards the waiting blue and white

Skoda Superb. Slamming the doors, the officer started the engine and the car roared into life. Then placing the gears into first he pushed his foot down on the accelerator and the car sped away.

WEDNESDAY 4.07PM REYKJAVIK, ICELAND

IN THE EXECUTIVE lounge on the eighth floor of the Hilton Nordica, Dougie Allan paced up and down nervously waiting for the arrival of the Prime Minister, James Walton. Sat opposite an open fire waiting with him were Doctor Quest and Professor Moore. Glancing for a moment at her colleague the Professor sipped a glass of orange juice and returned her gaze to the pacing Scotsman.

"Dougie, there's no need to be anxious ... he's really quite approachable."

"Aye, I'm sure he is lass, but this is a first for me. By the way, have ye seen Miss Harding? I thought she was supposed tae be here."

Glancing awkwardly across at Quest, Moore shook her head. "No I'm afraid not. In this case she's classed as a civilian and as such was not invited. It's probably something to do with the fact that she's a reporter. They, er tend to make politicians nervous."

"Aye, that may be true, but after what she's been through, I thought they'd give her the benefit of the doubt."

Suddenly the door to the lounge swung open and a rather flustered looking James Walton stepped inside along with Lisa Harkins and the Home Secretary.

"I'm so sorry you were kept waiting. Unfortunately we were delayed. Please accept my apologies."

As the Prime Minister walked across to the group, Dougie turned and stood nervously behind the two scientists who had now stood up to face Walton. Extending his hand, Quest shook Walton's hand.

"It's no problem Prime Minister. I believe you know the Professor."

Walton smiled and shook hands with the young woman, "Nice to see you again Professor. I believe you both know my assistant Lisa and, of course, the Home Secretary."

Acknowledging the women with a smile, Moore stepped aside and motioned Dougie forward. Walton never quite imagined himself meeting a 300-year-old man. Despite his mental preparation for the encounter and years of political service, when the moment finally arrived, he could only think of two words to describe his feelings, "Intimidation and awe."

For him gazing at Dougie was like meeting a great historical character from the past, say Winston Churchill or Abraham Lincoln. Standing silently waiting for the Prime Minister to speak Dougie got the impression that perhaps the leader was as nervous as he was. Taking the lead he smiled and extended his large hand. "I'm glad tae meet ye Sir."

"I can't tell you how pleased I am to finally meet you Mr Allan, I've heard so much about you. Thank you so much for your help, I appreciate that this whole experience must be daunting for you."

"Aye, you could say that."

After shaking the big man's hand, Walton motioned the group to sit down. "Please have a seat."

Leaning back on the leather couch Walton sighed, "Dougie I have so many questions, I'm not sure where to begin."

Glancing at the group Dougie smiled, "Well just ask me what ye want, I'll do my best." Glancing across at the Home Secretary, Walton nodded.

"Thank you. Well firstly I know your basic story, but maybe you could fill in the details for me."

Shrugging his shoulders, Dougie nodded, "Aye of course. For me it all started a week ago ... er that is in 1710 of course. I manage a silver mine in Alva, er well at least I used tae. I had been employed because the previoos manager disappeared amid suspicions of skulduggery. I was his replacement."

"I see."

"Well. The men and I had just finished eating lunch when I was informed that MacArthur, that was his name, Alexander MacArthur, had been seen entering the mine from another entrance."

As Dougie described the events in detail, the Prime Minister sat spellbound. When finished he took a deep breath and sat forward.

"And the pyramid Dougie, how did you come across the pyramid?"

"By accident actually, after falling through the mine floor I landed on my backside and because of the intense light, it became almost impossible tae tell which direction I was walking."

Pausing, Dougie leaned across to the table, picked up his glass and took a sip of orange juice. "That was when I found the pyramid."

"And this is when this McArthur fellow attacked you?"

"Aye, but it was strange. When he appeared, it was almost as if he wasn't expecting me and that I'd somehow stumbled on something that I wasn't supposed tae."

Sitting back for a moment, Walton took a sip of juice and glanced across at the Home Secretary before returning his attention to Dougie. "And that's when the attack came?"

"Well he didn't attack me as such. He had this, I suppose ye would call it a miniature black rock which appeared to dissolve into a liquid and …"

"Liquid?"

"Aye, all I remember is being unable tae move as this liquid came alive and somehow swallowed me up. The next thing I knew I was on the ground outside the mine entrance. Then Tom appeared and well, ye ken the rest."

"Tom?" interrupted the Prime Minister. Leaning forward in her seat, Professor Moore cleared her throat, "Tom Duncan Sir, the man who found Dougie.

"Ah of course."

As the group relaxed into the conversation Anne Petrie leaned across and opened her briefcase retrieving a blue A4 folder that she placed on her knees and took out an A4 sheet of paper.

"Dougie in your police interview you mentioned the appearance of a stranger, I believe you described him as gaunt faced with piercing blue eyes."

Flipping the sheet over Dougie nodded in recognition at the chillingly familiar drawing of the gaunt faced hooded figure. Glancing across at Professor Moore, Dougie nodded apprehensively.

"Aye, that's him. As I explained I first saw him outside the mine, then at the pyramid …"

"Any other sightings since you arrived?"

"Only in nightmares – visions, call them what ye will."

Glancing briefly at the Prime Minister and then gazing back at Dougie with questioning eyes, the Home Secretary repeated, "Visions?"

Sitting forward, Dougie sighed and lowered his voice, "Aye, at first I thought I was going out of my mind. But since my arrival, these visions seem tae be getting stronger, more intense. So much so, that it's sometimes been difficult to distinguish between the dream and reality." Walton placed his glass down and cleared his throat. "Well, Dougie after all you've been through perhaps …"

"Perhaps I'm seeing things? That's what ye were thinking? I disagree. What I've experienced, I should say what I'm experiencing seems bloody real tae me. In the cemetery in Alva, one of them appeared and told me who they were and why this insane decision had been made."

Walton shuffled in his seat uncomfortably, "Yes, I read about your experience. However, from what I understand, you originally said that it was your wife in the cemetery and not one of these beings. "

"Aye that's true, but as I mentioned she told me that by taking on a familiar face, it would make interaction easier."

"Shape Shifters"

Walton turned his head towards Quest and murmured, "I'm sorry, but what?"

"Shape shifters Sir, the ability for a life form to change or morph its appearance into anyone, or anything."

Sitting back, Petrie rolled her eyes and sighed, "Oh please Doctor, really!"

Quest objected, "Why not? We have them here on Earth already. Well sort of. Look at the Chameleon with its ability to blend into its surroundings. And there are countless others plants and animals. These beings, whatever they are, they are obviously far more advanced than us."

For a moment the group sat in silence until Walton continued, "So what you're saying is that they could be out there right now, living among us?"

Before Quest could respond, Dougie interrupted, "Doctor I think you're perhaps getting the wrong idea. I don't think ye should think of them as alien, Mary told me that they have been here from the beginning, now what exactly that means I'm nae entirely sure. But one thing I do know is that they see humanity as a serioos threat tae the planet, almost like an infection, or disease. And this process which has been activated will essentially er …"

"Cure the disease?"

Looking serious, Dougie nodded in agreement, "Aye, exactly."

Moore stood up and began to pace up and down.

"But from what Dougie has said, he believes that his encounter in the cemetery could be seen as some kind of olive branch," she said.

Walton screwed his eyes in confusion, "Professor?"

"Dougie was handed a piece of parchment which contained symbols."

Gazing in amazement at the group, the Prime Minister repeated, "Symbols, what kind of symbols?"

Turning to face her colleague for support, she continued, "We believe that the symbols contain some kind of message, but so far we've had little success."

"So, you think that they're perhaps giving us an opportunity to save ourselves?" the Prime Minister asked.

For a moment Moore looked a little unsure as how to respond, but as she opened her mouth, Dougie jumped in, "I don't know, perhaps. But I got the impression that the decision had already been made. Whatever the meaning of this message is, I'm unsure. All I ken is that whatever's going happen it's going tae be soon."

Placing the picture of the hooded creature back inside the folder, Petrie then put the folder back inside her briefcase and closed the metal clasp.

"Have you had anything back since you emailed the symbols out?"

Both Quest and Moore shook their heads simultaneously.

"We've had a couple of possible ideas back, but nothing concrete I'm afraid," Quest said.

"I see."

Returning to her seat, the Professor picked up her glass and gulped down the remaining few drops of juice. "And what of us, humanity, is that it?"

Gazing around at the grim faces of the group, Walton fixed his glance upon the gentle flames of the lounges gas fire and sighed. "Well, unlike the movies we don't really have a contingency plan for this. Along with Russia, the US and China we're launching three of four flights to the International Space Station – hopefully to create a kind of Noah's ark if you like. It's not much but it will allow the essence of who we are to survive, at least for a while." As his words faded, Walton got to his feet and motioned his assistant and the Home Secretary to follow him.

"Well Dougie it's been an experience. However, if you'll excuse us we have other meetings to attend. I'm just sorry we couldn't meet under better circumstances."

Standing up, Dougie extended his hand and shook Walton's. "Aye."

With a nod to Quest and Moore, the Prime Minister turned and moved towards the exit. As the large door swung open, he suddenly stopped and turned.

"That reminds me, President Bryant has asked to pass on a request meeting. He unfortunately is a very busy man, but wondered if you would perhaps meet him in a day or so. I believe he's the outdoors type. He seemed keen on seeing you away from this madness. I trust that would be okay?"

Glancing once more at the two scientists Dougie nodded and shrugged his shoulders, "Of course."

"Excellent! I'll have Lisa make the arrangements."

As the group departed, Quest rose to his feet and beckoned his colleague, "Well Dougie, unfortunately we also have to get back to work, so if you'll excuse us?"

Following Quest, Moore stood and placed her hand on Dougie's shoulder. "I'm sorry it wasn't better news Dougie."

Glancing up at the young woman he smiled, "Aye lass, but dinna give up just yet."

FORTY FOUR

WEDNESDAY: 7.55PM THAMES HOUSE, LONDON

IN HER UNUSUALLY quiet office, Hammond sat gazing out of her second-floor window and surveyed the threatening storm clouds as they moved ominously across the skies of central London. Having been sitting at her desk for most of the afternoon she was frustrated at her lack of progress.

Turning to her monitor, she refocused her gaze to an image of Bill Peterson, the former *Chronicle* reporter and apparent CIA mole who was arrested while attempting to flee London Heathrow a day earlier. Reading the interrogators report, she was disappointed to learn that Peterson had refused to answer any questions, arguing that as an employee of the Central Intelligence Agency he had the right of diplomatic immunity. Rubbing her tired eyes she gazed once more at the "Classified" status of Peterson's file. Why had he been undercover for so long and, more importantly, what was his link to Brooks the man who so callously murdered so many people including three members of the *Chronicle*'s news team?

Leaning across to her phone, she dialled and waited for a connection. After a moment the line clicked as the call was picked up. "Hello …"

"Yes this is Claire Hammond, I wondered if any progress had been made with Bill Peterson? I thought that perhaps. "

"I'm sorry Miss Hammond but he's been released – About half an hour ago."

Standing up in a state of shock she shouted out, "What!"

"I'm sorry but I was just following orders I, I thought …"

"Wait a minute, orders, from whom?"

"Deputy Director Marshal. If you like I can …"

Claire slammed the phone down and stormed across towards the elevator and pushed the call button. As the doors hissed open, she stepped inside and pushed the button marked 4.

Arriving moments later she stomped out of elevator and strode down the corridor towards the Deputy Directors office. Stopping outside his door, she paused for a moment to gather her thoughts. Her father always warned her that "There were times when losing one's temper can be useful. But losing it in front of your boss is unprofessional and never a good idea".

Taking a deep breath, Claire slowly exhaled and knocked on the door and waited for a reply.

"Come in."

She opened the door and stepped inside. The Deputy Director was alone, his assistant had gone home for the evening and as she walked through the door, Marshal was in the process of pouring himself a generous glass of brandy.

"Claire, come in, I was beginning to wonder how long it would take. Would you like one?"

Closing the door behind her, Claire followed Marshal into his office. "Sir?"

"A brandy … You look like you could use one?"

Claire shook her head, "No thank you."

Returning to his desk, Marshal sat down, gulped down a mouthful of the amber liquid, placed the glass down and sighed.

"Go on, you can say it."

"Sir?"

"Let me guess. You've come to enquire why I gave the order to release Peterson."

"Well frankly Sir, yes."

"Simple, it's called diplomatic immunity."

"Yes Sir, I know that, but if I could just be allowed to have ..."

Raising his hand Marshal cut the analyst off in mid-sentence.

"You've already had him for 24 hours and achieved nothing. On top of that, I've got a bloody CIA section chief screaming down my neck threatening an international incident because we're holding one of his agents."

"Yes Sir, but ..."

Suddenly Marshal stood and raised his voice, "Enough! Miss Hammond I understand your frustration. I really do, but under the circumstances there was nothing I could do. Also, to be quite frank, the world's turning to shit. Haven't you seen what's going on? Don't you read the bulletins? Tomorrow the government is planning to invoke a state of emergency and I've been ordered to co-ordinate with the military to send our people to help. I just don't have enough people – France, Germany, Italy and possibly us. I tell you Claire, I don't know where this will end. I really don't."

For a moment the room went silent as the Deputy Director took another mouthful of brandy. "Do you have family?"

"Yes of course but ..."

"Then do yourself a favour. Go home; go home now. If there is a tomorrow we can worry about Peterson then, but for now go home and be with your family."

For a moment the reality of the situation fell over her like a shroud and after taking a deep breath she nodded and gave a sigh. "Yes Sir. I will, thank you."

Standing, she walked over to the door and pulled the handle downwards. As the door swung open, Marshal called out, "Claire."

"Yes Sir."

"Good luck and keep your pass with you. If there are road blocks, it should get you through."

Giving a sober nod she sighed, "I will Sir, thank you."

By the time ex-*Daily Chronicle* reporter and apparent CIA mole, Bill Peterson, reached the doorway of Oxford Street tube station, a London Underground employee had just finished padlocking the pair of large yellow metal gates and another man was busy erecting a sign which read, "Piccadilly Line Closed until Further Notice."

Rolling his eyes in disbelief Peterson shook the gates in order to get the men's attention. "Excuse me … It's urgent that I get to Heathrow. Is there any chance?"

"No … It's all shut down mate."

"What!"

"It's all shut down, the whole network, government orders or something. Don't you watch the bloody news?"

Banging the gates in frustration Peterson raised his voice. "Please, you have to help me; I have to get to Heathrow."

Ignoring Peterson's pleas the two men turned a corner and disappeared out of sight.

"Damn it!" he screamed as he turned back towards Oxford Street. Walking away, his heart leapt as he spotted a black cab coming towards him. Then thrusting his hand out to get the driver's attention, he sighed in relief as the taxi came to a screeching halt opposite the station entrance. Reaching out, he stepped forward, opened the door and climbed in.

"Where to Guvnor?"

"Heathrow please."

"Sorry Mate, it closed about an hour ago."

Shaking his head in disbelief, Peterson could feel the frustration growing. He had to get out of the country, but as time rolled on, it was becoming seemingly impossible to get away. "Okay, do you know of any other airports that are still open?"

"Yes, Gatwick I think. But I can't guarantee it."

Slamming the door closed, Peterson buckled himself in and nodded, "That'll do, take me there, but please hurry."

As the cab sped away, Peterson reached inside his coat pocket and pulled out his cell phone. After checking for a signal he pushed a button on the side of the cabbies door that read, "Push for Privacy", which when pressed, immediately disconnected the cabs intercom system. After pushing redial on his handset he waited for the call to be answered. "Code in please." Speaking quietly Peterson responded, "One, Alpha, Five, Charlie, Zulu, Seven."

After a moment the voice on the other end continued, "Conformed. Peterson, I thought you were supposed to be on a flight yesterday."

"I was, but I've had problems."

"I've heard, in fact everyone's heard."

Before the man could continue, Peterson yelled out, "Will you, just shut up man and listen. I need to pass on a message to the President. It's urgent he gets it, understand?"

After a moment of silence the voice came back, "I understand."

"Good, tell him that the bird has flown the nest; understand? The bird has flown the nest!" Pressing the call end button the line went dead and Peterson placed the phone back in his pocket. As the cab sped along Regent Street, Peterson released the privacy button and shouted to the driver, "Can't we go any faster?"

Feeling flustered by his passenger's apparent lack of patience, the driver blurted out. "Alright guvnor, keep your bloody hair on. I'm doing my best. What's your rush anyway? Are you afraid it's not going to be there?"

Peterson didn't respond, but merely gritted his teeth and muttered to himself, "Come on move."

WEDNESDAY: 10.40PM CENTRAL POLICE HEADQUARTERS, ROME, ITALY

BELOW THE STREETS of Rome's Central police headquarters, Father Antonio Demarco sat in a small interview room that had been hurriedly converted into a makeshift office. Although dimly lit, Antonio had access to a computer and paper for taking notes.

Given the dreadful events of the past 24-hours, he felt not only lucky to be alive, but also grateful to the young officer who arranged this safe haven for him.

He had been staring at the page of symbols for the past three hours, but Antonio felt no closer to finding a solution than he did a day earlier. In the dim light of the small room, the strange markings looked nothing more than a jumbled mix of lines and circles. How he was supposed to decipher these into tangible numbers he did not know. As he looked up for a moment, his train of thought was interrupted by a knock on door and the entrance of a young officer carrying a small wooden tray containing a mug of coffee and what appeared to be a ham and cheese bruschetta.

"Padre. We thought you might be hungry."

Leaning back in his chair, Antonio smiled and gave a nod of gratitude, "*Sì, grazie.*"

Placing the tray down, the officer nodded and left, closing the door behind him.

As the room again fell silent, Antonio leaned across and picked up the mug. Then, after pausing for a moment he slowly gulped down a mouthful of the hot liquid. As he slowly swallowed he took a sigh of satisfaction and placed the mug down.

Then, as he reached across for the bruschetta, a small beam of light suddenly caught his eye and he glanced up to see where it was coming from. He could see that it was emanating from a high-placed air vent on the far wall of the room, no doubt, he thought from the floor above. As he gazed down at the long shadows being cast on the floor from the vent, he excitedly reached across and grabbed the crumpled sheet of A4 paper. Staring first at the symbols, he then returned his gaze to the floor and threw his hands up into the air shouting, "Eureka!" Suddenly, from outside he heard footsteps approaching and the large wooden door to the room flew open and two concerned looking officers ran into the room.

"*Padre … Va tutto bene?*"

Antonio stood and raised his hand, "*Sì, mi dispiace bene.* I've solved it, I know what they mean."

"Padre, solved what?"

Smiling broadly, Antonio looked at the officers and held up the sheet of paper. "He knew. My father, he was right all along. They were numbers after all. "

"Numbers?"

"*Sì* … Binary numbers!"

FORTY FIVE

THURSDAY: 4.10AM CAMDEN TOWN, LONDON

IN THE EARLY morning half-light, Claire lay in her bed staring upwards at her bedroom ceiling, her mind reeling with recent events. She had been restless for most of the night and had eventually decided that it was pointless staying in bed any longer and as such had decided to get up.

There was just something about the *Chronicle* case that made no sense and no matter how many times she cross-examined the facts in her mind the more distant the result appeared to be. After the previous evening's conversation with Marshal, she had been astounded at how quickly he had yielded to external pressure and prematurely released Peterson from custody, especially after hearing from colleagues about his "Formidable and supposedly uncompromising nature".

She could only conclude that it was perhaps the burden of current events that had dictated his actions. Whatever it was, Claire was convinced that with a little more time and effort, Peterson would have yielded. In hindsight though, she was also the first to admit that his recommendation for her to visit her parents was a good idea and after tying up a few loose ends she would later drive the 50-minute journey to Dunstable later that afternoon.

Once dressed, she poured herself a large mug of black coffee, buttered two slices of wholemeal toast and walked across to her small desk and switched on her laptop. As she waited for the computer to warm up, she took a seat and sipped another mouthful of coffee. As the Security Services welcome page appeared, she placed her mug down and entered her user credentials. Reaching across her desk she picked up a notepad and pencil and began to write. She first listed what she considered to be her "puzzle points", the names of the murdered *Chronicle* reporters, the Icelandic scientist and Herman Brauer. Then she added the names of the two CIA agents, the mole Bill Peterson and the murderous David James Brooks, the man who so callously carried out the killings. Pondering over the list for a moment, she then jotted down Donald McPherson's name, the reporter from Stirling and finally she added Harding's name at the bottom, as she would have been Brooks' final victim. Staring at the list, she took another bite of toast and wondered whether or not to write down the names of the innocents, the unfortunate individuals, who just happened to be in the wrong place at the wrong time. In the end, she decided against it. As tragic as these deaths were, they were clearly unrelated to the case in hand. Placing the pencil down, she glanced once more over the list and asked herself just what was the connection between these people and the CIA.

Once her login credentials were authorised, Claire shuffled in closer and began to type. She began by entering Harding's name into the search box. Within moments the screen flickered and displayed the results. Claire began to read.

"Kathryn Anne Harding also known as Kate. Age 38. Current address: 12 Shrewsbury Lane, Richmond, SW14. Current Position and Employer: Editor, *The Daily Chronicle*, London."

Glancing at the record, nothing overtly unusual leapt out as to why she had been targeted in such a brutal way. For Claire, however, something tingled inside. A niggling thought that something was amiss here.

It was well known that newspaper editors often made enemies. Perhaps it was a story from her past which had come back to haunt her, or someone with a grudge. Whatever it was, something inside Claire was gnawing away at her, pushing her to dig deeper. Sitting back, Claire rubbed her eyes, glanced across at the list of names on her notepad and whispered, "Come on … What's the link here?"

Sighing, she scrolled through what she considered to be the more mundane pieces of information, previous employers, schooling, and political affiliations and so on. On the surface though and to Claire's frustration, the woman appeared squeaky clean. Pushing her chair back, Claire stood and stretched out her arms before picking up her empty coffee mug and walking through to her compact but functional kitchen.

Placing the mug down, she opened a cupboard and took out a tall glass. After filling it with cold water, she returned to her seat. Taking another glance at her notepad she had the sudden thought that perhaps it was somehow significant that Harding's name was last on the list. Perhaps it was something to do with the fact that she knew most of the victims. Indeed, most of them had worked for her in one form or another, but this still did not explain the connection with the CIA.

Scrolling to the bottom of the page, Claire spotted an additional information link and moved her mouse to click on it. As the results appeared, Claire starred in disbelief as a now all too familiar message appeared, "CIA: Unauthorised Access – Level One, Top Secret clearance required."

"What the hell. You've got to be kidding me! "

THURSDAY: 5.20AM REYKJAVIK, ICELAND

IN ROOM 211 of the Hilton Nordica, Helen Moore was woken by a sudden knock on her hotel room door. Taking a deep breath, she reached out and grappled with a small alarm clock at the side of her bed. Reading the time, she placed the clock down and sighed loudly in annoyance. Swinging her legs out of bed, she placed her feet down onto the cool laminate floor slowly walked across to a large mirrored wardrobe, unhooked a white hotel robe and wrapped it around herself before moving to investigate who was at her door. Peering through a small peephole, she groaned as she caught a fleeting glimpse of a familiar but agitated looking Richard Quest standing on the far side of her door. Muttering, "This better be good …" she turned the deadlock and opened the door.

She didn't have a chance to speak as an excited looking Quest barged past her.

"Richard please, have you seen the time? I …"

Before she could continue, Quest pushed the door closed and eagerly held up a sheet of paper containing the text of an email.

Excited he grinned at her like a Cheshire cat, "I know … I know. I'm sorry but I just found out and I wanted to."

"Found out what? Richard what are you talking about?"

"Dougie Allan's symbols Helen. They are not symbols at all, they're numbers, look!"

Moore's look of annoyance melted away into one of bewilderment, as she took hold of the piece of paper and scrutinised the markings followed by a series of distinct binary numbers and their decimal counterparts.

"Numbers, but how? Where did you get this from?"

"Demarco, Father Antonio Demarco. He's a priest in Rome. He was one of the 11 mathematicians that I sent a copy of Dougie's symbols to. I thought that perhaps they could have helped. Well it appears I was right. He's suggested that they appear to be numerical in nature … look!"

Gazing at the email she saw 100000000010 = 2050 then she took in Demarco's findings. "Binary? But Richard this is absurd. How is that even possible? The parchment has to be thousands of years old."

Quest shook his head, "I don't know, but there they are as clear as day. The question is what does 2050 mean?"

"Richard, you'll have to tell the Prime Minister. He has a right to know."

Stepping forward, Quest shook his head, "No, not yet …"

"What? But you must?"

For a moment Quest said nothing as he walked across to the room's large glass wardrobe and pondered over his reflection. Taking a deep sigh he turned back towards his colleague and continued, "Helen, I simply meant that it would be a little premature to bring it to the PM's attention until we are sure of all the facts. I promise you that if these findings are indeed correct then I'll be the first to knock on his door. You can be sure of that."

THURSDAY: 9.40AM CAMDEN TOWN, LONDON

"CLAIRE, I THOUGHT I told you to leave this case alone. You're putting me in a very difficult position."

Holding the telephone handset away from her ear, Claire winced as Marshal's voice roared angrily from the earpiece. But what was done was done, and no matter what Claire said, it couldn't change the situation now. She just couldn't simply let go. People had died – been murdered – and for some reason the CIA, and now her own boss, the deputy head of British Intelligence, were trying to hide the truth from her.

"I'm sorry Sir, I just thought that perhaps with a little more time and effort I could have uncovered …"

"Uncovered what Claire, some deep, dark conspiracy involving little green men? Claire you are a good researcher, but you are reaching for truths beyond your pay grade here, you really are."

Although she may have already crossed the line, she couldn't stop herself now. It simply wasn't in her nature to just walk away, especially after making such progress. She wanted answers to why so many of the *Chronicle's* files had been sealed as "Level One, Top Secret" and why Marshal had released Peterson so quickly. He was the one man whom she believed knew the truth. What was he afraid of?

Ignoring the voice within her head to just shut up and save her job, Claire drew breath and continued.

"Sir, I appreciate what you're saying but without having full access or even knowledge of what level one clearance is and why it's been applied to so many records, I am unable to do my job. Harding's name was last on the list and I think she was perhaps last for a reason."

"Miss Hammond …"

"Sir, if I may?"

"No Claire."

The line went silent and Claire heard Marshal give a frustrated sigh.

"Claire I promise you nobody's hiding anything from you. It's just that I don't know. In fact I spoke with a contact in the agency, Gerry Garcia. He confirmed that both Peterson and Brooks were not members of any of the teams under his command."

"Sir, did you discover why the files had been sealed?"

"No, I'm afraid not."

"That's a pity."

The line went silent and Claire heard Marshal cough.

"Although I can't tell you why those records were sealed and the mission authorised, I can tell you that according to Gerry, nobody in his team had the clearance to authorise it. In fact, after digging a little deeper, it appears that nobody in his team even knew about it."

"Sir?"

"Nobody knew about it, because the clearance required to seal those records could only come from the highest level."

Claire sighed and shrugged her shoulders, "Which is from where Sir?"

"It could have only have come from the President of the United States."

FORTY SIX

ONE BY ONE, each of the seven cloaked figures emerged from the shadows and walked into the intense light. Standing motionless for a moment, they stared upwards at the enormous mass of the black marblesque pyramid. Its rhythmic pulsating power reverberated through the chamber as if they were inside the chest of some giant sea beast that was about to rise up rapturously from the ocean depths. Each of the figures simultaneously lowered their dark hoods and stood together facing the pyramid, each pair of eyes blazing like blue diamonds. Then each individual reached under his cloak, took out a small black pyramid shaped object and placed it onto the palm of his hand. Stepping closer, each member raised his hand up and positioned it against the surface of the pyramid. Without warning the objects began to dissolve and transform themselves into a semi translucent state.

"No wait!"

Suddenly one of the figures flinched, pulled his hand back and stepped backwards. As he moved, the small black object in his hand reformed back into its original state. The remaining members of the group turned and stared at him with empty questioning eyes.

"You hesitate brother, why? You know what has to be done."

"I know, but this just seems wrong."

As he spoke, a taller, more muscular looking member of the group stepped forward and said, "Our instructions have been clear on this matter from the beginning."

"But this time it's different. They are different. Last time our actions were warranted. We understood that if the reptilians were allowed to evolve and travel, there would have been far reaching consequences. But this species, although apparently aggressive, has evolved to be so much more, and now even at their apparent end, they show great resourcefulness and courage. To deny them of a future, just seems, immoral."

For a moment the group stood silently until the tall figure stepped a little closer and lowered his voice.

"I understand your misgivings brother, but as they are already aware of our existence we cannot delay farther. To do so would risk too much."

The figure that flinched raised his head, "Have you considered that perhaps it was no accident that the human found us. Could it be that he is the one?"

The tall figure shook his head and sighed, "Ah Brother, I once believed as you do, but we've even lost one of our own to such thoughts. I am telling you no good will come of such things."

As the tall figure spoke, another member of the group stepped forward and placed a hand on his shoulder and interrupted, "Our lost brother. He was banished because he became twisted and cruel, nothing more. The decision was made and we did what had to be done."

"But what of his threats. The consequences would be unimaginable. We must …"

The tall figure turned to the group and raised his hand, "Calm yourselves my brothers, such speculation will be your undoing. We all knew this day would come. Just as it did before."

As his words faded, the cloaked figure turned back to face the pyramid and returned his hand to the cold surface.

"Brothers, we must not hesitate. What we do today will correct the imbalance, surely we must see this task through to the appropriate conclusion."

As before the black marble began to transform and liquefy when a sudden and unified shout bellowed out from the group, "No. Stop!"

As their voices faded, the tall figure removed his hand and turned in surprise, "You agree with him?"

The remaining members turned to one another and nodded, "We do. Without consensus this action cannot be warranted."

The tall figure sighed and nodded reluctantly, "You have been living among them for too long. It has made you weak. Very well, I agree to a short recess to review the evidence. However be aware that events in motion cannot be terminated – only delayed."

"And what of the missing keys? If they should turn up and fall into the wrong hands …,"

The taller figure turned to face the group and grimaced, "Then … we will have no choice but to proceed."

THURSDAY: 4.40PM REYKJAVIK, ICELAND

THURSDAY AFTERNOON'S BRIGHT skies soon faded, as a heavy rain shower descended over Reykjavik from the mountains. Outside the Hilton Nordica, the throng of reporters and news crews that had converged for an early evening press conference were hurriedly dismantling and packing camera equipment away before the onset of the heavier rain. Inside the hotel's lobby, Dougie Allan sat alone on a brightly coloured but comfortable chair opposite the hotels fashionable lobby bar.

Because of the threat of bad weather, a planned golden circle excursion had been cancelled and instead, the chaperone, Herman Michelson, had offered Dougie and Kate a tour of the University's volcanic research department. However, after the drama of the past few days, Dougie wanted time to collect his thoughts and was in no mood for a tour so had politely declined, which to Kate's annoyance meant that she had to go alone.

Gazing in amazement at the plethora of bottles behind the bar, Dougie had finally decided on a whisky which had been recommended by the young twenty something bartender. She called it Glenfiddich. After sipping a mouthful of the twelve-year-old amber liquid, he sighed with satisfaction as it glided smoothly down his throat with relative ease.

"Ah …"

The young woman grinned. "You see … I knew you'd like it."

Dougie took another sip, slowly swallowed and smiled, "Aye lass, there's no doubt, that's the good stuff alright."

Smiling once more, the young bartender refilled his glass and turned away to serve a small group of reporters who had just arrived at the far side of the bar.

Taking another sip of whisky Dougie sighed as he pondered over his recent adventure, his arrival in Alva glen and of the friendship formed with the Duncan family, not to mention his strange experiences in the mine, as well as the drama at the lighthouse.

Placing his glass down on top of a small round table, he reached inside the fold of his kilt and took out the small black pyramid object and rolled it between his fingers for a few moments. Like its larger brother, its surface was abnormally cold to the touch. Staring at the object he sighed and whispered to himself, "What the devil are ye?"

"What's that Dougie?"

Looking up surprised, Dougie was confronted by a rather wet and confused looking Wilkes. "Huh. Och nothing lad, something I picked up. I was just thinking of Tom and wondered how he was."

Wilkes gave a nod, "Well, as a matter of fact I have some news."

"Really?"

Motioning his hand towards a nearby seat, Wilkes cleared his throat. "Do you mind if I join you?"

Dougie nodded enthusiastically, "Aye lad, please."

As Wilkes pulled up a seat, Dougie quickly returned the black object to the fold of his kilt and looked up as Wilkes slipped off his khaki raincoat, placed it over the seat and sat down.

The young bartender suddenly reappeared and gave the two men a smile. "Would you like something, Sir?"

Glancing at Dougie's glass he nodded and responded, "Yes please, I'll have whatever he's having."

With an efficient nod, the woman turned and moved quickly towards the bar.

"So what's the news Mr Wilkes?"

"Well I'm pleased to report that Jane is making a good recovery and has been released from hospital. The family have returned to the house in Alva."

As he listened, Dougie got the impression that although the news was good, he couldn't help feeling that Wilkes was holding something back.

As Wilkes was about to continue, they were interrupted by the smiling bartender returning with a glass of Glenfiddich. Placing the drink down, she glanced across at the kilted Scotsman and at his half empty glass.

"Would you like a refill?"

"Nae lass this one's grand for the moment thank you."

As she nodded and walked away, Wilkes picked up his glass and briefly raised it up, "Cheers."

"Aye, cheers."

"So how are you settling in here Dougie?"

Giving a wry smile Dougie sighed, "Too be honest lad, I feel like a fish out of water. It's so strange tae wake up one morning with your wife beside ye and the next tae find yourself in a place that is so different to everything ye ance knew."

"I can't begin to imagine what you must be going through.

To be flung 300 years into a world which now seems to have no future."

Glancing across at the bartender, Dougie watched as she cleared a table of its glasses and placed them on the bar. Then, returning his eyes to Wilkes, Dougie sighed, "I was thinking, I'd like tae send Tom a message if that's possible?"

As he spoke, Wilkes smile faded and he picked up his glass and took another mouthful of whisky. Watching the young officer's uneasy expression, Dougie once again got the impression that the subject of Tom made Wilkes feel uncomfortable.

"Laddie, that's twice you've looked away when I've mentioned Tom. Is there something you're nae telling me?"

For a moment Wilkes wasn't sure how to respond. Placing his glass down, he gazed at Dougie with a sombre expression.

"I, I'm sorry Dougie but I'm not sure how to say this. It appears that Tom volunteered yesterday to accompany a survey team into the mine."

Suddenly Dougie's stomach churned and for a moment he feared the worst.

"And?"

"Well it appears that after the group had finished the survey, they were making their way out when there was an unexpected landslide."

"Landslide?"

"Yes, and it appears that although most of the team got out, Tom unfortunately became trapped."

Dougie leapt to his feet in alarm and raised his voice in concern, "Then ye have tae do something. We have tae get him out!"

Wilkes lowered his voice and motioned Dougie to sit down. "It's already underway I promise. The last I heard was that the team had already made their way through to the cavern."

Glancing briefly towards the bar, Dougie caught a glimpse of the bartender as she turned with a look of concern. In an attempt to avoid causing farther alarm Dougie sighed and returned to his seat. "Thank God, did they find him? Is he alright?"

For a moment Wilkes remained silent. That was it. In that moment of pause, that Dougie knew, he knew that something was wrong. Lowering his head, Wilkes now sensed that whatever he said was now only going to make the situation worse.

"No, I'm afraid that despite an extensive search he's not been found."

"Not found! What do ye mean, not found? Where is he?"

"Well that's just it I'm afraid we don't know. He seems to have just disappeared."

FORTY SEVEN

THURSDAY: 6.10PM REYKJAVIK, ICELAND

THE DOORS TO the Grand Ballroom flung open and an unyielding looking Professor Helen Moore came storming out, followed by a red faced Richard Quest.

"Helen, for God's sake stop. Please don't be so unreasonable."

Stopping dead in her tracks, Moore turned heel, her face seething with anger, "Unreasonable? Unreasonable? Richard don't you dare call me unreasonable again. I've just sat for three hours trying to explain our findings and despite the clear evidence those fools refuse to accept our results."

Grasping her shoulders with both hands, Quest said, "Helen, that's maybe the case but there was no need to act so childishly. They weren't attacking our evidence. It was our conclusions they were having trouble with. Even you admitted there were parts of it which are hard to swallow."

Moore rolled her eyes. "That's exactly what I'm talking about Richard. I expected more support from you. "

"Helen, I totally support you, but think about it, if what we are implying has any kind of truth about it, then none of this is going to mean a damn anyway. I honestly believe that whatever is happening here, it's somehow connected to Dougie Allan and we have to work with him to find a solution."

Pausing for a moment, Moore's hard expression melted into one of despair.

"I'm sorry okay. I admit it I'm scared. I just expected more from the Prime Minister. "

"Helen, that's politicians all over. We've seen it a thousand times before. Whatever this nightmare is, our best chance of success is to work with Dougie directly. Don't you see, he's the key?"

Moore stared at Quest for a moment, her eyes filled with stinging tears. Then in an instant she flung her arms around him as if her whole life suddenly depended on this one moment.

"I'm sorry Richard, I'm so afraid."

Quest cupped her delicate face in his hands and wiped away the tears rolling down her cheek. Then gently kissing her soft lips, he whispered, "I won't leave you Helen I promise. Everything's going to be okay. Come on, let's get some food and start focussing on what exactly those numbers mean."

By the time Herman Michelson had returned Kate to the Hilton Reykjavik, the afternoon's rain shower had turned into a deluge of heavy rain. As scientists and leaders headed through the doors of the hotel's Vox restaurant for dinner, Kate picked up her key from reception and wandered across to the elevators. As she was about to step into an open car, a familiar voice shouted out from behind, "Kate!"

Turning she smiled wryly as she caught sight of Dougie and Wilkes sitting on chairs next to the lobby bar. With a disapproving look she strode across to where the two men were sitting.

"I might have known I'd find you here."

Standing in front of the two men, her smile quickly fell away as the men's expressions painted a grim picture.

"Dougie what is it? What's wrong?"

Before he could answer, Wilkes stood and offered her his seat.

"Here Miss Harding, you may as well have my seat. I've got to go and change for dinner."

Kate nodded in appreciation and sat down, "Thank you Mr Wilkes."

As the officer picked up his raincoat and walked towards the elevator, Kate's face and voice simultaneously softened.

"What?"

"It's Tom lassie, it seems he's disappeared."

Kate's mouth fell open and for a moment she looked genuinely stunned.

"What ... but how?"

"For some reason he agreed tae accompany another crew back into the mine and somehow became separated. Apparently there was an accident and he became trapped. When they finally made it through to him, he'd gone."

"Gone? What does that mean?"

"I mean gone lassie ... they looked for hours yesterday but he was nowhere tae be found."

Grasping the big man's hand Kate sighed, "Dougie we've both been down there. That cavern is massive, and it wouldn't take much to get lost. Tom's a resourceful man, I'm sure he will turn up. Like he said to you, you just have to have faith. Remember?"

Dougie looked across at Kate and gave a reluctant nod, "Aye, I suppose you're right, at least I hope so anyway."

As they were about to stand, they were interrupted by the sudden arrival of an excited looking Quest and a somewhat subdued looking Helen Moore.

"Dougie ... Kate, do you have a moment?"

Returning to their seats, Dougie glanced across at Kate and pursed his lips, "Aye, what can we do for ye lad?"

As the advisors sat down, Quest reached inside his pocket and pulled out the familiar piece of parchment that was given to him by Dougie only a few days earlier. Handing it back, Quest smiled.

"I have some news. I think we may have discovered the meaning of the symbols. Turning to Dougie, Kate's eyes widened.

"Really, that's wonderful. Isn't it Dougie?"

Dougie didn't respond but merely continued to gaze apprehensively at the ancient symbols. "And what did ye discover, Doctor?"

Glancing across at his colleague, Quest smiled, "Well for one, they don't appear to be symbols. We think, that the markings may be numerical in nature."

"Numerical?"

Turning to Kate, Quest nodded, "Precisely, Miss Harding."

Moving his eyes over the faces of the group, Dougie had the strange sensation that everything was beginning to fall into place, almost as if he had been aware of Quest's findings before he'd opened his mouth.

"Numbers, but what do they mean?"

Quest's smile was replaced by a more puzzled look and he shook his head.

"We don't know yet, but hopefully with a little luck we'll find an answer."

Glancing at the group, Dougie grimaced and gave a heavy sigh.

"I hope so lad, I've an unpleasant feeling that we haven't much time."

Bryant stood quietly by a double set of glazed balcony doors of his suite and stared out solemnly at the heavy rain and the lights of the city below.

"Excuse me Mr President, I'm sorry to disturb you."

Bryant sighed and turned to find a tired looking Obrien holding what appeared to be a large glass of brandy.

"I thought you could use one of these."

"You read my mind Ethel. How do you do that?"

"Years of practice, Sir."

As Bryant sat, Obrien took a tall glass, filled it with orange juice and took a seat opposite the President and took a sip of her drink.

Placing his glass down Bryant rubbed his eyes and yawned, "So have they finished?"

Suddenly their conversation was interrupted as a knock came to the door.

"Yes, what is it?"

As the door swung open, a secret service agent stepped into the room and approached the President.

"I'm sorry to disturb you Mr President, but I have a message for you from Langley."

Handing the envelope over, Bryant nodded and thanked the young agent who turned heel and smartly left the room. As the door closed, Bryant opened the envelope, took out the message and began to read.

From his expression, Obrien gauged that it was bad news. As she looked on she speculated that it was perhaps another quake or tsunami, or perhaps worse.

"More bad news?"

Slowly folding the paper in half, Bryant returned the message to the envelope and placed it inside his jacket pocket and shook his head. "No. No Ethel. But it is personal. "

"I hope it's nothing serious?"

Suddenly, to Obrien's surprise, the President appeared to become agitated.

"It's not. However, it is a matter I need to take care of personally. So if you don't mind."

He stood and began to usher his speechless Chief of Staff towards the door, and practically pushed her out into the corridor. As the door slammed behind her, she shook her head in quiet disbelief.

Back inside, the President's expression turned to one of frustration as he took the envelope out of his pocket, pulled out the paper and re-read the message.

"*Top Secret – For Presidential eyes only. Message from Bill Peterson in London: Message reads: The bird has flown the nest! Message Ends. Routed via Langley HQ.*"

As he finished, Bryant gritted his teeth, scrunched up the message and tossed it into a nearby trash bin. Then sitting behind the desk, he reached across, picked up the handset to a specially installed secure line and waited for a moment to be connected.

"Yes, Mr President."

The voice on the other end was that of a female operator, possibly in her twenties.

"Put me through to Langley please?"

"Yes, Mr President. Hold please."

After a moment the line clicked and the call was again picked up, this time by a gruff sounding military-type male.

"Mr President."

The man's voice was clear and to the point, which told Bryant that whoever this was, he was used to both giving and receiving orders.

"I received a message about 10 minutes ago from an agent in London, Bill Peterson. Are you familiar with him?"

"Not personally Sir, but I apologise for the delay in getting that message to you. You were supposed to have received that yesterday but I …"

Bryant cleared his throat and impatiently cut the man off from saying what he was sure to have been a well-rehearsed excuse. In his opinion, now was not the time for excuses, the damage had already been done. Now it was time to limit the fallout.

"With all due respect I'm not interested in excuses. I need to speak to him, as soon as possible."

"Of course Mr President. I'm sorry. When I've made contact I'll have the call patched through to you as soon as possible."

Bryant replaced the handset, stood and walked across to the large double glazed balcony doors and looked across the city lights below. Catching sight of his normally handsome reflection, he stared as it suddenly began to change. His hair became darker, cheek bones rose higher and his skin tone appeared paler. Finally the eyes that were reflected back through the glass were not those of a normal human being, but could almost be mistaken for those of an animal, a wolf perhaps, or some other large predator with its eyes, eerie and piercing through the darkness.

FORTY EIGHT

FRIDAY: 9.30AM CAMDEN TOWN, LONDON

"IT'S 9.30AM, AND now the headlines from the *BBC*. From midnight last night The United Kingdom has been placed under a state of national emergency readiness following the series of recent earthquakes and natural disasters, which have struck many parts of the world. From today the police and UK military forces are putting into action the government's contingency response plan that will see the evacuation of London's population and its surrounding areas to higher ground. The public are being reminded that this is being done as a precautionary tactic only and that there is no need to panic. Viewers are also reminded that they must leave London by 9pm, after which time the city will be placed under lockdown. For more on this story and the evacuation plans let's go to our special correspondent David Drummond live in central London …"

Claire had seen enough, she picked up the remote control and pushed the off button. As the screen went dark, she continued to stare at the blank screen for a few moments, feeling terribly guilty for allowing yesterday's best-laid plans to fall apart. As many times before, morning research slipped unnoticed into afternoon report writing and by 10 pm, she had finally glanced up from her laptop screen only to sigh in disbelief at the lateness of the hour.

"Today, however," thought Claire, "was going to be different."

After days of endless trolling through case files, she was determined to finally find answers to her list of puzzle points. Despite her discoveries, she still couldn't shake off the gnawing suspicion that although Harding was to be Brooks' final victim, and her record appeared squeaky clean, she was clearly the centrepiece of something sinister, but what, she was still unsure.

Firstly, Harding either knew Brooks' victims or had at some point worked with most of them," she thought. "Secondly, as far-fetched as it sounds, perhaps Harding was the reason that the CIA planted an undercover agent in the employment of *The Daily Chronicle*. But, if so, why?

Finally, and most importantly, she wondered why the President of the United States would sanction such a seemingly brutal covert operation without the backing, or apparent knowledge, of the agency's Director.

As she picked up her pen, Claire's train of thought suddenly shifted as her cell phone began to ring. Glancing across at the phone she rolled her eyes as the caller ID of Mum & Dad appeared on screen. Picking up the phone, she reluctantly pushed the answer button. For a moment she didn't say anything, she didn't need to. The irate voice on the other end gave her little chance to explain, never mind apologise.

"Mum ... Mum ... Please don't be angry ... Something came up and I just couldn't get away ... I'm sorry, but it's my job. Look, my pass is still good. I'll be able to get home ... Don't worry I'll see you soon, I promise."

Ending the call, she returned the phone to the table and refocused her attention to Harding's on screen record. Gazing at Kate's picture, she suddenly thought that although she had little experience in the field, perhaps a visit to her apartment would yield more information. Even a chat with a neighbour might reveal something she hadn't thought of.

FRIDAY: 11.05AM CENTRAL, LONDON

WITH MOST CITY hotels closed and an unwillingness to stay in his apartment overnight, a rather rough and unshaven looking Bill Peterson was worried. Unable to return to the US, Peterson concluded that his best course of action was to get to either the US embassy in Grosvenor Square or to board a train northwards from King's Cross or European ferry from Hull or Liverpool. But to his dismay, all central London public transport appeared to have been either suspended or commandeered by the Military for evacuation purposes.

As he emerged from a small back street adjacent to Euston station, he was startled by the sudden appearance of an army checkpoint that had been placed opposite the stations entrance overnight. Realising that his recent arrest might complicate matters, he nervously turned away to avoid detection.

"You there, just a moment."

It was too late. Turning around as instructed, he found himself confronted by two young armed soldiers. His first thought was to fight his way out, but then considered that the consequences could be somewhat "unfortunate". "No," he thought, perhaps under the circumstances a more diplomatic approach would work better.

"Yes Sir."

"This area's closed. Don't you watch the bloody news?"

"I'm sorry, but I'm, er, supposed to meet my wife outside King's Cross. Please, she's all alone, you've got to let me through."

The young soldier glanced across at his comrade, who semi-sympathetically tilted his head. Then turning back to Peterson the youngster sighed. "Go on then, but hurry up and get to an evacuation point as soon as possible."

Peterson nodded in appreciation, "I will, thanks."

Walking past the checkpoint, he continued down the eerily quiet street towards Euston Road and as he crossed a normally busy junction his cell phone began to ring. Reaching inside his pocket he pulled out the phone and pressed the answer button.

"This is Peterson."

"Peterson, this is Langley, where the hell have you been. We've been trying to get through to you for hours."

"I'm sorry but I've …"

The voice on the other end snapped back, "Just hold the line I have the President for you." The line clicked and went silent before the operator returned.

"Mr President, you can go ahead now."

"Peterson, is that you?"

Peterson detected a sense of anxiety, almost urgency in the Presidents voice, that up until now he had not been accustomed to.

"Yes Sir, I'm sorry for not …"

"Just tell me what happened."

"I was intercepted at Heathrow by MI5. They've linked the *Chronicle* operation with me and Brooks but are currently unaware of the details. I've also had difficulties in getting back to the US."

The President hissed angrily, "Unbelievable, just unbelievable. Between you and Brooks what was supposed to be a simple surveillance operation has turned into a nightmare."

"Sir, I revealed nothing about the operation. I feel just terrible for what's happened. I should never have recommended him for this job, his methods have been … questionable."

"Questionable? Peterson, I said surveillance … not a bloodbath across Europe."

Peterson took a breath and exhaled, "Yes Sir, I'm sorry."

"I assume you are aware by now that the Scotsman is here in Reykjavik?"

"What! No I didn't know that Sir."

"No, I thought not. So it's possible that she could be here as well?"

Peterson rolled his eyes feeling a pang of guilt, "Yes sir, I guess that is a possibility. Do you want me to…?"

"No, It's too late for that now. I'll take care of it myself. For now just disappear. Understand?"

"I understand, Sir."

The line clicked and the call was over. Placing the phone back inside his jacket pocket, Peterson sighed, glanced once more around at the empty streets and continued walking towards King's Cross.

FORTY NINE

HAVING NAVIGATED THROUGH numerous army roadblocks and police check-points, Claire finally arrived in Richmond. Parking her red Mini Cooper adjacent at the entrance of number 12 Shrewsbury Lane, she climbed out of the car, glanced up and down the quiet street, and took a deep breath.

On her own and clearly out on a limb, she had taken the precarious decision to place protocol aside and visit Harding's home. She knew full well that if Deputy Director Marshal caught wind of her actions, she'd probably lose her job, but it was too late for that now. It was a chance she had to take. Harding was in her opinion the centrepiece of something important, but what it was still eluded her.

Slamming the car door shut, she walked up to the front door of the three-storey town house and looked around. Apart from her, the street appeared to be empty. To the left of the front door was a small ornate iron gate that appeared to lead to the back of the property. Opening the gate, Claire walked along the gravelled path and around to the rear of the house. Other than finding a well-kept city garden and a small timber garden shed, there was nothing out of the ordinary.

Returning to the front of the house, Claire walked up to the black glossed front door and pushed a small brass doorbell. After waiting a moment, she knocked and simultaneously tried the handle while shouting out, "Hello. Is there anybody home?"

There was no response and the door was locked, so she was satisfied that the house was empty. Then, stepping across to a lower ground-floor window she stooped to peer inside.

"Can I help you dear?"

Startled, Claire almost jumped out of her skin. "Jesus!"

Turning, she found herself confronted by an elderly woman, perhaps in her mid-seventies wearing a cotton patchwork dress, navy cardigan, large rounded glasses and leaning against a walking stick. Realising that the woman was a neighbour, Claire reached inside her pocket, pulled out her identity card and stepped forward.

"Yes. I'm sorry to disturb you. My name's Claire Hammond and I'm with the, police. I was looking for Miss Harding."

She was about to say MI5, but decided that by identifying herself as a police officer would not only be easier to explain but also understand.

"Oh, I see, I hope everything is alright?"

Claire nodded and gave a comforting smile, "Oh yes, it's just a routine call. Mrs …?"

"Wilson dear, Margaret Wilson. That's good dear, you can't be too careful, especially in these times."

After the old woman had inspected her ID, Claire returned it to her bag and gave a nod.

"Too true. But what are you still doing here, you should have been evacuated."

The old lady smiled, "Oh don't worry about me dear. My son is picking me up around 3 pm and I'm travelling to Scotland with the family. But what about you, shouldn't you…?"

"Oh I will, I'm just tying up a couple of loose ends and I'll be off." Do you know Miss Harding well?"

The woman exhaled and shrugged, "Oh, not really dear she's a busy woman, always coming and going, what with the newspaper and all."

"When was the last time you saw her?"

Stopping in her tracks the old lady rubbed her head, trying to remember.

"Oh, I would say a couple of weeks ago. Yes, that's right about two weeks ago. My son had just left and that's when he arrived. Oh dear, now, it's not for me to pry, but with friends like that who needs enemies."

Claire looked at the lady with inquisitive eyes, "What do you mean?"

The old woman gave an awkward, almost embarrassed look, "Well, as I said, it was the Friday night about 8.30 pm and she had a caller, a man. I saw him through my living room window. Anyway he went inside, there was an argument and a short time later he left."

Claire thought for a moment and continued, "Did you see Miss Harding again?"

The old woman shrugged her shoulders, "No, I think that was probably the last time. Too be honest I can't really remember dear. Age, it plays havoc with your mind."

Claire smiled and gave a sympathetic nod, "I don't suppose you caught the gentleman's name?"

The old woman hesitated for a moment, trying to remember. Nodding, she replied, "Will … er, no Bill, yes that was it. I think his name was Bill. Sorry I didn't get a surname although I think he was somebody she worked with. She appeared to be very angry at him for some reason, but I'm not sure what."

Claire's eyes widened and she breathed in, "Don't worry Mrs Wilson, you've been very helpful."

The old woman gave a shaky smile and coughed, "Oh don't mention it dear. I'm glad to help."

Having got this far without a warrant, Claire decided not push her luck any farther and made a move towards her car. After thanking the woman she opened the driver's door and climbed in.

As she was about to start the engine the old woman suddenly called out, "I meant to ask dear, do you need access? I have a spare key."

Claire couldn't believe her luck. The offer was too good to be true. As she opened her mouth to respond, an unpleasant image of a furious Marshal flashed through her mind. Not having a search warrant gave her a moment of indecision, but after considering the amount of work she'd already put into this case, she would be crazy to look this gift horse in the mouth and walk away empty handed.

"No, to hell with protocol," she thought as she climbed out of the car, slammed the door shut and walked back to where the old woman was standing.

"Are you sure it wouldn't be too much trouble?"

"Not at all, I'm sure Miss Harding won't mind. Just a moment dear and I'll get the keys."

Mrs Wilson turned away and disappeared down her hallway. A minute or so later she returned clasping a BMW black leather key ring complete with two brass keys attached. "There you are dear. I'm just off to check up on my son's progress. When you've finished, just pop them through the letterbox."

Taking the keys out of the woman's frail hand she smiled, "I will and thank you."

As the neighbour turned and disappeared inside, Claire stepped across to number twelve, took a deep breath and placed one of the keys into the lock of the black front door. As she turned the key and swung the door open, her relaxed expression changed into one of sheer revulsion as the most awful putrescent smell drifted outwards.

Whispering "Oh my God" to herself, she covered her mouth with the back of her hand and made her way slowly into the property. Once inside, she glanced around the hallway in an attempt to locate the source of the rotten smell. Her initial thought was that it was perhaps a piece of rotten meat that had been left, but this was quickly replaced by a more disturbing and sinister thought.

Although she had never personally experienced death, she had always thought that when faced with the situation, she would be ready, but now, and at this moment, she was not so sure. She carefully opened a door to her right that revealed a bright modern living room complete with large, flat-panel television and a chocolate coloured leather couch. Closing the door, she again edged forward and opened another door, this time on her left. This door was fronted with frosted glass. Once inside, she found herself in a bright, spacious modern kitchen. Stepping towards a tall American-style fridge, she took a deep breath and closed her eyes in trepidation. As she pulled the door open, she looked and took a sigh of relief at the sight of nothing more than clean empty shelves.

However, as the door shut, Claire stood momentarily fixated, almost numb with the grim realisation that if the fridge was not the source of the smell, then something else, something even more ghastly lay ahead. As she returned to the hallway, she felt a new and sudden rush of adrenaline, combined with nausea and pure cold fear. Almost as if an icy finger was at work stroking the back of her neck. With her throat becoming increasingly tight and dry, she licked her lips and moved slowly towards a carpeted stairwell and began the slow climb upwards. Arriving on the first floor, she again placed her hand over her mouth to prevent herself from gagging at the progressively unbearable smell.

Just up ahead, Claire almost threw up in disgust as she caught sight of a mass of flies buzzing around the base of the door.

Almost too afraid to open the door, Claire summoned up all her strength, took a deep breath, grasped the door handle and swung it open. Claire's eyes widened with sheer disbelief as she thrust both hands over her mouth to stop herself from gagging. There, lying face down on the bedroom floor was the fully clothed, decomposing, but definitely recognisable, body of Kate Harding.

After a moment of staring at the body, the urge to throw up became so overpowering that she leapt from the bedroom, bolted downstairs and stumbled out through the front door to finally fall to her knees.

When she stopped being sick, Claire took out a tissue from her pocket, wiped her mouth and slowly pulled herself up to her feet. Shaking and breathing heavily she opened her bag and pulled out her cell phone. Flicking through her list of contacts she finally selected Deputy Director Marshal and pushed call. After a moment's delay, the call was answered by an angry but familiar sounding voice.

"Claire I thought I told you to …"

Wiping back tears, Claire didn't give Marshal a chance to continue, "Sorry Sir, but it's Kate Harding …"

"Miss Hammond I told you to leave that case alone."

"I know Sir. But I'm afraid she's dead, Sir."

For a moment Claire could sense Marshall's confusion in the silence.

"Dead? But that's impossible I've just spoke with Reykjavik, she's alive and well."

Wiping her forehead she took a deep breath. "No Sir, I'm currently at her home in London. I spoke with her neighbour who told me of an argument that she had a couple of weeks ago with a man – a man named Bill."

The line went quiet for a moment then Marshal continued, "But that's impossible. Are you sure?"

Claire sighed and gave a nod. "Sir, I'm absolutely positive. The body matches Harding's appearance exactly."

"Well if Harding's dead, then who the hell is in Iceland?"

"I don't know Sir. Do you want me to call Robert Wilkes in Reykjavik?"

"Yes, you're bloody right I do!"

FIFTY

ICHARD QUEST WAS tired and frustrated. Leaning back in his chair, he stretched out his arms and sighed. He was sitting alone in one of twenty makeshift meeting rooms that the hotel had hurriedly assembled for the summit. Quest had been looking at the same computer spread sheet for hours in an attempt to decipher Father Demarco's string of binary numbers.

To his annoyance, knowing the binary of 100000000010 seemed to only be part of the puzzle. After thousands of permutations he still felt no closer to discovering as to what 2050 actually meant. He tossed out numerous ideas including a grid reference point, a year, a specific time. He even considered at one point that it could be a biblical reference.

After working for many hours, he tried sequencing the numbers into blocks, and contemplated that perhaps they represented some form of simple calculation like 20+50 or 20-50 and so on. After each attempt, he ran the result through a self-designed, pattern-matching algorithm in the hope that it would detect and extract any potential patterns. Unfortunately, with no success.

Tired, exhausted and almost at breaking point, he made one last effort. 20=50, twenty individual numbers that when added together equalled fifty. Running with this idea he ran the formulae against the pattern-matching algorithm to search through thousands of variations until his screen finally displayed one hopeful result, 160814635209902240530.

Rubbing his eyes, he sat forward and stared wide eyed at the first six digits. "160814 … Oh my God! It's a date, It's tomorrow's date!"

As he moved in for a closer look, the door to the small room suddenly burst open and a grim faced Moore rushed in carrying a plastic A4 folder.

Seeing Moore's distress, Quest sat up in preparation to receive what he suspected was going to be more bad news.

"Is everything alright Helen? You look a little shaken?"

Walking across to his desk she pulled up a chair and sat opposite him. "No it's not. It's worse than we thought."

As she spoke, she opened the folder, pulled out a document – *Confidential: Eurasian Seismology Survey* – and placed it in front of him.

"The earthquakes are getting stronger Richard. The evidence, everyone agrees that we're looking at the build-up to some kind of major event."

"Helen I think we're already going through that, don't you?"

Shaking her head in disagreement, she opened the document and fingered her way to a point on a map of the world, which had been overlain with symbols showing recent volcanic activity and a table of figures. Taking hold of her companion's hand she gazed into his eyes.

"No Richard, the earthquakes are only part of it. You know that. Throughout history nearly every major volcanic event has been preceded by an earthquake or tsunami. Looking at these figures, they show a definite expansion of the pacific ring into the Eurasian and North America regions. Don't you see Gylfadóttir was right! We're looking at some kind of Wilson Cycle, but on a scale that I've never seen before."

Gazing at the chart, Quest shook his head, "Come on Helen, a Wilson Cycle? You're starting to sound like some of those …"

"Those what? For God's sake Richard, look at the evidence for yourself. Whatever this is, it's enormous."

Without really giving Quest a chance to review the data she grabbed the document and returned it back inside the plastic folder.

"I knew it, if you're not going to take me seriously …"

"Helen, wait. Let's, for the sake of things, say that you are right, when …"

For a moment Quest's voice faded away and his face turned pale.

"Richard what is it?"

Staring at the numbers on the screen he suddenly turned to Moore with a look of urgency. "Wait a minute, let me see that survey again."

Opening the folder she and took out the document, unfolded it and laid it down.

Staring at the world map, Quest then turned to his computer, reached across to his mouse and clicked on the number result 160814635209902240530. Then omitting what he now considered to be the next day's date of 160814, he selected the remaining portion and ran it against his pattern-matching algorithm.

"Richard, what is it? What are you looking for?"

"It's just a hunch but …"

Waiting for the result the pair watched in anticipation as the small on-screen egg timer turned as the computer processed the instruction. Then after what seemed to be an unbearable amount of time the result was displayed – "N 63° 52.099 W 022° 40.530"

Throwing his fist up in triumph he screamed out, "Co-ordinates. I knew it!"

"Co-ordinates to what though?"

Quest glanced up at Moore, "I don't know, but let's find out." Turning back to the computer, he opened an internet browser, navigated to Google and pasted the co-ordinate results into the search box. As "Midlina – Iceland – Places of Geologic Significance" appeared on the screen, Moore gasped, "Oh my God Richard, that's here!"

Stunned and momentarily speechless, Quest quickly stood, folded the survey document and handed it back to his stunned partner.

"Midlina, the Mid-Atlantic Ridge. It's the mid-point that separates the Eurasian and North America tectonic plates. There's even a bridge you can walk across, but why there? It doesn't make any sense. It's not a volcano. What possible significance could it …?"

Something suddenly clicked in his mind and turning to Moore with a look of dread he whispered, "Oh my God Helen, don't you see. It has to be the location of another pyramid!"

With his adrenaline kicking in, he suddenly bolted for the door.

"Richard, where the hell are you going?"

"Helen, we've got to warn them. Whatever's going to happen it's going to happen tomorrow."

As he opened the door, Moore suddenly sprang forward and grabbed his arm. "Richard. Wait! Dougie Allan. We have to tell him. Perhaps there's a chance."

In the Presidential Suite of the Grand Hotel Reykjavik, an anxious looking President Richard Bryant was pacing the floor. Stopping beside the room's drinks trolley he took a moment to pour himself a tall glass of spring water and was about to take a seat when there was an abrupt knock on the door.

"Come in."

A secret service agent stepped inside. Tall, in his thirties and well built, Bryant acknowledged the agent with a respectful nod.

"Come in."

"You sent for an agent, Mr President?"

Bryant smiled, "Yes I did Agent ..?"

"Reynolds Sir. Special Agent Mark Reynolds"

"Please, take a seat."

Reynolds pulled out a chair from under an adjacent table and sat opposite the President. "Well, Agent Reynolds I have a small, off-the-record favour that I need your help with. Interested?"

As he spoke Reynolds smiled inwardly at being given the honour to serve the President personally. "Of course Mr President, anything."

. "I'm looking for a woman."

"Sir?"

"No. It's not like that. Finding this particular woman is important to national security. Her name is Kate Harding, she's a reporter and I believe a guest at the Hilton."

"I understand Sir. What action would you like me to take if I find her?"

Bryant gave him a stern look and cleared his throat, "Now, I want to make sure you absolutely understand this."

"Sir?"

"I want you to do nothing! Under no circumstances do you talk to her, in fact the only thing I want you to do is report her movements directly to me and nobody else. Is that clear?"

"Absolutely crystal Sir."

"Good."

Reaching inside his suit pocket, the President pulled out a card with what appeared to be a cell phone number written on it.

"Take this. It's my personal number. If you do find her and she attempts to leave the hotel, call me immediately."

Leaning across the agent took the card and stepped back. "Is there anything else Mr President?"

Bryant thought for a moment and nodded. "Yes, I'd like to go for a drive tomorrow morning and I need a car. Can you arrange this for me?"

"Of course Sir ... and an escort?"

"No, that won't be necessary. It'll just be me, understand?"

"Of course Mr President."

Rising to his feet, the President stepped up to Reynolds and extended his hand. As the two men shook hands Bryant smiled "Thank you Agent Reynolds, that'll be all for now."

"Yes Sir … Thank you Mr President."

Stepping back the agent turned heel and quickly exited the room closing the door behind him. Leaving the President alone once more, Bryant walked across to the room's large glazed balcony doors, gazed out and hissed, "At last my brothers, I think I've found him."

FIFTY ONE

FRIDAY: 6.40PM REYKJAVIK, ICELAND

"*GO TO THE light and find the key to join the world only then can I guide you home.*" Dougie's body twitched and his eyes opened.

"Mary. No, don't go!"

As her image dissolved into nothingness, his disorientation cleared and he sat up to find himself once again alone in his hotel room. Climbing out of bed, Dougie sighed and grunted with guilt as he caught sight of an empty whisky bottle sitting beside his bed. Standing up, he picked up the bottle, walked into the room's adjacent bathroom and placed it into a small waste bin. Then after rinsing his face with cold water, he dried himself and stepped across to the room's large picturesque window.

Gazing across Reykjavik he pondered at how, until his arrival, he had enjoyed fresh Scottish air and walks through Alva Glen and his beloved Ochil hills. But now the prospect of spending his life, let alone another day, in this unnatural, pampered world was, in his opinion, becoming intolerable.

In what now felt like a lifetime ago, he would have kissed his wife goodbye and gone hunting or fishing for food, but now all that he had to do was ask for something and it would miraculously appear as if by magic. Of course, this is not to say he didn't appreciate the efforts of the hotel staff. On the contrary they could not have been more accommodating. But at least when he was staying with Tom and his family he was free to explore, but here he felt as if he was becoming a virtual prisoner.

Gazing at the distant mountains with envious eyes he'd finally had enough and snapped. "Ach tae hell with this."

Spinning around he strode across to his door, turned the handle and pulled.

As the door swung open he jumped with fright, for standing directly in his path was a stern faced Kate Harding.

"Kate … lassie, you gave me quite a scare."

Giving him a somewhat frosty, unapologetic smile she replied, "I'm sorry Dougie , but I wondered if you had a minute to spare?"

Not wishing to appear rude, Dougie nodded reluctantly and stepped aside. "Aye lass … of course come in."

Dougie closed the door and looked on as she sat down in what was now becoming her usual seat. For a moment Dougie stared at her solemnly, thinking that although in Scotland he had enjoyed her company, her frequent visits here were becoming a little uncomfortable.

Stepping across to an adjacent chair, he sat down and said, "So what is it lass? What's troubling ye?"

Before she could speak there was another knock at his door. Standing up, Dougie rolled his eyes and stomped angrily across to the door, pulled the handle and swung the door open to reveal two familiar but concerned looking science advisors. "Doctor, Professor, what can I do for ye?"

As Quest and Moore entered, Kate rose to her feet, "Is everything alright?"

Quest glanced across at his partner and cleared his throat. "We've successfully translated the symbols."

Kate glanced at Dougie, her eyes wide with anticipation.

"Really that's great news, isn't it Dougie?"

Dougie's sense of relief soon dissolved into one of concern, as Quest's expression remained unchanged.

"It is good news, isn't it lad?"

Quest frowned and replied, "Not really. As you know we were correct in our assumptions that the symbols were in fact numbers. But we had no idea as to what it was they meant. That is until now."

Glancing at the scientists in anticipation Dougie shrugged, "Well please tell us lad, what have ye found?"

"When translated we believe the numbers reveal a date and a set of co-ordinates; a set of co-ordinates that point to a location right here, in Iceland. I, that is to say we both, think it may be a possible location of another pyramid, similar to the one you discovered in Alva."

Kate interrupted, "Which date exactly?"

Quest stared at Moore with an invariable grim expression and swallowed hard, "It's tomorrow."

"Tomorrow!"

Looking briefly at Kate, Dougie shivered as he thought for a horrible moment that he saw her mouth curl upwards, almost as if she sneered in wicked relief. Disregarding the feeling as being somewhat absurd, he immediately turned his attention back to the scientists and continued.

"This discovery can't be a coincidence. In Alva, Mary – or whoever she was – told me that I was here for a reason. Now, if there is the remote chance that these beings are indeed offering us a lifeline, then surely we have tae grab it with both hands."

With his heart thumping and his mind racing, Quest gazed at Moore who nodded in agreement.

"He's right Richard. You saw the survey data. If we are looking at some kind of Wilson Cycle, the effects could be devastating. We have to at least give him a chance."

"Helen I agree. But if it is another pyramid we have an obligation to inform the Prime Minister. He'll want to send a survey team in."

Dougie gave an exasperated sigh and began to pace up and down.

"Survey teams! What are ye talkin' about! This could be it, game over; we don't have time for bloody surveys. Ye have tae evacuate these people and I have tae get out there as soon as possible."

Quest reluctantly nodded his head in agreement, "Okay, let's not jump to conclusions Dougie. The Professor and I will speak to the Prime Minister. I'll see if we can arrange transportation and a team for first light. In the meantime, sit tight and I'll let you know the result as soon as possible."

Pausing for a moment Quest then turned towards Kate, a stern expression on his face.

"Miss Harding I appreciate you are a reporter and that your first obligation is to your readers, but given the sensitivity of the situation I would appreciate your continued restraint in this matter."

Suddenly Kate threw her arms into the air and shrieked, "You're insane! Do you have any idea of the shit I've been through this week? I've been shot at, strangled, chased halfway around Scotland by a bloody maniac and now you're telling me that the world is going to end tomorrow and that I've got to put all my faith in a time-travelling Scotsman. Look no offense, but I have a duty to inform people .You have to evacuate them or whatever it is you people do."

"Miss Harding, I know you're afraid, we're all afraid, but you have to understand that whatever's happening here is global and will possibly affect everyone. Reporting these events right now will only cause worldwide panic and undue suffering. That is something I can't allow. If you can't restrain yourself then I'll have no choice but to have you restrained. Do you understand?"

Gritting her teeth in anger, Kate stormed towards the door and pulled the handle, "Yes I understand, but if you ask me you're all crazy. I'll stay silent but I don't like it."

As the door swung open Kate stormed out and slammed the door behind her.

FIFTY TWO

AS HEAVY RAIN fell over central London, the security services moved through the streets for one final sweep of the city before the nine o'clock lockdown was due to come into effect. After that point, both the police and the military were under orders to withdraw north along with the rest of the population. Anyone unfortunate enough to find themselves left in the city after 9 pm would not be evacuated.

Outside King's Cross Station, the atmosphere was becoming increasingly tense and confrontational as people jostled and pushed their way through the line, almost as if they were passengers on board a doomed ocean liner desperately queuing for the last few places aboard a life boat.

Inside the station's concourse, Bill Peterson was exasperated at having made so little progress in the seemingly endless queue that stretched far outside the station and about halfway down Euston Road. With little to eat or drink and all the forecourt stores empty or abandoned, tempers were beginning to fray. Even the police, who up until now had been relatively patient with the crowds, were starting to handle disagreements in a more aggressive manner. Only moments earlier, Peterson had witnessed an argument between two male family members which had been brought to a brutal conclusion by four baton wielding officers who dragged the two individuals blooded and screaming away.

Now that he was inside the station forecourt, he was hopeful that he would soon be sitting on a train and speeding northwards out of this nightmare. Peterson's thoughts were suddenly interrupted as two soldiers appeared and placed barriers and a makeshift sign that read, "Edinburgh – Please Q Here" just behind where he was standing. As the crowd waited in anticipation, a soldier stepped forward and announced the train's immediate departure.

In response the group surged forwards and Peterson gave a sigh of relief as he ran towards platform 15 and an eventual seat on a waiting train.

As Claire Hammond's Red Mini Cooper sped out of the Bell Common Tunnel onto the M25 she glanced frantically at her watch with a mixture of disbelief and anxiety. Disbelief at how stupid she had been in delaying her departure out of London, and of the anxiety she felt at upsetting her parents. What should have been a routine journey northwards turned out to be a rather long-winded affair. As she approached exit 27, Claire was suddenly forced to hit the brakes and slow down due to a sudden build-up of traffic at the junction ahead.

As she brought the Mini to a halt behind an empty dark blue Hyundai with its driver's door wide open she muttered, "What the hell?" Claire's initial thoughts were that perhaps the driver had gone to assist someone up ahead, or perhaps it was some kind of accident.

As she waited for the driver to return, she reached across to the passenger seat, opened her bag and pulled out her cell phone. Then after scrolling through her list of recently called numbers, she stopped at Robert Wilkes. Having already tried the agent twice, she decided to make one final attempt. Pressing the call button, she waited a few moments to be connected. But as Wilkes phone rang out, Claire rolled her eyes in annoyance as once again the call was diverted to voicemail.

"Hello, this is Robert Wilkes. I'm unable to take your call at the moment so please leave a message and I'll come back to you as soon as possible."

As the line beeped, she cleared her throat and spoke clearly into the mouthpiece. "Mr Wilkes it's Claire Hammond again. I've tried calling and you've still not returned my call. Anyway as I mentioned before it's critical that you follow my instructions. We believe that the journalist Kate Harding is an imposter and dangerous. She is to be placed in custody as soon as possible. Hang on a minute."

As her voice fell silent, she thought for an awful moment that she had felt the ground tremble. "Mr Wilkes I'm sorry I'll have to call you back."

She flung the phone back inside her bag and quickly opened her car door.

Jumping out of the car, she slammed the door and slowly moved forward past the parked Hyundai, momentarily stopping to glance inside for signs of life, but there was none. Then it happened again, but this time she was in no doubt, it was a definite rumble. Her eyes widened in fear as once again she felt the ground shake and a definite sense of dread reverberated through her. With each passing moment, the shuddering grew in intensity. Suddenly and with no warning there was an almighty bang from behind as a huge block of concrete fell away from an enormous pillar, holding up the roof of an overhead bridge.

As the block crashed to the ground, Claire screamed in terror. Dust and debris began to rain down all around her. With her heart racing and the ground shaking violently, she leapt towards her car, pulled open the door and scrambled inside. Then choking on thick dust, she wiped the tears out of her eyes, slammed the door and started the engine. Forgetting to place the gear stick in reverse, she pushed her foot hard down on the pedal. She screamed wildly as the car lurched forward and slammed into the back of the abandoned Hyundai.

As Claire recovered and frantically attempted to regain control of the vehicle, she gazed up in horror, as the giant concrete leg above her began to crumble and the colossal bridge overhead began to collapse. She whimpered, realising that there was now no possibility of escape. So taking a deep breath, she closed her eyes and waited for what she now saw as her inevitable fate, whispering, "I love you Mum and Dad."

A moment later, and with an almighty roar, both the bridge and Claire Hammond were gone.

As the Edinburgh bound train finally pulled out of King's cross, any sense of relief among the passengers was soon replaced with one of shock and concern as an almighty thud suddenly rang out from the front of the train, bringing the journey north to a sudden and abrupt stop. Inside, Bill Peterson and many of the other passengers lurched forward uncontrollably out of their seats and crashed into fellow passengers and luggage racks.

Dazed, disorientated and with blood oozing out of his left eye, Peterson struggled to pull himself up. Once he was able to stand he began to move slowly forward along the carriage, carefully climbing over injured passengers in a desperate attempt to get to a set of emergency doors, which were now only meters away. All around, hurt and bewildered passengers began to panic. Then as the ground trembled, Women and children who had become separated began screaming and clambering over each other in a frantic bid to be reunited.

Again, the ground began to shake. But this time it wasn't a mere tremble, this time the shaking was so violent, that the majority of passengers, who had managed to stand after the first impact, now lost their footing and again crumpled to the floor. People were screaming for help and crying with fear.

Peterson realised that this could only be an earthquake and that his only chance of survival was to get off the train as quickly as possible. With the shaking becoming almost unbearable, he finally arrived at the emergency door only to gaze out in horror at the scene. The train appeared to have come to a stop opposite the Emirates football stadium, or at least what remained of it. What had been the heart of the Arsenal Football Club was now nothing more than a grotesque pile of twisted metal and smouldering rubble. Wiping the blood from his head, he took a deep breath, pulled down hard on a red emergency handle and the double set of doors hissed slowly open.

With no platform to step out onto, Peterson jumped out of the train and onto the rough ground below. Now outside, he began to comprehend the damage that had been done. Along with the stadium and a number of apartment blocks, the scene was one of sheer devastation. Glancing backwards he grimaced with shock as he saw the front of the train lying on its side. It had apparently collided with a fallen block of concrete.

As the shaking finally subsided and the ground once again became still, Peterson breathed a sigh of relief and turned back towards the middle section of the train to offer assistance. However, as he reached the carriage doors he became aware of another sound – a low rumble, almost like that of distant thunder. Looking puzzled, he raised his hand towards a couple of teenagers who were about to jump down from the train, "Hang on. Just wait a minute will you?"

Then turning back towards the stadium, his mouth fell open in horror as he caught sight of a huge wall of water approaching from the east. The Tsunami moved like nothing Peterson had ever seen before, engulfing mercilessly everything in its path. Cars, offices, homes … anything … everything.

Staring bewildered at the oncoming torrent, he knew that there was absolutely nothing he could do. So with a remarkable sense of calm, Peterson turned towards the train, gazed up at the two teenagers in the doorway and smiled at them before finally closing his eyes for the last time.

FRIDAY: 9.25PM - REYKJAVIK, ICELAND

For some reason sitting opposite the President of the United States always made the British Prime Minister feel intimidated. It was true that the man was just another leader, like himself, who had been voted in to represent his people. But as he stared into Bryant's eyes he wondered if it was something more. It wasn't that the man was any smarter than he was or better looking, but for some reason the man just intimidated him.

Sitting around a table which had been carefully laid with crisp white linen, crystal glasses and fine silverware the pair were among a small group of four leaders who had come together for dinner to discuss the day's affairs. Sitting in a cordoned off area of the Hilton's stylish Vox restaurant, Walton and Bryant were joined by Russian President Sergey Belanov and Chinese Premier Wu Chen. Picking up his glass of New Zealand Sauvignon Blanc, Walton cleared his throat, "Gentlemen, this is a historic day. I'd like to propose a toast. Who would have ever thought that in our darkest hour the four of us would come together and sit around a dinner table like this? Of course like you, I wish that it was under better circumstances, but whatever the outcome of this week's events are, I honestly believe that it will bring us all closer."

Belanov smiled and raised his glass. "Here, here, Mr Prime Minister I completely agree. This is a new dawn between us all."

Bryant nodded, raised his glass and also reciprocated, "Indeed it is."

As Walton raised his glass in salute, the group were interrupted by the sudden arrival of a grim faced Harkins.

"Prime Minister, Mr President, I'm sorry to disturb you but I need to speak to the Prime Minister for a moment."

Smiling at the ministerial aide, Chen nodded courteously, "Of course."

As Walton stood and excused himself, he followed Harkins away from the group to a quieter area of the restaurant and gave her a concerned look.

"What is it Lisa, what's wrong?"

For a moment the pale Harkins said nothing, but then handed a note slowly over to the Prime Minister. "It's, London Sir. It's very bad news I'm afraid."

FIFTY THREE

SATURDAY: 5.00AM REYKJAVIK, ICELAND

AFTER COMPLETING 40 laps of the Hilton Nordica's swimming pool, Robert Wilkes was confident that he had finally expelled the majority of yesterday's alcohol out of his system. Not that he regretted it, on the contrary he believed he now understood Dougie a little more and rather enjoyed sitting at the bar listening to his stories. The man almost had a purity about him, innocence perhaps, that in his opinion was a very rare thing.

Taking a deep breath, Wilkes pulled himself out of the pool, picked up his towel and stepped into an adjacent changing room. Leaving the health spa, he ignored the temptation to take the elevator and walked up the stylish spiral staircase to the second floor instead. A heavy workload left him with precious little personal time. So an opportunity for an early morning swim had provided the perfect excuse, not only for exercise but also some private time.

Outside his room, Wilkes placed his key card in the lock, pulled down firmly on the brass handle and swung the heavy door open. Once inside, he threw his swim towel onto the tiled bathroom floor and walked across to his suitcase. Flipping the lid open, he took out a clean casual shirt, blue sports sweater and a pair of casual khaki trousers.

As he was about to close the case, he caught sight of his cell phone, semi obscured among a pile of clothes. Realising that it had been some time since he'd checked in, he decided to take advantage of the opportunity and as such he picked up his phone, walked across to a nearby chair and sat down.

Restless and unable to sleep, Dougie climbed out of bed and got dressed. After listening to Quest's revelations about the possibility of another pyramid, Dougie decided that enough was enough. He was tired of running from his nightmares and that it was time to confront them head on.

Opening the heavy door to his room, Dougie glanced down the corridor for signs of life. Confident that he was alone, he stepped slowly out into the quiet corridor and closed the door behind him. Kate Harding had been right about one thing, he thought, since his first fateful encounter with James Ritchie, his life had turned upside down, and if the omen from Mary was indeed correct, this may be his only opportunity to get home.

Moving swiftly but quietly along the third floor corridor, Dougie came to a stop outside room 323 and took a deep breath. If he were going to fulfil his destiny, he would need help. Waiting for authorisation from the authorities would take too long. Whatever he was going to do, it he had to do it now.

After knocking a couple of times on Harding's door, Dougie waited patiently for an answer. Moments later he heard the lock turn and the door swung open to reveal a heavy-eyed Kate Harding. "Dougie? What is it? What's wrong?"

Dougie took a deep breath and shook his head, "Nothing lass, I just need your help that's all."

"Of course, with what?"

"Midlina. I need tae get out there and I wondered if ye wooldn't mind taking me?"

Kate shook her head, "Midlina? Dougie are you crazy? What about Doctor Quest and …"

Dougie raised his hand and shook his head, "That's the whole point, I don't want them involved. I don't ken why, but this is something I've got tae do myself. Surely ye must understand?"

Lowering her head, Kate sighed and gave a reluctant nod, "All right. Herman kindly arranged a car for me today. It's in the car park, give me five minutes to get changed and I'll meet you downstairs."

"Aye of course lass, thank ye."

As Dougie turned away, Kate closed the door and got changed.

"Mr Wilkes it's Claire Hammond again. I've tried calling and you've still not returned my call. Anyway as I mentioned before it's critical that you follow my instructions. We believe that the journalist Kate Harding is an imposter and dangerous. She is to be placed into custody as soon as possible. Hang on a minute. Mr Wilkes I'm sorry I'll have to call you back ..."

Having listened to all of his messages, Wilkes pushed the end call button, placed the phone down and sat up, feeling somewhat numbed by the revelation that Kate Harding may not only be an imposter, but in some way may also dangerous.

"This is crazy," he muttered to himself, "It has to be a mistake."

In all of his years as an agent, Wilkes had never questioned or disobeyed an order. Or for that matter, allowed himself the luxury of becoming emotionally involved in a case, but this time he was sure that it had to be a mistake. He had spent almost a week with the woman; he'd even saved her life from a crazed maniac. What kind of imposter would put her life at risk in such an extreme way?

On the other hand, he was an agent of the British Government. If she was indeed a villain with some kind of covert agenda, then he had a duty to find out what it was and stop her. Experience had taught him that in operational matters, personal feelings had to be placed aside. After much deliberation, Wilkes decided that if he had to arrest Harding, it should be done sooner, rather than later, this would then ensure that any disturbance would be kept to the minimum, as well as allowing him to show a little more discretion.

Once dressed, he sat down on his bed, slipped on a pair of brown leather shoes and getting to his feet, he gazed ominously across to his desk and to the leather briefcase that was given to him only days earlier by Corporal Jarvis. With a heavy groan, he reluctantly walked across to the case, picked it up and laid it down on top of his bed.

After opening the security lock, the case opened and he stared despondently at the automatic pistol inside. Struggling internally, he couldn't believe that he was even contemplating picking up the weapon, let alone actually arresting a woman that he had got to know personally.

In his mind his superiors had to be wrong, but as an old instructor had once told him, "You're not paid to think. You're paid to do a job and follow orders."

Wilkes reluctantly reached inside, picked up the weapon and, after carefully checking the chamber, he discretely tucked it away under his belt. Then closing the case, he picked up his blue sports sweater, put it on and pulled it down, ensuring that the weapon was adequately concealed from view.

FIFTY FOUR

STEPPING OUT THROUGH the hotel's revolving entrance door, Dougie stood for a moment, gazed outwards in awe towards the foreboding summit of Mount Esja and sighed with a growing sense of trepidation. Apart from the faint smell of sulphur, the August morning air was cool and crisp. Fortunately, due to the time, the daily horde of television crews and reporters had not yet converged in the hotel's car park and as such it was still relatively deserted.

As he waited for Kate to appear, Dougie went over the events of the past week as images of lost friends and loved ones began to once again torture his mind. Then the images slowly morphed into scenes of a more disturbing nature. The frightening game of cat and mouse at the lighthouse, the nightmare involving Alexander McArthur and, perhaps the most disturbing, his on-going struggle with the gaunt, bright-eyed stranger.

As his mind cleared, Dougie gritted his teeth, determined to remain focused and not let fear overcome him. If today were indeed the beginning of the end, then he would stand tall and hold his ground, not just for himself but also for Mary, Tom and his family and, more importantly, for all those lives which now hung in the balance.

"Dougie, are you ready?"

Turning, Dougie sighed and gave a hesitant nod as Kate

emerged from the hotel wearing a pair of blue jeans, red lamb's wool sweater and khaki rain jacket.

"Huh … Aye lass … I guess I'm as ready as I'll ever be."

"I'm sure you'll do fine. The car's just over here."

Stepping away from the hotels entrance Kate led Dougie across the semi empty car park towards a bronze-coloured Honda CRV.

"It was really kind of Herman to arrange this for me."

As she opened the driver's door, the pair were suddenly interrupted by the arrival of a rather gruff looking Icelandic police officer.

"Good morning, I assume you have a pass for this vehicle?"

Kate sighed, "Darn it, yes I do but I've left it in my room. I can show it to you on our return if that's okay?"

Even before her words faded, Kate knew from his sly expression, that this officer was not exactly the yielding type. Shaking his head the large Icelander licked his lips and gave a wry smile. "Under normal circumstances yes. But these are not normal circumstances. So I'm afraid I'll need your pass."

Giving a reluctant nod she turned to Dougie and sighed, "Yes, yes, alright. Dougie you can wait in the car if you like, I'll only be a few minutes."

As she turned away, Dougie opened the passenger door as instructed, climbed into the car and slammed the door shut.

With his heart thumping, Wilkes unenthusiastically opened the door to his room and slipped outwards into the empty second floor corridor. Quietly closing the door behind him, he once again checked the weapon under his sweater, took a deep breath and made his way back along the hallway towards the spiral staircase.

Emerging from the elevator into the third floor hallway, Kate hurriedly made her way along to her room. Feeling somewhat irritated by the Icelander's inflexibility, she angrily thrust her key-card into the reader, pushed down the door handle and swung the door open. Once inside, she stomped across to her bedside table, picked up the pass and walked back towards the door.

Outside Kate's room, Wilkes noticed that the door was slightly ajar and was about to knock, when to his surprise the door flew open and he found himself confronted by a somewhat shocked looking Kate Harding.

"Mr Wilkes! Jesus! You scared me half to death man. What are you doing creeping around the hotel so early in the morning?"

Swallowing hard Wilkes took a deep breath and motioned Kate back inside her room.

"I'm very sorry, but I need a quick word? Would you mind?"

"Yes, of course."

As Kate turned back, Wilkes followed her inside and closed the door.

"Alright, would you mind telling me what this is all about?"

Still struggling internally with the idea of arresting the woman, Wilkes took a deep breath and exhaled. "Perhaps you should take a seat and we …"

Kate shook her head, stepped across to the room's large picture window and glanced down towards the car park below. Conscious that Dougie was sitting waiting, she was in no mood for a delay. "No thank you. I'm fine right here."

"Very well. In that case I have to regretfully inform you that I'm placing you under arrest on suspicion of impersonation. You do not have to say …"

"What! Have you lost your bloody mind? Impersonation? What the hell are you talking about?"

"I'm sorry Miss Harding, I'm simply following orders. My Superiors have asked me to take you into custody and await farther instr …"

Kate shook her head in frustration, "You're insane, you've seen what's going on here and all you want to do is arrest me."

Wilkes stepped forward, "I'm sorry Kate, but until we get this sorted out, I must insist that you come with me."

Turning her back to Wilkes she sighed and returned her cold gaze downwards towards the waiting Honda.

"No, Mr Wilkes, I'm sorry but I can't go with you. Not today."

Taken aback by her surprising response, Wilkes found himself momentarily unsure how to handle the situation. He didn't want to take the heavy approach. On the other hand, he kept hearing Claire Hammond's recorded message replaying over and over in his mind.

"We believe that the journalist Kate Harding is an imposter and dangerous ..."

"Miss Harding please don't be unreasonable. I'm sure with a little co-operation we'll get this all sorted out. "

"No Mr Wilkes, not today. I've waited too long for this."

Watching her figure standing silently by the window, Wilkes suddenly felt an icy chill creep up his spine. As he fought for words, he began to feel uncomfortable, almost afraid.

"Miss Harding, Please I ..."

As he spoke, Wilkes suddenly caught a glimpse of her reflection in the window and froze in horror. There before his eyes, her face was no longer that of the Kate Harding he knew, but was morphing into something different – something gaunt and hideous with vile bright eyes. As he watched the shocking transformation, Wilkes grimaced in fear, reached under his sweater and quickly pulled out the pistol.

"Are you going to shoot me Mr Wilkes?"

The voice that spoke was not Kate's but of something else. Its grotesque voice rattled and hissed, almost like a serpent's.

"What the hell are you?"

Continuing to stare out of the window, the figure remained motionless and seemingly unperturbed by Wilkes presence.

"I have so many names. It would take too long to explain and I'm afraid I just don't have the time."

Taking a deep breath, Wilkes raised the pistol towards the figure and gritted his teeth, "Then it's all true, what Dougie said? Where's the real Kate Harding? Is she dead?"

"Of course. They killed her along with all the others because they were looking for me, but this time I managed to stay one step ahead. That is until now of course …"

Wilkes suddenly screamed in agony as a piecing pain shot through his chest like a knife. Unable to breath, he clutched his ribcage and collapsed in agony onto his knees. As he fell, the pistol tumbled out of his hand and bounced onto the hardwood floor with a dull clatter. "You see Mr Wilkes, it's my turn now. This is my time."

Struggling to catch his breath and writhing in agony, Wilkes turned his head upwards, only to see a pair of terrifying bright eyes staring mercilessly down at him like two eerie campfires burning in the darkness. "What … Arghhh."

"It's remarkable don't you think? The pain, the way it grips you. It's so pure."

Wilkes screamed in agony, "You're insane!"

The creature gave a cruel sneer and hissed, "No, it's just I can't have any complications today."

As his body began to go into shock, Wilkes spluttered and desperately gasped for air.

"Help me, plea …"

But his efforts were in vain. With one final gasp, MI5 officer Robert Wilkes crumpled face down on to the floor, his body limp and lifeless.

For a moment the creature gazed at the body with a sense of callous satisfaction, before, once again morphing back into the familiar shape of *The Chronicle* editor Kate Harding. Staring at Wilkes body, her expression was now a combination of pure hatred and revulsion as she raised her right hand to her lips and blew, what appeared to be a kiss towards Wilkes lifeless body. "Disgusting Creatures."

But this was no ordinary kiss, Wilkes body began to break down and slowly disintegrate. Dissolving into what appeared to be a fine grey powder and then into nothingness, almost as if he had never existed.

"Ashes to ashes Mr Wilkes. Dust to dust!"

With all traces of his body gone, Kate walked calmly across the room to face a small wall mounted mirror, then after checking her makeup, she gave a cold sneer before collecting her bag and making her way back towards her door.

Rather than sitting in the cold discomfort of an empty car, Dougie had taken the advice of the Icelandic policeman to wait inside for Kate. Indoors, he poured himself a large mug of black coffee and sat opposite a large wall mounted television. As she emerged from the elevator, Kate spotted Dougie and strode across the marble floor to where he was sitting.

"I'm sorry to have kept you waiting Dougie, I met Mr Wilkes. He wanted a quick chat."

Swallowing a mouthful of coffee, Dougie placed the mug down and looked up at her with questioning eyes, "Really, he's not coming with us is he?"

Shaking her head Kate responded, "No, he's busy. Perhaps we should just get going?"

Standing up, Dougie nodded with a smile, "Aye lass, of course let's."

Suddenly Dougie's words faded and a look of alarm appeared on his face, almost as if he had seen a ghost.

"Dougie. What is it, what's wrong?"

"Oh my God, it can't be, it's him!"

Kate watched as he raised his right index finger and pointed it directly towards the television. On screen, a BBC news reporter was interviewing a familiar looking politician, so familiar in fact that Kate knew immediately that the dark-suited man was in fact Richard Bryant, the President of the United States.

"Dougie what are you talking about, that's the President of the United States, Richard Bryant."

Turning Dougie grabbed her sleeve and stared at her fearfully.

"Nae lassie, it's nae! It's him … it's Alexander McArthur!"

"What? You've got to be …"

Stopping her in mid-sentence, Dougie turned and sharply barked, "Do I look like I'm joking?"

As a thousand images started pouring through his mind he grabbed Kate by the arm and roughly dragged her towards the large revolving glass door.

"Dougie. Wait, you're hurting me."

Conscious of suddenly being more than a little forceful, Dougie stopped and released her, gazing at her apologetically, "I'm so sorry lass, but that bastard's destroyed my life. If there's a chance that I can stop him, then it's a chance I've got tae take. Will ye help me?"

Placing her hand on his arm, she exhaled almost in relief and gave a cold smile. "Of course Dougie. That's what friends are for."

As the pair bolted through the doorway towards the parked Honda CRV, neither one of them noticed a solitary figure emerging silently from the shadows. Watching the Honda pull away, Secret service agent Mark Reynolds reached inside his jacket pocket and pulled out his cell phone. Then taking a deep breath, he dialled the number given to him personally by Bryant. After a moment the call was picked up and a familiar voice answered, "Yes Agent Reynolds?"

"Mr President, I'm sorry to disturb you so early Sir, but you said to call if …"

"That's alright, what did you find out?"

Sensing that the President was in no mood for idle chat,

Reynolds cleared his throat and continued. "Kate Harding and the Scotsman have just left the hotel and Sir they appeared to be in a bit of a hurry."

"I see."

"Mr President, do you want me to take a car and follow them?"

For a moment the line went silent and then the President replied. "No, that won't be necessary, I can take it from here."

"Sir?"

"You heard me, I'll deal with them."

Reynolds nodded feeling somewhat rejected. "Yes Sir of course, I understand. I meant to mention just before they left. The Scotsman said something unusual."

For a moment Reynolds hesitated, almost biting his tongue with regret. After all, in his opinion what he heard was ridiculous, not even worth mentioning. But it was too late now; he was committed to tell the President. "What was it?"

Reynolds took a deep breath and swallowed hard, "Well Sir, it sounds ridiculous and I'm sure it's nothing more than a case of mistaken identity, but when he saw you on television, he called you …"

"Called me what Reynolds?"

"Well Sir, it was rather bizarre. He called you Alexander McArthur."

FIFTY FIVE

SATURDAY: 6.10AM REYKJAVIK, ICELAND

ON THE THIRTEENTH floor of the Grand hotel Reykjavik, Bryant pressed the call end button and placed his cell phone down with a heavy sigh. Swinging his legs out of bed, he stood for a moment in the early morning half-light, before walking across to the large balcony window and pulled its thin net curtain aside.

Gazing outwards with a sense of mild satisfaction Bryant caught a fleeting glimpse of a bronze Honda CRV pulling out from the Hilton's car park and heading eastwards onto Suðurlandsbraut. As he stood back form the window, the curtain fell back into place and he walked across the room to where a casual blue shirt, pair of chinos and navy blue raincoat were draped over the back of a chair. Once changed, Bryant walked across to the door to his room and pulled down on the door handle.

As the door swung open he was met by a pair of somewhat startled looking Secret service agents.

"Mr President … I'm Sorry I wasn't expecting …"

Without uttering a word, Bryant simply raised his right hand and the two men collapsed onto the ground like a pair of freshly felled trees. Stepping over the sleeping men, Bryant continued across the hallway and pushed the elevator call button.

When the elevator arrived and the doors slowly hissed open, he momentarily gazed at the two unconscious men before stepping inside. As the elevator descended, he gazed coldly at his own reflection opposite and hissed, "I was right my brothers. It's time!"

As the CRV sped off along Route 41 Dougie fidgeted in his seat looking nervously across at Kate, before glancing to the rear in order to check that they weren't being followed. "Something wrong Dougie?"

Anxiously, Dougie shook his head, "Nae lass. For a moment I thought I saw a man in the hotel watching us. It was probably nothing." With her eyes fixed on the road Ahead, Kate gave a cold sneer and pushed her foot down harder on the accelerator.

"I wouldn't worry about him."

Stepping out of the elevator, Bryant stood for a moment next to the Hotel's impressive reception desk and glanced around. Apart from himself, the only others in proximity were a teenage porter, a middle aged receptionist and two security guards huddled over a pot of coffee in the far corner of the lobby.

Aware of the elevator doors suddenly re-opening behind him, Bryant turned to see his somewhat flustered looking Ethel Obrien emerge carrying a navy blue gym bag and a white cotton towel. "Mr President! I'm sorry. I had no idea that you were coming down I would have …"

As she spoke, she noticed that the President's skin appeared unusually pale and his expression somewhat distant. Afraid that that her leader was perhaps unwell, she stepped forward to offer assistance. "Mr President, you look unwell Sir, are you alright?"

Without saying a word, Bryant took a deep breath and calmly raised his right hand. As with the agents on the top floor, the effect was instantaneous. Obrien, the receptionist, porter and the security officers all suddenly went limp, like a set of child's rag dolls before collapsing unconscious onto the polished tiled floor.

Staring coldly ahead, Bryant stepped over his unconscious chief of staff before walking across the lobby and straight out through a revolving side exit door. Once outside he made his way across the car park towards a black Land Rover parked nearby. Walking around to the driver's door, he pulled down on the handle, only to discover that it was, unsurprisingly, locked. Seemingly unperturbed, he reached out again and touched the handle. This time, the door was unlocked and the door opened easily. Once inside, Bryant shut the door, took a breath and with the absence of a key placed his hands on the leather bound steering wheel.

Suddenly, tiny sparks of brilliant white light began to emanate from his fingertips, like miniature bolts of energy. Then, as the car roared into life, he pushed he foot down hard on the accelerator and the Land Rover sprang forward and sped away towards Route 41.

FIFTY SIX

EXHAUSTED AND BREATHLESS, Dougie frantically ran down the steep grassy slope, desperately trying to escape from an unknown assailant. Then, scurrying forward through dense woodland, he suddenly cried out in pain as he stumbled over a protruding tree stump and came crashing to the ground in agony. Struggling to his feet, his mouth fell open in horror as a foreboding cloaked figure suddenly emerged from behind a clump of trees. Wincing in pain, Dougie climbed awkwardly to his feet, staggered forward and once again began to run.

Then everything changed, he was no longer in dense woodland, but found himself back in 1710 in the familiar surroundings of his beloved Scottish homeland. His heart leapt, as up ahead he caught a glimpse of his home. His simple self-built stone cottage, with its thatched roof, surrounded by the imposing landscape of the magnificent Ochil hills.

Arriving outside the cottage, Dougie shouted "Mary" and ran forward pushing the simple timber door open, once inside he dropped to his knees in sheer disbelief as there before him stood his beautiful Mary. Dressed in a familiar, but simple, green dress with lace bodice, she stood for a moment, puzzled as to why her husband was on his knees.

"Dougie what is it? What's wrong?"

Standing, Dougie flung his arms around her neck and began to sob uncontrollably. "You're alive … Mary, is it really ye lass?"

"What on earth are ye talking about? Of course it's me, who else would it be?"

"I'm … I'm sorry, it's a long story. I just thought that I'd never see ye again …"

As he spoke his face turned pale and his words faded, as there was a knock at the door.

Mary gently pushed away from her husband's embrace and Dougie leapt forward and grabbed her arm, "Stay here lass, don't answer it!"

Mary's expression now turned to one of annoyance, "Dougie don't be silly, I've got tae answer the door. Ye can't just leave folk outside."

As she stepped forward to open the door, Dougie pulled aside the large tartan blanket that divided the room and stood behind it in order to conceal his presence.

"Mrs Allan I'm sorry tae trouble ye, I was hoping for a quick word with your good man."

Although obscured from sight, Dougie immediately recognised the voice as that of James Ritchie. The young man from Hardies of Falkirk who had secured his employment with Sir John Erskine, in what now felt like a lifetime ago.

"Aye, nae bother Mr Ritchie, just hold on a moment while I get him."

As Mary backed away from the door, Dougie sighed in quiet relief as he emerged from behind the blanket and moved forward to greet Ritchie. But as the door swung open, his expression rapidly turned to shock as there, standing in the doorway, was not the expected James Ritchie, but the frighteningly ominous hooded figure from his nightmares.

"No, it cannae be …"

With no warning, the figure sprang forward and seized Dougie by the throat. Choking and thrashing his arms wildly, Dougie frantically tried to break free, but the creatures grip was just too powerful. With little chance of escape Dougie's eyes flickered as a lack of oxygen began to take hold and he began to drift in and out of consciousness. Almost succumbing to his fate, he suddenly found himself free and reeling backwards, crashing onto the ground. As his eyes refocused, Dougie's heart sank as he found himself no longer in the warm familiar surroundings of home but in the middle of a cold, vast snow covered wilderness. "Mary. No!"

Turning a slow full 360 degrees, Dougie gazed at the bleakness of the frozen landscape and shivered as icy winds whipped coarsely around him. In an attempt to keep warm he blew into his hands and vigorously rubbed them together, but to no avail.

The cold was just too intense, bitter and raw, unlike anything he'd experienced before. For Dougie it became quickly obvious that he had to move, otherwise …

Moving forward his thoughts were suddenly interrupted as the ground beneath his feet began to tremble. Without warning, the very spot where he was standing suddenly gave way. Screaming in terror, Dougie found himself falling into a terrifying crevasse along with a deluge of deadly powdery snow. His journey downwards came crashing to an abrupt halt as he landed on his back in a pile of deep, freezing snow. Unhurt, but visibly shaken, his eyes flickered open and for a moment he lay motionless gazing upwards at a great wall of ice towering above. Then as he sat up and slowly climbed to his feet his eyes widened and his expression changed to one of horror. There, standing before him was the eerie-cloaked figure from his nightmares. Its hideous pale skin, gaunt expression and glistening eyes gazed at him as if he was nothing more than an insect.

But for Dougie, this was too much. He raised his arms in anger and screamed at the figure, "Who, what the hell are ye? What do ye want with me?"

Remaining still and unnervingly silent, the shadowy figure suddenly stepped forward and raised its clenched fist. Then, showing little emotion, it opened its fist to reveal a familiar small, black marblesque pyramid, identical to the one that Dougie had received in Alva.

Then, for a moment, Dougie thought that he heard a woman screaming. Gazing at the cloaked figure in bewilderment, he heard the scream again.

"Dougie!"

Then the scene began to melt away, almost as if he had been a figure positioned at the centre of a painting that was in the process of being whitewashed away by its artist.

"Dougie … Wake Up!"

Then the scene was gone, replaced with an empty void bereft of substance and colour. "Dougie, please for God's sake wake up!"

Opening his eyes, the dream was over and Dougie found himself back inside the car with Kate, speeding along route 41.

"Dougie."

"I'm awake."

Glancing quickly across at Kate, her eyes showed a combination of panic and fear. "What is it?"

Glancing into her mirror she screamed, "Can't you see, behind us? Look!"

Glancing back, Dougie's eyes widened as he caught a glimpse of a large black car about half a mile away speeding towards them from the rear.

"Dougie, what will I do?"

Dougie swallowed hard and tried desperately to think.

"Well, you'll have tae make this contraption go faster, that's for sure."

She nodded, pushed her foot down hard on the accelerator and the Honda lurched forward and sped away like a hungry cat. "He's still gaining …"

As the car thundered across the disconcerting moon-like landscape, Kate yelled out, "Wait look at that sign, Bridge America! That's surely got to be it, hang on!"

With little notice she thrust her foot down on the brake pedal causing the car to come to a screaming halt. As both driver and passenger violently lurched forward and with little time to recover, she pulled the gear stick into reverse, slammed her foot down hard onto the accelerator and the car suddenly shot backwards. Dougie yelled out "What the hell ..." as Kate frantically changed gears again and the car lurched awkwardly forward and sped away down the dusty road.

Anxiously looking into her mirror, Kate's eyes widened as the black Land Rover that had been following them suddenly turned in pursuit.

"Dougie!"

As the Honda raced away in a desperate bid to put distance between the two vehicles, Dougie had a sudden thought.

"How far is this Midlina, do ye ken?"

"I'm not sure, but that looks like a car park. That's got to be the place."

Taking a deep breath Dougie pointed towards an approaching clump of rocks.

"What about there?"

"What?"

"Aye, that might work."

Suddenly in a combination of frustration and anxiety Kate shrieked, "Dougie for Christ's sake, what are you talking about. Just tell me what to do?"

Taking a deep breath, Dougie turned calmly towards Kate and pointed towards the approaching rocks.

"Alright. You want a plan? Drop me off over there by those rocks and drive away."

"What!"

"Lassie, it's the only way, if it's who I think it is, then ye ken it's me that he's coming for and ye ken what I have tae do. If ye can get him tae follow me then I might have a chance."

Kate's alarm suddenly turned to despair and she burst into tears.

"No. What are you talking about? You're crazy I won't let you. "

"Kate! It's the only way. I have tae do this. It's our only chance, now let me off over there."

Wiping her eyes with the back of her hand, Kate reluctantly nodded and slowed the car, eventually coming to a stop opposite the large clump of grey volcanic rocks beside the road. As Dougie opened the door and jumped out, he pursed his lips into a forced smile and said, "Thank ye lass for everything, I'll not forget ye."

Swallowing hard to fight back tears, Kate smiled, "No Dougie, thank you. I think you're the bravest man I've ever met."

Anxiously aware of the approaching vehicle, Dougie nodded in acknowledgment, "Okay, well then, just keep going. Whatever happens, don't come back. Do ye understand?"

As he slammed the door shut, Kate gave a nod and again pushed her foot down on the accelerator causing the car to roar angrily and speed away in a flurry of dust leaving Dougie standing alone.

With barely time to think, Dougie scrambled off the road, flung himself on the ground and covertly crouched down low behind the clump of large grey rocks. Moments later and just as he had hoped, the large black Land Rover sped past and continued its pursuit of the bronze Honda, seemingly unaware that it no longer had a passenger.

FIFTY SEVEN

AS THE LAND Rover disappeared over the horizon, Dougie stood and gazed around at the desolate eerie lunar like landscape with an uncomfortable sense of familiarity. Approximately one hundred meters away the normally busy tourist attraction of Midlina, its bridge and adjacent car park were quiet and deserted. As he looked out over the foreboding landscape, Dougie could just make out what appeared to be a range of distant mountains and volcanoes to his west and the angry grey waters of the North Atlantic to his east. Now completely alone, he began the short walk along an adjacent tarmac path, took a deep breath and began the short walk towards the bridge.

Stepping on to the steel and timber structure, he took a moment to look downwards in awe at the enormous volcanic chasm below. Then, walking up to a blue and white sign attached to the middle section, he read with interest that this was indeed Midlina or the "mid-point" that uniquely separated the two continents of Europe and North America. As he read he smiled inwardly at the seemingly appropriate quote just above the name Midlina, "*In the footsteps of the gods.*"

Reaching inside the fold of his kilt, he pulled out the small, marblesque black pyramid, placed it onto the palm of his right hand and muttered, "Well this seems tae be the right place … What do I do with you?"

"Mr Allan, I knew you would come."

Clenching his fist around the object, Dougie spun around to find himself no longer alone. Directly facing him on the far side of the bridge was a solitary, but all too familiar looking figure.

"Mr President I assume, or should I call ye Alexander MacArthur?"

For a moment the figure remained motionless, merely gazing at Dougie in silence, almost as if the pair were gladiators about to face each other in the arena for the first time.

"Names do not matter Mr Allan. What does, however, is the object that you now hold in your hand. It belongs to us and was never meant to find its way into your world."

Glancing at the figure, Dougie opened his clenched fist and looked at the pyramid. Then placing it back inside the fold of his kilt, he gritted his teeth as the anger began to swell inside him like one of the many gurgling hot springs nearby. He hated this man, despised him with every fibre of his being. McArthur had stolen his life. Ripped him away from everything he held dear, his friends, his home, his wife, – all gone because of him.

"Ye have taken everything from me and now you, whatever the hell ye are, ye want tae take everything else. Well I ken the truth, I ken what ye are. Ye might see us as insignificant. But we have lives, families and ye have nae right tae destroy them."

As Dougie's words reverberated across the chasm, McArthur suddenly raised his right arm, opened his clenched fist and revealed an identical miniature black pyramid.

"The object, give it to me now."

As McArthur's demand also reverberated across the chasm, Dougie angrily recollected the pair's first confrontation in Alva, where his life had been so brutally torn apart. Shaking his head, Dougie hissed, "I don't think so laddie. I am nae going to fall for that one again."

Without warning he suddenly threw himself furiously towards McArthur. As the pair collided, the impact sent both men careering onto the wooden deck of the bridge. Before McArthur had a chance to recover, Dougie was already on his feet and inbound with a second blow. As his fist smashed into McArthur's cheekbone, Dougie screamed out in fury, "Ye bastard, you've taken everything from me. I hate ye!"

As Dougie lunged forward to bring his fist down for a farther blow, McArthur suddenly rolled aside causing the blow to be ricocheted of the wooden deck. Howling with rage, Dougie glared at McArthur, his nostrils flaring with hatred. As the two men stood facing each other, McArthur unexpectedly raised his right hand and the Scotsman shrieked as he was lifted clean of his feet and thrown into the air with an incredible wave of invisible energy. Tumbling onto the dusty path, Dougie sat for a moment visibly shaken before slowly climbing to his feet.

Gritting his teeth, he barked "Enough of your parlour tricks ... do ye have no honour? Can ye not fight me like a man?"

Stepping onto the bridge, Dougie glared at McArthur as he again moved forward to continue his attack. Dougie's eyes widened in alarm as the ground suddenly began to tremble and the bridge began to sway. As the shaking intensified, Dougie screamed out in alarm, before stumbling backwards and careering uncontrollably off the bridge to land on his backside only metres from the edge of the chasm.

Within moments, the shaking had become so ferocious, that on either side of the precipice rocks and debris were crashing downwards. Struggling to regain his balance, Dougie caught sight of McArthur on the far side of the bridge – from his unusual behaviour it became apparent that something was wrong. For a moment Dougie couldn't understand what he was seeing. McArthur was on his knees, scrambling around in the dust, desperately searching for something. As he watched, Dougie's eyes suddenly widened with the realisation that McArthur's miniature pyramid must have fallen during their fight.

Dougie gave a wry smile and yelled, "What's the matter laddie, lost your weapon have ye?"

Glaring at Dougie, McArthur climbed to his feet and hissed, "Fool! You don't know what you've done?"

Without warning the bridge began to creak and groan as if was being pulled by two unseen forces. From within the blackened chasm below a crack suddenly appeared, followed by another and then another.

Looking into the crater, Dougie's expression turned to horror as the fissures began a sudden and deadly metamorphosis from dead, blackened rock into a lethal writhing sea of molten lava. Scrambling backwards in a desperate bid to avoid being hit by lethal plumes of boiling hot steam, Dougie looked on as the raging red mass began to rise.

As the haze cleared, his eyes looked on in alarm as he caught a glimpse of McArthur frantically clinging for life at the centre of the bridge. With no warning there was a deafening roar as an enormous plume of deadly molten lava exploded upwards from the chasm. As lethal fireballs rained down, the bridge suddenly buckled and began to fall into the fiery abyss. McArthur screamed in terror as he suddenly lost his footing and edged ever closer to certain death.

For a split second, watching McArthur squirm for life gave Dougie an immense sense of closure and satisfaction. This man, who had destroyed his life, was about to get his comeuppance. But somehow watching the man die in this way seemed wrong. He had no way to defend himself. If he let MacArthur die here, it would be an empty death, an honourless death. No, it would just be wrong.

As the bridge collapsed and McArthur screamed, Dougie suddenly leapt forward and literally threw himself at McArthur, grabbing his arm just as the bridge disappeared into the nightmare below. Dougie held on tight and with all of his strength and began to pull the dangling man up to safety.

"Climb up, come on lad!"

A battered and bruised looking McArthur emerged from the deadly precipice and fell forward onto his knees exhausted and clearly relieved.

As the pair gazed at each other McArthur's expression turned to puzzlement, "Why?"

Dougie looked at the battered man and sighed, "Is it not obvious? It was the right thing tae do. I just couldn't let ye die like that, not here."

McArthur smiled, "Thank you Dougie I ..."

Without warning, another massive explosion rocked the ground where they were sitting and a plume of lava shot into the air only meters away, forcing both men to scramble backwards to safety. While McArthur stood, Dougie suddenly shrieked in alarm as an explosion of brilliant white light erupted from the chasm like an exploding star. Shielding his eyes from the intense light, Dougie desperately tried to focus in on the cause. But it was impossible, the brilliance and intensity were overwhelming.

After a few moments, the brightness subsided and Dougie found that he was able to open his eyes. Climbing to his feet, he stood gazing in disbelief at what he saw. Midlina, the bridge and the fiery chasm were gone. In its place the volcanic activity had ripped open the ground to reveal the top of an enormous, black marblesque pyramid sitting just below the surface. Bathed in brilliant white light, its exterior appeared almost alive, as sparks of white light and fiery orange danced off its surface. Watching in wonder, Dougie had no doubt that this pyramid was identical to the one he discovered in Scotland.

Turning to McArthur he suddenly recalled the words spoken by Mary in the cemetery back in Alva. "Find the key to join the world ..."

Looking across at McArthur he whispered to himself, "I did it?"

"As I said Dougie, the object, was never meant to find its way into your world."

Dougie shook his head and stepped forward angrily, "Aye that may be so, but what about me! I was never meant tae be here either."

"Actually you're wrong Dougie. This is exactly where you're meant to be."

"Huh?"

Turning around, Dougie's expression turned to shock as standing only meters away was a familiar, but unemotional looking Kate Harding.

"Kate, what the hell are ye doing' here? I told ye tae keep going."

Ignoring Dougie's comments, she turned to McArthur and gave him a callous smile, "It's been a long time brother!"

FIFTY EIGHT

"**B**ROTHER? WHAT THE? Kate what are ye talking abo …"
Dougie's expression turned to utter disbelief, as Kate suddenly began to change. Her face, hair, eyes and even her clothes, everything recognisable about her was now morphing into something grotesquely different. Within moments, the person that Dougie had known as Kate Harding was gone and in her place stood a fearsome, cloaked figure. Its skin was pale, its face gaunt and eyes glimmering like diamonds.

"My God, what are ye?"

Walking closer it turned to Dougie and hissed, "I have many names … and so many … faces." Dougie watched in horror as the creatures face morphed once again. But for Dougie, this transformation was the cruellest yet. For now, standing in front of him was Mary, his beautiful wife, with her soft complexion, loving eyes and flowing long dark hair.

"Mary … no!"

"Find the key Dougie …"

When she spoke, it was not the soft voice of his wife, but of the creature, cold and callous. "Find the key to join the world. Well Dougie it appears that congratulations are in order. You did it, look!"

Metamorphosing back into its hideous natural form, the creature raised its hand and pointed towards the range of distant volcanoes to the west, which had begun to violently erupt in the distance. "You see Dougie, it was always your destiny. You were the key and you've joined the world."

"Oh my God, the ring of fire. They were right. What have I done?"

As Dougie spoke, McArthur stepped forward and gazed at the gaunt figure in disgust.

"Caius! I should have known. You are truly reprehensible, using a human in this way. Like your own personal plaything and for what? Vengeance? Conquest! You forget brother, we are keepers, we were never meant to expose them to our world."

Clearly agitated by McArthur's comments, the sinister figure began to pace back and forth like a wolf stalking its prey. "I was a keeper. You forget brother, it was you who brought him here."

"Only because you gave me no choice."

Laughing out loud Caius snapped back, "We all have a choice brother and you made yours. It was your choice to collude with the others to banish me, remember?"

Looking briefly at Dougie, McArthur's expression softened.

"Those were dark days brother and you left us with little choice. But it doesn't have to be that way this time. You could come back and re-join us."

For a moment Caius paused and looked almost tempted. Then, just as McArthur thought a compromise might be a possibility, the creature's expression slowly changed into a cruel sneer.

"Brother, there may have been a time when that might have been possible, but not now. You see I've waited so long for today, so very long.

"But Caius I …"

"I once told you that these … humans were dangerous but you didn't listen. Now look at them. They infest this world, like a disease. You've been living among them for too long and it has made you weak. Call it redemption brother, but now it's time to pay the price."

Dougie stepped forward angrily, gritting his teeth, "Ye mean it was all lies, all of it. Ye lied. Ye used me, ye used all of us? It was ye in the cemetery that morning. The lighthouse … everything, it was all a masquerade tae get ye here."

Glaring at Dougie, Caius gave a cold laugh, "Of course and you played your part perfectly."

Dougie was furious and had heard enough. Clenching his fist he rushed towards the creature in blind fury. But he stood little chance. Caius had already anticipated his move and as he lunged, Dougie found himself suddenly gripped by an invisible force which hurled him brutally up into the air and down again. As he hit the ground with a thud, Dougie howled out in a mixture of pain and frustration.

As Dougie lay stunned on the dusty ground, Caius turned to McArthur and cackled heartlessly.

"Do you see how weak they are, how pathetic?"

As he tried to stand, Dougie suddenly grasped his chest and fell forward screaming in agony as a piercing pain shot through him like a deadly blade.

"Arghhh."

Gazing at Dougie writhing on the ground in agony, McArthur stepped forward and raised his hand.

Although invisible, the blow to Caius was overwhelming, he was hurled ten meters into the air, before finally crashing down, narrowly missing a pool of deadly molten lava. As Dougie recovered, McArthur bellowed "Enough! They are not your playthings anymore!"

Watching McArthur with his gleaming blue eyes, Caius rose menacingly to his feet. He turned and clasped his hands together roaring with callous laughter.

"You're so wrong Brother, that's exactly what they are. This is my time now and I'm afraid you're not part it." As Caius spoke, he pulled his hands apart to reveal a small ball of flickering white light between his fingers.

Stepping forward the creature pulled his palms apart and as he did, the pulsating ball of light began to grow. Sneering at McArthur with a sense of vengeful hatred, Caius raised the object above his head, and with a cruel smile hurled it directly at him.

Gasping in awe, Dougie covered his eyes from the blinding light as the energy wave hit McArthur directly in the chest, imprisoning him within the field. All around light intertwined with crackling and popping sparks of electricity as they danced viciously off his body.

For a moment, McArthur appeared hopelessly trapped with little hope of escape until he suddenly closed his eyes, raised his hands and for a moment appeared to be completely at peace. As Dougie lowered his arms, he watched as small orange sparks of energy materialised from McArthur's hands and the energy bubble began to transform. Within moments it was no longer energy, but had altered its state into a solid black sphere, almost like a surrounding protective shield.

Suddenly the area around Midlina and the sphere went deadly quiet. Glancing threateningly at Dougie Caius gave a cruel smirk and licked his pale lips in callous anticipation.

"Behold human! Behold your new master. You like the rest of your disgusting race will soon learn respect."

As Caius began to pace back and forth once again, Dougie gave a shallow laugh.

"Oh laddie, Caius or whatever the hell your name is. You've a lot tae learn about human beings … we're survivors."

Dougie paused for breath as, the fearsome cloaked figure suddenly turned and with a vicious gaze, walked across to where he was sitting and hissed, "I know exactly what humans are. I don't need lessons from you. The only thing I want from you is the object which you have in your possession."

Gazing up at the hideous figure, Dougie shrugged his shoulders and spat out, "I don't have it any longer. I've lost it."

Caius gave a hollow laugh and snarled, "Don't lie to me … I know you've got it and I want it now."

"Why ye …"

Caius sneered menacingly and Dougie suddenly felt his chest beginning to tighten with pain. Then as quickly as it had started, the pain was gone as Caius's attention was suddenly drawn away to the sphere, which had begun to tremble. He slowly approached the object, and then was suddenly thrown brutally backwards onto the ground as the object exploded.

Hastily scrambling backwards, Dougie bolted to avoid being hit by falling debris. As the dust cleared, his eyes widened in alarm, as standing in front of him were not just one of the fearsome cloaked creatures but now two. For a moment, neither spoke, but merely gazed at each other almost as if they were baiting each other to make the next move.

"I thought you would have learnt from your past mistakes Brother. You must know that we can't allow you access to humanity. You would cause untold damage."

As the sneering Caius rose ominously to his feet, the creature suddenly pulled his hand back and pushed out an intense beam of green light. As the wave hit, Caius reeled backwards in apparent pain. Then writhing on the ground the beam suddenly exploded around him into a plethora of brightly coloured sparks.

Morphing back into a familiar looking McArthur, he glimpsed cautiously back across at Dougie and looking anxious raised his hand, "Get back and keep out of the way …"

With his back to Caius, Dougie's expression turned to alarm as Caius suddenly sprang to his feet and quickly moved towards the fiery gorge. Then, with a heartless smile he plunged his hand into a deadly pool of flaming hot lava – but with no cries of pain or obvious burns. Dougie watched in amazement, as Caius pulled his hand out.

From a distance it appeared to Dougie that Caius had something in his hand, some kind of weapon, a whip perhaps. But amazement soon turned to horror as Dougie realised that this was no ordinary whip. This whip had been forged out of the fiery lava pit. It resembled a deadly fiery serpent, shimmering, glowing and writhing in preparation to strike.

As McArthur turned, Caius cackled, "Did you know the ancient people of these lands once believed that this was a gateway to hell? Well brother perhaps it's time to release its full potential."

With a flick of his wrist and with little effort, McArthur gasped as Caius moved forward with intense ferocity. Raising the whip above his head, the fire licked the early morning air like a deadly snake tongue. Then, as the flame came crashing down, it didn't just strike once, but quickly entwined itself around him, like a deadly coil of fire. His eyes burning like diamonds, Caius wrenched the whip again and McArthur was hoisted high up into the air like a child's toy.

"There's no need to worry about the humans any longer brother. I'll take care of them."

Without warning, the sky suddenly exploded with an incredible white light as the top of the pyramid began to slowly open outwards like a poisonous flower. "You see Brother, it's beginning, all over the world the devices are opening!"

Momentarily shielding his eyes from the brilliance, Dougie watched in horror as McArthur swayed helplessly in the air like a caged bird, his life force slowly being drained from him. Turning his head downward, McArthur spluttered and then screamed out, "The pyramid … You must cl … close it."

He watched in sheer disbelief at Caius's brutality, and Dougie knew at that moment that this being was a true manifestation of evil. It would never compromise or be negotiated with. It would never stop.

Watching McArthur slowly die, Dougie knew in his heart what had to be done. Reaching inside the fold of his kilt, he pulled out the miniature black pyramid and placed it onto the palm of his hand.

"Caius I have what ye want. I have your key! If ye want it, then ye have tae release him."

Glancing up at McArthur's writhing body, Caius roared with laughter, "You see Brother, how weak they are. They'll make perfect slaves."

Suddenly, the fire whip vanished and McArthur was free. As he crashed painfully to the ground, Dougie sighed with relief. Caius turned to face the Scotsman and sneered, "Very well, I shall spare his life if you give me the key."

Taking a deep breath and with a look of utter defeat, Dougie began his slow walk to the chasms edge where Caius was waiting for him with a cruel look of anticipation. As he stood opposite the creature, Dougie looked into its cold heartless eyes and gazed at the cold marblesque object in his hand.

"This was what it was all about wasn't it, the key? I know now. Ye were banished by your people and they took your power away ..."

"Enough. Give it to me now or I will kill you."

Glancing across at the unconscious McArthur, Dougie gave a hollow laugh.

"I'm nae stupid laddie, you were with me in Alva remember?"

Suddenly the creature stepped forward and snapped angrily, "What are you talking about human?"

"At Tom's house in Alva remember, when that Brooks' fellow was about to shoot you. Mr Wilkes tried to negotiate with him to release you. But he wouldn't compromise, he couldn't compromise."

With a cruel growl, Caius extended his pale bony hand in anticipation of receiving his prize. "I've had enough of your stories. Now give me what's mine."

"That's it though, don't ye see? For all your power ye can't take this. I have tae voluntarily give it tae ye. The thing is that if I hand this over tae ye now, you'll probably kill us all anyway, so I'm thinking that if ye want this, then ye should go and get it yourself!"

"Noooo …"

Dougie suddenly leapt sideways away from the furious creature and bolted at top speed towards the chasm. Standing by the remains of the Midlina Bridge, Caius watched in disbelief as Dougie raised his arm and flung the miniature black pyramid into the blinding light.

A moment later, an explosion of brilliant white light ripped across the Midlina skyline and a massive energy wave erupted from the crater that lifted Dougie clean off his feet and into the air. As he crumpled onto the ground, he looked on with satisfaction as the black pyramid began to close.

"What have you done?"

Caius was furious and although standing directly behind with his back to him, Dougie knew that his fate was sealed.

As he slowly turned to face his inevitable punishment, Dougie had already accepted the fact that he was probably going to die. So without saying a word, he took a deep breath, closed his eyes and with an image of his beautiful Mary in his mind, waited for the inevitable.

FIFTY NINE

WHEN NOTHING HAPPENED, Dougie slowly opened his eyes. Caius was standing about five meters away, but there was something different about him. Although obviously still seething at Dougie, he seemed somewhat humbled in manner, almost fearful perhaps. Then as Dougie raised his head to look around, he immediately understood why. From within the light of the pyramid, six cloaked figures were beginning to slowly materialise around him.

"Dougie."

Suddenly remembering McArthur, Dougie spun around and ran across to where the badly burnt McArthur lay. Kneeling beside him in the dust, Dougie looked down as the man coughed and spluttered, desperately trying to find the strength to talk.

"Dougie I'm sorry, I'm sorry for involving you in this. I had … little choice."

As McArthur's appearance began to regress back to his original form, Dougie placed his hand on the creature's shoulder and shook his head.

"It's okay lad, I understand."

"Wait, help me up, I want to see him."

Suddenly McArthur grabbed Dougie's arm and began to pull himself up so that he could see Caius. Watching the other six-cloaked figures appear, McArthur wheezed, "It … It's over you've lost. Plea … Please reconsider, it's still not too late."

With his head hung low the apparently defeated Caius sighed. Then Dougie looked on in disbelief as the creature's mouth slowly curled upwards into that familiar cruel smirk. Then raising his hand, he gazed first at the emerging cloaked figures and then at the wounded McArthur and hissed, "You've won nothing Brother. This is only the beginning!"

Suddenly the ground shook and McArthur opened his mouth to protest. But it was too late. The spot where Caius had been standing suddenly exploded into a shimmering vortex surrounded by brilliant white light.

Gazing at the light-filled turbulence, Dougie lowered his arm, glanced up at the six other figures and then at McArthur.

"He's getting away? Ye have tae stop him."

Spluttering, McArthur lay back down in the dust and wheezed, "For now … there is nothing we can do. There will be other chances."

"B … But what about you … I thought ye couldn't die."

Gazing at the others, McArthur winced in pain and gave an uneasy smile.

"Th … this body can die, but what we are will live on. That's the foundation of all life Dougie."

Gazing down at the dying creature, Dougie desperately glanced up at the other cloaked figures, hoping, almost praying, that they would intervene.

"Please, you must help him."

But getting no response, Dougie's gaze fell back to McArthur as the creature took a final breath and close his eyes.

"No! McArthur wake up … Please!"

As Dougie stared silently at McArthur's lifeless body, he swallowed hard, climbed to his feet and turned to the shimmering but now dwindling vortex of light and sighed.

"I can't believe you're going let him go."

As he turned to address the group, one of the cloaked figures stepped forward and said. "Dougie, it was his request that we send you home."

Dougie had a sudden vision of being reunited with beautiful Mary and of being able to sit by his fire on cold nights or to walk through the flower filled glen in mid-summer.

It was a fine vision, but looking down at McArthur's lifeless body and across at the shimmering remains of the portal, he realised that he had now indivertibly become entangled in a war, and that in this war, Caius had just won his first battle.

"If I go back now, he'll have won ... I would live, but I'd be living a lie. Knowing that he was still out there, I'm sorry but I can't let that happen."

"Dougie ..."

Before the others could respond, Dougie suddenly bolted towards the shimmering portal and hurled himself into the dazzling white light. With a sudden burst of brilliance the portal closed and Dougie Allan was gone. As silence began to fall on Midlina, one of the figures stepped forward and sighed.

"Everything has transpired as I have foretold my brothers. The prophecy was correct."

SIXTY

TUESDAY 11TH FEBRUARY 1710 ALVA, SCOTLAND

AS THE HEAVY skies over the Ochil's began to finally clear and the night's snow stopped falling, chinks of early morning sunlight began to break through the bleak skies over Alva. Dougie Allan's simple cottage was covered with a thick blanket of brilliant white snow. Inside, Mary Allan smiled as she felt the warmth of her husband's breath on the back of her neck and his muscular arms entwined around her.

"Are ye alright my love?"

Turning to face him she sighed and gave him a smile, "Aye I'm fine my …"

Mary's body suddenly twitched and she woke with a start.

"Dougie!"

As her husband's image faded into a misty white fog, the harsh realisation that he was gone, once again fell over her like a dark veil. Taking a deep breath she slowly exhaled, sat up, rubbed her eyes and swung her legs out of bed and down onto the cold wooden floor of the empty cottage.

As she sat motionless staring into space, memories of that awful day came rushing back. The day when Fraser McAndrew and two other lads came calling to inform her of the accident and of her husband's disappearance in the mine. Of course she wasn't stupid, she knew full well of the dangers of mining. Every local woman did. But the harsh reality was that every time a husband, father or brother went out to work, there was a chance he might not return. But like every woman, when news of an accident came, she would just hope and pray that it was no one she knew.

Sometimes luck could step in and a man who was once thought lost could miraculously turn up. But with eight days having now passed since the accident, the chance of that happening here was unlikely. Still she wouldn't give up yet, she couldn't!

Once dressed into her dark, green dress and bodice, she ate a light breakfast of bread and cold porridge. Afterwards she decided to brave the icy morning to take milk from household's two cows and feed the chickens with the scraps of yesterday's leftovers.

By 9.30 am, and having collected firewood and five medium-sized brown eggs, she returned inside and was about to light a fire, when she was startled as a knock came to the door. Taking a deep breath she stepped across and opened the door to reveal a sweating and rather flustered looking Robert McRae. Even before the youngster spoke, Mary knew that something was wrong. Firstly he was armed with a broadsword and second his face was a deathly shade of pale.

"I'm … I'm sorry tae bother ye Missus Allan but yer needed at the mine."

"What is Robert? Is it my husband?"

Remaining silent and grim faced, Mary's initial sense of elation subsided back into panic. "For god's sake man, is it my husband?"

Robert shook his head. "Nae Missus Allan it's not. But, you'd best come quick."

With a nod, she turned heel, grabbed a thick woollen shawl from the back of a chair, placed it over her shoulders and bolted for the door. Once outside Robert directed her towards his waiting horse. "Here lass, let me help up." As he cupped his two hands to form a makeshift step, she then climbed up onto the animals back.

Once positioned, Robert climbed up and sat in front of her. "You'd best hold on."

As instructed Mary grasped the youngster's waist and the horse began to slowly trudge forward through the thick powdery snow. Moments later and after a harsh kick, the beast neighed and surged forward into a steady gallop upwards towards Alva glen.

"If it's not Dougie, then who the hell is it? McArthur?"

The youngster just gave the harness another tug and shook his head, "You'll see."

Minutes later the horse and its passengers made their way upwards through the glen towards the mine.

"What's that noise?"

Even as they rode at speed towards the mine, Mary could hear loud voices. No, not voices at all. More like the enraged shouts of an angry mob. At the mine, Robert was first to dismount and then Mary down. Her face turned to revulsion as she made her way towards a mob of angry jeering men.

At first she couldn't see what was causing the commotion. They all appeared to be huddled around something on the ground, an animal perhaps. But as she stepped in closer her face turned to horror as she now saw that it was not an animal but a cowering, blood-soaked figure with a cloth sack over his head.

"What the bloody hell's going on here!"

As the sound of her angry voice shrieked above those of the men, the group suddenly fell silent.

"I said what is this, what's happening here?"

As she spoke one of the men turned and she recognised him instantly as Fraser McAndrew, the very man who had only days earlier informed her about her husband's disappearance. "Get yerself away Mary, this is none of your business."

"What? My husband disappears and I find you here kicking this poor man half tae death. What has he done tae deserve this."

Before McAndrew could respond a voice yelled out from the

group, "This bastard's in league with the devil. He just appeared oot of thin air."

Mary shook her head in disbelief, "What the hell are ye talking about man, let me see him." Before McAndrew could object, she had stepped forward and was in the process of removing the sack hood.

"Now just wait a minute woman, I don't think ye should …"

"Don't tell me about what I should or shouldn't do, less ye forget who my husband was."

As the hood came off the group stepped back as the blooded, cringing excuse for a man raised his hand to shield his eyes from the brightness. His head was badly bruised and his right eye bleeding and swollen. Cowering and breathing heavily he slowly lowered his hand and tried to speak. "Pl … please help me …"

"There's nae help for ye here laddie …"

As McAndrew spoke, the group roared with a cruel and unanimous "Aye".

Then surging forward, one of the men lashed out at the snivelling figure with a wooden stick and was about to deliver another blow when Mary stepped forward and shrieked, "Put yer bloody stick down man!"

As instructed the man reluctantly lowered the stick and stepped back.

"At least let's find oot about the man before ye condemn him."

Turning back, Mary stepped closer and knelt down beside the man who had now turned to face her. Breathing heavily, and nursing what she suspected was a bruised rib.

"Who are ye, and where did ye come from?"

"I don't know. One … one minute I was in the c … cavern and the next, a bright light and I found myself here."

Staring at the terrified figure, Mary couldn't help notice the man's clothing. His breeches were of a strange light blue material and on top he wore an unusual navy blue woollen cloth, almost like a shawl but with fitted sleeves. Even the man's shoes were like nothing she'd seen before. Not leather but some kind of white material with a strange symbol.

"What's your name laddie?"

For a moment the blooded figure said nothing. Finally he took a deep breath and wincing with pain said softly, "T ... Tom, Tom Duncan."

Glancing uneasily up McAndrew for a moment and then back at the stranger she continued, "So what are doing in the mine and dressed so strangely?"

"You're wasting your bloody time Mary, I'm telling ye he's in league with the devil!"

"Be quiet man."

Suddenly at the mention of her name the man raised his head and glared at her wide eyed.

"Oh my God it's really you, Mary!"

With a look of shock on her face she stood up. "How do you know me?"

"Dougie. You're Dougie's wife."

Without saying another word and with anger smouldering inside her, she slowly shook her head. "How would you know that? You know what I think they're right, I think you are in league with the devil. My husband's dead and I don't know who the bloody hell ye are."

Tom looked at her in sheer disbelief, "What! No wait, please!"

At that moment the young Robert McRae stepped forward. "What'll we do with him Fraser? Take him tae Stirling?"

Glancing around at the multitude of angry faces, McAndrew glared at the cringing figure and shook his head, "Stirling! Nae laddie, if he's a demon then there's only one thing tae do."

"What's that?"

"String the bastard up."

Lightning Source UK Ltd.
Milton Keynes UK
UKOW04f2220150415

249719UK00001B/2/P